DOUBLE EXPOSURE

DOUBLE EXPOSURE

ALFRED GOUGH &
MILES MILLAR

GRAND CENTRAL
PUBLISHING

New York Boston

Grand Central Publishing
Hachette Book Group
1290 Avenue of the Americas, New York, NY 10104
grandcentralpublishing.com
twitter.com/grandcentralpub

First Edition: March 2019

Grand Central Publishing is a division of Hachette Book Group, Inc. The Grand Central Publishing name and logo is a trademark of Hachette Book Group, Inc.

The publisher is not responsible for websites (or their content) that are not owned by the publisher.

The Hachette Speakers Bureau provides a wide range of authors for speaking events. To find out more, go to www.hachettespeakersbureau.com or call (866) 376-6591.

Library of Congress Cataloging-in-Publication Data

Names: Gough, Alfred, 1967- author. | Millar, Miles, author.
Title: Double exposure / Alfred Gough & Miles Millar.
Description: First edition. | New York : Grand Central Publishing, 2019.
Identifiers: LCCN 2018044405| ISBN 9781538731369 (hardcover) | ISBN 9781549143212 (audio download) | ISBN 9781538731376 (ebook)
Subjects: | GSAFD: Suspense fiction.
Classification: LCC PS3607.O883 D68 2019 | DDC 813/.6--dc23
LC record available at https://lccn.loc.gov/2018044405

ISBNs: 978-1-5387-3136-9 (hardcover), 978-1-5387-3137-6 (ebook)

Printed in the United States of America

LSC-C

10 9 8 7 6 5 4 3 2 1

We dedicate this book to the cinematic greats
who inspired this story.

"The more successful the villain, the more
successful the picture."
—*Alfred Hitchcock*

DOUBLE EXPOSURE

PROLOGUE

November 1961, Brandenburg Gate Checkpoint, East Berlin

Winter had come to Berlin. Iron-gray days turned keen and brittle in the quickening dark. For three nights, Tarkovsky took a place among the workers at the wall, masquerading as one of them.

Some of the men whispered, on clouds of frozen breath, of a bricklayer shot on the Friedrichstrasse in the weeks before Tarkovsky arrived—a young husband, separated by unlucky timing from his wife and unborn child. The wife had been visiting friends in the West when the barbed wire sprang up overnight like a thorny hedge, dividing the city in two. The bricklayer finally attempted a jump across the border from the roof of a construction shed. He'd died bleeding a few paces from the wall, still in the East.

The story did nothing to adjust Tarkovsky's aim. After all: The bricklayer's child would be born safely in the West, father or no father. And the Communists had no shortage of bricklayers.

Sergei Tarkovsky had only secrets to trade.

Each night he worked himself raw, moving block after cold heavy block into place as the Volksarmee—the "people's army"—stood guard. Tarkovsky watched the soldiers and learned. When spoken to, he responded in perfect German; when issued a command, he complied. He attracted no attention. He caused no delays. And on the third night, at last, his opportunity arrived.

"Sie da," the young guard said. *"Tanken sie da generatoren."*

You there. Refuel the generator. The guard was blond and blue-eyed beneath the rim of his helmet, his cold-reddened cheeks hardly in need of a regular shave. He'd been among the first Tarkovsky had noticed—impatient, imprecise, easily distracted. A mirror to his generation.

Tarkovsky snapped a salute and grabbed up the jerrycan, setting off toward the wheel-mounted light tower illuminating the work underway.

While the young guard smoked his cigarette, rifle slung on his shoulder, Tarkovsky sabotaged the generator with a pocket full of sand from the mortar silo.

Half an hour later—just as the season's first dry snowflakes began to swirl in the bright beams of the work lights—the generator coughed, shuddered, and finally died, plunging the wall into darkness.

By the time the young guard shouted to the others, Tarkovsky's boots had already touched ground on the other side. He crouched with the foraging rats in the gritty narrow space between the wall and the outer barrier—a screen of fireboard three meters high, braced with lumber. On the other side of the fireboard: the hedge of barbed wire. On the other side of that: the Americans.

Tarkovsky listened. He waited.

He thought briefly of Nina, and of Moscow. He thought of the bricklayer.

And then he ran.

*   *   *

First Sergeant Morse and PFC Robinson had just lit their Luckies when the Kraut came over the wall.

Half a minute before that, all the lights had gone out on the other side. Robinson—a gangly farm kid from Nebraska, not the brightest of Morse's bunch, but pretty good behind the wheel of an M48 when

2

tasked—shook out his match and said, "Maybe Ulbricht forgot to pay the electric bill."

Morse was about to tell the kid to clam up and look sharp when he saw the dark silhouette appear atop the panel fence fifty yards down the line. He slapped Robinson's shoulder and pointed. "Climber. There."

They tossed their smokes and unslung their rifles as a clamor rose from the other side. Now a spotlight raked along the top of the wall, splashing the climbing figure in a sudden bright pool: not a soldier after all, Morse saw, but a worker making a break for it.

Morse could hear the GDR soldiers shouting; he heard the pounding of boots on brick. He realized that he was holding his breath for the guy coming over. Hoping he'd make it.

Then came the sudden hard crack of rifle fire.

Morse heard a single shot, followed by half a dozen more. Mists of blood drifted in the spotlight beam as bullets struck the fleeing worker in the back, punching shreds of fabric from the front of his coat as they exited his body. The worker twitched as though stung by wasps. Morse heard a final shot and the worker jerked upright. Then he pitched forward, limp as a rag.

By the time they reached him, the worker's body steamed in the cold, cruelly tangled in the snarl of barbed wire along the base of the panel fence. His open eyes stared at nothing. PFC Robinson said, "I think he's a goner."

"Good observation, Private," Morse said. "Now help me get the poor bastard out of there."

They reslung their rifles and went to work, peeling back the stiff, cold wire as best they could using only their gloves, until Morse finally gave up and radioed for support and a pair of cutters. He was lighting a new smoke when Robinson—still crouched with the body amid the toothy bramble—said, "Whoa. Top, look at this."

Morse looked. Snowflakes had already stopped melting on the worker's blood-spattered face. He thought, *At least close the man's eyes, Robinson, for crying out loud.*

Then the private pulled some kind of strap from beneath the worker's bullet-tattered coat, stood to his feet, and handed Morse a dented metal disc about the size of a hubcap. "What's this?" he said.

It was a film container, that much Morse could see. With bullet holes in it. And Robinson's bloody thumb prints on the metal.

Along with a crusty, faded filing label bearing a single word: *СЕКРЕТНЫЙ*.

Peering at the label over Morse's shoulder, Robinson said, "How's your German, Top?"

"That isn't German," Morse told him, calling upon the few minutes of language training he'd managed to stay awake for back at Bragg. "It's Russian."

"Yeah? What's it say?"

Morse glanced at the body of the worker in the wire as the first growling jeep from checkpoint arrived. He rubbed the label on the battered film can with his thumb and thought: *I'll be damned.*

"It says classified," he finally answered, though Robinson had already run off toward the jeep, and there was nobody but the dead man to hear him.

PART I

Resurrecting the Wolf

CHAPTER
ONE

December 1961, Washington, DC

Ten minutes into the class period, David W. Toland realized that no matter what he said, no matter how he said it, there was no way on God's green earth he was going to be able to make his job sound interesting to a bunch of fourth graders.

"Have you ever met Marilyn Monroe?" the girl with the braids and the freckles wanted to know. "Is she nice in person?"

Patiently, David explained again that as director of preservation for the National Film Archive at the Library of Congress, he did not himself make movies, and only rarely did he meet the people who did.

A stocky, towheaded boy in the back piped up: "My granddad was in the Air Force with Clark Gable."

This provoked such a reaction from the rest of the class that David wondered if the towheaded boy had some prior record of telling tall tales. The other boys all scoffed or called baloney; even the freckled girl rolled her eyes and said, "Oh, he was not, either."

Through all of this, David couldn't help noticing that the class teacher—one Miss Megan Jenkins, slim and pretty, perhaps five years his junior—didn't exactly seem to be rushing to his rescue. Instead, she leaned against the wall behind her desk, biting back a grin while David sweated bullets near the Christmas tree at the front of her class. He had to do something to right this ship, and quick.

So Toland abandoned the lecture he'd planned about film stock and substrates, the deleterious effects of mold. He said to the towheaded boy, "Clark Gable, that's interesting. What's your name, son?"

"Martin Ellroy," the towheaded boy said.

"Okay, Martin Ellroy, here's something you might not know about Clark Gable." The class settled down a notch, waiting to see what he had up his sleeve. David said, "While he was in the Air Force with your granddad—this would have been during World War II—Gable made recruitment films. That is, short movies designed to attract young men to the war effort. It so happens that my office has restored and archived those particular recruitment films starring Clark Gable. You might think of them as pages in the scrapbook of our nation's history." David spread his hands. "And that's film preservation in a nutshell."

Looking around the room, he could see plainly that nobody—including and perhaps especially Martin Ellroy—seemed as impressed by film preservation in a nutshell as David had hoped they might be. A pale boy with horn rims raised his hand and said, "Did you fight in the war?"

"Not in that one, no," David told him. "I was only around your age then, believe it or not."

"What war did you fight in?"

"Well, I went to a different war in Korea, although that's not what I came to talk..."

"Were you in the Air Force?" Martin Ellroy asked.

"I was in the Marine Corps," David answered, once again struggling to keep things on track. "But as long as we're speaking of war and movies..."

The freckled girl wrinkled her nose. "Marilyn Monroe was in *The Misfits* with Clark Gable. But my folks wouldn't let me see it."

"Nobody cares, Stacy," Martin Ellroy said.

Stacy replied, "Nobody cares about your grandpa, how about that?"

Then everybody started jabbering at once. David sighed and

glanced to his right, where Miss Jenkins—still visibly amused at his expense—appeared ready to bail him out at last.

At the sight of her gathering herself, David felt compelled to go down swinging. For Pete's sake, he'd survived combat—was he going to let a gang of freckle-faced schoolkids get the better of him? In his most authoritative tone, he said, "Okay, troops, listen up."

The din of high voices squelched. David squared his shoulders, nodded, and surveyed the room like MacArthur at Inchon.

"Let's cut to it," he said. "Who likes war stories?"

Martin Ellroy shot up his hand. The other boys in the class followed suit.

"That's what I thought. Now, who likes to laugh? Don't be shy."

The boys looked at each other and kept their hands in the air; one or two at a time, the girls gradually joined them.

"Perfect," David said, removing a film can from his battered leather satchel. "Then you're all in for a treat."

He gestured to the teacher as he moved toward the projector at the center of the room. While David pried open his can, Miss Jenkins pulled the classroom's rollaway screen down over the dusty blackboard.

"My office also recently completed the restoration of this film," David said, loading the projector while he talked. "Which makes it possible for me to show it to you today. It starts during the war that happened just before the one Martin's granddad and Clark Gable were in together. It's very funny. And," he added, winking directly at Stacy, "you might find it interesting to note that the son of this film's star once dated Marilyn Monroe. Enjoy."

With that, David fired up the projector. Miss Jenkins moved toward the door and turned out the lights. Within moments, Charlie Chaplin's *The Great Dictator* flickered to life on the screen.

Soon after that, the fourth graders of George Washington Elementary had given over to regular bursts of laughter as Chaplin pratfalled his way across the canvas. Standing with Miss Jenkins at the back of the room, David Toland finally breathed a sigh of relief. He felt like he'd been through a wringer.

"Clearly, nine-year-olds are not my forte."

"I'm not so sure about that," Miss Jenkins whispered. "Personally, I was impressed."

She really did have a very pretty smile. "I think we have to give Chaplin the credit," he whispered back.

Without turning her eyes from the screen, Miss Jenkins leaned an inch closer and said, very quietly, "You know, you look a little bit like Clark Gable. Without the mustache."

At first David wasn't completely sure he'd heard her correctly. Then he caught the way her eyes twinkled in the flickering dark, and he thought: *This day might be improving.* Matching her volume, he said, "Is that a good thing or a bad thing?"

"I don't like them, myself. Mustaches."

David studied her profile and found himself at a loss. He said, "Miss Jenkins, I'm afraid you may be toying with me."

There was that smile again.

"Call me Meg."

*   *   *

When class was over, after the students had filed out for the day and he'd gathered up his things, David worked up his nerve, took a chance, and asked Meg Jenkins if she'd care to join him for a piece of pie and a cup of coffee at the diner around the corner. She said she'd like that, then added, "It's right on the way to my apartment, actually."

"Oh," he said. "Perfect."

She blinked her lashes at him. "How so?"

David faltered. "I . . . no, of course, I only meant . . ."

She laughed. "I'm sorry, I've got to stop teasing you. You should see your face."

"I don't need to see it," he said. "I can feel it."

"That's okay," she said. "You're cute when you're embarrassed. I guess that must be why I keep teasing you."

While he'd never been particularly smooth with the ladies, it occurred to David that spending most of his days alone in a film lab, hunched over damaged Kodachrome with a magnifying loupe, hadn't made him any smoother. "I'm afraid you're matching wits with an unarmed man."

"Nonsense." She put on her scarf and coat. "You're doing fine."

Meg Jenkins unplugged the Christmas tree at the back of the room and they left together, David with his heavy satchel slung over his shoulder, Meg with her folder full of class homework in her arms. The halls were decked with ropes of garland and colorful snowflakes cut from construction paper. David couldn't help thinking back to his own fourth-grade days at D. W. Griffith Elementary in Burbank, California, where he supposed he'd probably been the Martin Ellroy of his class. His own parents really had known Clark Gable. They'd known D. W. Griffith, for that matter. Wallace and Evelyn Toland had known everyone in their day.

David, on the other hand, couldn't recall ever having had a teacher quite as appealing as Meg Jenkins. As they pushed open the doors and emerged into the crisp, overcast December afternoon, she said, "I can truthfully say that I've never met a film preservationist before. Tell me, how on earth does an ex-Marine become interested in such a unique line of work?"

"At a young age," he said. "My folks were in the business."

"The movie business? Really?" Her whole face brightened with curiosity as they descended the stone steps outside the building. "Were they actors?"

"My mother tried very hard to be," he said. "She was a studio player at MGM for a short time in her twenties, but she never quite made it. My father was a composer. He worked with Busby Berkeley a time or two. Though his favorite claim to fame was getting in a fist-fight with Otto Preminger over a card game."

Meg's breath frosted in the air when she laughed. "Is that really true?"

"As far as I know."

11

"Incredible! Who won?"

"The fight, or the card game?"

"Either."

"I imagine that probably depended on who was telling the story."

They turned up the sidewalk, lined on both sides with bare trees. A light snow fell, fuzzy flakes drifting gently all around them. A group of kids ran past, bundled up against the cold, weaving in and out of lampposts wrapped in red ribbon for the holidays. Meg Jenkins looked around, inhaled through her nose, and said, "Well. Isn't this lovely?"

"A good day for coffee and pie," he said, offering his arm.

She smiled and hooked her mittened hand in the crook of his elbow. "Play your cards right, soldier," she said, "and I might let you walk me to my apartment afterward. It's on the way, you know."

David was still trying to think of an appropriate response to that when he noticed the black sedan trolling along on the street half a block behind them. Meg caught him glancing over his shoulder and asked, "Is that car following us?"

"I wouldn't think so," he said.

"Those are government plates," she said. "You're not wanted, are you?"

"Not to my knowledge. Are you?"

She grinned, wrapping in a little closer with her arm. "If we were in a movie," she said, "you'd be a secret agent, and that car would be from the CIA. What would they want with you?"

"I can't imagine."

"Oh, come on," she said. "Play along."

"Lady, I don't write the movies. I only fix 'em and put 'em on the shelf."

She made a face as she reached out to press the crosswalk button. "Party pooper."

Just then the government sedan sped abruptly and rounded the corner, braking to a quick stop in the crosswalk, directly in their path. Two men in dark suits got out, both wearing sunglasses despite the cloudy day. One took up a post near the front bumper, hands folded in front of him. The other came around and opened the rear passenger door.

From the back seat came a dark high-heeled shoe, followed by a shapely calf, followed by an extremely attractive brunette in a belted black overcoat. In the spy movie Meg Jenkins had just attempted to postulate, David thought, Meg herself was the adorable, coffee-and-pie, young Judy Garland type; this woman from the government sedan was more snowflake-melting Sophia Loren. No sunglasses for her. She said, "Captain Toland?"

David felt as though he'd stepped into a hallucination. "I . . . yes. I'm David Toland," he said. "And you are . . ."

"CIA Special Agent Lana Welles," the woman said. She produced an identification badge. "Your government needs your immediate assistance."

He glanced at Meg Jenkins, who stood open-jawed, her eyes as big around as the film canister tucked away in his satchel. He said, "I'm sure I don't understand."

"I'll fill you in on the way, Captain Toland."

"Stop calling me Captain. I'm a librarian."

"Yes." CIA Special Agent Lana Welles nodded sharply. "We've requested your services through your office via the chief of staff."

"My services?"

"We really are on quite a tight schedule, David," Agent Welles said. "If you'll come with us, I'll explain everything."

One of the agents in sunglasses approached. He nodded politely to Meg, then offered to take David's satchel. David said, "Thanks, I'll hang on to it."

The agent nodded, stood aside, and gestured toward the car.

David looked again at Meg Jenkins. For the first time since he'd met her, she appeared to be at a loss for words. "I really have no idea what to say, either," he told her.

She said, "Looks like no pie today."

"You have no idea how disappointing to me that is."

"Another time." She shrugged and patted his shoulder. "It seems your government needs you."

Three minutes later, sitting next to Agent Welles in the back seat of the warm dark sedan, clutching his satchel awkwardly in his lap, David watched Miss Megan Jenkins through tinted glass. She stood alone on the sidewalk as they pulled away from the curb, snow falling around her, shaking her head as though she couldn't believe what had just happened.

David knew how she felt.

"Wow," Agent Welles said. "That was quite a look she gave me back there. I think she really wanted that pie."

Up front, Sunglasses #1 and Sunglasses #2 shared a quiet chuckle. Irritated, David turned from the window. "Do any of you know the last time I had a date?"

Agent Welles smiled. "You've got one now."

CHAPTER
TWO

Langley, Virginia

They'd finished the new CIA headquarters in May—a big, broad-shouldered, H-shaped building situated on a wooded parcel on the Virginia side of the Potomac, some ten miles from George Washington Public Elementary. The facility would consolidate, for the first time, operations from a scatter of antiquated offices around Foggy Bottom and the National Mall. President Kennedy had dedicated the new building only a few weeks ago; David had watched the ceremony on television. But he'd never seen the joint in person before now.

"What do you think?" Agent Welles asked, leading him through the soaring foyer, her heels clicking along the polished floor.

David looked at his feet as they crossed an enormous Central Intelligence Agency seal set into the granite tile. "Impressive," he said. "And empty."

"Yes, well. We're still moving in."

"It always takes longer than you think."

"Based on your file, I understand that this could have been your workplace as well," she said. "If you'd wanted it."

"I suppose that's true."

"Tell me. How does a decorated war hero with his choice of appointments end up in a library basement?"

David couldn't help wondering what Meg Jenkins was doing at

that moment. "Do you know that you're the second woman in an hour to ask me that same question?"

"What did you tell the first one?"

"I was right in the middle of that when you showed up," David said. "And you still haven't told me why I'm here."

"Of course I did," she said. "You're here to provide emergency consultation on a matter relating directly to national security."

"I don't believe I've ever run across a film preservation emergency, Agent Welles. Certainly not one that relates to national security. Directly or indirectly."

"No," she conceded. "I don't suppose you have."

"So you haven't really told me anything."

"Call me old-fashioned," she said, "but I prefer showing."

Agent Welles pushed through a tall glass door and led him into a maze of interior hallways. Glass, steel, and granite gave way to carpet and soft, indirect light. David marveled at how eerily quiet the heart of this building seemed; he heard no voices, no telephones, no typewriters or mimeographs or fancy new Xerox machines—no evidence of human activity anywhere within earshot. At one point, a man in a sport coat pushed a potted tree past them on a handcart; the man nodded to them, said nothing, then rounded a corner and disappeared. Just like that, they were alone again.

Agent Welles stopped before a set of unmarked doors. She pulled the doors open and ushered David into a conference room paneled in honey-colored wood. A long, burnished oval table surrounded by office chairs dominated the space. In one of the chairs sat a man in a charcoal suit reading from a stack of papers—mid-fifties, handsome, graying hair neatly trimmed. A film canister rested on the table in front of him.

"Mr. Toland, welcome," the man said as they entered. He stood and removed his eyeglasses. "Roger Ford, Assistant Deputy Director. Thank you for coming."

David shook the man's hand. "Pleased to meet you. I remain confused as to why I'm here."

"Of course." Roger Ford gestured to the chairs. "Can I offer you anything? Coffee or a soft drink? Something stronger?"

"I'm fine, thank you."

"Then let me explain why we've hijacked your day." They all sat, Ford on one side of the table, David and Agent Welles on the other. Ford pushed the film canister an inch toward David. "We have something of a restoration project on our hands. We need an expert."

David looked at the can. Except for the dents, bullet holes, and rust-colored stains marking its surface, the canister resembled the one in David's satchel. He said, "I think it's only fair to tell you, Deputy Director, my projects don't normally involve bloodstains."

"Assistant Deputy Director. And believe me, this is an atypical situation for all concerned."

"Doesn't the CIA have its own experts?"

Roger Ford smiled. "Our experts sent us to you."

David couldn't imagine how that could possibly be true. "As Agent Welles previously noted, I've been a private citizen working in a public sector basement with no windows for half a decade and change. How'd a lowly strip-cutter like me make it onto CIA radar in the first place?"

"We heard you worked cheap," Agent Welles said.

Before he could ask, *Heard it from who?*, Welles reached for the can, pried off the lid, and positioned the open container in front of David.

"So," she said. "How bad is it, doc?"

David peered at the roll of film inside the bullet-ventilated can. "Somebody shot it. No pun intended."

"Wow," Agent Welles said. "You are good."

David looked closer. "Russian?"

"Yes. How did you know?"

"It's nitrate stock," he said. "Used commonly up to fifty-one or so, but this is in sixteen millimeter, which is rare. The only nitrate sixteen I've come across is Soviet."

Agent Welles looked impressed. She glanced at her boss.

Roger Ford slipped his eyeglasses back on. "And who said Operation Barbarossa was a failure?"

While David puzzled over that comment, Ford opened a blue folder and removed a single sheet of paper. He slid the sheet across the table to David. "The man you see in that photograph was a KGB agent named Sergei Tarkovsky," he said. "For the past six months we've been developing him as a resource, primarily via Agent Welles, who recruited him personally, and who served as his field contact."

David looked at the paper while he listened. The photo depicted a man in his thirties drinking coffee alone at an outdoor café.

"Tarkovsky was funneling Communist intel to us," Agent Welles said, "in exchange for asylum in the States for his wife and himself."

"Was?"

"Three weeks ago, Tarkovsky was shot and killed by German Democratic Republic soldiers in Berlin," Roger Ford explained. "He was attempting to defect through East Germany. And he was carrying that film with him at the time."

That explains the bullet holes, David thought.

And perhaps a few other things. He thought again of Roger Ford's strange comment: *Barbarossa*. The operational code name for Nazi Germany's ill-fated invasion of the USSR in 1941. He discovered that he'd leaned forward in his chair without realizing it.

"We need to confirm what's on it," Welles said, indicating the film between them.

David nodded toward the canister. "May I?"

"By all means, please."

He took out his handkerchief and carefully lifted the roll out of the can. Holding the roll by the spindle core, he used a corner of the cotton handkerchief fabric to lift a few inches of film.

"Well," he said, "there's the obvious mechanical damage to contend with. But the larger problem is that this appears to have been improperly stored."

"Can you fix it?"

"That all depends." David held the film segment up to the light.

"Without putting you to sleep, I can tell you that nitrate decay occurs in five stages. Once the decay reaches stage three, the film can no longer be duplicated."

"Meaning..."

"Meaning we'd be out of luck," David said.

Roger Ford said, "Are you able to tell by looking what stage this particular material might be in?"

"Based on the blooms I can see in the emulsion, I'd say we're definitely well into stage two," David said. "But it's not what I'm seeing that worries me."

Agent Welles said, "What can't you see?"

Gently, David replaced the reel back into its container and held the container toward her. "Smell that?"

Agent Welles wrinkled her nose and held up her hand. "I smelled it when I opened it, thank you."

"That's what stage three smells like, in my experience."

Welles and Ford exchanged glances.

"Is there any way you can predict," Roger Ford asked him, "how long it might take to provide a full assessment of the damage?"

"Again, that depends," David said. "I gather you're in a rush?"

"That's a fair inference, yes."

"I'd say a skilled technician with nothing else to interfere should be able to complete the work within the week," David said.

Ford nodded. "Very well. We'd like to hire you, Mr. Toland," he said. "The agency will pay your office a significant retainer for your undivided attention, with a few provisos. Are you able to accept the job?"

"Provisos," David said.

"As a temporary contract employee of the Central Intelligence Agency," Agent Welles informed him, "only you will be allowed access to this material. No assistants. No outside processors. You alone. You'll perform the work at your lab, but under my supervision, with the signed understanding that any images and/or sound you may be able to recover are Level 1 classified secrets of the federal government of the United Sates."

"We presume that a man with your background remembers how to keep a secret," Ford said.

"I thought it was my foreground you needed," David said. "Exactly what kind of images and/or sound are you expecting to find on this thing?"

Roger Ford folded his hands on the table. "If that film contains even half of what Tarkovsky led us to expect that it might," he said, "the kind of images and/or sound that rewrites history books."

David looked back and forth between them. He half expected Allen Funt and his *Candid Camera* crew to poke his head around a corner and reveal that this had all been some kind of joke. But no hidden cameras appeared, and neither Agent Lana Welles nor Assistant Deputy Director Roger Ford cracked a smile. David looked at the film on the table.

"I guess we'd better get started, then," he said.

CHAPTER

THREE

The week before Christmas, David W. Toland did the last thing he'd ever have predicted: he went to work for the Spooks again.

The first time, he'd been a twenty-four-year-old US Marine training South Korean guerilla fighters to kill their fellow human beings more effectively. Agent Lana Welles seemed unable to comprehend this fact about him, historical though it was, but David could hardly fault her for her skepticism. Some days he could hardly imagine it himself.

"According to your file, you were tapped for JACK straight out of jump school," she said, her first morning in his lab, while David hunched over the splicer. She was referring to the Joint Advisory Commission, Korea—a CIA-sponsored program that had operated out of Yong Do Island in the spring of '52.

"Then it must be true," David said, applying solvent to his cut ends with a linen swab.

"You led a Special Mission Group on a demolition raid that took out a railway bridge north of the thirty-eighth parallel," she said. "For which you received the Bronze Star. You also led a three-man POW extraction mission, also successful, for which you received the Navy Cross."

"Yes, and yes." David applied the splice tape. One more bullet hole edited out.

"And now you do...this?"

He looked at her as he straightened his back. Agent Welles wore a sharp dark suit today, indistinguishable from the sharp dark suit she'd worn yesterday, even to David's relatively attuned eye for detail. But he had to admit she wore them well.

"You say that like it's some kind of punishment," he said.

From her stool, she surveyed the array of equipment in front of him. "It does seem a little dull for a commando. No offense."

"None taken." David worked the rewinds with both hands, carefully transferring another few inches of film from the feed reel to the take-up reel. "I find it soothing, actually."

"Don't you ever miss serving your country?"

"I was under the impression that I was doing so at the moment." He put the loupe to his eye and leaned down to examine an individual frame over the light box. "National security, my government needs me, et cetera."

Agent Welles smirked. "Fair enough." She watched him work a moment, then added, "I'd apologize, but I don't believe in it."

"No apology necessary. Though I would like to hear more about our Hitler movie."

"Excuse me?"

"*Der Führer.*" He lowered the loupe, gesturing toward the light box. "That's the subject here, yes?"

Agent Welles sat to immediate attention on her stool. "You can see that?"

"Hard to miss the mustache." David couldn't help thinking of Chaplin playing Adenoid Hynkel in the film he'd screened for Meg Jenkins's fourth-grade class just before this strange detour began. There seemed to be some kind of irony there, though he couldn't put his finger on why.

Agent Welles clearly didn't care to discuss it. The expression on her face became very serious very quickly. "Let me remind you, Captain Toland, that you are bound by Executive Order 05148 . . ."

"Level 1 classified state secrets, yes," he said. "Don't worry, I'm just the lab guy. You're the spy."

"As long as we're clear on that," Welles said.

"Anyway, I'm only working frame-by-frame at this point. None of this will make narrative sense until after I transfer to new stock and we can project it. Your Level 1 secrets are safe at least until then."

Agent Welles took a long look at him. Then she looked at her wristwatch and sighed. "And how long is that supposed to take, again?"

"Patience," David told her, returning to his loupe and light box. "Adolf's not going anywhere."

*   *   *

While his staff enjoyed an unexpected three-day vacation leading into their regular end-of-year break, David worked twelve-hour shifts in the lab, cleaning and repairing the film a KGB mole named Tarkovsky had died delivering.

Lana Welles lasted exactly half of day one before deciding that the only thing duller than the process of film restoration was observing the process of film restoration, and that either David was trustworthy enough to leave alone with her spool of top-secret nitrocellulose, or babysitting him was below her pay grade after all.

She did leave yet another stout, stony-faced man in a suit and sunglasses in a chair outside David's office door. This one answered to the name Collins, unless it was David talking to him, in which case he didn't answer at all. David presumed that the man was too busy reading his newspaper and making his suit coat strain at the shoulder seams.

"Call my direct line the moment you finish," Lana told David upon her departure, "and remember: my eyes only. That includes yours."

"I'll work blindfolded," he said.

By day 3, however, even Collins had gotten bored or reassigned, leaving David to complete his work unattended. He gathered that he must have earned himself an unexpectedly high view from inside the walls at Langley. Either that, or nobody could bring themselves to view him as a credible threat to homeland safety.

Either way, finally, late on that third evening, he trudged through the deserted archive vault to his small office in the back. He used his desk phone to dial Agent Welles, expecting to leave a message on her Code-a-Phone. She answered in person on the first ring.

"Is it ready?" she said.

David said, "I guess I'm not the only one working late after all."

"You're finished?"

"And quite sleepy, thanks. I'll be here at the lab first thing tomorrow. You bring the popcorn."

"No," she said over the line. "Meet me here with the package in thirty minutes. I'll have everything ready."

She hung up before David could reply.

He sighed and put the receiver back into its cradle. A command engagement, then. Back in the lab, he wound the clean new print onto a permanent reel, placed the reel into a new can with hardly any bloodstains or bullet holes at all, collected the patched-up original, and set about packaging the footage for transport.

He was almost finished when the power went out.

"You've got to be kidding," David said to the empty lab. Disoriented by the sudden darkness, he felt his way around the work table, toward the door.

On his way, he heard movement outside, in the archive room. David thought of the night custodian and called out, "Hello?"

No reply.

As he reached the doorway, David saw a shadow move in the vault's dim emergency lighting. The back of his neck prickled. David tensed instinctively. He had just enough time to call out, "Who's there?"

Then the shadow was on him.

CHAPTER
FOUR

David felt the blows before he saw them: first to one side of his head, then the other. Psychedelic blooms of light crossed his vision in the dark, and by the time they faded, he could no longer breathe.

He became aware of a burning pain encircling his throat like a fiery rope. David pawed with his fingers. Felt the thin, tough cord cinched across his larynx. As he followed the cord back to a pair of gloved fists, his adrenaline spiked. The fists clenched, drawing the garrote tighter, and David finally understood what was happening: he was being strangled to death.

His neck veins bulged like pinched hoses ready to burst. He thrashed but had no leverage. He struggled to push his fingers under the cord. Little by little, his consciousness grew fuzzy around the edges. David imagined a heavy black curtain lowering over a screen.

Then some long-forgotten circuit breaker tripped inside him. Old training disconnected his higher brain from the animal fear signal deep within. Instead of panicking, David became calm.

He drew up one leg and thrust it back like a piston. He felt a hot, breathy grunt in his ear as his heel connected with his assailant's knee. The cord loosened just enough to allow David to turn his head to one side, letting the muscles and tendons of his neck bear the brunt of the choking force, rather than his windpipe. He managed to sip in a breath.

In the next motion, David raised both arms above his head and twisted his body, breaking his attacker's hold. In the low haze of the emergency lighting he glimpsed a silhouette clad in black from masked head to booted toe. Then he saw motion and reacted a moment too late, catching a rib-crunching kick to his side, followed by another cinder block blow to the head.

David sagged to the floor, dazed. He looked up a split second before the assassin's outline descended like a great black bird of prey.

David pressed himself flat onto his back and raised his feet. The attacker's full weight landed on his soles, driving his knees into his chest. With a roar of effort, David drove his legs up again, launching the attacker back through the air, away from him. There came a shattering crash as the figure in black stumbled over a work table, sending a raft of perfectly good lab equipment to the floor.

David was up and out the door in an instant, into the vault room and its maze of floor-to-ceiling shelves. He slipped into the nearest aisle, gathering his senses as he moved.

He was at a tactical advantage out here in the stacks, in the semidarkness, putting a little space between himself and his attacker. He'd bought himself a moment to recover. A moment to think. Most importantly, David knew every square foot of this space by feel; he could have located the copyright print of Disney's *Fantasia* blindfolded, if circumstances required.

The print he needed, however, was still neatly packaged on his work table back in the lab. *Unless he's got it already*, David thought, certain beyond doubt that it was the film this sudden assassin was here to claim.

Just then, through the shelves, he saw movement pass like a shadow just on the other side of his aisle, and he understood another thing clearly: whoever had just tried to kill him meant to finish the job first.

David slipped around the end of his aisle and up the next, creeping along, watching the adjacent aisle in flickering glimpses through the stacks. He paused, listened, and crept on, slipping into the next aisle, then the next, drawing his stalker away from the lab. Whoever wanted this film wanted it badly, and there was still enough soldier left in David to understand that whoever wanted the film this badly should probably not be allowed to have it.

So he moved silently toward a break in the shelves, trying to put his eyes everywhere at once: ahead of him, behind him, through the shelves on either side. He slipped into the break and down the next aisle, then the next.

Then the hair on the back of his neck prickled. David spun.

In the next instant, he found himself leaping backward, arms flailing, before his mind fully registered what his eyes had seen: the flash of a knife blade slicing the air inches in front of his face.

David barely had time to steady his balance before the assassin lunged again with the knife, thrusting forward and up in a gutting maneuver. He stepped aside and trapped his attacker's arm against his own ribs; in the same motion he grabbed the elbow and spun around, back into the assailant's chest.

He shoved back with all his weight, driving the assassin into the shelves behind them. Film cans rained down in a deafening clatter, spilling their contents around their feet like glossy entrails. The two of them grunted and panted and trudged around through tangles of film stock, slipping and tripping on yards of history in an absurdist tango, each fighting for control of the knife. Then all at once the knife was gone, clattering to the floor and skittering away, and David thought: *Enough.*

He dropped his center of gravity, stepped one leg behind his opponent, and shoved the attacker back, tripping him to the floor. Then he gave up the cat-and-mouse nonsense and bore straight back to the lab.

Just as David crossed the lab door's threshold a crashing weight slammed into him from behind, driving him forward, stumbling, then down into the jackstraw pile of broken equipment still littering the floor. His fingers closed around an object the size of a pencil as the assassin wrenched his foot, flipping him over and leaping atop him, arms raised. David had time enough to recognize the bulky object in the assassin's gloved hands: his 16mm film splicer, poised for a skull-crushing blow.

David shot up his arm and plunged his own object into his would-be killer's side, just beneath the other man's armpit: the X-Acto knife from his splicing table.

He heard the man grunt, then wheeze out a breath that seemed to come from somewhere in the very bottom of him. *The lung*, David thought as the film splicer fell from the man's grip, banging a gouge in the tile floor an inch from David's head. *I got the lung.* He tried to imagine the location of the man's heart, shoving the slender knife as far as he could make it go. The man shrieked and convulsed as David worked the knife's handle, trying to make the most of the small razor at its tip; he imagined running an old hand-crank Vitascope film projector as he sat up, dumping the other man's weight off his lap.

David shoved the man away with his foot, disentangled his legs, and collapsed to his elbows amid the rubble of equipment, panting. Coughing. Utterly spent.

Two feet away, the assassin in black sat splay-legged against the base of the wall cabinets, arms loose at his sides. His chest lifted slightly as he sipped a few shallow breaths.

Looking at him, David knew the blade had been sufficient after all. He gathered himself, crawled through the mess. With a blood-covered hand he yanked off the shadow figure's balaclava to reveal the craggy, pockmarked features of a face he'd never seen before—a man roughly David's own age. The man's eyes were open, staring at a spot somewhere on the other side of the room.

David's voice came from his bruised throat in a clotted rasp. "Who are you?"

As if with great effort, the dying man raised his eyes.

"Who are you?" David repeated. "Who sent you here?"

Slowly, the man smiled. A bubble of blood emerged from his lips and burst there, turning the grin black in the gloom.

Then his eyes went dull.

And then he was still.

*   *   *

"Where on earth are you?" Agent Welles said over the line. "And what's wrong with your voice?"

"Be quiet," David told her. "And listen to me."

Sagged over the desk in his darkened office, blood-smeared phone clutched to his ear, David told her as much as he could manage as quickly as he could manage it. His throat felt crimped and raw. His whole body ached. As the last of the adrenaline drained from his bloodstream, he found himself making a fist with his free hand to keep it from trembling.

"This man," she said, her voice taut with a quality David couldn't interpret. Skepticism? Disbelief? Or just the opposite? "Where is he now?"

"Still in the lab," David repeated. "Bleeding into his own chest cavity. At least he was."

"He's not there anymore?"

"I mean he's not bleeding anymore."

After a long silence, she said: "Have you called the police?"

"I called you first."

"Good," Agent Welles said. "Are you armed?"

"Of course not," David said. He thought briefly of the X-Acto knife still lodged in the assassin's rib cage, but his stomach turned at the thought of claiming it. "This is a library."

"I'm going to give you an address," Agent Welles said. "Do you have a pen?"

"Pens I have."

"Then write this down. You'll find a pay phone at this location. I'll call you there in twenty minutes."

David scribbled on a pad in the dark as Agent Welles recited an intersection of streets. *None of this,* he thought, *can possibly be happening.* When she finished, he said, "What am I supposed to do about..."

"Nothing. Just get out of there," she said. "Twenty minutes. And, David?"

"What?"

"Bring the package with you."

The line went dead in his ear.

*   *   *

Toland exited the lower level of the building at half past ten, just as he had the night before, and the night before that.

Meanwhile, a man who answered to the name Jeremiah—among other names, depending on circumstances—kept watch from his spot at the curb, undetected. Just as he had the night before, and the night before that.

But tonight, something was different. Toland hustled up the concrete stairwell onto C Street, bare-headed, wearing no scarf or gloves, his overcoat flapping open behind him despite the winter chill. As always, he carried the same battered leather satchel on his shoulder—but tonight he clutched the bag to his body like a thief. He moved stiffly, with a noticeable limp, sticking to the shadows as he skirted the pools of light from the overhead streetlamps. He didn't walk to his '53 club coupe, waiting at its regular parking spot at the curb up the block.

Tonight, for some reason, Toland ran.

Jeremiah watched Toland fumble with his keys as he opened his car. He watched Toland climb in behind the wheel without removing his bag.

The coupe's headlights flared, illuminating the bare trees lining the empty street ahead. White clouds of exhaust began to curl from the coupe's tailpipe; brake lights pulsed red through the clouds as the coupe dropped into gear.

Jeremiah started his own engine. He kept the headlights off.

When Toland finally lurched from the curb and careened away up the street, Jeremiah checked the street behind him, pulled away smoothly, and followed.

CHAPTER
FIVE

David found the pay phone at the intersection of O Street and 37th, at the edge of the Georgetown University campus. The campus, already deserted for winter break, felt eerily barren as he hurried up the sidewalk, heavy satchel slung across his body, clutched under his arm. He felt like the last student at the end of the world, late for final exams.

In reality, he was just in time. As the Romanesque spires of Healy Hall came into view, the pay phone started ringing—a thin, plaintive trill in the cold.

David jogged the last few paces and snatched up the receiver from its cradle. "I'm here."

"Do you have the..."

"I have it, yes." David realized he was clenching his jaw. "I'm fine, by the way, thanks for asking."

"I'm glad. Do you need medical attention?"

"What I need is a drink."

"You're not the only one, I assure you. Now. Listen carefully."

"Please start by telling me why I'm standing at a pay phone in the cold instead of making a beeline toward your fancy new Langley building."

Agent Welles paused. "I'm afraid it may not be advisable for you to come in right now."

"Not advisable? What does that mean?"

"Not safe."

David stood alone on the sidewalk, staring at the darkened clock tower of the Healy building, wondering what the hell he'd gotten himself into.

"I'll explain more in person. But not on the phone. I'm not far from your location now. Wait where you are and I'll come for you."

"You're not calling from your office?"

"No."

"Where are you?"

"I'll be there soon."

Even though the street was vacant in both directions, campus empty as far as he could see, David couldn't shake the sudden sensation that he was being watched.

"I won't," he said.

"You won't what?"

"I won't be here when you get here."

"Wait a minute." Her voice hardened. "Captain Toland, I want you to listen very, very closely to me..."

"I'm all done listening," David said. "And if you call me Captain again, I'll hang up on you."

Silence.

"Come here like you planned," he said, "and wait. I'll call this phone within the hour. If you're here to answer it, I'll let you know where *you* can meet *me*."

Before she could respond, he did hang up on her.

David took a deep breath and stood there a moment longer, one hand on the phone. Looking up at the Healy clock tower, he thought briefly of the library's own Thomas Jefferson Building; it so happened that the very same architects who'd designed it had also designed this building here a decade earlier. David once heard a story that the building's construction had left the university in such debt that for years they couldn't afford to remove the enormous pile of dirt they'd dug up. He wondered if that story was true.

He wondered what he was going to do next.

A thought came to him.

David dug quickly into his trouser pocket for spare change. He picked up the phone, dropped a dime into the coin slot, and placed a single call.

He felt a welcome pang of relief at the sound of the gruff voice on the other end of the line: "What?"

"Myron, it's DT," David said. "I need a favor."

CHAPTER

SIX

W hen he'd first moved to DC, David Toland had made a priority out of finding two things: a reliable auto mechanic and a good movie theater. He was still searching for the former, but the latter he'd found almost immediately: the Uptown Theater in Cleveland Park.

It was a thing of Art Deco beauty, the Uptown, with its ornate finishes, 1,100-seat auditorium, and, most importantly, its gorgeous, curved, seventy-foot screen. He'd become fast friends with the theater's proprietor, a crusty old grump named Myron Burbage, who'd started as a popcorn sweeper in 1936, the year the Uptown first opened its doors. Myron claimed he'd quit drinking in '41, and within five years he'd been running the place. *Give me another ten and I'll own her*, he liked to say. David wouldn't be surprised if one day that turned out to be true.

In the meantime, he continued to attend, at least once, every film the Uptown screened. Three years ago, he'd privately consulted with Burbage and the Uptown's current ownership on renovations to accommodate the new Todd-AO widescreen format, unveiled to the public with a seven-month run of *South Pacific* in 70mm Technicolor. He bought Myron Burbage lunch once a year on Myron's birthday, and Myron let him use the place for his own special screenings from time to time.

"It's midnight," Myron said when David arrived. He was a short man, built like a padded fireplug, with caterpillar eyebrows and wiry hair growing untended from his ears like tufts of steel wool. He wore the same threadbare cardigan sweater winter and summer and smelled, at all times, like aftershave and Listerine. "I was home in bed resting comfortably."

"No you weren't," David told him. "I called you here, remember?"

Myron shrugged and held the alley door open. "Yeah, well. I was thinking about being home in bed. Come in out of the damned cold already."

David clapped him on the shoulder as he squeezed past, into the musty stairwell. "Thanks, Burb. I owe you one."

"Uh-huh." Myron pulled the door closed behind them. "Three ain't enough I guess?"

"Sorry?"

"This silly thing." Myron made a vague gesture over his shoulder as he jingled his ring of keys and locked the bolt. "You've seen it three times already."

He was talking about the Uptown's current film, David realized—a musical called *West Side Story*, which had been running since October.

"Bunch of fruitcakes dancing around with switchblades," Myron said. "I don't get it."

"Actually, I brought my own." David patted his satchel as they climbed the creaky wooden stairs to the main level. "You've still got that old Bolex in the storage room?"

Myron glanced at David's bag, then at David. He rolled his eyes and led David on into the warmth of the theater.

The lobby was empty, so quiet that David could hear the faint hum from the neon tubing in the windows up front. Bits of popcorn and ticket stubs littered the carpet outside the auditorium, leftovers from the nine o'clock show that gave the place a lonesome, recently vacated vibe—not unlike the campus he'd just left behind, David thought. At least here he had Myron.

"Where is everybody?" David asked, looking around at the mess still waiting to be cleaned up.

"Sent 'em home," Myron grumbled. "It's Christmastime."

"You left all this work for yourself?"

"Hell, no." Myron waved a hand. "It'll keep 'til morning."

"I think you're getting soft in your old age."

"I ain't that damn old." Myron grabbed his coat from the concessions counter and shrugged into it. "What's wrong with your voice, anyway? You sound like you swallowed a toad."

David cleared his abraded throat. "I think I might be coming down with something."

"It's the damp."

"Probably."

"Scarf would help."

"Probably."

Myron jammed his well-worn homburg onto his head. "So," he said. "Who is she?"

"Who is who?"

"The girl you're showing off for."

"What makes you think there's any girl?"

"When a guy with a head cold needs the biggest movie screen in the District of Columbia at this hour for whatever that is," he said, gesturing toward David's satchel, "I figure there's a girl involved."

David thought for a moment about how to answer. "She's a CIA agent," he finally said. "I've been hired to repair a top-secret film. Level 1 state secrets, very sensitive. I needed a safe place to screen it for her."

Myron gave him a long look, his face expressionless beneath the narrow brim of his hat. "Fine, don't tell me. What do I care?" He tossed his keys to David. "Lock up when you're finished. Leave the keys in my office, I got extras."

David promised he would. "Thanks again, Burb. Like I said: I owe you one. Merry Christmas."

"Uh-huh."

With that, Myron Burbage shoved his fists in his coat pockets and headed for the doors. David could hear the man whistling lightly to himself as he exited onto Connecticut Street, out into the cold. David couldn't be positive, but after three viewings of his own, he felt reasonably certain that he recognized the tune: "I Feel Pretty" from *West Side Story*.

*   *   *

By the time the knock at the front doors came, David was ready and waiting. He could see Agent Lana Welles through the windows, stamping her feet and rubbing her gloved hands together as she waited outside on the sidewalk. He used Myron's keys to open up for her.

"What the hell is this?" she demanded.

"This is a movie theater," David said. "Manager's a friend of mine."

She stalked past him, into the lobby, then turned on a heel. "Tell me something. Are you having fun?"

"I don't understand the question."

"Obviously you think this is some kind of game," Agent Welles said. "So I'm just curious: are you enjoying yourself?"

Turning his back, David took great time and care in relocking the front doors. He breathed slowly through his nose, afraid that if he opened his mouth just then, he might say something to Lana Welles that he'd regret later. When the doors were locked tight, he took another moment. Counted to ten.

Then he turned around again.

"Somebody tried to murder me tonight. I killed him instead. With my hands." He heard an angry tremble creeping into his own voice. He took a deep breath. Straightened his shoulders. "I understand that you wouldn't know this about me, because we've only just met and it's not in my file, but killing another human being is something I promised myself I was never going to do again. So, to answer your question, no. I don't think this is a game."

Agent Welles seemed momentarily taken aback by his response. But only momentarily. "Can I assume by the fact that you've brought me to a movie theater that you have the package here with you?"

"Ready to roll," he said.

"Show me."

"First tell me why it's not safe for me to come in to CIA head-quarters."

Agent Welles met his eyes, then looked away. She busied herself, taking off her gloves, stuffing them into the pockets of her overcoat.

David said, "Shall I repeat the question?"

"I have reason to believe," she said, "that my operation has been compromised."

"Compromised how?"

"That's what I don't know yet," she said. "But for some time I've suspected a breach."

"What kind of breach?"

"A mole."

David took a moment to absorb this news. Given the events of the evening so far, it didn't come as much of a surprise. He said, "You mean a mole like Sergei Tarkovsky?"

"Exactly like Tarkovsky," she said. "Only alive and well. And working from inside *my* organization."

David looked at Lana Welles. She stood there and let him look. There seemed a kind of defiance in her posture.

He put Myron's keys in his pocket and walked past her, toward the auditorium. "Welcome to the Uptown," he said. "Right this way."

CHAPTER

SEVEN

D avid led Agent Welles down the center aisle to the front of the empty auditorium, where he'd positioned Myron's old Bolex projector on a wheeled cart at the center of the screen. Except for the screen itself—seventy feet wide by forty feet high—and the lavish Art Moderne décor, not to mention the thousand empty seats behind them, it was very much the same setup as he'd used to screen *The Great Dictator* for Martin Ellroy and his fellow fourth graders just a week ago. The days since already seemed like a lifetime.

Lana Welles went straight to the projector, unconcerned with the grandeur around her. "Is it intact?"

"Not entirely," David said. "But I tried to keep the major surgery to a minimum. I saved and cataloged the fragments, per instruction." He gestured to the film cans stacked on the cart. "Along with what's left of the original."

She reached out and touched the projector's rear spool.

"That's the new print," David said. "The good news is, the nitrate decay wasn't as severe as I'd predicted. And I'm hopeful that the wet gate took care of most of the lesser damage to the emulsion. Scratches and so forth."

"Let's find out."

David gestured to the nearest seat in the front row.

Lana Welles shook her head and faced the screen. "For this, I think I'll stand."

He shrugged and switched on the projector. The reels turned. Sprockets clicked and clacked. A flickering window of light appeared at the end of the projector's beam, a meager square frame in the center of the massive screen. White letters on a black card appeared: CIA LEVEL 1—ITEM #1031-A—16NOV1961.

Then the movie started.

*   *   *

The first clip began in sunshine.

A man in a knit shirt and jodhpurs played catch with his dog at the shore of a mountain lake. The dog, a beautiful German Shepherd, bounded and barked, its voice reduced to a thin, monophonic warble over the projector's small speakers.

The man, quite obviously, was Adolf Hitler in civilian clothes. He looked like a soul at peace. Absently, David thought, *I'm watching Hitler's vacation movies.* It was the latest surreal turn in an evening that already felt like a dream.

"Blondi," Agent Welles whispered, staring at the screen.

"What?"

"His dog," she said. "That has to be Blondi. Which dates this between '41 and '45. Just as Tarkovsky claimed."

The image quality, David felt a certain sense of self-satisfaction to see, was generally very good, at times even better than he'd hoped. The film skipped frames occasionally, quick jump cuts where he'd removed bullet-torn frames from the original. Occasionally the black-and-white images faded to ghosts; sometimes they darkened to murky blots. Every so often, an emulsion bloom turned a series of frames to illegible sludge. But for the most part, the content on the screen was clear to see: Adolf Hitler—aka Der Führer, aka Herr Wolf, aka the most notorious mass murderer in human history— playing fetch with his dog.

The next clip featured a small gathering of people in what looked to be a modest, windowless sitting room. Three men—including Adolf—were decked in their military best. Hitler stood next to a lovely woman wearing a buttoned, black silk dress.

Eva Braun.

"The Führerbunker," Welles said. "Also as Tarkovsky promised. We could have used that man."

David still didn't know much about Tarkovsky, but he definitely knew of the Führerbunker—the subterranean complex in Berlin where Hitler had spent the last days of World War II.

Lana began to point out the figures on the screen. "That's Goebbels. And Bormann. Which must make the third man Walter Wagner."

"Who's Walter Wagner?"

"The man who married them." She stared at David a moment, then turned back to the screen. "This is footage of the marriage of Adolf Hitler to Eva Braun. The day before they committed suicide together." She glanced at him again, quickly, then back to the screen. "Honestly, there's a part of me that still doesn't believe what Tarkovsky told us about this film. And I'm seeing it with my eyes."

As an artifact it was, David had to admit, remarkable. On any other day, he'd have been enthralled by these images that he'd been tasked to restore, images previously unseen by history.

But today, he only wondered what any of these images could possibly have to do with national security. And why the hell they'd nearly gotten him killed.

The scene cut again, this time to a handheld view down a dim, concrete corridor. There was a sense of commotion and disarray as uniformed SS officers crisscrossed the frame.

Then came a jump cut—more bullet damage—and they were looking at a wood-paneled study. Hitler, still decked in his wartime finest, sat on a printed sofa next to Eva's slumped, motionless form.

Over the audio track came the sudden, sharp crack of a single gunshot.

The Führer's head snapped back.

Then he collapsed forward, dead.

This, David realized, with mounting awe, was the scene of the famed double suicide Agent Welles had just mentioned. Actually captured on film. It was beyond incredible.

But who had shot Hitler?

As the camera panned quickly to the source of the gunshot, David became aware that he and Lana had unconsciously taken seats next to one another in the front row, utterly absorbed in what they were seeing. He imagined observing the two of them as a bystander, from a distance—as Myron Burbage, perhaps. Out of context, they looked almost comical. The strangest movie date in history.

Then two things happened.

First, the camera settled on the sneering face of a second Adolf Hitler, this one holding the smoking pistol in one hand. The *real* Adolf Hitler, David immediately theorized, remembering all the stories he'd heard of look-alikes and decoys the Führer had employed. And with that theory, the significance of this film clicked into place all at once. Here, before him, was the answer to all his questions: the real Hitler. And his freshly murdered double.

Then, the flimsy mono soundtrack of the Führerbunker film resolved into a sudden, deafening roar as machine-gun fire erupted from the back of the Uptown Theater, stitching a line of jagged holes across the screen.

CHAPTER
EIGHT

David pulled Agent Welles to the floor, covering her with his body as bullets chewed up Myron's beautiful screen, the proscenium, the seats above their heads.

Immediately he recognized military training in the three-round bursts coming from the back of the theater; it was a demonstration of controlled fire right out of the field manual, tied together by the occasional long, blatting spray designed to discombobulate the senses, create panic among targets. The sound put him back in Korea, behind enemy lines, as immediately as if he'd never left—as if he'd only dreamed the near-decade separating that life from this one. For a moment, all he could think was, *Why is this happening to me?*

Then the fire ceased abruptly. In the flood of sudden silence, David heard the unmistakable sound of a spent magazine hitting the deck, followed by the metallic *chack* of a new magazine being slapped into place, a receiver bolt engaging.

He felt Agent Welles writhing beneath him and whispered, "Are you okay? Are you hit?"

"Get," she panted, her voice muffled by his sweater, "the *hell* off me."

He rolled to his side just as the gunfire resumed, this time focused on the projector cart. Bullets *whinged* and metal *whanged* as reels came unsprung, film cans hopped and spun, as the projector itself flew apart into pieces.

David stared at the carnage in progress, feeling a sharp pang of loss. Then Agent Lana Welles was up and running along the front row in a crouch, her overcoat flapping behind her, a Walther PPK in her hand.

The gunfire shifted, trailing her badly, gnawing through the seats behind her, sending tufts of upholstery batting into the air like dandelion chaff in summertime. *Not so good with a moving target*, David thought smugly. It didn't make him feel all that much better. Meanwhile, Lana reached the end of the row and dropped to a knee, motioning urgently toward him: *come on*.

Then she popped up and fired three quick shots catercorner across the middle rows, toward the unseen gunman at the back of the theater.

As David gained his feet and prepared to run, he looked back over his shoulder to see that the projector cart had fallen over sideways, spilling the demolished projector and all its contents into a pile. Even as he watched, the pile caught fire, sparks from the damaged projector lamp sifting down into the volatile nitrate scraps of original footage, leaping into an instant conflagration on the carpet in front of him.

He heard Agent Welles yelling *"Get the film!"* before a fresh burst of gunfire drowned out her voice.

David was already crawling toward the heat of the fire, circling it on all fours, looking for a place to dart his hands in. He finally plunged them straight into the flames, cutting his palm on a sharp curl of metal as he tore the mangled front spool free from the projector. He burned his fingertips on the hot metal of an overturned can, felt the hair on the backs of his hands singeing and curling. Then he dropped flat to his belly as a bullet whined past his ear, an angry wasp with a lethal sting in its tail.

David reached up and grabbed the strap of his satchel as he elbow-crawled toward Agent Welles, who remained crouched in the aisle at the end of the row.

When he got there, she hopped to the end of the next row to make room for him. "You let yourself be *followed*?"

Seared hands stinging, David shoved what little material he'd managed to recover into his satchel as another burst of ammunition thudded and clanged through the seats near their spot. "Tell me something," he called through the noise. "Exactly who is trying to kill us right now?"

"I don't know!"

"Then what makes you so sure it was *me* who was followed?"

Agent Welles barked in frustration, turned, fired three shots. Then she crouched again, calling back to David through the hammering whine of return fire. "Where's your car?"

"Alley!" he said, particles of wood, plastic, and fabric dancing in the air between them.

"Exit?"

"I'll lead us out."

Agent Welles nodded sharply. "I'll cover you. Go!"

With that, she popped up and snapped five more shots toward the back. David hugged his satchel and ran like a fullback up the aisle toward the ornate, hand-carved auditorium doors leading out. In his peripheral vision, he caught sight of a figure diving into a row for cover, just as he heard the impotent click of Agent Welles's hammer falling on an empty chamber.

Somehow, she was only steps behind him as he reached the doors. They burst through together, out into the foyer, then sprinted toward the alley exit, David leading the way. He heard the sound of the auditorium doors banging open behind them; he grabbed Agent Welles by the arm and hauled her around the corner to the stairwell as bullets shattered the wall sconce near his head.

They tromped down the stairs and blasted through the service door, out into the cold. Alley grit crunched under David's shoes as he ran to the car, dove in, unlocked the passenger side.

The moment she could open her door, Agent Welles piled in and shouted, "Drive!"

David cranked the engine, dropped into gear, and mashed on the gas. An oncoming swarm of bullets perforated his trunk in a staccato *thonk* of punctured steel, shattered his back window in a cymbal crash of glass.

Agent Welles ducked down beneath dashboard level; David crunched and drove with his hands on the wheel above his head, tires squealing as he cornered out of the alley, onto Connecticut, away.

* * *

Jeremiah lowered his Kalashnikov and watched, bracing the theater's alley door open with his body, as Toland's club coupe cornered onto the cross street, scratched its tires, and disappeared.

He listened to the high wine of the revving engine as the coupe sped away.

He listened to tires squall as the car took the next corner.

The engine revved again in the distance, finally fading to nothing, restoring the neighborhood to sleepy silence.

Somewhere in the quiet, a dog barked.

Somewhere beyond the end of the alley, a porch light came on.

Jeremiah cursed softly, retreated back into the shadows of the empty theater, and pulled the alley door closed behind him.

CHAPTER
NINE

Following instructions, David drove them south out of Cleveland Park, down Connecticut, around Dupont, and onto Massachusetts heading southeast. Agent Welles stared ahead, arms folded, clutching her coat around her neck as David clenched his jaw to keep his teeth from chattering. Cold wind from the shattered back window whistled and swirled around them inside the car, a traveling echo of the bedlam they'd just left behind. But the discomfort was fine with David.

Better wind than bullets, he thought.

Neither of them spoke another word to the other, though David developed an idea about where they were heading without needing to ask.

He just couldn't work out why.

Finally, Agent Welles said, "Take Columbus," and he complied, steering them on—indeed—to the very destination he'd predicted: Union Station terminal, lit from ground to gable in all its triumphal Beaux Arts glory.

Only after he'd parked and switched off the engine did David look over at Agent Welles and say, "Planning a trip?"

She pushed open her door and got out of the car without looking back at him. "Bring the film," she said over her shoulder, "and come on."

*   *   *

Twenty minutes later, David sat alone on a bench in the soaring, vaulted Main Hall while Agent Welles spoke on a pay phone nearby. Satchel open beside him, he contemplated the material he'd managed to rescue from the projector fire back at the Uptown.

He'd cobbled together a mismatched film can: the bottom from the new print and the lid from the old one, both scored now with black licks of char. Inside the can, what remained of the acetate safety stock had melted together and hardened again, fusing itself into a useless wheel of plastic.

David stared at the molten wreck on his lap. He felt numb. Disconnected. Far afield. The terminal's Main Hall seemed like a great stone cavern, shared only between himself, Agent Lana Welles, and a few scattered souls awaiting the day's final train out of town. He felt as though he were observing the whole of it from a remove. He might have been back at his lab, monitoring a train station sequence from Meg Jenkins's imagined spy picture on a tabletop viewer without color or sound.

"We've got to go."

He looked up to find Agent Welles standing before him in her overcoat.

"Who were you talking to?" he said.

"I attempted to make a number of contacts."

"Deputy Director Ford?"

"Assistant Deputy Director Ford," she corrected. She looked as if she'd swallowed something that hadn't tasted pleasant. "Among them, yes."

"What did he say?"

"My orders are to bring you to Langley immediately for debriefing."

"So why are we at the train station?"

"My operation has been suspended," she said. "Effective immediately."

He studied her. David had never seen Agent Welles look this way before now. She almost appeared...vulnerable. Slowly, it dawned on him what she was trying not to say.

"You mean *you've* been suspended," he said.

"I'm not clear on my current status," she said. "Or yours, for that matter."

"I thought I was just the lab tech."

Agent Welles said nothing.

"But I've seen something I shouldn't have seen," he said, speaking as much to himself as to her. He thought about it, then added, "Of course, you'd have prepared for that already. The CIA."

Again, no response.

"That's why you didn't use your own people for this." He looked at her. "I was a loose end the moment I sat down in Ford's office, wasn't I? Designed to be snipped." Another way of phrasing it occurred to him. "Edited out."

She met his eye directly at last. But still she remained silent.

David realized that he should feel angry. Manipulated. Betrayed. Alarmed. But he felt nothing. It was as if his emotional circuits had melted into an inarticulate lump like the one on his lap.

"He was yours," he said. "The man who came to see me in the lab. Ten minutes after I called to tell you my work was finished. The man I killed."

"Yes," Agent Welles said simply.

David waited for more, then remembered that she didn't believe in apologies. "And at the theater?"

"Yes," she said. "At the theater, I was going to finish the job myself."

"Jesus."

"Nothing personal."

"As much as I appreciate your candor, I meant the other guy."

"Oh," she said. "I don't know who that was."

He had absolutely no reason to believe her. Except perhaps for the simplest reason of all. "But he was there for both of us."

"I was left with that unmistakable impression, yes."

"And now here we are." He glanced around. "At the train station."

"For the moment." She checked her watch. "The last train out of the District leaves in ten minutes. I'll be on it. I'm inviting you to travel with me, at least long enough for me to get us somewhere safe. I owe you that much."

David suddenly couldn't help laughing. It just bubbled up and out of him—a harsh bleat that echoed back to them from the vaulted ceiling. "Gee, thanks," he said. "Are you sure that's all you owe me?"

Agent Welles glared at him. "I will not explain my actions to you," she said. "And I'm not going to defend myself. Not to you or anybody else. I will acknowledge that you've been treated poorly, Captain Toland…"

"And you wondered why I didn't want to come work for the CIA."

"And I'm acknowledging my role in that treatment."

"I imagine that must be easier for you," David said, "now that we're both in the same boat."

Agent Welles closed her mouth and set her jaw. Once again, she stood silent.

"What about Deputy Director Ford?" he asked her.

"Assistant Deputy Director Ford," she said. "What about him?"

"He's your boss, isn't he?"

"He's superior to me in the chain of command."

"You're not planning to defend yourself to him?"

"Not for serving my country, no." She grimaced, then muttered something else. David wasn't quite sure he'd caught it all. But it sounded like she'd said, *He's the one who ought to be defending himself to me.*

"So where does that leave us, exactly? Being in the same boat and all. I'll need to go home and feed my cat at some point in the future."

"I don't know!" she said, with a sudden sharpness and volume that startled David. A few of their fellow travelers turned their heads briefly, then went back to their newspapers.

Agent Welles took a step closer, dropping her voice. "All I know is that somebody in the Company is doing their best to hang me out to dry. Over *that*." She jabbed a finger at the ruined film print in David's lap. "I don't know who, and I don't know how. I don't even know why. But I'm pretty sure *that*"—she jabbed her finger again—"was the only chip I had to play. And now it's gone." At this point she straightened her spine, rolled her shoulders, and took a deep breath. "So. Until I can get to ground and dig into this, your cat is the least of my concerns."

David didn't really have a cat. He didn't even have any house-plants. What he had was a job that he liked and a life that he resented being forced to abandon, even temporarily.

But he didn't tell Agent Lana Welles any of that. All he said was, "Ford thinks you're the mole. Doesn't he?"

Calmly, she said, "I'm forced to assume that's a possibility."

"Are you?"

"I'm assuming that anything could be a possibility at this point, yes."

"I mean, are you the mole?"

Her eyes flashed, then narrowed. After a long beat, her garnet-red lips pressed together into a rather chilling smile. In that moment, Agent Lana Welles struck David as both gorgeous and terrifying.

"If I were," she said, "I can promise you three things: you'd be dead, that film would be intact, and I'd be long gone."

David searched her face. She waited.

Eventually, he sighed, closed the film can, and stuffed it back into his satchel. Then he stood and shambled past her. His whole body felt heavy.

Agent Welles said, "Where are you going?"

He pointed wearily toward the barred ticket window on the far side of the terminal, then showed her his wristwatch. "Train leaves in seven minutes," he said over his shoulder.

CHAPTER
TEN

Their line ended in New York City—normally David Toland's favorite city on earth at Christmastime. Tonight, that city he'd come to know so well as a visitor seemed very far away. And not just in miles.

He sat with his head back against the seat, staring out through his own reflection as the city lights of DC gave way to the snow-dusted fields of the southern Maryland countryside. The rhythmic thrum of the train gradually worked its way into David's tired bones— a hypnotic counterpoint to the flat, open landscape beyond the window, cast in a silver-white glow by the light of the moon.

He'd nearly dropped into a doze when Agent Welles, across from him, said, "Nora Charles?"

He opened his eyes to find her looking at her ticket in the overhead light.

"I figured we shouldn't put them in our own names." He shrugged. "It just popped into my head."

"I get that part. I'm just curious to know where you came up with the name," she said. "Someone you know?"

Good grief, he thought. *Sacrilege.* "You might say that."

"Who is she?"

"Nick and Nora Charles?" David shifted in his seat. "William Powell and Myrna Loy, *The Thin Man*, 1934. Adapted from the novel by Dashiell Hammett." He stifled a yawn with his fist. "Husband and wife who solved mysteries together."

Agent Welles raised an eyebrow. "And I take it you're Nick?"

"Like I said. It just popped into my head."

She made a vague shape with her mouth that might have been a smirk. Or maybe she had heartburn. She reached up, switched off her light, and turned to her window. "Dream on, Captain," she said.

David nodded in the dark. "I expect to be reimbursed for those tickets, by the way."

*   *   *

He tried again to fall asleep but found that he couldn't. He gave up around Baltimore.

Later, as the lights of suburban Philadelphia began to flicker through their windows, strobing across their seats, Agent Welles—unprompted, and without preamble—said, "The man you killed tonight was a highly trained operative."

David didn't know what sort of a response she expected. "Sorry for your loss."

"My point," she said, "is that you obviously remember how to handle yourself."

"Depressing thought, isn't it?"

"And at the theater," she continued. "Under fire. You were calm and deliberate. Yes, of course, I'm aware of your file. But even so: After nearly a decade in civvies, I suppose I find it somewhat impressive that . . . I'm sorry, am I boring you?"

She was, but that wasn't what had turned David's attention. Somewhere between Baltimore and Philly he'd taken the film can from his satchel again, impatient with the ride but unable to keep his eyes closed. Now he found himself staring at the can's lid—the bullet-riddled, bloodstained lid from the original print Sergei Tarkovsky had smuggled to the West.

He reached up and switched on his overhead light, picking the lid up in his hands for a closer look. David felt along the curled edges of the classified tag, apparently loosened from the metal by the heat of the fire. When he pinched an edge and gave a gentle tug, the label's baked adhesive crackled and gave way. The tag came away easily in his fingers, revealing a second tag beneath.

Agent Welles said, "What are you doing?"

He flipped the lid around to face her, holding it under the cone of light.

Her eyes widened. She switched on her own light. "May I see that, please?"

He handed it over. Agent Welles inhaled sharply as she studied the exposed tag. "When did you notice this?"

"You watched me notice it," he said. "Just now. What is it?"

"Don't you know?"

"I don't speak Russian."

She sat back with the lid in her hands, appraising it like an excavated treasure. "This is a Kremlin filing tag."

Indicating clearly, if David's interpretation of the printed numerals was correct, that the film can in Tarkovsky's possession had contained not one ultra-secret reel of history-changing film footage, but rather, the first reel of two.

"Huh," he said. "I guess they had another one."

They rode on in silence, overhead lights still on, blacking out their windows. David could see her reflection in the glass. In another context, Agent Welles might have been a pensive young woman traveling by train to meet a lover. Or leaving one behind. He wouldn't have been able to tell the difference.

At last, just as the glittering New York cityscape pierced their reflections, she turned to him with what might have been the first genuine, unguarded smile he'd ever seen on her face. She raised the lid an inch from her lap.

"You don't understand what this means, do you?"

"To me?" He shrugged. "Not really, no."

"Well. The first thing it means—to both of us—is that Tarkovsky was telling the truth."

"You already knew there was a second reel." It didn't surprise him.

"It was part of our negotiations. One reel delivered up front. Information about the other after we brought him in." She held the lid in her hands like an empty plate waiting to be filled. "We presumed it to be a bluff, but that didn't matter."

"Our side still wanted the reel he had."

"The one he claimed to have. Yes." She tapped the secret label with her finger. "But if Tarkovsky's stories keep bearing out the way they have so far, the second reel could be even more valuable than the one you restored."

Considering the state of the first film, it also could turn out to be worth less than the stock it was printed on. Either way, what was the point? "I still don't see what good it does us."

"Absolutely no good at all, if I don't find the second reel. Tell me something, Captain Toland."

"Only if you stop calling me Captain."

"How would you feel about a little field trip to the Soviet Union?"

He didn't realize he was laughing until he tried to stop. Agent Welles waited patiently for him to collect himself.

"Sorry," he said, pressing the heels of his hands into his tired eyes. "At first I thought you were offering to show me around the USSR."

"As long as we're stuck together." She waggled the lid. "You do realize that you've found an actual lead we can use?"

David thought, *Are we stuck together?* He said, "A lead to what, exactly?"

"Is that a serious question?"

"Look. Let's be crazy and say you could manage to get your hands on this second reel. In Russia or wherever the hell else on planet Earth it might happen to be. Operating outside the agency. As a fugitive, no less. Then what?"

"Well, let me think." Lana raised her hands and began counting rhetorical points on her fingers. "I jump the command chain like a damned subway turnstile and deliver Tarkovsky's second film straight to the DCI, clearing my name. Which clears your name as a matter of course. I . . ."

"My name? Why would *my* name need clearing?"

"Refresh my memory," she said. "Was it you who was telling me something about murdering a man in a government building earlier this evening?"

"You mean the man you sent to kill me?"

"That's the man I mean, yes."

"That was self-defense. Not murder. And it was your fault, not mine."

"Ah," Lana said. "I presume you left some kind of clearly worded note to that effect before you fled the scene? Preferably somewhere near the corpse? Because it would be a flat-out American tragedy if Assistant Deputy Director Roger Ford were to draw the mistaken conclusion that you and I were somehow in league with one another as enemies of the state."

"Very funny."

"Is it? You're not laughing anymore."

David sat back in his seat. She was right: he didn't feel so much like laughing now. He'd been so focused on staying alive that his own appearance of guilt in this situation had never even occurred to him.

"And just in case you've lost sight of the larger picture, Captain Toland, we're still talking about documented proof that the most notorious war criminal of the modern age may be alive and well." Lana appraised him openly. "God only knows where. Planning only God knows what."

A new level of aching fatigue settled over him like a blanket. "Why don't we do each other a favor," he said, "and cut the baloney?"

"How do you mean?"

"We're not talking about a big picture. Just a bunch of little ones, all strung together. That's the only reason in a million you'd propose what you're proposing."

"I'm not sure I understand."

"The second film." He pointed at the lid in her lap. "You think you might need me."

"Well, of course. I'd have thought that was obvious."

"The only thing obvious to me is what happened the first time you thought you didn't need me anymore."

Agent Welles rolled her eyes. "Honestly, I'd hoped we'd put all that behind us at this point."

"Uh-huh. And what about the next time?"

She turned back to her window. "If you'd prefer taking your chances with Roger Ford, that option remains open to you."

They didn't speak again until the train clattered into the main terminal at Pennsylvania Station in New York City, two-hundred-odd miles from where they'd clattered out of the main terminal at Union Station in DC. As their fellow passengers began to disembark, Agent Welles gathered her things, rose from her seat, and handed the lid back to him.

"A souvenir. I've memorized the number. Good luck to you. And, Captain Toland?"

David sighed. He was getting tired of correcting her, so he didn't bother.

"If I could do it all over again," she said in parting, "knowing what I know now, there's a chance I wouldn't order your assassination."

David looked at the lid.

He looked at Agent Welles, who had already turned away.

She was halfway down the aisle to the open doors before he finally said, "Russia, huh?"

PART II

In the Cold

CHAPTER

ELEVEN

New York, New York

In the autumn of 1952, David Toland led a three-man Force Recon team on a black operation in the Nangnim Mountains of North Korea, deep behind enemy lines. Their objective had been to extract two American GIs and a South Korean intelligence operative from a POW camp maintained by a KPA guerilla unit—a mission they'd completed successfully, in a downpour of bone-chilling rain, under breakpoint personal strain.

David and his crew had earned medals over it. One of the two GIs they'd brought back had gone home to Wichita, Kansas, where he'd fathered a brood and opened a successful Oldsmobile dealership; the other had gone home to drink himself to death by the age of forty-five. Meanwhile, the South Korean spy had supplied information to United Nations Command that helped lead US infantry forces to victory on Pork Chop Hill in April '53.

And now you do this? Agent Welles had asked him in the lab, nearly a decade later.

Don't you ever miss serving your country?

David could have reminded her that in July '53, the other side took the Chop right back again. A couple thousand men had died with their guts hanging out, and nobody on either side could say, from a military perspective, what was so all-fired important about that damned hill anyway. People in crisp uniforms signed the armistice three weeks later, which would have happened anyway; if everybody on what the brass simply called Hill 255 had put down their guns and had a picnic instead of shooting each other to death like they'd been told, only the gravediggers would have suffered.

He hadn't said any of that to Agent Welles, of course. David hadn't been on Hill 255 himself, and none of it had much to do with what she wanted to know anyway. Not really.

All Lana Welles really wanted to know was how any man could throw away all of Captain David Toland's talent and training and still call himself a proud American. The answer to that question was basically pretty simple, and he imagined Agent Welles would have found it unsatisfactory.

Captain David Toland was sick and tired of killing people. That was all. Sick and tired of seeing them killed, sick and tired of making decisions that caused them to be killed, sick and tired of teaching others how to kill them, sick and tired of killing them himself. Tired in mind and body. Sick all the way down to his soul.

Of course he still loved his country. Warts and all. He'd simply come to believe that there were other ways to fight for it. Other ways to preserve it.

Sometimes you had to destroy what you hated in order to save what you loved. Okay, sure. He supposed there was no way around it. Freedom, as they said, was never free.

But David himself had personally done enough destroying to last a lifetime. And he had other talents to offer. Hell, two years ago, United Artists made a Pork Chop Hill picture. It starred Gregory Peck, Rip Torn, and George Peppard, and one day it might even end up in David's lab. To be prepped for posterity in the very basement Lana Welles seemed to hold in such low regard.

She booked them adjoining rooms at the Stanhope on Fifth Avenue, across from the park. So much for the Nick and Nora Charles routine. Under the circumstances, David couldn't claim to be disappointed.

The room smelled nice, though he didn't get a look at it until morning, when he awoke facedown in the middle of the bed, atop the covers, banded in sunlight, still in his clothes.

David turned over and sat up, blinking, unsure at first where he was. He felt rich, heavy fabric beneath his hands. He looked around and saw high-end Louis XVI furniture. Near the bed, he spotted a chinoiserie lamp on a side table and what looked like original art on the walls.

Then, finally, he remembered what had brought him here. David yawned, stretched, threw his legs over the edge of the bed, then sat there for a long while, head in his hands.

He felt like he'd been thrown off a bridge. His entire body ached from tip to tail. His throat felt like he'd swallowed a mouthful of pea gravel; his bruised neck muscles complained when he lifted his head. He had slick red stripes and stinging sprocket marks on his palms and knuckles where he'd burned his hands on the flaming film projector back at the Uptown.

David forced himself up and into the lushly appointed bathroom, where he relieved his aching bladder into the gleaming porcelain bowl. He splashed water on his face and looked at himself in the mirror over the sink, hardly recognizing the stubbled, bleary-eyed wreck looking back at him. He cupped his hands under the faucet and took a long, gloriously cooling drink.

When he felt moderately restored, or at least fully conscious, David shambled back out to the bedroom, marveling again at Agent Welles's apparent idea of "getting to ground." He peeled back a curtain to look out the window, down at the bare trees of Central Park eight stories below, thinking, *The CIA must pay better than they used to.*

It was only then that David turned from the window and realized that the door separating his room from Agent Welles's room stood ajar.

And that his wallet was missing.

Satchel, too.

*   *   *

By the time David returned to his room, he'd turned Agent Welles's room upside down; searched the hotel lobby, restaurant, and lounge; spoken with the front desk, the concierge, and the bellmen; even taken a rapid, figure-eight walk east around a two-block radius— from 78th to 76th between Fifth and Madison, ending back at the Stanhope where he'd begun. At this point, he finally admitted the obvious to himself: Agent Lana Welles had robbed him of his cash and identification and left him there.

Perhaps she didn't feel she needed him so badly after all. *Be glad she didn't put a bullet behind your ear while you were facedown, sawing logs on a two-hundred-dollar bedspread*, he thought.

Then he thought: *Jesus.*

Now what?

David stared out his window at the world passing by down below. He watched cars and motorbikes jostle with cabs and couriers, all working their way south on Fifth. He watched men in suits tip their hats to bundled-up women pushing bundled-up carriages on the cobbled walkway alongside the park. He even watched a man in a grime-stained Santa Claus suit sit on a bench, panhandling for spare change. *I should join him*, David thought.

It was eleven a.m., three days before Christmas, and he'd never felt stupider. Or more alone.

He was still standing there at the window at noon when he heard the sound of a tumbling lock from the room next door.

David rushed in to find Agent Welles entering, casual as a breeze, room key dangling on a pinky finger. She carried a garment bag over one shoulder, his satchel on a hip, and a bulging, grease-stained deli bag in her other hand. She saw him, smiled, and said, "Ah. You're up."

"Where the hell have you been?"

She scrunched her brow. "Wow. Married one day and the honeymoon's over already." She kicked the door closed with one heel, saw him glaring, and said, "Good grief, relax. I had a few errands and wanted to start early. I didn't realize you'd need a babysitter."

"Errands?"

"That's right." She held up the deli bag. "And I assumed you'd be hungry."

"So you broke into my room and pickpocketed me?" he said. "While I was sleeping?"

"I didn't want to wake you." She came into the room, draping the garment bag onto the bed. "And 'broke in' is putting it strongly, don't you think? Especially considering I paid for both rooms." She looked around. "Which aren't the worst, really."

David began to feel exasperated. He pointed toward his satchel hanging bandolier-style across her torso. "You needed the film for your errands?"

"The film is in your top dresser drawer, if you can still call it a film." Agent Welles rolled her eyes. "I just needed the extra carrying space."

David turned and stalked back into his room, where he immediately saw the film can exactly where she said it would be. He stared at the can as though it were a mirage, unable to believe he hadn't noticed it there before.

When he walked back to her room, hands stuffed in his pockets—still angry, but starting to feel silly for still being angry, now feeling angry for being made to feel silly—he found Agent Welles seated at the round burlwood table in her small dining area, digging into the deli bag. As he stood there watching, she pulled out a sandwich the size of a clock radio, bundled up in waxed paper.

"Maybe you're not hungry," she said, "but I sure as hell am."

*   *   *

It turned out he was hungry.

Ravenous, in fact. David caught one stray whiff of Lana's sandwich—piled high with steaming corned beef and pastrami on aromatic marble rye bread—and began to salivate.

It was his body's reaction to the stress of the previous day more than anything resembling genuine need, he knew, but knowing didn't change the reaction. His stomach growled audibly, giving his weakness away to the world, and when she pulled out a second sandwich for him, he sat down as much to join her as to hide the fact that he'd gone a bit loose in the knees.

"God, I love New York," she mumbled through a mouthful, her cheeks bulging with food.

David closed his eyes involuntarily as the mingling flavors of cured meat and mustard and toasted rye hit his pleasure center. He would not have gone so far as to kiss Agent Lana Welles out of gratitude for a corned beef on rye. But three bites in, he reluctantly conceded that certain things could be forgiven.

"Okay, then," she said, a few minutes later, dabbing the corners of her mouth primly with the corner of a napkin, having polished off her heaping lunch like a lumberjack on whistle break. "On to the good news and the bad news."

David kept eating. "You mean there's good news?"

"Actually, first things first." She dug into his satchel and tossed his wallet across the table. "That's yours."

He resisted the urge to flip the wallet open and count what was left of his cash. It would have meant putting down the sandwich. "So, what do you owe me for lunch?"

Agent Welles smirked. "Don't worry, Rockefeller. Your fortune's intact. But that brings me back to the good news/bad news." She wadded up her empty sandwich wrapper and stuffed it back in the sack. "The not-surprising bad news is that my operations account has been frozen."

"I was going to say start with the good news."

"The good news is that I still have access to Diners Club, AmEx, and a fair amount of personal cash under various names," she said. "So we'll be funded. At least for a while."

David couldn't help noting her sudden ease with the word *we*. "So why did you need my wallet?"

"Right. Next item of business."

She dug into his satchel again, this time retrieving two fat brown envelopes. She handed one across to him, kept the other for herself.

David shoved the last of his sandwich into his mouth, wiped his fingers on a napkin, and chewed while he opened his envelope.

Inside, he found a New York state driver's license and an international travel passport, both bearing his photograph, accompanied by the name John Davis. Folded around the phony IDs were a certified copy of a Massachusetts birth certificate, also for a John Davis—born on David Toland's birthday, as coincidence would have it—and a certified Connecticut marriage certificate: Davis, Mr. John and Mrs. Irene, of New Haven.

"You had a good instinct with the husband-and-wife thing," Agent Welles said. "It makes sense, traveling together. Fewer looks, fewer questions. It just needs to be less cute. That's all."

David held up the driver's license. Without a loupe, it was indistinguishable to his eye from an authentic one. "Where on earth did you get all this stuff?"

She smiled. "I still have associates outside official channels."

David turned the passport over in his hands. "Your associates work fast."

"I try to associate myself with reliable talent when possible." She dug into the satchel again, this time retrieving a pair of long blue envelopes with the white Pan Am airline logo printed on the side. "Now. Given the global climate at present, the Soviets don't permit individual entry into the USSR. So I've booked us a late-afternoon flight to Amsterdam out of Idlewild. We'll join a tour group to Moscow there."

David opened the passport, flipped through it. The work really was impeccable. John Davis appeared to be quite the world traveler. "Christmas with Khrushchev," he mused.

"Something like that."

"Forgive me for questioning," he said, "but what do we plan to do when we get there? Ask around if anybody's missing any top-secret intel?"

Again, Agent Welles smiled. "I have an idea or two where to start," she said. "Anyway, neither one of us can go home for the moment. We may as well go to Moscow."

Once more, she dipped into the satchel. She brought out one item after the other and placed them on the table: men's deodorant, a can of Barbasol and a razor, a comb and a pair of grooming scissors, a bottle of talcum, a tin of shoe polish.

"I don't want you to take offense," she said, "but you could do with a clean and press before venturing out."

He found his eye drifting over to the garment bag on the bed. "Do I dare ask what's in there?"

"Just a pretty dress." She batted her eyelashes theatrically. "And a few changes of clothes. A girl on holiday needs to be presentable."

He looked down at his rumpled clothes reflexively.

"I didn't want to guess your size," she said. She removed a crisp stack of bills from her pocketbook and handed them across the table. "You'll have time to shop for yourself before we go. I've seen how you dress: neat, respectable, boring. Perfect."

"That's me."

"And one formal outfit," she said. "Black, obviously." She appraised him. "You do have nice shoulders. Single-breasted for you, I'd think. Tie, cummerbund, no tails, for God's sake no ruffles—Saks should have everything you need. Do you know how to get there?"

"You mean Saks Fifth Avenue?"

"Exactly."

"No. Where is it?"

She smirked. "Very funny. Our luggage is to be delivered here, to the hotel, by three o'clock. Our car to the airport leaves at three forty-five. Can I answer any other questions before you go back to your room so that I can get under the shower?"

David sat and looked at her. Agent Lana Welles seemed like an entirely different person this morning. It was almost hard to believe that just over twelve hours ago she'd sent a man to his lab to assassinate him.

"Actually, just one," he said.

"I'm waiting."

"As long as you're buying my toiletries and clothing, and we're traveling abroad together as husband and wife, do you think I should start calling you Lana? Or do you still prefer Agent Welles?"

"Actually, John, darling," she said, "I think you'd better get used to calling me Irene."

CHAPTER

TWELVE

Amsterdam, The Netherlands

They lifted off the runway at Idlewild Airport just before five o'clock that afternoon. They touched down at Amsterdam Airport Schiphol just after midnight.

In between, David Toland (aka John Davis) took the opportunity to ask Lana Welles a number of questions about herself. He had a hundred more pertinent questions he could have been asking, but just then— with nowhere to go and nobody to kill them for at least the next several hours—he was curious to know who he was traveling with. Agent Welles (aka Mrs. Davis) took the opportunity to answer none of them.

"Oh, come on," he said. "I'm not looking for your innermost hopes and dreams. A harmless fact or two, that's all. You already have all of mine on file."

"Had," she reminded him.

"Semantics."

"The past is semantic," she said.

But in the sleepy, pressurized quiet of the darkened cabin— spotted here and there by the glow of an overhead reading light, punctuated now and then by the scratch and flare of a cigarette lighter, or the soft *bing* of a passenger calling for a stewardess—he began to enjoy making a nuisance of himself.

Finally, somewhere over the Atlantic, she sighed, shifted in the seat beside him, and said, "Fine. I was born a small girl."

David nodded. "Go on."

Her mother, she told him, had been a prominent Washington socialite with philanthropic tendencies. Her father, meanwhile, had been in the intelligence game himself, first as an OSS officer in the European Theater during WWII, later as a special advisor in Truman's State Department. Lana Welles had grown up in a very nice house in Silver Spring, Maryland, where her parents had entertained important people often and memorably.

"So," David said. "You were born to be a spy, then."

"No," she said, displaying a flash of irritation. "I paid more dues than my share, as a matter of fact."

He hadn't meant it that way, but David didn't correct himself. Maybe he'd try that "no apologies" policy of hers. See what that felt like for a change.

It was a quiet ride from there.

*   *   *

On the ground, David loaded their sturdy new Airstream luggage into the back of an airport taxi while Lana directed the driver to the city center. They took a room at the Hotel Estheréa— a very cozy, very charming, very Dutch converted row house on the Singel Canal, a few minutes' ride from Amsterdam Centraal Station.

Then there was the bed question, but David was too tired to discuss it. He slept on a pile of blankets in the bathtub.

Saturday morning, he woke up with knots between his shoulders and a kink in his neck. Later, he'd remember that morning as the first time he glimpsed Lana Welles in her nightgown—an impractically sheer affair for winter in the Netherlands, it seemed to him, though not an easy sight to forget.

They took turns in the bathroom, dressed, and had coffee at the window. Instead of making small talk, they watched ice skaters glide along the canal, scarves trailing behind them as they carved their way toward a festive-looking Christmas market on the corner of Singel and Wolvenstraat.

An hour later, on their way to the train station, a light snow began to fall. The cab passed a stone pillar on David's side of the street; set into the pillar was a cast brass plaque pointing the way to a historical address: HUIS VAN ANNE FRANK, PRINSENGRACHT 267.

Anne Frank's house. He felt a vague stitch of unease as they passed the monument. David couldn't help seeing the plaque in light of this pursuit they'd undertaken: to track down proof about the fate of the very man who had made that address—Prinsengracht 267—historical in the first place. And somehow save their own skins in the process.

He turned to Lana, prepared to voice his renewed misgivings about the whole operation. But at the last moment, he kept it to himself. They rode on in silence, gazing out their respective windows at the gingerbread city around them, the storybook snow falling over the frozen canals.

Two hours after that, they were on a train to Magdeburg with a motley crew of retired Europeans, organized by an eccentric Belgian named Vermeersch, who called themselves the Galloping Merry-makers.

CHAPTER
THIRTEEN

J oren Vermeersch had been a minor-league footballer for Royal Antwerp before an unfortunate collision in the 1928 Belgian Cup championship left one of his knees folding both ways. After a number of surgeries, he took up bicycling for therapy and cannabis for pain, became interested in Mexican folk art and American jazz music, discovered that he'd always been interested in men more than women, and eventually began his own business leading cycle tours along the Scheldt. Over the years he'd grown this business into the small but thriving international touring concern he now operated single-handedly, claiming to have abandoned the concept of long-term partnerships some happy time ago.

David and Lana learned these things within five and a half minutes of meeting their tour coordinator, a smiling, moon-faced fellow who, at fifty-three, showed a zest for life in both deportment and waistband. Yet David saw vestiges of athleticism in the way Vermeeersch carried his somewhat overburdened frame, and he liked the man quickly.

Under Vermeersch's jolly directorship, the Galloping Merrymakers numbered more than a dozen in total, most of them well into their sixties, all brought together by a shared appetite for travel, adventure, and the desire to be far from their homes and families during the holidays.

Among them, David and Lana met Klaus and Lita Diefenbach from Cologne. Klaus had been an orchestra conductor, Lita his first chair oboist. They met Charles Bibieau, a florid-faced poultry baron from Reims, and his wife, Olly—the jovial wife of a poultry baron from Reims.

They met Andres and Natalia Lucero, who owned a silver shop on Majorca. They met the buxom Federspiel twins, silver-haired sisters from Lucerne, who had never married but had, as they claimed proudly, placed internationally as a pairs cross-country ski shooting team in their younger days.

They also met—to David's rather embarrassed yet thorough delight—one Simon Lean: a handsome, single Englishman in his forties, traveling alone.

"I think that's Simon Lean," David whispered to Lana.

She plucked the olive from her martini and said, "Who?"

"Simon Lean. The author."

She squinted through the crowded club car as she popped the olive into her mouth and chewed it down. "Who?"

"You've got to be kidding," David said, and before he could stop her, Lana was leading him over by the hand, slipping easily between shoulders and around conversations, her drink held high to avoid jostling.

"Wait a minute!" he hissed, pulling back halfheartedly.

But she was already busy tapping Simon Lean on the shoulder. "Excuse me, but aren't you Simon Lean, the author?"

Lean turned from Olly Bibieau and received Lana Welles with a polite, practiced smile. "I'm afraid you've found me, my dear," he said. "And you are?"

"Irene Davis." Lana allowed Simon Lean to kiss the back of her hand lightly, then said, "This is my husband, John."

"Ah," Lean said. "John. A pleasure."

"All mine, Mr. Lean." David shook the author's hand with more vigor than he'd intended, feeling profoundly idiotic. "I've read all your books."

"Good God. How unfortunate for you."

"I'm so embarrassed that I hadn't even heard of you," Lana said, adding a self-deprecating flutter to her voice that David might have fallen for himself, if he'd only just met her. "I suppose I'm not much of a reader. What kind of books do you write?"

"Third-rate thrillers," Lean said amiably, "that fetch top-rate advances." He winked and sipped his whiskey. "It's quite appalling, really."

He was, in fact, traveling to research his latest novel—the plot of which, he assured them, was too preposterous to divulge.

"Well, I'm a fan," David said. "Your books certainly passed the time when I was in the service."

"Ah! A military man. Where did you serve?"

"Korea," David said, and immediately felt Lana's fingernails digging into the flesh of his wrist. Her face showed absolutely nothing amiss; she merely carried on watching Simon Lean, smiling and friendly, as if fascinated by the international bestseller's every word. Braced by the sudden pain, David recognized that his two stiff gin and tonics had lubricated him a bit more than he'd realized.

She's right, he thought. *Pull yourself together.*

"But I never actually left Fort Stewart," he added quickly. "I was 3A. In my case the A stood for asthma."

Lana's talons loosened slightly. David wondered if his wrist was bleeding.

"And what did you do at Fort Stewart, then?"

"Payroll, mostly."

Lana's grip disappeared. He felt her pat the back of his hand: *Good boy, honey.*

"Ah, Savannah," Simon Lean said. "A beautiful town. I love the way the Spanish moss hangs from the trees like…Spanish moss hanging from trees, I suppose. Well." He raised his whiskey glass. "Let it be said that the Georgian coast of the United States never fell under attack while John Davis was on watch."

Lana giggled breezily and raised her glass. "I'll drink to that!"

David stared at her. She ignored him. After they'd polished off their drinks and ordered a fresh round, Simon Lean said, "And what do you do these days, John?"

"Payroll, mostly."

Lean barked out a laugh. "Good God, we should get you on with my publisher immediately. They could use a good man in the accounting department."

And that was the company David Toland kept, as Mr. John Davis of New Haven, Connecticut, in the smoky, convivial club car of an eastbound passenger train, creaking and clacking over the frozen lakes and through the dark snowy forests of central Poland.

*   *   *

He couldn't trace the exact moment things changed between himself and Lana Welles.

Of course, as husband and wife, they'd shared a sleeping car for a night; David had taken the upper berth, Lana the lower, and they'd each vacated the car entirely for the other when it came to personal grooming and changes of clothes. But it was still a small space, paneled all around in cozy cherrywood, intimate whether they meant it to be or not. Maybe waking up together that morning had subconsciously paved their eventual path back that night.

Or maybe it was the lively camaraderie of the party that second night. The conversation, the laughter. The food and the drink. The bawling, impromptu Christmas carol sing-along led by Joren Vermeersch with a skinful of wine.

Or maybe it was the husband-and-wife act itself, working a bit of a spell after the heightened tension of the past few days, gradually taking on a life of its own. They'd played their roles convincingly, David had to admit, eliciting more than one toast to young love from their travel mates, and by night's end he'd sensed that he and Lana had become something of a wistful memento to the elder couples in the group.

All he could say for sure was that as the party burbled on—
and as the alcohol continued to flow—it seemed to him that Lana
began to laugh at his dumb jokes just a little bit easier. Occasionally,
he caught her glancing at him when she thought he wasn't paying
attention; often, he felt the glances lingering. Sometimes, while
chatting away with this person or that, he found her fingers resting
lightly on his arm.

Maybe he was imagining it, or maybe Agent Lana Welles was just
that good at her job, but as her alabaster cheeks took on a flush, and
her cinnamon eyes gained a slightly over-moist twinkle in the warm
low light, David would have sworn that he was in the presence of a
very serious young woman relaxing—genuinely enjoying herself—for
the first time in a very long while.

God only knew he was doing a fair bit of relaxing himself. In
fact, after matching Charles Bibieau and Simon Lean whiskey-for-
whiskey for the better part of two hours, he found himself relaxed to
the brink of major motor failure.

David showed his palms in surrender the next time Simon raised
his hand for another round. "Under no circumstances," he said.
"I know when I'm licked." He stood from the table and collected
himself. "Gentlemen."

Then the car hit a rough joint in the track and he canted suddenly
off to the left. Lana, deep in conversation with the Federspiel twins
nearby, stepped over quickly to offer a steadying hand.

But she was none too steady herself, by that point. They
stumbled, swayed, attempted to help each other, and somehow
ended tumbling backward into one of the upholstered settees—
laughing, legs in a tangle, Lana's drink sloshing over both of them.
The Merrymakers cheered and toasted their tipsy spectacle. David
felt the heat of embarrassment in his cheeks.

"Oops," Lana said, and lost herself to the giggles again.

David braced himself with one palm on the cushion, the other
on her hip, extricating himself from their awkward arrangement and
pushing himself cautiously up to his feet.

"I think I need a jolt of fresh air," he said.

"Boo," Lana said. "You're no fun."

"Your drink's empty anyway."

She regarded her glass. "You're right."

"Upsy-daisy," he said, offering her his hand.

She took it. He helped her up. They bid their companions good night and left the car together, arm in arm, accompanied by a round of good-natured cheers and applause.

"I think we're a hit," Lana said.

"I think everybody's drunk," David replied.

Out in the dim corridor, he could hear the party falling back into swing behind them. A muffled eruption of laughter from the club car faded and disappeared as they moved on, giggling and shushing each other, weaving and yawing from one wall to the other with the motion of the train.

The tail of Lana's blouse had come untucked, David couldn't help noticing, her skirt tugged amusingly off center. At one point, she said, "Oh, forget it," and held on to his shoulder for balance while she removed her heels. She carried them with her by the straps the rest of the way, thumping along in her stockings. She took his hand and allowed him to help her across the chilly vestibules in between cars.

At their cabin, David fumbled with the key, turned the lock, and pushed in through the door, flipping on the wall lamp as he entered.

Lana followed close on his heels, switching the lamp off again. "Too bright," she murmured.

"I knew it," he said. "You're a vampire."

"You don't know the half of it."

Hands on her hips, David steered them in a circle, trading places, so that his back was to the door. Silvery moonlight filtered in through the half-shaded window, silhouetting her figure as she turned and pulled out her hair. He watched her massage her own scalp with her fingertips. All at once, in close quarters, he became supremely aware of the scent of her perfume. Bergamot and spice.

He shook his head as if to clear it. Thought, *Get a grip on yourself.*

"I'll step out so you can get undressed," he said.

"Oh, don't bother," she said. "We're legally married. Sort of."

"It's okay," he said. "I don't mind."

She stood silent a moment, her back to him, hand-tousled hair draped around the collar of her blouse.

"Fine," she said then, turning again, stepping into him.

David felt a moment's discombobulation as she leaned forward, pressing him back against the door with the full length of her body. She was daintier than he'd realized. Lithe and firm. But soft in all the right places. He felt the door close behind his back with a soft snick of the latch.

"I thought you were going to step out," she said.

David didn't remember making the decision to kiss her. He'd done it before he'd known he was doing it. Softly. Just once.

Lana didn't close her eyes. He knew that because he hadn't closed his.

She looked at him curiously in the moonlight.

He was about to apologize when she tilted her head and parted her lips slightly, as if to say, *Is that all?*

CHAPTER
FOURTEEN

David awoke Christmas morning with a pounding headache and a mouth full of glue, alone.

He sat up in the upper berth, struck his head painfully, and remembered that he was still in the lower. It was the last thing he remembered, in fact: lying naked there, under the covers with Lana, spooned together in her narrow berth. Warm. Listening to the sound of her breathing in the dark while the train rocked along.

Now there was only a rumpled, roughly Lana-sized space beneath his hand.

David winced, swung out his legs, and sat very still for a moment, waiting for his head to stop swirling, his sour stomach to stop rolling. Or at least for them to start swirling and rolling in the same direction. He noticed the door to the darkened bathroom standing open. He noticed Lana's suitcase unzipped on the valet. He saw an outline of gray daylight around the shade over the window, which had been open to the moonlight last he recalled. Dimly, it occurred to him that she must have pulled the shade down for him on her way out.

He rose unsteadily and shambled into the bathroom, relieved his bursting bladder into the too-small bowl. In his condition, with the sway of the train, it was all he could do to aim successfully at such a meager target. He splashed his face at the sink, cupped his hands under the spout, and guzzled half a dozen large gulps of water from his palms.

Mistake.

Back to the toilet. Up came the water, and everything else in his stomach, followed by a dry heave or two for good measure. When his midsection had finally stopped convulsing, David sat on his bare ass, pressing his face against the cool porcelain pedestal under the sink, hoping to either feel better or die—either one, but soon.

When at last he reemerged into the main cabin—a bath towel wrapped around his waist in a gesture of decorum that seemed silly upon reflection—David noticed something that confused him: Lana's seamed hose and one of his wool dress socks, hanging side-by-side from a set of coat hooks inside the closed cabin door.

He puzzled over the sight a moment. Then he remembered: Lana had put them there. In between go-rounds. *Stockings for Santa*, she'd said, grinned at him playfully, and came snuggling back to bed.

David noticed something poking out from the top of his sock. He went over and found a curled piece of railroad company memo paper with a handwritten note in blue ink:

Went to breakfast. Join if you like.

~~*Lana.*~~ *Irene.*

*   *   *

He found her sitting alone in the dining car, one elbow on the table, head propped in her hand. She wore a loose sweater this morning, snug cotton pants, and a very large pair of very dark sunglasses. Her breakfast appeared to consist, at least as far as David could see, of a half-drunk cup of pitch-black coffee and a cigarette smoldering between her fingers.

He caught sight of Simon Lean sitting with Joren Vermeersch and the Bibieaus several tables behind her, on the other side of the aisle. Simon raised his coffee cup casually in greeting as David entered the car. Beside Simon, Vermeersch smiled broadly, pointed toward Lana, pressed his palms to either side of his head and rocked back and forth—the international pantomime for "splitting headache," David presumed. He put a palm ruefully to his own forehead, to which they all chuckled and returned to their plates.

By then he'd reached the free side of Lana's table. He stopped but didn't sit down. Lana lifted her head weakly.

"Merry Christmas," he said.

"Bah, humbug," she answered. But she attempted a smile.

He liked her without makeup. "You remain the early riser, I see."

"I didn't want to wake you."

"Where have I heard that before?" He made a show of checking his back pocket, pulling out his wallet. "Oh, there it is. Whew."

"Are you going to sit down or just stand there being funny?"

"Ho-ho-ho."

Lana sighed. "Suit yourself."

David stooped carefully, held the table for balance, and worked his way into the space across from her. It made his head spin to move any faster.

"You look like I feel," she said.

"You must feel awfully handsome."

She took a listless drag from her cigarette. "You're full of it this morning, aren't you?"

He flagged a passing waitress and begged her to bring him a cup of her very strongest coffee. Then he nodded toward Lana's hand. "I didn't know you smoked."

"One more for the very long list of things you don't know about me." She took another puff, blew the smoke up and to the side. "Though I suppose that list got significantly shorter in certain categories last evening. No?"

David opened his mouth to respond, then realized that he didn't really know what to say.

"I'm sorry." Lana dropped the cigarette into her coffee with a sizzle, gesturing vaguely over her shoulder. "I nicked one from Simon. I don't really smoke. Not very often, anyway."

"Ah," David said.

"I don't drink like that very often, either," she added. "Which may or may not have been evident. What's the matter with you?"

"I just realized that I owe you an apology," he said.

"For what?"

He took a deep breath, rubbed his palms over his face. "I'm not sure what to say for myself. I'm not normally the kind to take advantage. At least I didn't think so."

"Advantage?" She tilted her head. "Of what?"

"Of . . . situations," he said.

"Situations?"

"Last night."

She sat still for a long moment. *She's going to make me come out and say it*, David thought. *Of course she is.*

Then she lifted her sunglasses an inch, appraising him from beneath the dark lenses with red-rimmed eyes. "You're serious, aren't you?"

"Do I seem insincere?"

She dropped the glasses and shook her head, a broad smile spreading across her face.

"What's so funny?"

Lana folded her arms on the table and leaned across conspiratorially. "You do realize that I'm a trained CIA field operative," she murmured, "and not some fourth-grade schoolteacher with big dewy eyes?"

David opened his mouth. Closed it.

"For God's sake, I've infiltrated *governments*." She leaned back again, still grinning. "It was like pulling teeth to get you to take me to bed, by the way. If that makes you feel any better."

He could feel heat creeping into his face now. "Oh," he said.

A rustle of activity in the dining car distracted his attention momentarily. In the booth behind Lana, a middle-aged man folded his newspaper, signed his check, and rose to leave. David watched the man idly, noticing his white-blond hair and unusually clear blue eyes. The blue-eyed man noticed him in return, nodding in acknowledgment as he passed Lana and David's table, tucking his paper under his arm.

Lana tracked David's gaze over her shoulder just in time to notice Simon Lean, Joren Vermeersch, and the Bibieaus also leaving their table, now heading David and Lana's way.

"Time to get back into character," she said, turning to face him again. "Try and pretend you're married."

David collected himself. "Right."

"To me, preferably."

He gave her a smirk.

They went back to work.

*   *   *

Jeremiah unfolded his newspaper and waited in the drafty vestibule outside the dining car, choosing a spot at an angle to the windows where he could see, yet not be seen.

He'd caught up with them in Minsk, boarding the quiet train in the predawn hours while most of the passengers had still been asleep. He'd freshened, changed his clothes, then found his way around the slumbering train until he was satisfied that his ground-work was complete. When the dining car opened for service, he'd bought himself a cup of coffee. And the newspaper.

Now he waited, nodding occasionally to those who passed him on their way out or on their way in. He waited there, looking at his newspaper, until Toland and Welles had been served their breakfast on fine white China: Belgian waffles with syrup for her, boiled eggs and sausage for him. A plate of toast each. A pot of coffee on the table between them.

Plenty to keep them occupied for the time he needed. By the look of them together—Mr. and Mrs. John Davis indeed—he doubted he'd need very long.

Then, finally, once he'd recovered what he'd lost in DC—what he'd been sent all this way to bring back again to the men who'd sent him to get it—he'd fit the silencer to the muzzle of his pistol, find a spot behind the door of their sleeping cabin, and patiently await their return.

CHAPTER
FIFTEEN

At five minutes past nine, Jeremiah made his way down the carpeted aisle toward the closed, walnut-paneled door of Welles and Toland's empty cabin: number 548.

He scanned the aisle in front of him as far to the connecting vestibule as he could see. Then he glanced over his shoulder the way he'd come. All was quiet in both directions. He was alone.

Jeremiah put on his gloves as he walked. He worked the fingers snug. Then he slipped his lock-picking kit from inside his jacket, though he might not have bothered.

He never had a chance to use it anyway.

Ten paces from number 548, the door crashed open; Welles and Toland's cabin turned out not to be empty after all.

Jeremiah stopped in his tracks as a tall man in sunglasses hurried out. The man wore the lapels of a woolen sport coat flipped up around his chin, a gray flannel fedora pulled low on his brow. He took one quick look to his left, then one to his right.

He saw Jeremiah standing there.

Jeremiah narrowed his eyes and growled, "You."

The man turned and sprinted up the corridor without another pause. Jeremiah gave chase, calling upon all his reserves, narrowly brushing the back of his quarry's jacket just as the man slipped through the vestibule to the connecting car. Jeremiah pushed through, into the milling crowd of tourists collected there—a yammering herd mindlessly waiting to be led along to trough.

"Hey," one of the men said.

"Move!"

A woman: "My word."

Another man grabbed him by the back of the collar. Jeremiah reached behind his head, grabbed the unseen hand, and twisted the man's thin-boned wrist until he heard a yelp.

Another woman: "Hey! You can't just...Arthur, are you all right?"

Jeremiah was still shoving his way through them, cursing, when he saw the man he chased reach the far end of the car. The man jerked open the door to the next vestibule, then paused and turned briefly.

The man smiled. Tipped the brim of his hat with a finger.

And slipped away.

*   *   *

Around twenty past nine, David and Lana walked back to the cabin together, sluggish from breakfast but feeling marginally human again, to find the door to number 548 standing open.

"I guess the maid's here," David said.

Lana stopped instantly, removing her sunglasses. She slipped a hand in her purse. "You didn't leave that door open?"

"No."

"You're sure?"

David jangled the key on his finger. "Positive, dear."

She looked both ways, up and down the corridor, then put a hand on his chest and moved past him, her Walther PPK in hand.

"Have you been carrying that this whole time?"

She jammed a finger to her lips: *Shhh!* Then she pointed to the floor: *Stay.* Then she slipped inside the cabin.

David waited for about five seconds, felt utterly stupid standing there, and followed her in. He found Lana standing in the middle of the cabin: one hand pointing the gun toward the ceiling, the other hand on a hip, a scowl on her face.

"Jesus," he said, looking around.

Their quarters, at some point during breakfast, had been turned inside out and upside down: suitcases upended, clothing strewn everywhere, mattresses and linens torn from the berths. The vanity doors hung open. Bureau drawers had been torn out and flung. Even the window shades had been pulled free of their mounts.

Lana turned a circle in the rubble, then looked at him, eyebrows raised.

"The maid service on this train is terrible," he said.

She stooped and picked up his satchel from the floor. She pulled back the flap, held the bag open for him to see. "And they steal," she said.

David stood in place another moment, surveying the godawful mess they'd stepped into. He felt his headache coming back.

"Who?" he finally asked her. *"How?"*

"Unimportant questions at the moment, I think."

He tried another one: "What happens now?"

"Whoever took that can from your bag is about to discover that they've swiped a can full of melted scraps." She dropped his empty satchel back to the floor. "If they're even half smart, they'll take one look at the label and figure out where we must be going."

David closed his eyes. When he opened them, it was still Christmas morning. He was still on a train, their cabin was still wrecked, and whoever they'd been running from had apparently found them.

"What then?" he said.

Lana stepped around him through the mess and calmly pushed the cabin door closed. She locked the bolt. She popped the magazine from the butt of her pistol, counted her loads, and slapped the clip back in.

"Let's concentrate on getting off this train in Moscow alive. Then I guess we'll see."

*   *   *

Jeremiah spent a quarter hour in the frosty baggage car, breathing white plumes and watching through the windows until a conductor and a coach attendant completed their door-knocking patrol in the adjacent Pullman. The company men gestured to their own physical features as they spoke to each passenger; they indicated an approximate height relative to their own. They were searching, clearly, for the blue-eyed man reported to them by a babbling clutch of overexcited Europeans.

Once they'd finally moved on, empty-handed, Jeremiah slipped into the same car behind them and returned to his cabin. Also empty-handed.

Again.

Back in his roomette, he raided his rarely used identity kit for a salt-and-pepper mustache and theatrical-grade wig, feeling like a buffoon as he applied them over the narrow vanity. He was a twenty-year field man, not a Times Square Marx Brother; cheap disguises were for greenhorns and drama students. He popped in a pair of colored eye lenses anyway, hating the way the brittle, space-age polymethyl saucers grated against his corneas. There would be a cost for this indignity. A bill Jeremiah would relish collecting indeed.

But for now, he was consigned once again to recede. For the second time in four days, his best opportunity had passed. Toland and Welles were now restored to high alert. Meanwhile, there was a new operator in the mix. The package was still in the clear. His superiors would be unhappy. Jeremiah was unhappy.

Fortunately, he was also patient.

And it wouldn't be much longer before this train reached the end of the line.

*   *   *

All that Christmas Day, nobody came to kill them.

Nobody came to kill them for so long that Lana eventually got tired of waiting, tucked her Walther under her sweater, and went looking for somebody to kill them, fully intending to kill that somebody first.

David, for lack of anything more helpful to contribute, tagged along.

"If killing us was an objective," he suggested, "why didn't they just wait for us to come back from breakfast?" He thought about it, then added, "Better yet, why not strike in the night? While we were still—"

She glanced at him sharply.

"Sleeping," he said. "I was going to say sleeping."

"I wouldn't presume to know," Lana answered.

Nor did she seem inclined to speculate. Three cars later, he tried a different approach. "Can I ask how you'll know them if we find them?"

"The plan is to shoot anybody who looks at me twice. If they stay alive long enough to answer questions, I'll ask them a few."

"Almost everyone looks at you twice, Agent Welles."

"Aren't you sweet."

"You've always said it was the reason you married me."

Finally, as they made their way through the crowded observation car, David took her by the elbow and steered them into a pair of freshly vacated seats.

"What are you doing?" she hissed.

"It's a crowded observation car," he said. "If anybody's coming to kill us, couldn't we observe them coming from here?"

Lana scowled, closed her eyes, and drew in a deep breath through the nose. She exhaled slowly.

Beyond the large, frost-glazed picture windows, the eastern flat-lands of the Byelorussian SSR stretched off toward the horizon, a crusted field of new-fallen snow twinkling in the morning sunlight. It wasn't a bad view, David thought, all things considered. Nice and empty. Peaceful.

Lana turned in her seat, scanning left to right, then slowly back again, watching the interior of the car instead.

Two hours later, they pulled into Belorussky Station, tense and on edge, more than slightly confused.

Upon debarking, the Galloping Merrymakers swept them back into the fold. Captained along under the enthusiastic guidance of Joren Vermeersch, the group chittered and chattered among themselves all the way to the platform, then up to the street level above, ready for anything that Moscow might have in store.

CHAPTER
SIXTEEN

Moscow, USSR

At the heart of the city, within the Garden Ring, upon a slender urban island in the historic Zamoskvorechye District, stood the Hotel Bucharest: seven stories of old-world opulence between the Moskva River and the Vodootvodny Canal.

Lana—as Mrs. Irene Davis—paid extra for a suite that featured grandiose views of Red Square, just across the river. Upstairs, after an early dinner with the Merrymakers in the hotel restaurant, he stood at the window while Lana showered. Across the river, atop Borovitsky Hill, bathed in skyward rays of surreal white light, were the storybook spires of St. Basil's Cathedral; the Gothic turrets and gold-limned clock face of Spasskaya Tower; and the dramatic, Imperial façade of Grand Kremlin Palace itself.

It almost seemed to be waiting for them.

Lana eventually emerged from the bathroom wrapped in steam and a complimentary robe stitched with the Hotel Bucharest coat of arms. She spent the rest of Christmas night looking out the same window in silence.

David fell asleep trying to judge her reflected expression in the inky glass.

*   *   *

The next morning didn't seem to break so much as fade in, a hard gray day beneath a low concrete sky.

Once again, David woke alone in a strange bed, Agent Lana Welles nowhere to be found. He stood at the window, bleary-eyed, watching a foreign world carry on about its business five stories below. Motorized vehicles of various unfamiliar makes and models passed on the streets, trailing clouds of frozen fog behind them. People huddled along the boulevards, small dark jots against the snow. Ice floes gave the vacant river the look of shattered pavement.

Once again, Lana returned on her own eventually. She was well-bundled today, head wrapped in a woolen scarf, her nose and cheeks raw from the cold.

"You're up," she said. "I was hoping that would be the case."

David sipped his coffee from a delicate gold-rimmed cup. "You've been shopping again."

Closing the door with her hip, Lana strode purposefully toward him, heels clicking along the marble entryway. Shopping bags hung from her shoulders. In her arms she carried what looked like a small dog wrapped in striped tissue paper.

"Here," she said. "I bought this for you."

"I thought we agreed we weren't exchanging Christmas gifts this year." David placed his cup onto its saucer so that he could accept the bundle. Peeling back the tissue paper, he found in his lap a boxy fur hat with ear flaps tied up at the crown.

"What do you think?"

David looked at the hat. "I don't know what to say."

"Try it on. Let me see."

He did as instructed, catching a glimpse of himself in the dressing table mirror. He looked like a villain from a Simon Lean novel. In pajamas.

She frowned at him. "What's so funny? That's sable."

"Sorry," David said. "I appreciate the thought. I just can't decide if it's my style."

Lana dropped her other bags, stripped her gloves, and unbelted her overcoat. "Even if you had a style, that's not what I'm concerned about at the moment."

"You're right. We need to blend. Sorry, I'm still getting used to being a spy."

"Don't worry," she said. "You're still the lab guy."

"Then what am I missing?"

"First of all, there's not a man, woman, or child within the borders of the USSR who won't peg us for Americans at twenty paces, hat or no hat."

"Then why did you buy me the hat?"

"Because the average temperature in Moscow this week has been negative fifteen degrees Celsius," Lana said. "And because at the shop where I purchased that hat, there was a man. Would you like to know what the man was doing there?"

"What was he doing?"

"Preparing to spend an entire month's salary on a hat just like that one." She pointed at David's head. "That's how important a good hat is here."

"Oh."

"It's called an *ushanka*, by the way."

"I didn't know that."

"Now you do," Lana said. "Thank me whenever you're ready."

His new *ushanka* really was about the softest thing he'd ever touched that wasn't alive. David's head was sweating already. "Thank you," he said. "It's an excellent hat."

"Now the bad news: the Merrymakers spotted me downstairs."

"Why is that bad news?"

"Because it ruins the excuse I'd prepared," Lana said. "So now you're the one who's stuck in bed with the flu."

"I am?"

"Far too ill to tour Red Square today, obviously. I'll need to stay back myself to look after you."

"That doesn't sound so bad, actually."

"Simmer down. We're not actually staying here."

He sighed and took off the that. The room suddenly felt ten de-grees cooler. "Where are we going?"

"To visit Sergei Tarkovsky's widow," Lana said.

*   *   *

Late in the morning, after the Galloping Merrymakers had galloped off to make merry without them, David and Lana boarded the Metro train at Arbatskaya Station, a frigid ten-minute walk from the hotel.

Their agenda: to call upon the wife of a dead Russian spy in search of clues to the whereabouts of a top-secret film. If Lana's thinking proved sound, then succeeding in this mission could go some distance toward, first, saving their skins and, second, altering the course of world history.

David breathed through the nose as they walked, warming the ice-shard air as much as he could before it pierced his lungs. He found himself wondering what the people he knew back home were doing today. The archive would be closed, along with the rest of the Library, not to mention Capitol Hill proper; he imagined his colleagues nursing mulled-wine hangovers. He imagined Meg Jenkins enjoying time with her family somewhere, perhaps in a house with a fireplace. He imagined men in suits and sunglasses out shaking the bushes, searching high and low for a rogue agent and a fugitive film restoration expert.

Around him, he saw men in business attire and long wool over-coats, heads covered by their own fur *ushankas*, chatting on street corners or hurrying along their way. He saw women in babushkas wielding flat-bladed shovels, filling potholes in the street with cold-patch asphalt. He saw dressed-and-pressed officers of the MVD *militsiya* replacing frazzled Soviet propaganda posters with crisp, colorful fresh ones. A block from the station, they passed a cinema playing a World War II double feature. Both films were Soviet treasures David knew well: Chukhrai's *Ballad of a Soldier*, and Kalatozov's *The Cranes Are Flying*. The sight of the theater made him think of the wreck they'd left of the Uptown back in Cleveland Park. Poor Myron.

They caught the train to a blighted suburb at the end of the line. From the terminal, they followed an off-kilter network of buckled sidewalks, lined by bare trees on one side, chain-link fencing on the other. Here—in stark contrast to the city center they'd come from—they appeared to be the only people out and about at this time of day. Soon enough, David found himself surrounded by an entire neighborhood of five-story apartment buildings built of concrete block, many of which appeared to be deteriorating where they stood.

"*Khrushchyovka*," Lana said.

"What does that mean?"

"It means slum." She gestured at the buildings around them. "Khrushchev built most of these rat traps within the last five years, if you can believe it."

He followed Lana into the building she chose, noticing immediately that Khrushchev's housing authority seemed unburdened by a heating bill for this particular address. Their breath frosted in the vestibule.

"This way," Lana said.

The stairwell wasn't any cozier. They climbed three floors to an empty hallway with cracked walls and a creaky subfloor. Prior foot traffic had worn a threadbare track into the paper-thin carpeting; every so often, David glimpsed patches of plywood showing through the grimy weave. He also saw what looked like rodent droppings along the scuffed baseboards. Lana hadn't been exaggerating when she'd called the building a rat trap.

They could hear sounds coming through the walls: voices, general clatter, a state radio broadcast crackling with static. The sounds seemed to disappear in time with their footsteps as the groaning hallway announced their approach.

"Did you hear the one about the talking clock?" Lana asked him, continuing before he could answer. "Ivan invites a friend to see his new apartment. They stay up late, talking and drinking vodka, until

Ivan says, 'Now let me show you my talking clock.' He knocks on the wall behind his head. The person in the next apartment yells back—"

"'It's two in the morning!'" David finished.

"I guess you've heard it."

"Guy in my outfit was from Wisconsin," he said. "It was an Ole and Lena joke when he told it."

They stopped at the end of the hallway. Lana turned to the unit on their left and raised her eyes, scanning along the edge of the ceiling. "Let's see if this is a talking door," she said.

CHAPTER
SEVENTEEN

The first thing David Toland saw of Nina Tarkovsky—indeed, the most indelible thing he would remember about her later—was an alert, sea-green, deeply wary eyeball. The eye appeared in the two-inch gap between the apartment door and the jamb when Nina finally, reluctantly, responded to Lana's insistent knocking.

"Go away," she said. She spoke the words in English, but with a thick Russian lilt, keeping the rest of her face hidden behind the door. "No Americans."

Lana raised an eyebrow at David. "See what I mean?"

"Maybe I should have left my hat on."

To the eye in the doorway, Lana said, "Nina. My name is Lana Welles. Sergei must have spoken my name to you."

"There is no Sergei here."

"Your English is far better than my Russian," Lana said. "So I hope you won't mind my telling you in English how very sorry I am for your loss."

"I have lost nothing. I have nothing. Please go away."

The door closed in their faces.

Somewhere inside the apartment, David could hear elderly voices complaining in Russian, Nina Tarkovsky's voice snapping back in her native tongue.

Lana knocked on the door again, raising her own voice. "Nina, please invite us inside. It's very important that I meet with you."

Silence.

"Sergei spoke of an operator in Moscow. He used the identity of this resource in bargaining our arrangement, but he was killed before putting us in contact. It's imperative that I make contact now. Nina: Your part of Sergei's deal is still in play if you can help me. Will you help me?"

More silence.

"Listen to me carefully, Nina. I'll leave, if that's what you want. But I'll come back tomorrow. And the day after that. The day after that, perhaps it will be Semichastny's men who knock."

David whispered, "Who's Semichastny?"

"The new head of the KGB."

"Oh." He thought about that. "Do you really think it's necessary to threaten the poor..."

The door opened. All the way this time. There, across the threshold, stood a young woman with statuesque features already worn beyond their years. But her striking eyes gave away a fierceness of spirit that seemed to exist in defiance of her obvious hardships. She wore loose, dark woolen clothing, and she was—undeniably—somewhere in the middle stages of carrying a child.

Lana took a long look at her. "I see that congratulations are in order."

No response.

"Did Sergei know?"

"There is no Sergei here." Nina Tarkovsky wiped roughly at her eyes with the heel of one hand, then set her jaw and straightened her spine. "Please leave my family in peace."

She closed the door again. David heard the sound of locks tumbling.

Then he heard a growling animal. It took him a moment, imagining a slavering German Shepherd on the other side of the door, before he realized that the sound was coming from Lana.

And that she had her Walther in hand.

As she took aim at the door jamb, David reached out quickly, placing his hand on her wrist. "No," he said. "There's some other way."

Lana jerked free, the hammer of the compact pistol clicking back beneath her thumb. She steadied the weapon with her other hand, resetting her aim.

He tried an animal sound himself then, barking, *"Agent Welles."*

She sucked in a breath and blinked at him.

"Please," David said. He showed her his palms: *See? No touching. Don't shoot.*

She looked back at the door.

After a long minute, she finally decocked the Walther, which somehow disappeared from her hand. "It's possible that you're not wrong," she said.

She turned on a heel and left him standing there, her footfalls reverberating through the muffled plywood flooring as she strode away down the hall. David realized that his pulse was racing. He took a deep breath, thinking, *How did I get here?*

He knocked softly on the apartment door. "Nina?"

No answer.

"I didn't know your husband," he said. "But I'm told that he was a good man. He didn't deserve to die the way he did, and we don't deserve an invitation into your home. But if there's anything you can do to help us, we'll do everything in our power to finish what Sergei started. That's my promise to you."

Nothing. David put his ear to the door. Utter silence. *Leave her alone*, he thought. *You tried. Now let the poor woman mourn in peace.*

He was just about to follow Agent Welles to the stairwell when he heard a faint rustling at his feet. Something tapped against the sole of his shoe. David looked down, honestly expecting to find a rat gnawing on his shoelaces.

Among the many things he did not expect to see was a torn scrap of butcher's paper, which someone inside the apartment had just slipped beneath the door.

*   *   *

Lana's mood had improved considerably by the time they'd found seats at the back corner of the next available Metro car. That alone seemed like a minor victory. David still would have liked more credit than he seemed to be getting, however.

"Why so happy?" he asked.

"Who says I'm happy?"

"You keep smiling."

"Be ready," she said. "We're getting off at Tverskaya."

"At least tell me what it says." David raised Nina Tarkovsky's scrap of paper, which bore a single word hand-printed in large, bold Cyrillic characters, then underlined:

БРОСНЯ

"It says Brosnya."

David attempted to copy her pronunciation of the word aloud. When he did so, an elderly woman looked up from her newspaper, found him with her eyes, winked mischievously, and returned to her reading.

He looked at Lana. "What's Brosnya?"

"A local legend," she said. "That's all."

But she was still smiling.

CHAPTER
EIGHTEEN

A few hundred kilometers from Moscow, in the Tver region of western Russia, near the hilly logging town of Andreapol, there existed a freshwater lake that, for some undiscovered reason, supported two different kinds of saltwater fish. This mysterious lake also served as home—according to reports dating back to the twelfth century or so—to a monster. The lake was called Brosno, and its monster, Brosnya, aka the Brosno Dragon.

"But in our case, it's a code name," Lana told him.

"A code name for what?"

"For a man named Yegor Aspidov."

"Who's Yegor Aspidov?"

"Arguably the most successful KGB double agent our country has ever recruited," she said. "Though I'm sure there are those who would describe him differently. If he really is still alive, we'll find him here."

Here turned out to be a small stone house in the far northern outskirts of the city, almost into the countryside. A belching, Stalin-era transit bus deposited them a mile from their destination late that afternoon, pulling away with a labored wheeze and a black diesel cloud that hung in the wintry air.

They walked the remaining distance, picking their way arduously along a treacherous bed of grimy snowpack seeded with clods of ice. A footbridge took them over a slender frozen creek. A narrow shoveled path led to the house through high banks of cleaner snow—just wide enough for a single person walking carefully. David had the sense that the house had existed in this spot since long before the city had come out to meet it. Window-high stacks of firewood lined the exterior walls. Smoke curled from the chimney.

Somebody was home.

"It would be dishonest of me," Lana said as they approached the front stoop, "if I claimed to know what we can expect to encounter at this location. My advice is to be ready for anything."

"Does that mean I get to carry the gun for a while?"

"Fat chance." She lifted the lid of a scarred wooden box attached to the exterior stone of the house, retrieving a small wooden mallet from inside. She used the mallet to rap on the door.

Nothing. Lana rapped again.

This time, from inside, a voice called, *"Podozhdi minutu, pozhaluysta."*

David pulled out the pocket translation book he'd bought for himself at a market they'd passed. Lana saved him the trouble, whispering, *"Wait a minute, please."* A few moments later, the door opened with a heavy creak.

David judged the man who opened it to be somewhere in his seventies. He was slight of frame for such a legendary creature, with an afghan blanket draped around his shoulders. His yellowed dentures appeared to be one size too large for his mouth. But he'd retained an impressive mane of silvery-white hair, which stood out from his head in flyaway tufts. The man looked back and forth between David and Lana, then said, *"Da?"*

"Comrade Aspidov," Lana said. "My name is Lana Welles. You were a friend to my father."

Aspidov's rheumy eyes widened, then narrowed. He leaned forward. In an astonished whisper, he said, "Lanechka?"

Lana smiled at him. "I was certain you'd have forgotten me after so many years, *Dya.*"

The sight of her appeared to leave the older man at a loss for words. Before the moment could languish, Lana held out the gift she'd purchased at the same market where David had picked up the translation book: a frosted glass bottle of Moskovskaya vodka in an embossed velvet bag. "I brought afternoon tea."

Now the eyes twinkled.

"Then by all means, *myshka*," the Brosno Dragon said, "bring your American friend with you inside."

*   *   *

Yegor Aspidov's small home was tidy and well-kept, with spare but well-made furnishings and stout oaken bookshelves on every wall. The stone walls themselves seemed to retain the heat of the fire. It seemed to David a comfortable lair for a toothless old dragon to live out his days in relative peace. The vodka wasn't bad, either. He reminded himself to go easy.

Meanwhile, the man himself had disappeared into the cellar through a trapdoor, previously hidden from view by a woven rug in the far corner of the room. David gathered that they'd made some important, exciting progress since their arrival here, although he couldn't precisely say how much, or in what way. What little he understood was based almost entirely on what he could piece together from the snippets of English Lana occasionally lapsed into while speaking with this man she called *dya-dya*.

Uncle, according to the translation book.

While they waited for him, David availed himself of another short sip of vodka from the chipped ceramic mug on the table near his hand. "May I ask how this man and your father came to know each other?"

"My father was Aspidov's handler," Lana told him. "Before his time in the State Department, of course."

Like father like daughter, he thought. Although he couldn't help observing that her father's recruit still counted himself among the living. Unlike Sergei Tarkovsky.

"Is it reasonable to presume that Yegor Aspidov was one of the important people your parents entertained back in Silver Spring, once upon a time?"

"It wouldn't be unreasonable." Lana's smile seemed softer around the edges than usual. "Yegor has always been a friend of the family. Although I haven't seen him since I was small."

"He called you *myshka*. What does that mean?"

"Look it up in your book if you're so curious."

"It's still in my coat. And my coat is way over there."

Lana sighed. "*Little mouse*. It means little mouse."

They heard creaking footfalls ascending the cellar stairs. Aspidov's head appeared above the opening in the floor. He grew taller and taller again.

"Our contact will present himself," he said. "His payment has already been arranged."

"*Dya*," Lana said, rising to meet him. "How can I thank you when you've done so much more than I could have asked?"

"To wake up from this dream and go home, *myshka*. That would be thanks enough."

"I should have imagined that you'd ask me for the only thing I can't give."

Aspidov smiled ruefully as he returned to the sitting area. "Be alive when you're finished, then."

She embraced him. Aspidov returned the gesture, patting the back of her head softly. After a moment, he looked at her face as though taking one last photograph with his mind.

"So beautiful." He kissed her three times, alternating cheeks: right, left, right. He glanced briefly toward the ceiling. "Your father is proud."

David couldn't be sure, but he thought Lana's eyes looked the slightest bit glassy in the firelight. Maybe it was the vodka.

"Thank you," she said.

"*Na zdorovie, myshka.*" Yegor smiled. He broke their clinch, then shuffled over to the bucket of snow he'd placed inside the door. From the bucket he retrieved the open bottle of Moskovskaya. He poured more into each of their mugs.

David, already feeling considerably looser than he'd intended—deeply confused about what they'd accomplished here—raised a palm. "Thank you, sir, very kindly, but I . . ."

"How do you Americans say? *Yesche odin* . . . One more for the road." He raised his mug, grinning. "For luck. *Za vashe zdorovie.*"

Lana matched him. *"Za vas."*

David shrugged, raised his own mug. "Here's mud in your eye."

*　　*　　*

Cold did not bother Jeremiah. He came from a place where, in the dead part of any typical winter, a person could sling a bucket of warm water into the air and watch pellets of ice hit the ground.

He watched the stone house from the mouth of a nearby tunnel, where the frozen creek passed beneath a rutted roadway leading out of the city. Daylight had turned to dusk in the time since Welles and Toland had entered. Now the landscape glowed with the silvery light of a full moon reflected on the snow.

He resisted the urge to treat himself to a warming nip from the flask he carried in his parka. That kind of warmth would be short-lived and, ultimately, a lie. The truth was that spirits reduced a person's core body temperature, even while providing the illusion of heat. It was a danger masquerading as a comfort.

So he waited. And he watched.

After a time, he became aware of the sensation that he was being watched in return. A brief scan of the area uncovered the counter-surveillance: A trio of elk—a bull and two cows—had wandered out of the timber to graze the trash barrels atop the embankment opposite his position. They'd detected Jeremiah's presence and now stood motionless, on alert.

Jeremiah watched them back. Nobody moved.

After a time, he removed one of his fur-lined tactical mittens, dug out his cigarette lighter, and scraped up a pale flame. The flint wheel made a crisp, flat sound in the cold air, like a twig crunching underfoot.

The bull snorted and pricked his ears.

The cows bolted.

The bull tested the air with flaring nostrils, then followed after them. Jeremiah watched all three animals disappear over the embankment, then returned his attention to the stone house.

Eventually, Toland and Welles reemerged, picking their way back along the narrow footpath single file, the same way they'd gone in. Welles led the way. Toland followed her. They enjoyed the illusion of warmth in the cold.

At what passed for a street, they turned left and carried on their way, arm in arm.

Jeremiah let them go for now.

He left the mouth of the tunnel. Trudging through shin-deep snow in his pac boots, he followed the banks of the frozen creek toward the stone house. When he was finished here, he thought, he would have time enough to return to the *Khrushchyovka*. Where the traitor Tarkovsky had lived with his wife and the two old *babushkas*.

He changed his mind, then. Dug inside his parka. As the narrow creekline led him closer to the embankment leading up to Aspidov's home, he stole a drink from his flask after all.

His evening was only just beginning.

CHAPTER
NINETEEN

They carried their ruse into the following day, staying back at the Hotel Bucharest while the Merrymakers set off for the Tretyakov Gallery without them.

It was to be the group's last full day in Moscow, capped off by a black-tie soiree at the Bolshoi Theater in the Tverskoy District, a short cab ride north of the hotel. John and Irene Davis had vowed to attend the ball, given another day's rest and recuperation, claiming that David's fictional fever had broken during the night.

In reality, they would use the event as cover for a meeting with Yegor Aspidov's contact. According to Joren Vermeersch's tour schedule, the Merrymakers would depart first thing the next morning, ride the railway four hours northwest to St. Petersburg for a late lunch, then board the Baltic Empress passenger ferry to Helsinki. Once they'd made it back to sovereign democratic soil, David and Lana would break away and secure passage back to the States with the second film in hand, ready to bargain their names back to good standing. Between now and then, they faced their biggest challenge so far: waiting.

David supposed that any number of things may have led to the way they ended up passing the time: stress, boredom, the same kind of nervous energy he'd always felt before jumping out of a perfectly good airplane into a combat zone. But by nine thirty a.m. on

December 27, 1961, he'd learned that he could pretend not to notice Lana Welles lounging in a bathrobe only for so long.

It wasn't entirely clear which one of them finally made the first move since their night together on the train. It seemed simply to happen. But somehow the rest of that morning disappeared around them, and then the afternoon, and when it was finally time to dress for the evening's festivities, he didn't want to get out of bed.

"One more hour," he said.

Lana patted his bare shoulder. "You have stamina. I'll give you that."

"You ain't seen nothin' yet."

But she scooted out from under the covers before he could nab her, escaping into the shower alone. Eventually he took his own turn, then unpacked the tuxedo he'd purchased in New York. It was the first such garment he'd ever owned, and the tailor had done yeoman's work. While Lana applied her face at the dressing table, he spent the remainder of the time left to him trying to figure out the bow tie.

"I'll do that for you," she said, finally joining him at the window, "if you zip me the rest of the way up."

"At your service." He zipped her the rest of the way down instead.

"Very funny," Lana said. "Come on. I don't want to be late."

David slid his hands into the opening at the back of her dress, resting his palms on her hips. Her skin was warm. At least as soft as his new hat. Much less furry.

She sighed a little. He took that as encouragement, kissing the curve of her slender neck. While his lips did that, his hands went off on their own, sliding a little farther down, toward the tops of her stockings.

She dropped her hair and slapped at his hands. "All right. That's enough out of you."

David gripped her hips and turned her to face him. Her breath smelled of warm cider stirred with peppermint sticks. "We can always go to a gala at the Bolshoi next year," he said.

She smirked and pushed away gently. "Optimism. That's good. We'll need plenty."

CHAPTER

TWENTY

The Bolshoi Theater was easy to recognize: take away the dramatic uplighting, which cast the old landmark's neoclassical columns in brilliant white relief against the onyx Russian sky, and it looked just like its printed portrait on the back of the one-hundred-ruble note.

Lana, David, and their fellow partygoers arrived in a caravan of taxicabs. They queued in a wood-paneled anteroom, where a smartly dressed attendant took their invitations and outerwear, then passed them to a different smartly dressed attendant, who escorted them on. The Merrymakers—the lot of them already tipsy from the hotel cocktail bar—made plenty of merry at David's expense, donning sterile masks they'd purchased as a joke from a druggist at the GUM earlier that afternoon.

At least until they approached a grand divided staircase, where they encountered a pair of conscripted *militsya* public patrol officers in full dress, their white falcon shoulder patches unmistakable even from a distance. The staircase became something of a temporary checkpoint as the Merrymakers were relieved of their masks, briefly inspected, then ushered along their way, bare-faced and giggling like grade-schoolers.

"They do know how to make an impression," Lana groused.

"Kind of like you in that dress."

"Aren't you a sweet talker."

They followed along up the right-hand staircase, arm in arm. David considered the wide marble steps and the plush red carpet running the center aisle; it struck him as a reverse image of the worn track running the hallway of Nina Tarkovsky's apartment building.

Also unlike the *Khrushchyovka*, where the sounds of meager daily life disappeared upon their arrival, here the more festive sounds of laughter and clinking glasses grew louder until they ascended into the White Foyer, where they found the introductory cocktail hour already in full swing.

"Wow," David said. He took in the arctic-white walls and soaring archways; the intricate parquet floor; the carved stucco arabesques and gilded relief work; the ornate, multitiered chandeliers shimmering with golden light.

"Say what you will about Stalin," Lana said as the Merrymakers flowed around them and disappeared into the crowd, "but he did talk Lenin out of demolishing the joint once upon a time."

A server passed by, offering them crystal flutes of sparkling wine. Lana accepted two glasses, handing one to David. *"Sovetskoye shampanskoye,"* she said. "Soviet champagne, if you forgot your language book."

"Oh, yes please," David said. "This I can use."

"Go easy. It's mostly for show."

"I never thought I'd I say this, but…here's to Joseph Stalin, I guess."

They clinked glasses, the thin crystal chiming musically amid a sudden eruption of laughter nearby. A well-heeled crowd had gathered around a hale, handsome young man in a sharply creased, heavily decorated Soviet Air Forces ceremonial uniform.

David nodded in that direction. "I wonder who he is."

"You don't recognize him?"

"Should I?"

"That's Yuri Gagarin. Joren tells me he'll be giving a slideshow in the rotunda later."

"Surely not."

"Quite surely so."

David gaped at her. In April of this year—a mere eight months prior to this evening—Gagarin had climbed aboard the Vostok 3KA space capsule to become the first person in human history ever to orbit the planet Earth. Now here he was, back on terra firma: a national hero, a name for the history books, a Communist thorn in the collective side of the US space program, and the very face of Soviet triumph at the dawn of a brand-new year. With a very tall, presumably hard-earned glass of vodka in his hand.

"This," David said, "is truly exciting."

Lana smiled at a passing couple. "Get a grip on yourself."

"What do you mean?"

"This whole trip you've been goggle-eyed. Look, a famous author! Look, an astronaut!"

"Cosmonaut."

She waved dismissively. "He was only in outer space for a hundred and eight minutes anyway."

Before David could think up a reply, a hand fell upon his shoulder. He turned to a trim, tuxedoed man in his sixties who smiled broadly, greeting them both in heavy Russian. The man shook David's hand, kissed Lana's cheeks in the alternating fashion, and moved on to the next guests he spied, departing their company with the slightly off-kilter gait of a fellow already well-lubricated by *shampanskoye*.

David couldn't help chuckling at the encounter. "I think he thought we were somebody else."

When Lana didn't answer, he looked over and saw that her face had drained of all color. She stood ramrod straight, jaw clenched. Eyes vacant.

"What's the matter?"

No response.

He touched her arm. "Lana?"

She jumped as if startled. But she still didn't look at him. She only shoved a piece of folded memo paper into his hand.

David unfolded the square. On it was a single handwritten sentence:

THE DRAGON HAS LEFT SILENE ON FOUR OX CARTS.

It might have been written in English, but only one thing about it made sense to him: Uncle Yegor had just delivered on his promise.

Their contact had presented himself.

*   *   *

According to legend—as told by returning Crusaders in the swinging, cosmopolitan Middle Ages—the canonized Christian soldier Saint George had converted the entire kingdom of Silene to Jesus by killing their dragon for them and hauling the carcass out of town. Not just any dragon, either: specifically, a lake-dwelling dragon.

"Sound like anyone we know?" Lana spat.

David, who acknowledged that he had a lifetime of medieval hagiographies to catch up on, now understood the meaning of the delivered message all too clearly: Yegor Aspidov was dead.

He didn't know what to say to her. Hell, he could barely keep up with her, and she was the one in heels. "Lana. Slow down a minute."

"This isn't a meeting," she said, leading him right back down the red-carpeted staircase and straight past the guards, who stood by watchfully, their faces as expressive as stone. "It's a handoff. We need to move."

"Move where?"

She showed him a coat check ticket. "This was folded inside the note."

"But the man who gave it to you. Don't we—"

"Forget about him," she said. "We won't be seeing him again."

On that point, they would discover presently, she was entirely wrong.

No sooner had the coat check attendant handed them their

outerwear—along with an unfamiliar women's shoulder bag in rich oxblood leather, which Lana had most certainly not brought along to the theater with her this evening—than a rough hand grabbed David by the elbow hard enough to send sparks all the way to his fingertips.

He looked to find that they'd been flanked by a new pair of guards who seemed to have materialized out of thin air. Unlike the men posted back at the staircase, who appeared to be armed only with polished ebony truncheons on their belts, these two carried Makarov pistols. Much to the visible consternation of the guests still arriving.

"Hey," David said, jerking away instinctively. It was like trying to yank his arm from a blacksmith's vise.

The coat check attendant immediately averted her gaze to the countertop as the other guard tore the mystery bag from Lana's shoulder. He barked a command in Russian over the gasps and murmurs blossoming in the queue behind them. Then David and Lana were being shoved through a door with gun barrels jammed in their ribs.

"I knew this was too easy," David said.

"Just stay quiet," Lana told him. "And don't do anything stupid."

"You mean like die before we get to see Finland?"

"What part of 'keep your mouth shut' is unclear?"

The *militsiya* men—Officer Jaw and Officer Shoulders, David had already come to think of them—pushed them along down a dimly lit corridor, stopping at a plain wooden door with frosted glass.

Officer Jaw opened the door while Officer Shoulders shoved them through into some kind of administrative office, complete with a water cooler, filing cabinets, and a desk. At the desk sat none other than the trim, tuxedoed man in his sixties who had slipped Lana the note just ten short minutes ago.

"Ah," he said, rising and extending a hand. "I'll have that back now, please. Thank you, yes."

He spoke in practiced English this time, just like his handwriting, though his words were drenched in the same heavy Russian lilt.

Officer Shoulders seemed to take his meaning just fine, handing over the oxblood bag.

Lana said, "And I'll have your head, you double-dealing son of a bitch."

The man smiled his sympathies. "I understand that you might see me as such."

"But let me guess," she said. "Most people in my position would call you Foxtrap."

"Ah!" The man seemed impressed. "Sergei spoke well of me, then?"

"Sergei had a different name for you."

"Oh?"

"He called you the Weasel."

This brought a chuckle, followed by a sigh. "Sergei received less than he paid for, it is true."

"He paid everything he had."

"So he did." The man nodded solemnly. "And his poor wife as well."

Even from three feet away, David sensed Lana coiling like a spring. "What about Nina?"

"Perhaps your visit was not good luck for her," the man said. "It is a shame."

Lana took two steps toward him before Officer Shoulders pulled her back by the hair. David felt a sharp, immediate pang of rage. He lunged without thinking. Then came pain even sharper than the anger as he absorbed a gun butt to the back of the skull. He saw white light before the room disappeared behind a gauzy black curtain. When things came back into focus, he was on his knees. Officer Jaw pulled him roughly back to his unsteady feet.

"She was pregnant," Lana hissed.

Foxtrap raised his palms. "And I am but a messenger."

"Then tell me your real name," she said, "so I know who I'm killing."

"I, too, would not have preferred our first meeting to be this way."

The man lowered his hands. "And yet here we are. Our dragon is slain, Agent Welles, and a . . . how would you say? A *higher bidder* has emerged."

"Let me guess," David said, still woozy from his pistol-whipping. "About yay high. Blond hair. Blue eyes."

The man ignored him, gesturing to Officer Jaw and Officer Shoulders. David felt the grip tighten on his arm. The muzzle of the Makarov renewed its pressure against his rib cage. The man called Foxtrap passed between them and out the door; the soldiers clearly on his payroll marched David and Lana out on their string-puller's glossy patent leather heels.

David couldn't help noting that the son of a bitch didn't seem the least bit inebriated after all.

*   *   *

They exited the rear of the theater building into a private outdoor parking area, where a third uniform—Officer Bullneck—stood next to a black Mercedes sedan, waiting for them. As they approached, Officer Bullneck opened the car's rear door. The tuxedoed man hiked the oxblood bag onto his own shoulder and pointed to Lana.

"She comes with me," he said, then pointed to David. "Him you may keep." Then he shook his head as if he'd forgotten his manners and repeated the whole thing in Russian.

Officer Shoulders walked Lana toward the car as Officer Jaw kicked out the backs of David's knees, shoving him facedown onto the freezing pavement. David tensed as he waited for the handcuffs—or possibly the bullet—heart pounding in his temples. *Not like this*, he thought. *Not now.* He lifted his head, craning for a view. Tried to identify the options available to him. Didn't find many.

Then several things seemed to happen all at once.

First, there came a faint sound from somewhere in the shadows behind them. A brief, pneumatic *splurt*, like the sound of a person stifling a cough. He heard a grunt. Then a heavy, smothering weight landed hard on his back, pounding the breath from his lungs in a frozen cloud, pressing him flat into the ground.

He heard another cough, followed by a pop and a hiss. Ten feet away, the sedan settled back at a cant on its deflating rear tire. Foxtrap's eyes flew open wide as he yelped an alarm; Officer Shoulders spun Lana around, an arm around her throat, gun extended toward the source of the gunfire.

A third cough issued from the shadows, and a black hole appeared just beneath the soldier's left eye socket. The man's head snapped back, and he dropped to the pavement as if his strings had been cut, nearly dragging Lana down with him.

David wriggled his way free of the oppressive weight holding him down, finding Officer Jaw draped atop him, a bloody crater where his forehead used to be.

He scrambled to his feet to see that Lana had regained her balance. She hiked up the hem of her dress, drawing a six-inch tactical knife from a small scabbard garter-belted to her left thigh just as Officer Bullneck drew his Makarov and brought it to bear. David launched himself into the line of fire before Bullneck could pull the trigger, hitting the big soldier from the side like a linebacker.

The effect was embarrassingly ineffective. The larger, much stronger man spun him easily against the car and bore down, teeth bared, hot sour breath in David's face as they grappled each other for the gun. David held on with every pound per square inch his grip could muster; he forced his arms up, aiming the muzzle of the pistol toward the sky. He slipped an oncoming head-butt, then sensed Bullneck's knee coming toward his crotch and raised his leg to deflect. Bullneck responded by stomping hard on David's planted foot with the heel of his combat boot.

David shouted through clenched teeth in sudden, blinding pain. The whole world went wobbly for a moment. A wave of nausea rose up from the pit of his stomach as he felt the Makarov wrenched from his grasp. He panicked then, sagging back against the car, thinking, *This is it. I'm going to die in a tuxedo.* He wouldn't even need a funeral suit.

Then came another cough from the shadows, and Bullneck stumbled backward. Then fell.

David's vision cleared just in time to witness Lana climbing Foxtrap's back like a spider. She locked an arm around his throat, both legs around his waist, and plunged the blade of her knife into his chest from behind.

The older man's eyes flew open. He seemed to raise up on his tiptoes as he clawed frantically behind his head, grasping Lana's hair. When Lana gave the knife's handle a violent twist, he screamed, then gurgled, then coughed a fine mist of blood.

She rode him all the way to the pavement.

"Don't tell me your name, then," David heard her whispering to the dying man on the way down. *"Comrade."*

But he wasn't watching her anymore.

Now his eyes were fixed on a brand-new tuxedoed man, who emerged from the shadows holding a Welrod MKII pistol. He was smiling.

"This is some party," Simon Lean said. He blew across the long, fat barrel of the Welrod like a cowboy in an American Western. "Don't you think?"

CHAPTER
TWENTY-ONE

Lana never stopped moving. First, she crouched and used her knife to cut a strip from Foxtrap's shirttail. She plunged the rag into a nearby snow pile, then used it to wipe the dead man's blood from her knife, hand, and wrist. David thought that she did a pretty good job of it, considering it was dark out, and that she was glaring at Simon Lean the whole time.

"What in God's holy name," she demanded, "are *you* doing here?"

"We came as a group," Simon said.

David wondered if he was back at the Hotel Bucharest, having some kind of bizarre dream. "I don't understand."

"I didn't either, at first," Simon said. "Good thing I followed along. By the way, did either of you have the chance to speak with Yuri Gagarin before you so abruptly skedaddled? Captivating fellow. Drinks like a fish, but entirely charming."

While he was talking, Lana tossed the bloody rag aside and calmly picked up a fresh Makarov from the pavement. She pointed the gun directly at Lean. "Place your weapon on the ground. Slowly. Then step away."

"Oh." Simon looked at his own gun. "Well. I couldn't very easily do that, my dear. It's a collector's item."

David was familiar with the odd-looking Welrod by its nickname:

the assassin's pistol. It had been designed by the British during World War II, built around a long, noise-suppressing barrel, with no serial number or other markings. He was curious to know why a bestselling author happened to be carrying one.

But there were more pressing concerns at the moment. Namely, the certainty he felt that former CIA Agent Lana Welles was about to murder the same bestselling author where he stood.

He raised his hands and limped in between them, his stomped foot throbbing like a drumbeat. "I think it would be best," he said, "if we reserved the many questions I'm sure we both have for our friend Simon, who did just save our lives…"

"You're too kind," Simon said.

"And made our exit. Double-time."

Lana squeezed her eyes closed, still pointing the gun at Simon. In a moment she lowered the weapon, took a deep breath through the nose, and opened her eyes again.

"Fine," she said through gritted teeth. Then she glanced at the sedan, paused a beat, and added: "But was it *absolutely* necessary to shoot out the tires?"

"I only shot out one of them," Simon said. He glanced at David as if to ask, *How am I the bad guy?* "Quite by accident, mind."

Lana rolled her eyes, stooped again, and disentangled the oxblood shoulder bag from Foxtrap's dead shoulder.

David shifted his weight to his good foot. "Is it really in there?"

"Is what where?"

"Our item."

Simon said, "I was curious about that myself. What *is* our item, by the way?"

Lana plunged her free hand into the bag and pulled out an age-mottled film can. She waggled the can theatrically for David to see, sending him bolts of sarcasm with her eyes.

"There," she said bitterly, jerking her head toward Simon. "Now he knows. If we end up having to kill him, that'll be your doing. Happy?"

"Speaking as the only one of us who hasn't killed anybody yet tonight," he said, "I'll just have to hope it doesn't come to that."

"Oh, I agree completely," Simon said.

"I'm so glad." Lana reached into the open car and popped the trunk. "Stuff the bodies in there. We'll get a cab."

CHAPTER
TWENTY-TWO

Back at the Bucharest, they brought Simon with them into their room for a mutual debriefing while David and Lana took only enough time to gather a few essentials. Lana's idea of a mutual debriefing turned out to be much different than David's.

The moment Simon closed the door behind him, she turned and delivered a quick, sharp strike to his solar plexus through his open overcoat. As Simon dropped to one knee, gasping for air, she reached inside his tuxedo jacket, pulled the Welrod, and said, "Go over there and sit on the bed."

Simon did an admirable job of retaining his composure, David thought, in spite of his inability to draw oxygen. He waited patiently on his knees, bracing himself with one hand on the floor, head hanging.

"On your feet," Lana said. "Hands on your head."

David said, "Come on. He doesn't exactly seem to be a threat."

"Maybe he is and maybe he isn't," Lana said. "Either way, he can't talk if he can't breathe."

Then maybe you shouldn't have knocked the wind clean out of him, David thought, but he only stood by quietly. This was Lana's show. Besides that, he was forced to admit that she was right: they needed a few answers.

With some effort, Simon finally rose to a standing position. He winced and stretched his midsection, hands on hips. When at last his breathing allowed, he panted, "I'm the last person...to stand...on decorum, dear. But that bordered on rude."

"That was an appetizer. Rude is still in the kitchen." She waggled the Welrod. "Move."

Simon glanced at David. Finding no help for himself there, he sighed and walked over to the edge of the bed. With his back to Lana, he paused long enough to remove his overcoat, then his tuxedo jacket, revealing the empty shoulder holster he wore beneath. He folded each garment lengthwise and draped them on the bed. Then he turned and sat down.

"Now," Lana said. "Who are you?"

"A second-rate Ian Fleming, according to the *New York Times*," Simon said. He set about unfastening his bow tie. "But only a third-rate Patricia Highsmith. Alas."

Lana walked to the bed. She extended her arm and pressed the Welrod's muzzle to the center of Simon's forehead. "This is the last time I'll be repeating a question," she said.

Simon looked at her openly, without a trace of the twinkle David had grown accustomed to seeing in his eye. "Simon Lean is my pen name," he said. "My given name is Leonard Ziomak. I was born in Gdansk, Poland, in the autumn of 1911."

"I don't need to see your baby pictures, Leonard." Lana stepped back a few inches but kept the gun trained on Simon. "I just want you to tell me how..."

"In the autumn of 1943," Simon went on, "on my thirty-second birthday, I was taken in the back of a cattle truck to a place called Auschwitz." He unfastened his cufflinks as he spoke. "Along with my wife. And my twin daughters. And my son."

David forgot all about his throbbing foot for a moment. He even forgot about the men he'd seen killed this evening, and the man almost certainly yet coming for them. Everything in the room seemed to pause while Simon rolled up his sleeve and showed them his forearm. From where David stood, he could see the cloudy, blue-gray digits permanently inked there. *My God*, he thought.

Only one of the Third Reich's concentration and extermination camps had tattooed its prisoners with such serial numbers, and that camp had been Auschwitz. Simon Lean—David's favorite author, then his travel companion, and now his fellow fugitive—was showing them Leonard Ziomak's registration tag.

"My daughters were sick. My son was lame. And my wife..." He trailed off a moment. Rolled his sleeve back down. Cleared his throat. "I survived the march to Bergen-Belsen. Although I can tell you truly that, at the time, I wished I had not."

Lana displayed no discernible reaction at first. Eventually, she lowered the Welrod and held it at her side.

"I first heard the Führerbunker decoy theory a decade ago, while researching my first novel," Simon Lean said. "I've been investigating that theory independently ever since. The more popular my books have become, the better equipped I've been to fund my own efforts."

David limped over and put a hand on Simon's shoulder. The author gave him a wan smile.

Lana said, "How did you know what we were doing here?"

"All I knew at first," Simon said, "was that you were not who you claimed to be."

"How?"

"I'm an intuitive fellow," he said. "If you'll forgive me a moment of immodesty."

"And then?"

"And then what, dear?"

David stepped in. "That last morning on the train, somebody ransacked our cabin. That was you, wasn't it?"

"I'm forced to confess, old boy. And while I won't offer my apologies, I do hope you'll believe me when I say that I meant you no personal—"

"The first film," Lana interrupted. "You have it now?"

"What little of it remains," Simon said.

"Where?"

"In my room."

"Where in your room?"

"Hidden between the mattress and the box spring," Simon said. "But please, won't you tell me: Are the rumors true? Did the film really show proof?" He laughed to himself, shaking his head. "What am I saying? Of course it must have done, or you wouldn't be—"

"Let's go," she said.

David noted that she was pointing the gun again, but only from her hip this time: elbow bent, finger resting alongside the barrel, not on the trigger. Compared to the heightened tension of a few moments ago, her current stance seemed almost friendly.

But it still seemed clear enough to David that, as far as Agent Lana Welles was concerned, Leonard Ziomak's sympathy window—however briefly it had opened for business—was now closed.

*　　*　　*

He stayed back in the suite, on satchel duty, while Lana took Simon to his own room, one floor down.

David's first item of business was to look after his foot. In the quite likely event that the night ahead of him involved running for his life, being hobbled was tantamount to catastrophe.

So he found a chair, gingerly removed his torturous dress shoes, skinned out of his blood-sodden sock, and leaned forward on his knee.

Every one of his toes was skinned raw, but none of them appeared to be too flat, or sticking out at wrong angles, or severed entirely from his body. He could even wiggle most of them with minimal agony.

The source of his limp, however, was his big toe, which he judged to be approximately twice greater than its normal size. The skin was hot, stretched, and shiny, like a sausage ready to burst on a backyard grill. Droplets of blood oozed from a crack in the center of the nail, which had darkened to the color of an overripe plum. Touching it even lightly brought instant water to his eyes.

David hobbled to his toiletry bag. There he found nail clippers and a traveling first aid kit. The clippers featured a stubby, fold-out file attachment. He deployed the file, then sterilized it using an alcohol wipe from the med kit.

Then he hobbled back to the chair and sat down, grabbing a pencil from the phone pad on the side table. David stuck the pencil in his teeth, took three harsh breaths to pump up his adrenaline, and did what he had to do before he talked himself out of it.

He positioned the point of the file over the crack in his toenail and pressed down. The pain was atomic; he snapped the pencil in his jaws as if it were a strand of uncooked spaghetti. Eyes streaming, he worked the file attachment around in circles, opening a hole, then making it larger.

When David finally yanked the file free, blood spurted up from his toenail like a small fountain before settling down to a steady leak.

But the operation had been a success. The pain and throbbing subsided almost immediately with the release of pressure. David hoped that meant it was possible that the toe might not be broken after all. He disinfected the area, dressed his various toes in ointment and Band-Aids, and wrapped two layers of gauze around the whole shebang.

When he was finished, he gathered himself for a minute.

Then he dug into the oxblood shoulder bag and opened up the film can they'd somehow, against all odds, managed to retrieve.

Lana and Simon returned a few moments after he'd pried open the lid. Simon took one look at David's bandaged foot and the bloody towels he had yet to collect from the floor, and said, "Now that looks as though it must have been painful."

"Among the most painful ten seconds of my life," David said. "And I've been shot before."

"The film," Lana said. "What's your assessment?"

"No bullet holes," he said. "Otherwise, the condition is about the same as the first one."

She nodded. "I was afraid of that."

"Don't look so glum," he told her, unable to keep himself from smiling. "We just accomplished the impossible."

"Not yet, we haven't. I need to see what's on that film."

"If we can get ourselves back home, I can—"

"Now," she said. "I need to see what's on that film now."

"If you'll indulge me," Simon said, "I do have an alternate suggestion."

Lana and David both looked at him.

"First things first, has anyone else noticed that in all the excitement, we've all missed our dinner?"

"Just what I need," Lana said, pointing the gun at him once again. "Another man making wisecracks to go along with the one I have already."

Simon grinned, then walked casually around her, over to the bed. He put on his jacket and coat.

"Where do you think you're going?" Lana said.

He walked around her again, this time back in the other direction. "Come along."

"Hey." Lana marched after him, free hand swinging. "I asked you a question."

Simon paused at the door. Perhaps it was the feeling of his own gun in his back that brought him up short.

"It so happens," he said evenly, "that I know a man in Moscow who can help us."

"Who?"

"My dear, I'd be honored if you allowed me this opportunity to re-earn your trust. I think you'll find that we're on the same side."

"There are no sides," Lana said.

"I sincerely doubt you believe that."

She glanced back at David. If David hadn't known better, he might have thought that she was actually asking for his opinion on the matter.

He shrugged. "He could've shot us both in the cab and told the driver to step on it. If he'd wanted to."

Lana thought about that. She looked at the ceiling, then stamped her foot in frustration.

Then she gave the gun in Simon's back a shove, leaned close to his ear, and said, "The first sliver of a fraction of a moment that I sense you're playing me for a fool, I'll put a bullet in your storytelling, Mr. Lean."

"So well phrased that I instantly understood your meaning," Simon said.

After she'd left him to start gathering her things, he added, "For the record, though, I really am famished."

CHAPTER
TWENTY-THREE

They packed only what they could easily carry and took another cab to Ulitsa Gorkogo, one of Moscow's oldest and most prominent thoroughfares, still teeming with traffic even at this hour.

"For hundreds of years this street was called Tverskaya," Simon said, "until they went and renamed it for a writer. Can you imagine?"

"Gorky," their driver chipped in, smiling and nodding. "Is good Russian."

"Yes, wonderful, wonderful," Simon agreed. Then he cupped a hand around his mouth and whispered to the back seat, "Though I'd be willing to bet that I've already outsold him."

They traveled north to the Central Telegraph building, its Art Deco stone columns and modernist glass panes combining to form a looming monument to the Russian communications infrastructure. Simon instructed their driver to deposit them at the next corner.

"Is okay?" the driver asked. "For girls, *da*?"

"Don't worry about me, comrade," Lana said. "I'll be just fine."

"I don't think he's talking about you, dear," Simon said. To the driver, he said, "*Da*, my friend. This is our stop."

They disembarked and paid their fare, then followed Simon across Gorkogo, into a network of side streets. Within a few minutes they'd entered what David began to identify, from the cloudy shopfronts and the occasional, colorful strobe of neon, as a Moscovian red light district.

"They say that the telegraph girls earn so little during the day that they moonlight in this neighborhood as prostitutes," Simon told them. "I've no idea if it's true. Ah—here we are now."

He stopped in front of a sooty façade that featured a lighted cinema marquee. David couldn't read the titles on the bill, but he got the general impression that it wasn't another World War II double feature.

"Let me apologize in advance," Simon said, holding the door, "for any less-than-wholesome ambiance we may encounter."

They entered a chilly vestibule, where a tired-eyed girl in a negligée sat shivering behind a steamy ticket window. David saw an open toaster oven attached to an extension cord on the floor behind her stool, its crinkly wire elements glowing orange from within.

Simon smiled at her, held up three fingers, and purchased three tickets. Then he turned to Lana and said, "Would you mind telling her that we'd like to see my friend Nikolay Blyukher before the show?"

Noticing the girl's reaction, Lana said, "I think you just told her yourself."

"Perhaps I'm one to stand on decorum after all."

Lana conversed briefly in Russian with the ticket girl—a conversation David sensed that the ticket girl would prefer not to be having.

"She says he's not here," Lana reported.

"Would you please tell her my name? Oh, and that I have the money I owe him?"

Lana pursed her lips and did as requested. The ticket girl looked warily at each of them. Then she blew warm breath into her hands, dismounted her stool, and shuffled, stoop-shouldered, through a door in the back of the booth.

"Poor kid," David said.

"If a girl can't figure out how to make a living with her clothes on," Lana said, "then she won't find any sympathy with me."

"Personally, I heed the words of Mr. Scott Fitzgerald," Simon said, "and try to remember that not everyone has had the same advantages that I've had."

Lana scoffed at that. "Mr. Ziomak, I'd think that you of all people would find that sentiment rather extraordinarily naïve."

"Mr. Lean, if you please," Simon said. "And I may be paraphrasing."

In a few minutes, the main doors to the theater lobby opened. A short, impeccably groomed man stood at the threshold, backlit by a candy-colored glow. He wore round wire glasses with violet-tinted lenses and a long scarf over his shoulders like a shawl.

"Nikky B.!" Simon said, pumping his voice into a broad, gregarious baritone. "Chuffed to see you, mate. You look well as ever."

Nikolay Blyukher looked at David, then at Lana, and finally regarded Simon with a placid expression. His own speaking voice was almost delicate, as soft and articulate as Simon's greeting was bombastic, and delivered in well-spoken English.

"Mr. Lean," he said. "It surprises me to see you here."

"Pleasantly so, one hopes. But my goodness, Nikky, what's with this Mr. Lean business? Have we really come to this, after all these years?"

"Dominika informs me that you've come to rectify our imbalance," Blyukher said. "Is this information legitimate?"

"With interest, old boy. And if you're amenable, my colleagues," Simon said, introducing David and Lana after a fashion, "would like to rent your studio facilities for the evening. At the price you name, of course. My treat."

The faintest suggestion of a smile creased Nikolay Blyukher's fleshy lips as he turned his attention to Lana. After looking her up and down, he said, "I would imagine that to be a most interesting film. Perhaps a . . . deeper business arrangement could be made."

David saw Lana shove her hand deep into the pocket of her overcoat, where he knew her to be carrying the Makarov she'd rather recently acquired. He took a step to his right and slipped his arm around her, surreptitiously pinning her own arm to her side. He could feel her bristling against him. He only clamped tighter.

"Actually," he said, "we're in postproduction. On an unrelated film."

Blyukher's eyes flicked to David with reptilian languor as his smile disappeared.

"Pity," he said.

Without another word, he turned and disappeared into the theater, leaving the doors open behind him.

"Congratulations," Simon said. "You've now had the pleasure of meeting the adult entertainment czar of modern Moscow. I believe we're meant to follow him inside."

"Charming," Lana said. Her voice fairly dripped with disgust. "Let me guess: you met him while 'researching' one of your masterpieces."

"Nikolay? Why, no actually," Simon said. "I met Nicky at a card game. Although it's true that he's helped me with my fact-checking a time or two over the years." He stood aside and gestured to the open doors. "Shall we?"

"After you," Lana said.

Simon shrugged and entered the theater. David followed along. Sensing nobody else behind him, he paused at the threshold and looked back.

At some point during their exchange with Blyukher, Dominika had returned to her post in the booth. David caught sight of Lana Welles—she who claimed to hold no sympathies for the girl— slipping what looked like a fifty-ruble note under the ticket window. She spoke briefly to the girl in a voice too quiet for him to hear, then turned and strode toward lobby doors.

Finding him waiting there for her, she said, "What are you gawking at?"

David shook his head. "Don't worry. I didn't see a thing."

They went inside.

* * *

The adult entertainment czar of modern Moscow waited for them at the far side of a dimly lit, faux-Rococo lobby that smelled to David like mildew and stale perfume. The muffled but unmistakable sounds of the feature presentation drifted toward them through the walls.

Blyukher led them through a set of heavy tapestry curtains, then down a narrow corridor lined with framed lobby cards—most of the peekaboo variety, a few of them somewhat less coy. They followed him up a creaky wooden staircase to the second floor.

There, above the theater, they passed a suite of rooms, some with open doors, some doors closed. Through the open doors, David caught glimpses of lavishly furnished bedrooms that appeared to double as soundstages. From behind at least one of the closed doors came live sounds not unlike the recorded sounds they'd heard downstairs.

"Any of these spaces are available this evening," Blyukher said to Lana and David, "should either of you become...inspired."

"I'll be honest with you, Nikky," Lana said. "*Inspired* isn't the word I'd use to describe how I'm feeling."

"Nevertheless," Blyukher said.

He invited them into a small administrative office as organized and neatly kept as Blyukher's own personal appearance. The office served as the access point to a cramped warren of deeper rooms collectively outfitted to function as a bare-bones processing lab.

From the list of items David requested, Blyukher was able to supply David with a pair of cotton gloves, a jug of methyl chloroform cleaning solvent, a magnifying loupe and a package of swabs, and a basic set of darkroom equipment, including a Latvian-made Minox Model II enlarger.

Then—for an additional fee—he repaired to an outer lounge with Simon, leaving David and Lana to supervise themselves.

"Is it just me," David said, "or does that guy look exactly like a mid-career Peter Lorre?"

"The only thing I noticed about him is how much he makes

my skin crawl," Lana said. She handed him the film can from her satchel. "Roll it."

David took the can and opened it, turning his face away from the sickly sweet smell. "It won't be quite as simple as that, unfortunately."

"How much less simple is it?"

"Same story as the first reel," he said. "There's no way to mechanically project this footage without ruining it forever. If we want to see what's on it, we're going to have to work frame by frame, but we won't be able to do that without some prep."

"We don't have a week this time."

"I'm aware of that."

"So how long will it take?"

"One way to find out," David said.

With Lana observing closely over his shoulder, he set to work.

Almost immediately, he found that he'd been wrong back at the hotel: Even without bullet holes, this second reel was in an appreciably more advanced state of decomposition than the first. The nitrate had grown so brittle, and the emulsion so sticky, that simply unspooling the film risked irreparable damage with every inch.

In short order, the task became impossible. The inner layers of spooled film stock had already begun to congeal into a solid mass. After an hour's work, David was left with a scant twelve inches of film stock, containing just under forty frames in total, of which perhaps a handful of individual frames were legible.

"Lady's choice," he said, handing Lana the loupe.

"What do you mean?"

"I should be able to get a half-decent print out of these three," he said, pointing to a section of the film strip with his gloved index finger, "or this one, or probably this one here."

"Can't you print all of them?"

"I can," he said. "It just depends how long you want to wait."

Lana grimaced. "Fine. Let me see."

Gingerly, David held the strip in front of the bare overhead bulb, well away from the radiant heat. Lana put the loupe to her eye and studied the frames he'd indicated. Then she went back and studied them all again. At last, she pointed with her own ungloved index finger.

"Don't touch it," David cautioned.

"This one."

"Got it." He headed toward the darkroom with the film strip in hand. "I doubt he's got any Cibachrome around here, so I'll probably need to transfer this to negative, then…"

"Stop right there," Lana said, "and just give me a ballpark."

"Back in an hour. Please don't open this door."

*   *   *

When the small man with the purple eyeglasses stepped out into the freezing vestibule, he took a long look at the dead girl slumped against the cracked, blood-smeared ticket window.

Then, without expression, he looked at Jeremiah.

"May I help you?" he said.

"Where are they?"

"Perhaps you wish to speak with the proprietor of this establishment?"

"Your reputation precedes you, Mr. Blyukher. This will be better for you if we can agree to deal honestly with one another."

The small man nodded. He didn't appear particularly disturbed by the appearance of a gunman in his lobby. "Then perhaps you might tell me who you wish to locate?"

"A woman came in with two men."

"You'll have to be more specific, I'm afraid."

Jeremiah raised the silenced Tokarev TT-33 he'd liberated from Yegor Aspidov's cellar stronghold. "I doubt that."

Blyukher, standing otherwise motionless, raised his soft-looking hands simply by bending his arms at the elbows. He looked again at his former employee, who had been shivering in her nightie before Jeremiah had arrived. Now she'd never be warm again.

Still, Jeremiah believed he'd done her a favor.

"Perhaps, you're referring," Blyukher said, "to the woman and two gentlemen who wished to rent my production facilities?"

"Take me to them," Jeremiah said.

*   *   *

As a movie lover by predilection and a film preservationist by trade, David sensed some inevitable kind of symmetry in the fact that a can of decaying 16mm film had brought him to Moscow, while its mated pair would lead him out again.

It hardly seemed a tragedy. As vacations went, it hadn't been an especially relaxing one anyway.

But after an hour's work, he did find—in the grainy, yellowed, bloom-splotched eight-by-ten image he was able to print from the single frame of developed film Lana had chosen—that perhaps he brought a little something of worth to this operation after all.

"I know him," he said to Lana, showing her the print upon her return.

"Know who?"

"That guy," he said, pointing to the print still drying on the line. "I know him."

The frozen image depicted a group of men leaving the famous emergency exit of the Führerbunker through tendrils of battle smoke hanging over the Chancellery Garden. The photo print placed the fleeing group very near the hole in the ground, made by an Allied artillery shell, where Hitler and Braun were said to have been cremated following their suicides.

This print also placed Der Führer himself at the center of the group. Which gave the others the collective appearance of a protective detail, shuttling their leader away.

Lana squinted at the man David indicated. "What do you mean, you know him?"

"That's Nicholas Balcon."

"Surely you don't mean *General* Balcon," a new voice said.

They both turned to find Simon standing in the open doorway of the darkroom.

"One and the same," David said.

Simon invited himself in to peer over Lana's shoulder. "My goodness," he said. "I do believe you're right."

"I'm certain of it."

"Hmm," Simon mused. "Another Nicky B. What are the odds?"

Lana looked at Simon, then at David. "Are you two part of a fan club, or something?"

"One of my country's most beloved war heroes, Nicholas Balcon," Simon said. "Though perhaps not among the most prominent."

"Supposedly there are classified reports that say Balcon escaped from behind enemy lines on three separate occasions during campaigns in occupied Europe," David told her. "I've yet to hear about a report that names him as a Nazi collaborator, though."

"Although that would explain a few things," Simon said.

Lana seemed taken aback by the extent of David's knowledge. "Would it offend you too terribly if I asked how the hell *you* know so much about these alleged classified documents?"

"I don't know anything about them," David admitted. "I've heard stories, that's all. And I know that man to look at him."

"Why?"

"Because my team and I archived about ten miles' worth of footage from the Nuremberg trials last year." David shrugged. "I spent two months looking at his face through a magnifying loupe. I'd know it in my sleep."

Lana grabbed David by the elbow and pulled him aside, into the corner behind the Minox. Speaking softly, she informed him that the retired general was currently serving as the British ambassador to France. Her breath felt warm in his ear.

But Simon heard her anyway.

"Brilliant," he said, beaming. "I love Paris at the holidays."

"That's nice for you," Lana said. "I hope it hasn't entered your wildest imagination that you might be coming with us."

David said, "With us? Aren't we going home now?"

"But why not?" Simon said, ignoring him. "I'd say the three of us have made quite a team thus far."

"Then let me take this opportunity to thank you for your service," Lana said. "But we're not recruiting at the moment."

"Not to mention, we're going home now," David said. "Right?"

"That's a shame." Simon sighed theatrically. "I'll be sure and give Ambassador Balcon your regards."

"What's that supposed to mean?"

"Nothing, dear. I'm sure you already have a plan in place for getting out of Moscow without the Merrymakers."

Lana watched him a long time before she said, "Am I to infer that you have a more expedient option in mind?"

* * *

When the repellant, duplicitous little smut merchant finally returned to his office, Jeremiah sat up behind the man's desk, placed his tightly bound hands on the blotter in front of him, and said, "When I kill you, you might find yourself wondering what's taking me so long. I just want you to remember, while you're suffering, that you brought every moment of it upon yourself."

The two leather-jacketed goons who had been left to stand guard over him—neither one of whom appeared to be conversant in English—looked at each other as if wondering whether his comment required a response. The goon holding the Kalashnikov nodded his encouragement to the goon standing nearest the desk. The goon standing nearest the desk shrugged, stepped forward, and whipped Jeremiah in the back of the head with the barrel of the Tokarev he'd taken away.

There came a burst of sharp, clobbering pain. The office went dark for a moment, then wavered back into focus. Jeremiah clenched his fists, pushing himself upright again in the chair. The back of his scalp burned as if scalded. He could feel warmth trickling down the back of his neck.

"Only a fool," Blyukher observed, "still believes he holds the upper hand even after he's allowed himself to be led into an ambush."

"The line between foolishness and courage is fine and quite porous."

Blyukher did something with his mouth that seemed only vaguely akin to a smile. "Delightful. How do soldiers say it? Death before dishonor?"

"Something like that."

Blyukher removed his glasses and began to polish the lenses with one end of his ridiculous scarf, which he wore about his shoulders like a prayer stole. "Were you Special Forces?"

Jeremiah imagined taking the scarf and making a noose of it. "Were you a clergyman?"

Blyukher chuckled softly. He held his glasses to the light and inspected the lens. Finding them satisfactory, he slipped the frames back on, cosmetically shading his bulbous, amphibian eyes.

"But we digress," he said. "Let us discuss, instead, how you propose to compensate me for my ticket girl."

*　　*　　*

Simon grinned at Lana.

To the wilderness beyond the darkroom, he called, "Oh, Nikky? Hate to trouble you, chap, but would you mind answering a question for us?"

Somewhere in the distance, they heard the faint sound of a door opening, then closing again. A few moments later, Nikolay Blyukher reappeared for the first time since he'd parted their company. "What is the question?"

"How would you like to earn a great deal more money?"

Again, Blyukher's face registered that distant, vaguely bemused expression that David Toland disliked a little bit more each time he saw it.

On the other hand, the man's eventual answer explained how, just before midnight, David found himself, his favorite author, and the deadly spy with whom he'd been sleeping bound for France in the cargo hold of an Antonov air freighter owned by a Russian pornographer.

CHAPTER
TWENTY-FOUR

Paris

What the adult entertainment czar of modern Moscow happened not to disclose, prior to their departure aboard his illegal, contraband-laden aircraft, was that their itinerary included deliveries to shady, out-of-the-way airstrips populated by equally shady, heavily armed men in Ukraine, Moldova, Romania, and Czechoslovakia. All of this was scheduled to occur en route to their destination, Paris being the last stop on the list.

So it was just over fifteen hours later before they finally touched down—stiff as a trio of ice sculptures, and nearly as cold—at a barren demilitarized airfield somewhere outside the City of Light.

"Repulsive little worm," Lana said as they waited in the belly of the Antonov for the cargo ramp to lower. "If I didn't want to strangle him to death before, I'm ready to fly back to Moscow and do it now."

"For what little it's worth," Simon told her, "I took care of that job in my mind somewhere over Austria."

"You two should stop complaining and be thankful there are still three of us," David said. "I'm beyond starving."

Lana smirked, visibly shivering inside her coat. "I don't think you're in danger of expiring from hunger just yet."

"You misunderstand. I meant that you and Simon are lucky I didn't eat one of you on the way."

"I have to say that my conscience is clear on that score," Simon said, wagging a finger. "I did suggest dinner back in Moscow."

David heard a hollow bang as the ramp finally bridged the gap between the plane and the ground. They descended together, three sets of dress shoes clanging all the way down to the cracked, weedy tarmac below. Not a soul waited to meet or greet them.

It was a sunny Thursday afternoon. Next to Moscow, the last days of 1961 felt almost springlike here—a comparatively balmy six degrees Celsius, with a brisk but not punishing breeze. They had a clear view to the south over a rolling, snow-dusted meadow. David looked as far to the horizon as he could see, but he could not yet see Paris.

He shouted to Lana over the mechanical thunder of the Antonov's big turboprop engines: "Now what?"

"Now we get out of the way!" she yelled back, as the cargo ramp closed behind them again.

Nearby stood a row of abandoned aircraft hangars. The hangars were shaped like giant corrugated pipes cut in half and laid on their sides. The three of them hustled in that direction on stiff, creaky legs. Already the plane began pulling away, taxiing itself around in a slow, broad circle to face the same airstrip in the outgoing direction.

They reached the first hangar just in time to watch the Antonov chug, roar, then head back up the runway. The plane rolled slowly at first, slowly picking up speed, finally lumbering into the air 1,500 meters down the line. The runway grew quieter and quieter as the sound of the airborne plane's engines faded into the distance.

Then there was silence.

They were completely alone.

"So," David said. "France."

"Among the very best places to find an ambassador to France," Lana said.

"What do we need with an ambassador when we already have what we came for? Isn't it time for you to take that second reel and this print we've made and come in from the cold?"

"Are we *still* talking about this?"

"Have we talked about it?"

"Newsflash, Captain: We're not looking for films anymore," Lana said. "We're now following up with subjects."

"That seems off-mission, if you don't mind my saying."

"Not from where I'm standing, it doesn't. I still have no idea who I can trust. Besides. If you want something done right, do it yourself."

David looked around the decommissioned, dilapidated airfield. "What *are* we doing? And how do you think Nicholas Balcon can help us do it?"

"Nicholas Balcon," Lana said, "was among the men who helped Adolf Hitler escape the Füherbunker alive. Only the men in that photograph could tell us what happened next. The basic fact that Nicholas Balcon is still alive tells me that he can probably tell us what happened next after that, too. Maybe all the way up to what happens tomorrow."

"What do you imagine might be happening tomorrow?"

"I don't know, but I promise you this: If Hitler is still alive, I'm going to find him," Lana said. "And Nicholas Balcon is going to point me in the right direction. Even if he doesn't know it yet."

Simon finally joined the conversation. "Does anyone have any thoughts," he said, "as to what our next steps might be?"

"They might be numerous, if we have to walk all the way to Paris," David said.

"Does anyone have any better ideas?"

Lana said, "Aren't you supposed to be the one who thinks up ideas for a living?"

"The sedentary writer, yes. My point exactly."

She pointed to the meadow. In the medium distance, David saw a small farmhouse with a curl of smoke coming from the chimney. From this vantage, it looked almost like a painting of a French farmhouse. Even the smoke appeared stationary.

"Let's go ask them how *they* get to town," she said.

*   *   *

As far as David could tell, the owner of the farmhouse—a stocky fellow with muttonchop sideburns and a windburned chin—had little reason to give three overdressed strangers a ride to the nearest paved road in the back of his horse-drawn wagon. He didn't have much use for rubles, and they weren't exactly dressed to pay him back in chores.

But for whatever reason, he gave the ride anyway. The generous farmer even sent them on their way with a linen tea cloth tied in a bundle. The bundle contained a fresh baguette, a wedge of Gruyère, half a baton of dry-cured sausage, and a handful of dried apricots.

Stuffing his mouth greedily as they walked along the shoulder of the autoroute, David vowed—only partially in jest—that one day, as a small token of his appreciation, he'd return to the French countryside, find that farmhouse again, and give the windburned farmer with the muddy galoshes his entire personal life savings.

Until then, they thumbed for a ride in their increasingly rumpled evening wear. Within the half hour, a passing lorry driver agreed to take them as far as the northeastern suburb of Bondy, a ten-kilometer cab ride from the Parisian city center.

They arrived around six o'clock that evening. After an unusually colorful sunset—which David would have preferred to have viewed from, say, the Pont des Arts overlooking the Seine, rather than from a crowded sidewalk along Rue du Faubourg Saint-Honoré—they found themselves standing at a long, relatively unassuming limestone façade. Rooftop flagpoles bore the British Union Jack on all four corners of the building.

"This must be the embassy," David said.

"The embassy is there," Lana said, pointing a bit farther down the street. "This is the Hôtel de Charost."

"The British ambassador stays in a hotel?"

"It's not that kind of hotel," she said. "Come on. Let's try the garden entrance."

They went back to the corner, took a left onto the even narrower Rue de l'Élysée, and walked along the high wrought iron fence of the presidential palace. At Avenue Gabriel, they turned left again and came back the other direction.

The ambassador's residence had an iron fence of its own, canopied by trees the length of the street. But the trees were bare now, affording them the full garden view of an elaborate multistory, Empire-style home. The residence itself sat far back on a lot with more trees, and fountains, and sculptures, and a long, winter-brown apron of lawn.

"Whatever kind of hotel it is, it looks like a nice place to sleep," David said.

"A fine property," Simon agreed. "Napoleon's sister dumped it off to us for forty thousand quid. Personally, I think she'd have done well to find a better realtor."

"The question is, how do we get in? Ring the bell?"

Lana pointed and said, "Look there."

David followed her gesture but saw nothing of special interest. "Where?"

"Those two."

All he saw were a man and a woman huddled outside the residence, smoking cigarettes on the portico. The man wore black trousers and white shirtsleeves. The woman wore a black skirt and a white blouse. They both wore bow ties.

"What about them?"

"What do they look like to you?"

"Like staff grabbing a smoke out back," he said. "Why?"

"To me they look like caterers."

"Surely you can't be thinking," Simon said, "what I think you may be thinking."

"Maybe you should leave the thinking to me," Lana told him.

*   *   *

If there was an advantage to escaping Moscow with little more than the clothes on their backs, it was that the clothes on their backs happened to be tuxedos. Which meant that David and Simon had the pants, shirtsleeves, and bow ties covered.

Lana, meanwhile, used a fistful of francs to bribe a random, comparably sized woman on the street to exchange her black skirt and white blouse for a very expensive, not so gently used Givenchy evening gown.

They made the trade in the restroom of a nearby café.

"Honestly," Simon told David while they waited, "I wouldn't mind tagging along to observe this transaction."

"That's my pretend wife you're talking about," David said.

"Quite right. You have my apologies."

When Lana emerged from the restroom, David swore she looked even better in the secondhand skirt and open-collared blouse than she had in her gown. She put on her coat and scarf and said, "I guess I forgot my bow tie at home today."

"I hope they don't dock your pay," Simon said.

David said, "They wouldn't dare."

It was full dark now. The streetlamps along Avenue Gabriel all glowed with warm yellow light. They hurried back to the gate on the garden side of the Hôtel de Charost, which was exactly the same as they'd left it, except for one small difference: a guard with a rifle now stood there.

Simon looked at the guard, looked at their clothes, then looked at David and said, "You're the expert. Tell me: which Preston Sturges picture are we trapped in again?"

"Hey," David said. "I like Sturges. Anyway, this plan is more Marx Brothers if you ask me."

"Call me a traditionalist, but I'll have Chaplin over all of them, please and thank you."

"Funny story about Chaplin," David said. "Did I ever tell you about the time I screened *The Great Dictator* for a classroom full of—"

"Okay, you two, pretend you're a couple of idiots," Lana interjected. She glanced at them. "Perfect. Now follow my lead and don't speak."

Before either one of them could ask what she was planning, Lana hurried up to the guard. On the way, her body language transformed from cool and collected to urgent and flustered. When she spoke to the guard, even her voice had changed: higher, flightier, and significantly more French.

"Monsieur? Bonsoir, monsieur, bonsoir, nous sommes en retard pour le travail," she said. *"Tu peux m'aider s'il vous plaît?"*

Unlike Russian, David happened to know a little French. He'd forgotten most of it since his college year abroad, but he was able to pick up the gist of what Lana had said: she and her friends were late for work, and could the guard please help them?

The guard scowled, shook his head, shooed her away.

Lana tossed her hair and pumped up the desperation in her voice. *"Oo, monsieur, s'il vous plaît? Je doivent vous tant."*

Oh, sir, please? I need you.

The guard remained visibly disinclined to be needed. He barked at her to clear the area.

"Monsieur, s'il vous plaît, il se peut même que je perde mon emploi." She tossed her hair back the other way, taking her act to the incredible length of placing a hand lightly upon the guard's rounded shoulder. *"S'il te plait, s'il te plait, s'il te plait?"*

I might lose my job. Please, please, please?

Now the middle-aged guard was clearly growing uncomfortable with the scene developing at his post. Especially when Lana began sniffling. David couldn't be sure, but he thought that she was actually producing physical tears.

Her other hand flew to the right chest of the guard's uniform. The guard crooked his rifle in his elbow and attempted to brush all of her hands off his person.

"*Je vous en prie*," she said. *I beg you.* "*S'il vous plait?*"

Passersby began to take notice of them. Finally—as if to stop this gathering puddle of hysteria before it got any deeper around his ankles—the guard scowled again, looked both ways, then took a step back and quickly waved all three of them through the gate.

"*Allez vous en*," he hissed. "*Tout de toi. Dépêche-toi!*"

Everybody in. Hurry up.

Lana squealed like a college co-ed straight out of *Where the Boys Are*. The effect was surreal, even jarring; David would have never imagined Lana Welles to be capable of producing such a tone so convincingly.

She really had been good at her former job.

"*Oo, merci, monsieur,*" she said, clapping her hands and wiping her eyes. "*Merci beaucoup! Je te suis fortement redevable, tu m'as sauvé la vie!*" She bounced up onto her tiptoes and kissed his cheek. "*Merci, merci!*"

Blushing from collar to brim, the guard grumbled some more, pushing them one at a time through the gate, reserving a special nod of distaste for Simon and David. His eyes nervously scanned the sidewalk beyond his post all the while.

They hurried up the garden path toward the big house, where every window blazed with light—and where a new clutch of servers in shirtsleeves and bow ties smoked cigarettes on the portico. Simon said, "That, my dear, was brilliant. *Bravissima.*"

"Thank you."

"And more than slightly arousing, I must say."

"Please do keep in mind that I still have your gun."

"Yes," Simon said. "About that."

"You know, I haven't smoked a cigarette since Korea," David mused, only half-listening to them. "But after today, I think that if any of my new colleagues up there can spare a butt, I'm in for a pound."

"I'd say we're all in, thanks to Mademoiselle Gene Tierney, here," Simon said. "But, of course, I mean Irene Davis. Although, should I say...Lana something?" He tilted his head. "I'm sorry, dear, but what *is* your real name?"

"Tonight," Lana said, "you can call me Nicholas Balcon's worst dream."

David couldn't help noting that she sounded very much like herself this time.

CHAPTER

TWENTY-FIVE

A lavish function was already in full swing when David began his short career as a French waiter. He, Lana, and Simon hitched their way inside the ambassador's residence by tagging along with the smokers from the portico. No sooner had they stepped foot into the bustling kitchen than they were handed silver platters of hors d'oeuvres and sent out to circulate among the guests.

Of guests, there were many. Conversation and alcohol flowed in equal measure as those in attendance mingled beneath the ornate chandeliers of the ballroom and its parqueted outer corridor. All of the men looked more or less like David and Simon had looked in their full tuxedos the night before. Few of the women looked quite like Lana Welles, even in her bartered skirt and blouse. But they all appeared to be enjoying themselves.

David made the rounds slowly, scanning everywhere for a glimpse of their man Balcon. Every so often, Simon passed by him close enough to murmur some random fact about the Hôtel de Charost—his country's proud pearl in fashionable Rue du Faubourg Saint-Honoré. The author-turned-Nazi-hunter seemed unreasonably amused to sprinkle upon David the kinds of trivial items customarily delivered by a tour guide: the histories of the marble statues in the Entrance Hall; the provenance of the colorful silk damasks on the walls; even a few scandalous anecdotes from Sir Duff Cooper's library.

"Speaking of books," he said on his next pass, "Somerset Maugham was born in one of the rooms upstairs. His father was conscripted, you see, but he wanted his son to arrive on British soil, so he—"

"I'm pretty sure we're going to get in trouble if you don't stop talking to me," David said.

Simon laughed. "You're the one with the empty tray, dear boy."

It was true, David confirmed. Somehow, his tray of caviar and crackers had been thoroughly sacked while he wasn't paying attention. "I guess you're right," he said. "I'll be right back. Don't let Lana kill anybody while I'm gone."

"Then maybe you ought to stay here with me." Simon nodded across the ballroom. "And see what happens next."

David followed Simon's glance to one of the ballroom's three main entrances, where Lana moved through the partygoers like a whisper.

The sight of her required David to confront his own curiously jumbled priorities. In the space of these past twenty-four hours, they'd stolen ground-shaking history from a Soviet stronghold, escaped certain death, zigzagged across eastern Europe in a black marketeer's airplane, and ridden several deeply rutted kilometers in the back of a wagon. Yet all he could think about was his next opportunity to see that mystifying woman in bed. *Pull yourself together*, he thought.

Then Simon tapped him on the shoulder, redirecting his gaze to a corpulent, red-faced man pacing Lana through the crowd. The man looked like a drunken lion gone to seed, attempting to stalk a particularly svelte zebra.

He also looked like Ambassador Nicholas Balcon.

"Uh-oh," David said. "We'd better get over there."

"I'm quite sure she doesn't need our help. Or anyone else's, come to that."

"Come to whatever you like, just come on," David said.

He tucked his empty tray under his arm and worked his way through the crowd. Simon followed, passing out goose liver pâté on toast points as if unable to give up their ruse.

They were still a good distance away when Balcon finally caught up to Lana. David watched the ambassador lean in close to her, whisper something in her ear, then pat her on the rump with his meaty hand.

Oh, no, he thought. *No, no, no.*

But Lana responded in a manner he didn't expect. For starters, she did not break the man's fingers. She didn't even slap his face.

Instead, she glanced coyly over her shoulder. David saw her lips moving. In response, the ambassador threw back his large, round, sweat-dappled head and guffawed. He squeezed her shoulder, then made an ambling, somewhat unsteady line toward the ballroom doors.

Lana offered a sheepish smile to the guests now looking her way. She glanced around as if embarrassed, once again playing the flustered ingénue for the benefit of all who cared to observe.

Then she smoothed her hair and skirt coquettishly and followed along behind Balcon, her serving tray still perched atop her hand.

"Will you look at that," Simon said, finally joining David. "I do believe our hunter just became the hunted."

"I doubt it," David said. "But I still think this is our cue. Ditch the *foie gras* and let's go."

As Balcon took his leave of the ballroom with a terribly alluring waitress in tow, the ambassador raised a palm to two tuxedoed gentlemen with thin black wires trailing up from their collars.

The men—clearly members of Balcon's security detail, and perhaps not so gentle, by the look of them—glanced at Lana, nodded to their boss, and carried on with their duties, which appeared now to involve standing motionless at their posts and pretending they hadn't seen anything.

But they were bound to see David and Simon if they followed too closely.

"We should use the other doors," David said. "Let's hurry up before we lose them."

Which was, naturally, just what had happened by the time they made their way into the outer hall.

David turned in a complete circle as he scanned the area. He saw lots of guests. He saw one of his new smoking buddies from the portico carrying a tray of white wine. But no sign of Lana or the ambassador.

"This is less than ideal," David said.

Simon clapped him on the shoulder. "On the contrary. I'd say it's extraordinarily fortuitous," he said. "Couldn't have gone easier if I'd written it myself."

"If you say so."

"Again, I hardly think you need worry, chap. Whatever her real name is, that's a woman who can take care of herself."

"It's not her I'm thinking about. Wait—look there."

Up ahead, another white-shirted server snapped a cranberry-colored linen, then stooped, using the napkin to pick up a bit of dropped food from the parquet floor.

"The wealthy can be pigs." Simon sighed. "I should know—I'm quite wealthy."

David shushed him. "Hold on."

He waited for the server to move on, then nudged Simon with his elbow and hurried over to the spot. The spill had occurred at the corner of the main corridor and a smaller connecting hallway.

He scanned the smaller corridor. Carpet. Paneled walls. Lighted bronze sconces made to look like candlesticks.

And there: halfway up the hall. David pointed again and hustled toward another scatter of dropped food. He grinned at Simon.

"Unbelievable," he said. "She actually left us a trail of bread crumbs."

Simon looked down at the scraps of toast on the carpet at their feet. "And bits of dilled herring as well."

They continued on at a jog, following the trail Lana had laid out for them, a new scatter of crumbs every fifty feet or so.

At last, they rounded a corner and found, halfway down the next hallway, Balcon and Lana. The ambassador unlocked a set of carved wooden doors, opened them with a grandiose flourish, and ushered her through. He glanced furtively down the empty hallway to his right, double-checking to make sure the coast was clear.

Then he glanced back to his left. When Balcon saw David and Simon coming toward him, he jumped, startled.

The ambassador chuckled and shook his balding head. "Oh, no, thank you," he said, raising his palms to ward them off. "I . . . *je vais bien, merci beaucoup. Laissez-moi tranquille, s'il vous pl*—"

Balcon never had a chance to finish his sentence.

Simon Lean charged toward him at a sprint, holding his silver platter in front of him like a battering shield, bellowing, "Butcher's toad!"

Balcon's eyes widened as Simon rammed him in the chest with the platter. The collision knocked the larger man off balance, shoving him backward through the open doors. Balcon tripped over his own feet and fell to the carpet in a chubby pile.

Simon was atop him immediately, using the platter as a cudgel, whanging the ambassador about the head and shoulders with cacophonous, clanging abandon.

David ran after him, pulling the doors closed behind them, frantically throwing the locks. A few feet away, Lana hissed. "Idiot! Get off of him before you call every guard in the place!"

Balcon—mewling now in pain and panic—had managed to raise his forearms in defense. Simon tossed the platter aside and set to work with his fists instead, grunting and wheezing with the sustained effort of pummeling the United Kingdom's ambassador to France like a man-sized mound of dough.

David tossed his own tray into an upholstered settee and hurried over. He grabbed Simon under the armpits and dragged him off of the wheedling ambassador.

Rodeo steer wrestling may have been a simpler task. Simon had worked himself into a hot froth. He struggled wildly against David's grip, panting, "Unhand me. I'm not finished with him."

While David's hands remained full, Lana collected their discarded platters, stalked over, and brandished them at Simon. "Here!" she said, struggling to keep her own volume down. "Why don't you bang them together like cymbals? I don't think they heard you down the street at the embassy."

Meanwhile, Balcon labored to push himself up to his elbows. A blue knot had risen on his forehead. He had angry-looking scuff marks on his right jowl. A thin line of blood trailed down from one nostril over his fattening upper lip. He sputtered, "I...who...what is the *meaning* of this!"

"Excuse our associate," David told him, still straining to hold Simon Lean at bay. "He's planning a new novel. It's going to be about a friend of yours."

Lana turned to the still-prone ambassador.

"He has research questions," she said.

CHAPTER
TWENTY-SIX

Because neither Simon nor Lana could be trusted to touch the man on the floor without inflicting further violence, it fell to David to help the fat ambassador to his feet. *Fatbassador*, he thought to himself as he threw his back into the task. But then he thought, *No.*

War criminal.

They were in what appeared to be Balcon's private study: Turkish rugs, an antique floor globe in the corner, a wet bar in another. Floor-to-ceiling bookcases all around. There was an Empire-style desk the size of a Viking warship with a matching, thronelike chair. Behind the empty chair, a pair of tall bay windows looked out on the lights of Paris.

With David's help, Balcon collapsed into the chair with a slump-shouldered wheeze. David went to the wet bar, soaked a cloth in cold water, and tossed it toward the ambassador. The towel landed in his lap with a wet *splotch*.

Balcon picked the sodden towel from his lap and pressed it to the knot on his head. He squeezed his eyes closed, took a deep shaky breath, and said, "I'll have you drawn and quartered for this. The three of you. One at a time."

"But first, you're bloody well going to answer our questions," Simon said.

"*What* questions?" Balcon's eyes snapped open. "Who *are* you?"

David sensed movement and quickly stepped in front of Simon, blocking his path to the ambassador. "I think the important thing for you to be wondering right now," he said, "is what we want—"

"I say we should at least knock his yellow English teeth out first," Simon interrupted. "He'll still be able to speak well enough without them."

"This is an outrage!" Balcon countered.

"I couldn't agree with you more, you traitorous son of a—"

"And how quickly you can give it to us," David finished.

Balcon stared at him. "What in Queen Mother's Christendom *do* you want?"

Lana finally stepped forward.

"Why don't we start by telling you what we already have," she said.

*   *   *

A curious thing happened as Lana revealed to Ambassador Nicholas Balcon the nature and context of his situation.

Instead of becoming more pliable, the ambassador seemed to grow only more defiant as she went on. Even the threat of international exposure did little to bring the long-softened old soldier into line. It was as if the man could not have cared less about his legacy, or his future. Or, indeed, his immediate well-being.

"What's so funny," Simon Lean snapped at him, somewhere toward the tail end of Lana's spiel about secret films and filmed secrets.

Balcon merely dabbed at his injuries with the wet cloth, a look of smug detachment on his shiny, porcine face. "It entertains me to imagine," he mused, "that any of you still believes that the treaties ended the war. Typical American arrogance."

"I'm British," Simon said, "Unlike yourself."

Balcon only chuckled. "That's what you think."

"Would you like to know what else I think?"

"Pray, do tell."

"An old friend of mine has handkerchiefs monogrammed with the same initials as yours. He happens to be one of the most despicable pieces of human trash I know. But if both of you were on fire, I'd take at least a moment to consider pouring water on him."

"How terribly reassuring for me to know that you'll never be burdened by that decision."

While this exchange was underway, Lana walked calmly around to Balcon's side of the desk. She hopped up onto the edge and planted the point of her right shoe on the chair between the ambassador's legs.

Balcon returned to random sputtering as Lana gathered up the hem of her skirt, revealing the holster strapped to her thigh. The holster contained two items: the Makarov pistol on one side of her leg, her tactical knife on the other.

"Oh my," Simon said.

David nodded. "I admit it. I'm starting to love it when she does that."

"You're boring me," Lana said to the wide-eyed ambassador. "So, let's move this along. If you were given the opportunity to choose a weapon for yourself, which weapon would you choose?"

Balcon's doughy complexion had gone blotchy. He glanced at Simon and David, then returned his attention to Lana. "I'm quite sure I don't understand what you mean."

"I mean," Lana repeated, "if you were going to choose a weapon for yourself, which weapon would you choose? Go on." She raised a finger and added, "But no touching."

Tentatively, Balcon pointed at the gun.

"Good choice," Lana said. "Not necessarily any tidier, but certainly more efficient."

She pulled the gun from the holster, crossed her bare leg over her knee, and braced herself on the desk with one hand. When she pointed the gun at Balcon's moist, bloated face, David imagined a raven-haired Lauren Bacall packing heat.

"Now. The red button beneath the edge of this desk." She drummed her fingers on the blotter. "A silent alarm, I presume?"

"You presume correctly."

"And you've triggered it already, haven't you?"

Balcon's smile widened. "Indeed, I have."

Simon blurted, "Why you filthy…"

Lana shushed him over her shoulder, then turned back to Balcon. "Then in the short time left to us," she said, "I'd like for you to tell me what you think you mean when you say the war isn't over."

Balcon seemed more unnerved by Lana's exposed thigh than by his current vantage point, looking directly into the barrel of her gun. David was beginning to believe that the leg and the gun were in some ways equal weapons.

Not that either of them would be of much use for much longer.

You've triggered it already, haven't you?

Indeed, I have.

Only one door out of this office that David could see: the door they'd used coming in.

"The Party," Balcon said patiently, "began rebuilding even before the fall of Berlin."

"To what purpose?"

"To what other? To return, of course." Balcon licked his lips. "And this time, to prevail."

Even despite the filmed evidence he'd already seen with his own eyes, David could scarcely believe anything he was now hearing, standing here in Nicholas Balcon's personal sanctum, rooted in the real world. Somehow the medium of film itself—the intrinsic filter of celluloid—lent a sense of fiction to the idea that Adolf Hitler might be alive somewhere, hiding. Planning. Waiting.

"Impossible," Lana said, as if she could read his thoughts. "The Third Reich ended at Reims. The Party was abolished."

This prompted an oily chuckle. "Disrupted, yes. Underground? Necessarily so. But I assure you, my stunning, stupid girl, *very* much intact." Balcon's smug grin had returned, seemingly to stay. "Meanwhile, the recruitment opportunities within your so-called Cold War have been…how else can I say it? More than abundant."

"Now I'm the one feeling entertained."

"My advice would be to enjoy that feeling while it lasts." Balcon placed his towel aside and leaned back in the chair. "In the meantime, my 'abolished' Party has woven itself into the fabric of every formerly Allied power of consequence. Parliament. Congress. The Soviet of Ministers. MI6, KGB, your own CIA—even the boards of the world's most prominent corporations. Very soon now, our reach will have met our grasp. And then?" He made a pleasured humming sound as he sighed. "We will remake the world."

"Poppycock," Simon spat.

Balcon chuckled again, jowls waggling as he shook his head. "As you wish."

Now came the sound David had been expecting: thudding footsteps followed by a sharp rap at the door.

His pulse spiked. Beside him, Simon turned quickly, reaching behind his back for a Welrod that hadn't been there since Moscow. David thought: *And that concludes this interrogation.*

But Lana only sat up on the desk and said, "The top dog. What became of him? Tell me now."

"If you mean *Mein Führer*, I'm sure I wouldn't know."

Lana cocked the Makarov.

"You could ask a reconstructive surgeon in Madrid named Victor Herzog," Balcon said. "He operates a most luxurious private clinic in the Aravaca, near Casa de Campo. Perhaps, if you were not imprisoned, he would be able to enlighten you. Then again, perhaps not."

Lana scoffed. "That old rumor. You'll have to do better, General."

"As the woman who needed blood said to the stone."

"Shall we see how much blood you have to offer?"

The knocking came again, louder this time, accompanied by a male voice. The voice spoke English in a heavy French accent: "Ambassador Balcon. Are you there?"

Balcon consulted his pocket watch, clucking his tongue. "These men are slipping. Pity."

Lana held the gun steady. "Why would you tell me about Herzog?"

"Because you asked, Miss Whoever-You-Are. I'd have told you over espresso. None of this was remotely necessary."

"You seem awfully willing to divulge such sensitive information. I expected to torture you at least briefly before you turned coward."

"That's because you couldn't stop what's coming even if the Führer himself were sitting in this chair." Balcon licked his smile again, leaving his lips slick. "It gives me peace to imagine you agonizing over that knowledge until the three of you are murdered in your prison cells."

"Do you really think I'd allow that to happen?"

"When it does, I'd like for you to remember who led you to your deaths," Balcon said. "I only wish that you had longer to suffer."

David stopped listening. As the pounding on the door intensified, he found their silver platters and handed one to Simon.

Simon looked at it and said, "What am I supposed to do with this?"

"I don't know," David said. "Try to deflect the bullets, I guess."

"Ah. Quite."

Then the door to Balcon's office burst open on its hinges, shards of very old wood splintering from the jamb.

The last thing David saw, just before pandemonium erupted all around them—in the split second Lana's head turned toward the sound of the crashing door—was retired General Nicholas Balcon lurching forward in his chair to grab the gun out of her hand.

CHAPTER
TWENTY-SEVEN

As guards rushed into the room, shouting, the ambassador yelled, *"Heil Hitler!"* Then he jammed the barrel of the Makarov into his own mouth and pulled the trigger.

A deafening bang filled the room. David's ears rang. Gore painted the tall bay windows behind the desk with Jackson Pollock spatters. The spatters hung against the glass for a moment, as if in midair.

Then Paris ran red in the background.

Lana screamed and threw up her hands as Balcon's lifeless body slumped in the chair, double chin to chest. She began jabbering in breathless French so rapidly that David could only snatch bits and pieces: *Oh my God! He asked me to bring food! What's happening?*

David and Simon fell in with her immediately, dropping their trays and shoving their hands toward the ceiling. David couldn't help looking at Balcon slumped in the chair; the craven survivor had been a coward at heart after all. Given the few men of Balcon's ilk he'd encountered in the service, he didn't know why that should have come to him as a surprise.

The guards included two men in military uniforms brandishing MAT-49 submachine guns, followed by the same two plainclothes men in tuxedos David had gone out of his way to avoid back in the ballroom.

The tuxedos recognized Lana at once as Balcon's surreptitious conquest-in-waiting. They rushed to escort her from the room. One of the military men took David by the elbow, ushering him and Simon in the same direction.

They were left in the outer hallway under the supervision of a third man in military dress. David estimated this guard to be at least a decade junior to the others. He carried only his sidearm—a MAC 1950 autoloader—and looked almost as unnerved as David felt himself.

The tuxedos rushed back into the office to join the excited chatter already underway inside. The doors slammed shut.

More voices approached from another corridor. These voices were close enough to hear, but distant enough that David couldn't quite pinpoint their direction.

What he could pinpoint was the meaning in Lana's glance just before she set upon the young guard with the same breathless pleading she'd test-driven inside the office. She collapsed into his chest, sobbing.

The guard awkwardly holstered his weapon and took her gently by the shoulders.

David used that moment to attack the poor unwitting soldier from behind, applying a choke hold that performed—after a brief but vein-popping struggle across the corridor and back again—more or less exactly as designed.

He eased the unconscious guard to the floor as Lana stripped the sidearm from his belt.

"Oh," Simon said. "Bully."

"You were supposed to break his neck," Lana hissed.

"Just before the new year?" David said. "Not my style."

The approaching voices grew louder. Lana slipped the MAC 50 into the waistband of her skirt and untucked her blouse to cover it.

"This way," she said.

They followed her at a run, taking left turns and right turns, slowing to a brisk walk as they emerged into the state dining room.

Simon said, "May I presume by the confidence in your stride, dear, that you have an exit strategy?"

"Staff cloakroom," Lana said.

"That doesn't sound like an exit to me."

"First things first," she said. "My bag exits with us."

"And then?"

"The catacombs."

"Wait a minute," David said. "Not more tunnels."

"I figure they'll have this place locked down tight in about three more minutes," Lana told him. "That's if our luck holds out. But by all means, Captain Toland, if you'd prefer to try leaving on the ground level, that's your prerogative."

"If they were good enough for the French Resistance," Simon said, "then the tunnels are good enough for me."

"I'm glad you approve," Lana said.

"To the cloakroom, then!"

Simon quickened his pace until he was nearly jogging. Within moments, he'd put David and Lana twenty feet behind him and was still pulling away.

David said, "What the heck is he doing?"

"I know exactly what he's doing," Lana said, now speed-walking herself.

* * *

By the time they caught up with Simon at the cloakroom off the kitchen, he was opening their assigned cupboards and pulling out their things. He'd already buttoned his own coat.

"Here you are, dear," he said, handing Lana her coat and satchel.

"Gee, that's funny," she said. "This bag feels light to me."

"You're most welcome." Simon winked and patted his beltline. David thought he saw a bulge roughly the size of a Welrod MKII assassin's pistol beneath his coat. "There's simply no good reason for you to carry more than your share on this adventure."

An eruption of distant voices seemed to convince Lana that the time to argue was not now. "Kitchen," she said, shrugging into her coat. "We've got to move."

News of treachery within the dignified halls of the Hôtel de Charost had yet to reach the service areas of the residence, it seemed. The kitchen was filled with the same degree of hustle and bustle as when they'd first arrived. Except that this time, the chief steward—upon seeing three of his staff members buttoned up in their coats, heading in the wrong direction—showered them with a free-flowing, strangely musical fusillade of French invective that, if David interpreted correctly, seemed to call into question Lana's demurity, his and Simon's parentage, and their collective fitness to go on living if, indeed, they chose to walk out on him now.

David couldn't help feeling sheepish, even if he didn't actually work for the guy. *"Désolé,"* he called over his shoulder. The passing apology appeared to go unaccepted, and they left the steward fuming in their wake.

They wove their way through the swirling ballet of servers and prep staff, arriving at a large dry-goods pantry in the back. Lana went straight to a wire rack of canned items, grabbed an end, and said, "We need to move this."

David took the other end. "One-two-three-heave," he said.

Simon appeared content to supervise, although David got the sense that he wasn't really paying attention. In fact, he seemed to be busy looking over his own shoulder.

David and Lana slid the heavy rack aside with a screech of metal on tile. An industrial-sized can of yams fell onto David's bandaged toes; he bit his lip to keep from screaming.

But behind the rack, through the tears puddling in his eyes, he saw a half-height door fastened with a simple latch.

"You've been here before, haven't you?" he said.

"Once," she said. "During the previous administration. Long story." Lana stooped and opened the door to a rush of cold, musty air, revealing a flight of mossy stone steps leading down below ground level. "Last person through, pull the door shut behind you."

She ducked through the opening and was halfway down the steps when David heard an immediately recognizable *splurt* of air, followed by a rolling crash of pots and pans hitting the floor.

That was the first time he noticed that Simon Lean had withdrawn the Welrod and was, inexplicably, firing it into the kitchen.

A burst of commotion erupted behind them. A waitress screamed; the chief steward barked orders. Paths crisscrossed; people ran into each other. David saw a hanging pot rack, now empty of pots, hanging only by one of its chains. Someone tripped on a clattering saucepan and fell down, shattering a full tray's worth of filled wine goblets.

In the midst of all of it, David glimpsed a familiar figure angrily shoving his way through the chaos: blond hair. Piercing, iceberg-blue eyes.

The eyes narrowed as they locked on Simon Lean.

Simon grabbed David's arm and shoved him toward the pint-sized doorway. "No time for gawking, lad. Into the breach!"

David felt his way down the treacherous steps. He heard the half door slam behind him. He felt Simon's hot breath on the back of his neck in the cool darkness.

Lana waited for them at the bottom of the steps, her small penlight throwing long shadows against the damp stone walls. "What took you two so long?"

"We're being followed," David said. "Come on."

They were in a narrow underground tunnel. Puddles of water stood in the troughs and depressions of the worn stone beneath their feet. Their own gritty, splashing footfalls echoed all around them.

Simon cleared his throat. "Do any of us happen to know where we're going?"

"Left up here."

Following the meager glow of Lana's penlight, they ducked into a cramped keyhole passage lined with cobblestones. They hurried along in a crouch, duck-walking single file, splatting through rivulets of water, sediment grinding beneath their shoes. David could hear rats chittering in the darkness.

After a hundred meters that felt like a country mile, his chest began to tighten. For the first time in his life, he experienced a taste of what he imagined true claustrophobia felt like. A low-grade hum developed somewhere deep in his inner ear. He could feel his pulse thumping in his neck and temples. Little by little his breathing shallowed, until finally, for a few queasy minutes, he felt as if he couldn't draw in enough air to satisfy his lungs.

But at last they emerged into a larger tunnel. This one had smooth, barrel-vaulted walls and dim yellow modern safety lighting. Old lead and iron pipework ran overhead. A canal ran below, carrying a flow of water perhaps four feet in width, bordered on both sides by narrow concrete walkways. It still wasn't a place in which David cared to spend a minute longer than absolutely necessary, but at least he could breathe again.

"So, this is what the catacombs of Paris smell like," David said.

Simon said, "The brochure said we'd get to see bones."

"Nope," Lana said. "This is just the sewer."

"Lovely. Now which way?"

A deafening bang answered that question for them.

The echo of the gunshot filled the cavern as a round passed between David and Simon, chewing a divot in the wall on the other side of the canal.

"Come on!" Lana shouted, taking off at a sprint.

Simon fired a round back into the cobblestone tunnel: *splurt*. David shoved him with both hands after Lana, then fell in behind. Every step he took underscored his supreme awareness that bringing up the rear put him first in line for the next return bullet.

Which came momentarily, shattering a safety light just ahead of them with a pop and a shower of sparks. Now they could hear their pursuer's footsteps behind them—still distant for the moment, but certainly within firing range. And gaining ground.

They took another hard left into a connecting tunnel, then a right into a smaller tunnel, then a left into yet a smaller tunnel still, this one little more than a burrow in the sidewall.

Lana stopped just inside the entrance, the young guard's pilfered MAC 50 at the ready. She left just enough room for Simon and David to squeeze past her.

"In, in, in!" she hissed, shoving them along with one hand.

Then she snapped off three quick shots back in the direction they'd come. Her muzzle flashes strobed the darkness. Once again, the sound of gunfire in such an enclosed space left David's ears ringing. Fading orange streaks pulsed in his vision.

Silence.

Then, faintly: cautious footsteps crunching toward them in the tunnel grit.

Lana bobbed her head out long enough to fire another round. David heard a quick patter: running footsteps, moving several yards closer to their position.

Then silence again.

"There's three of us and one of him," he whispered. "We can take him. Then we can find out who the hell he is."

"I'd be more than happy to shoot him when we're finished," Simon offered.

"If you have a plan for sneaking up on him from here without getting shot, I'm all ears," Lana said.

"I was thinking more along the lines of staying right here," David said, "and waiting for him to come to us."

"Mr. Lean," she said. "How many rounds do you have left?"

"Counting the pot rack and the angry gentlemen you encountered at the Bolshoi—again, no need to thank me—I have five shots remaining."

Lana quietly released her clip and examined the count indicators. She held up four fingers.

Nine shots between them.

David had counted four shots from the pale assassin so far. But there was no telling how many he held in reserve. Or how many spare clips.

Lana shone her penlight farther into their tunnel. The thin beam stretched about ten feet before absorbing into the inky blackness.

"Let's head farther in and hold there," she whispered. "We'll be blind, but so will he. Which gives us the advantage."

"How do you figure?"

"If we're stationary, he won't be able to hear us. But we'll hear him."

David couldn't claim to love the plan, but he liked it better than standing here trading gunfire until they ran out of ammunition.

Simon agreed. "As long as he's not carrying a spotlight. And nobody sneezes."

"Plug your ears," Lana said. She stuck out her arm and fired two more quick shots around the corner.

Seven shots left.

Then they moved, heading farther into the tunnel as quickly and quietly as they could manage.

The air here grew slightly warmer and fouler the farther they progressed. Soon David could no longer see a thing in front of him, including his own feet. The tunnel opening became a dim gray circle far behind them.

All at once he heard a fleshy smack, followed by a grunt. Followed by Simon Lean muttering, "Bloody ouch."

At about the same time, the dim gray circle darkened.

David saw a distant flash of fire. There came another deafening bang.

Half a heartbeat later, a bullet ricocheted loudly off of something metal just over David's head. Lana responded immediately with two more shots in rapid succession—*blam-blam!*

In the temporary blossoms of illumination provided by the MAC 50's muzzle flare, David saw that they'd run up against a dead end. He glimpsed a rusty iron wheel mounted on the terminal wall of the tunnel, right next to an equally rusty ladder going up.

Five shots left.

Simon followed Lana with two more shots of his own. Now three remaining.

And footsteps running toward them.

So much for the advantage, David thought.

They were trapped. While Lana's Makarov finally clicked on an empty chamber, David felt in the dark with his hands, quickly stepping toward the spot in his memory where the wheel protruded from the back wall. He found the rough, flaky iron with his fingers and gripped it tightly. *What the hell*, he thought. He wrenched the wheel with all his might.

To his surprise, it turned easily in his hands. David heard a screech of metal, then the sound of rushing water.

Then the sound became actual water—a frigid, high-pressure gout of it, blasting him in the midsection with enough sudden force to knock him off his feet.

He choked and sputtered as the water swept him into Lana, knocking her off her feet on top of him. She yelped with the shock of the cold, landing squarely on his belly, forcing out what little air he had left.

David focused every ounce of his attention on finding his footing, then finding her hand. Somehow, he managed to struggle his way to a standing position, pulling her up with him.

Where previously they'd been trapped like rats in a concrete barrel, they now leaned together against a raging instant river they couldn't even see. They gripped each other like shipwreck survivors, coughing, drenched to the skin. Even in what might well have been his final moments, David thanked whatever gods ruled the sewer system that the water tasted, if not exactly clean, at least not biologically contaminated.

"I'm anchored!" Simon called. He'd found the ladder. "Take my hand!"

More gunfire rang out over the roar of the water, bullets whizzing and whanging all around them, David shoved Lana toward the sound of Simon's voice as Simon returned fire from above.

How the man managed to hang on to the ladder, repeatedly fire a bolt-action weapon, and grab Lana's hand in the dark, would forever remain a mystery to David. But he heard Simon yell, "I've got you!"

Then he felt Lana begin to climb. He put both hands on her rump and shoved her up.

"Hey!" she called back. "Watch it."

I would if I could see it, he thought, then found a rusty rung and climbed up after her.

A bullet *kerranged* off the ladder just a rung or two below his feet, sending vibrations all the way up into his palms. David tensed, waiting for the next bullet to find his back.

Meanwhile, above his head, he heard the heavy scrape of iron on pavement.

And street noises. Glorious, musical street noises.

A shaft of moonlight enveloped them as they ascended toward the open manhole above. David imagined a heavenly beam plucking them free of their earthly bonds.

Or at least out of the sewer.

CHAPTER
TWENTY-EIGHT

Paris may have been temperate for the season, but David's teeth chattered the moment he hit open air.

They found themselves on a short, narrow side street, walled in by buildings on both sides. The street was vacant but for a few parked cars, a single glowing streetlamp, and a young couple on a stroll. The couple seemed befuddled by the sight of three drenched waiters climbing out of a manhole at nine on a Saturday evening. They dipped their heads and walked even faster as Simon Lean racked the bolt on the Welrod and pointed the gun back down into the hole.

"Come on, you bugger," he muttered. "Show yourself."

After two minutes passed quietly—during which time the pale assassin proved himself wise enough not to climb up a ladder into a kill zone—David dropped to his hands and knees and shoved the heavy cover back over the hole. The scrape and bang of it rang out in the night, echoing up and down the street.

Simon helped David to his feet. "Any holes in you?"

"I don't...think so," David said between shivers.

"Good lad." Simon turned to Lana. "And you, my dear? Are you intact?"

Lana Welles looked like a half-drowned cat. Her hair hung in her face in loose wet curls, black tears of mascara running down her cheeks. She'd lost a shoe, her sense of humor, and yet another handgun.

But she still had her satchel.

"You and I," she said to Simon, hugging the bag against her body with both arms, "will be having words."

"I might have predicted so."

"But until then," she said, "thank you."

Simon blinked in surprise. Then he bowed his head. "You're quite welcome."

"I don't know about anybody else," David said, "but I could use a drink. Preferably somewhere well away from where we're standing at the moment."

"The stiffer the better," Lana agreed.

"I know the perfect hotel bar," Simon said. "The rooms aren't bad, either. Oh, and it's quite near Gare de Lyon as well."

"As long as it has a fireplace," David said.

"Gare de Lyon," Lana said. "Why? Are you taking a train somewhere?"

PART III

Cathedral

CHAPTER
TWENTY-NINE

Friday morning, David woke up from a dream in which he and Lana shared a picnic lunch beside a Bavarian mountain lake. In the dream, she wore a yellow summer dress with a dandelion behind her ear. She was smiling.

In reality, she was standing over him in the dark, shaking him roughly by the shoulders. "Get up," she said.

David braced himself on an elbow, muddled and groggy. "What time is it?"

"Time to go."

He rubbed his eyes and looked at the clock next to the bed. It was five a.m. The last thing he remembered was waiting for her to finish her turn in the shower last night; he'd been looking forward to drifting into oblivion with Lana Welles in his arms. But the covers on her side remained undisturbed. "Where did you sleep?"

"I didn't," she said. "Get up. I don't want to be late."

It was a twelve-hour trip from Paris to Madrid by rail. Before the ticketing window at Gare de Lyon had closed for the night, Lana—whose personal cash, David inferred, must finally be nearing depletion—had allowed Simon to book passage for the three of them to the last known city of residence for one Victor Herzog, MD. But their train wasn't scheduled to leave until 10:23 a.m.

"We don't have to be at the station for hours," he mumbled.

"We're not going to the train station. Come on."

*   *   *

They checked out of the hotel and took a taxi to Paris-Orly airport. Lana spoke scarcely a word for the duration of the ride. At the airport, she booked two coach-class seats aboard the 8:45 a.m. flight to Madrid-Barajas.

Apparently, she had money left after all. While they waited in line at the security gate, David said, "You still don't trust him, do you?"

She didn't look at him. "Trust who?"

He decided to leave the topic of Simon Lean alone for now.

When they arrived at their gate, however, they discovered none other than Simon Lean already sitting in the waiting lounge, near the windows, reading a newspaper. He looked up as they approached.

David sensed Lana fuming at the sight of him. He nodded to Simon, doing his best to keep from smiling. "Morning," he said. "Change of plans?"

Simon offered them a wry grin. "Well. This is awkward."

*   *   *

When at last their boarding call sounded over the public-address system, the three of them queued together as originally planned, with the minor substitution of a plane for a train.

It was perhaps fortunate, David thought, given the general tension level among their trio this morning, that Simon Lean went only as far as the first-class section.

"My readers often recognize me when I travel," he explained. "It wouldn't do to draw attention."

"I guess I'm lucky," David said as Lana pushed her way up the aisle. "I don't have that problem."

Simon winked. "We all have our own crosses to bear."

They watched Lana shove through the curtain and into coach, leaving them behind without a glance.

"On that topic, she appears to be feeling a bit cross with me," Simon said.

David nodded. "I don't think she likes surprises."

"Understandable. But what did *you* do?"

David had already asked himself that question. So far, he hadn't come up with any answers. "You said we all have crosses to bear," he said. "I think I'm hers."

Simon chuckled. "Quite."

David patted him on the shoulder. "Brush up on your Spanish."

"Ah. Yes. Well, *adiós* for now."

David limped onward. He was stiff and sore from the base of his skull to the tips of his bandaged toes. He dearly hoped that this gambit of Lana's did, in fact, mean that their money was holding out, because all he wanted in the whole wide world, other than his life back, was a change of shoes.

Lana didn't appear to be in the mood to discuss joint finances, however. She'd found their seats near the back of the plane and had taken the window for herself, clearly having slipped back into one of her pensive, melancholy moods. She was staring out at the tarmac when David wedged himself in beside her. He buckled his seat belt and got himself settled. He would have removed his shoes, but he hadn't had a change of socks in two days, so he left them on out of olfactory consideration for the rest of the aircraft. After a few moments of utter silence, he said, "Something on your mind?"

Lana looked at him as if he'd just asked the dumbest question in the history of human speech. Then back to the window.

"Well." He took her hand in his. "At least we'll always have Paris."

She jerked her hand away as if he'd burned her. "What's that supposed to mean?"

David raised his palms in immediate surrender. "*Casablanca*," he said. "Remember?"

"What the hell are you talking about?"

"I...never mind."

She went back to looking out her window.

David rested his head on the seat and closed his eyes.

*   *   *

Somewhere over the Iberian Peninsula, he awoke to find Lana watching him.

"Are we landing?" he said.

"Not yet."

"Why are you looking at me?"

Instead of answering, she asked him a question of her own. "Why did you give it up?"

"Why did I give what up?"

"The military," she said. "Your future."

This again. David normally found the line of inquiry tiresome, but under the circumstances, he was content simply to have returned to speaking terms.

"I didn't give up my future, Lana. I just chose a different one."

"Why?"

"Is wanting a different life so difficult to comprehend?"

She didn't answer that question, either. She only waited.

"My folks, I guess," David finally said. "They were at least partially responsible, anyway."

"Were your parents pacifists or something?"

"No. Well, yes, I suppose. But my father served. He was a Navy man."

"Then why blame your parents?"

"Blame them?"

"Credit them."

He shrugged. "They were the ones who taught me to love film."

"That still doesn't really answer my question."

"I suppose it doesn't."

The truth: For years he'd committed himself to the idea of

preservation over destruction—both as a livelihood and as an overarching philosophy. David loved his job, loved his life, loved the country that made both things possible. He didn't want to lose any of it.

Since meeting Lana Welles, however, he found himself once again butting up against that old, hard wall of truth: Sometimes saving what you love means a fight. And not a theoretical, figurative fight, but an actual fight-fight, with blood and tears and risk and fear and everything else that went along with it.

Sometimes, to save the flock, the shepherd actually has to confront the wolf.

Either that or find a new line of work. Film restoration, maybe.

He sighed. "I'm not sure I really know how to put it into words."

Lana faced forward in her seat. David got the impression that the conversation had ended.

Then, without looking at him, she said, "When I was a little girl, my father taught me a game. It was called *Am I Lying?* One of us would tell a story, and the other one would have to decide if the story was true or made up."

"The best games start with a simple premise."

"You never played *Am I Lying?* with my father," she said. "As I got older, we'd tell stories that were part truth and part fiction. Then you had to tell which parts were which."

"You're right, that doesn't sound so simple." *Or the least bit enjoyable*, he thought.

"We played until he couldn't beat me anymore."

"When did that happen?"

"Around the time I was twelve."

David looked at her in profile. For the first time, he wondered if he was beginning to move beyond whatever simple, animal infatuation he'd had for Lana Welles. That didn't seem like a sensible thing for him to be doing. He was afraid that he might be doing it anyway.

"Maybe that's one of the things I like about movies," he said. "They lie to tell the truth. Even the bad ones."

"That sounds awfully poetic for a jarhead," she said. "Or a lab guy, for that matter."

"Also, they don't shoot at you."

Lana turned to him and smiled for the first time all day. There didn't seem to be a great deal of joy in it.

"Then they're not telling you the whole story, are they?" she said.

*   *   *

They landed in Spain just after ten thirty that morning.

It was calm and temperate, the sky a bright blue, like a placid March morning back in DC. From the tarmac, the Sierra de Guadarrama was visible on the horizon—a distant, snow-tipped undulation beneath a wispy white ribbon of clouds.

Also, visible from the tarmac: one Simon Lean, duffel on his shoulder, waiting for them.

"I say it's far too lovely a morning," he called, "to carry on being duplicitous with one another. Don't you agree?"

In the bright sunlight, Simon's tuxedo finally looked spent. There were faint dark circles under his eyes. As many as five hairs appeared to be out of place atop his head. David found the overall picture oddly reassuring.

He expected Lana to walk right past him. But she stopped and looked him up and down, hiking her satchel on her shoulder.

"I agree," she said. "In theory."

Simon smiled at her, offering his hand. A truce.

"The only thing I ask," he said, "is that you allow me to be the one who kills him."

Reflexively, David glanced over his shoulder at the other passengers within earshot, all of them making their way across the tarmac toward the terminal. The terminal building was a wavy-roofed structure with colorful flying buttresses that put him in mind of a backyard tent blown up to institutional dimensions. Part of him wished that they really were in a backyard somewhere, playing international Nazi hunters, rather than standing here being international Nazi hunters.

But their fellow travelers appeared to take no special notice, parting around them as if they were no more consequential than stones in a stream. Meanwhile, Lana accepted Simon's handshake.

"And all I can promise you," she said, "is that I intend to see justice served."

Simon glanced at David, then looked off toward the mountains. After a moment, he said, "You realize, of course, that it's not possible?"

"Is it possible," she said, "for you and me to learn how to trust each other?"

"I'd certainly like to think so."

"Then maybe anything's possible."

Simon laughed. "Fair enough, my dear."

David said, "Where do we start?"

CHAPTER

THIRTY

They rented a car at the airport. Lana paid cash and drove them to the city center. There, they established a base for their operations in Spain at the Hotel Gran Meliá Fénix.

David had never stayed at a fancier string of places in his life. This one was situated on a leafy, lazy, sun-dappled stretch of Calle de Hermosilla in the exclusive Salamanca District. According to Simon, his publisher put him up at the Fénix whenever his appearance schedule took him to Madrid, and he could personally vouch for the establishment's adherence to—as he phrased it—the "heightened rules of discretion" required of its frequent celebrity clientele.

"Gary Cooper used to stay here, poor lad," he said, as if that were all the modern Nazi-hunter-about-town needed to know about the Fénix. "I can only imagine that Rita still does when she's in town."

David said, "Please don't tell me you're talking about Rita Hayworth."

"Didn't you think they were delightful together in *They Came to Cordura*? Gutted to hear the news this spring when he passed. Such a loss indeed. I bumped into Hemingway some time after the funeral, and I told him..."

"Hemingway," David said. "Ernest Hemingway."

"Well. He was too ill to attend himself, you know—the diabetes.

But they'd been the greatest of friends, loved the outdoors alike, even if Coop wasn't such an aficionado of the bullfights as Ernie. It *is* true that the two of them used to take day trips to the slaughterhouse together to watch the *novilleros* practice their killing. Of course, we've lost Papa now, too. But as I told him at the time—"

"Didn't I hear you say it was better," Lana interjected, "for you to avoid being recognized on this trip?"

"Whilst in transit." Simon affected a gravely serious expression as he waved off the bellman and held the door himself. "Amenities are another matter entirely."

They entered the upscale, Spanish-style lobby. Lana took one look around and said, "This place looks a bit rich for what's left of my operations account."

"Fear not," Simon said. "The rooms are on me."

"That won't be necessary."

"Nonsense. You paid for the car. It's the least I can do in return."

"I'm not keeping a ledger."

"Then consider it an unrecorded down payment on our mutual trust-building project."

Lana surprised David by relenting without further resistance. Simon, seemingly delighted that she'd come around to his generosity at last, booked them adjacent rooms overlooking the Plaza de Colón and its gleaming white monument to Christopher Columbus. After settling in, they met in his room.

"ABC Serrano is a walk up the street," he said. "What say we pop out for a bit of a shop, come back here, shower and change, then reconvene in the lobby for a late lunch while we plan our next campaign?"

"Sounds perfectly civilized," David said.

"The campaign is already planned," Lana said. "But you two get a head start on the shopping. I need to make a few calls."

*   *   *

The next time David saw Lana, she'd found for herself a cinnamon-colored, formfitting sweater dress that fit her form quite nicely indeed. David had chosen a light windbreaker, a checked button-down shirt, chinos, and the most comfortable pair of loafers he could find.

"You look terrific," he told her.

"Thank you," she said. "You look like a math teacher."

"Don't listen to her, old boy," Simon said, appearing from the wings in a herringbone sport coat and an ascot with an open collar. He wore an authorial-looking leather satchel on his shoulder. "Comfort is king."

"I didn't say it was a bad thing," Lana said. "I considered sleeping with my math teacher in college."

Simon chuckled. "I hope you passed the course."

"Glad to see you two getting along so well," David said. "Can we eat now?"

They took a table in the hotel restaurant and ordered as a group. By the time they'd finished their lunch—steaming bowls of *cocido madrileño* and a plate of calamari sandwiches they shared among them—David felt better than he had in days.

"Now then," Simon said, leaning back in his chair with a satiated sigh. "Someone was saying something about a plan?"

Lana wiped her hands on a napkin, dug into her fashionable new shoulder bag, and spread a map of the city out on the table before them.

"We're here," she said, pointing to a spot near the center of the map. She moved her hand a few inches to the west and tapped a new spot. "Herzog's clinic—also his residence—is here. This surrounding area is a chestnut grove, and this big green area to the west is Casa de Campo—four thousand acres of parkland." She traced a meandering blue band north and south on the map with her finger. "And this is Rio Manzaneres. The last water taxi runs at ten this evening."

"Ooh," Simon said, rubbing his hands together. "An amphibious assault. Tremendous."

"No," Lana said. "I'm pointing out the myriad lanes of approach, egress, and concealment at our blue-eyed friend's disposal."

David studied the map. "In other words, just about anywhere."

"What on God's earth makes you think that sodding fair-haired wankpot could possibly find us here?" Simon said. "He certainly couldn't have interrogated Balcon."

"The same way he made it onto our train in Amsterdam," Lana said. "Whoever he is, someone in what's left of my network has to be supplying him with information. There's no other way he could have tracked our movements."

"I admit it," David said. "I'm the tiniest bit offended."

Lana cocked her head. "In what way?"

"To not be considered a suspect."

"Why in the world would I consider you a suspect?"

"I've been with you every step of the way since DC," David said. "Maybe I'm a better spy than you think."

"The thought never occurred to me," she said, leaving David to wonder if he should consider it a compliment. "Now. Among my former resources, only two parties could possibly have been in a position to betray us effectively. The phone calls I made earlier were designed to plant misinformation with each of those parties. Where and when Blondie appears next will tell me who's working against us. What's so funny?"

David chuckled. "Blondie. Didn't you tell me that was Adolf's dog's name?"

"Perhaps an apt moniker, then," Simon suggested.

"Let's not get too far ahead of ourselves." Lana tapped the map again in three separate locations. "We need to keep an eye on these three locations as the most likely points of attack. I believe we stand a good chance of rooting out the traitor *and* eliminating the threat in the same maneuver."

"Uh-huh," David said. "One question."

"Yes?"

He waggled his empty hands. "Eliminate how? Urinate on him from close range?"

Lana reached for their drinks menu, unfolded it, and stood it on the edge of the table like a partition. Then she dug in her bag, retrieved an automatic handgun, and placed it on the table behind the partition with a heavy clunk.

"Merry Christmas," she said.

Simon whistled. "And happy new year."

"Jesus," David said, dropping his napkin quickly over the weapon and slipping it into his lap. "Where did you get this?"

"Same place I got the one in my bag," Lana said.

"His and her small arms!" Simon said. "How romantic."

David looked at her with amazement. "Where the hell did you go shopping, anyway?"

"That's a Llama Model IV," she said. "Spanish-made, but based on the Colt 1911. I presume you're more than passingly familiar with the latter weapon?"

"Whether I like it or not."

She nodded toward the gun under the napkin in his lap. "Hammer only—no safety. Also chambered for 7.63 millimeter, not .45 ACP. Ten in the magazine, one in the pipe, no extra ammo. So, fire effectively. And with finality."

"What about me?" Simon asked. "Don't I get a present?"

Lana dug in the bag again and produced a carton of nine-millimeter subsonic hollow points. "For the Welrod."

"My dear." Simon beamed at the box of bullets in front of him. "You shouldn't have."

"Don't be too appreciative. You'll have to gain much closer proximity with that contraption of yours, obviously."

"Perhaps," Simon agreed. "If I were a lesser marksman."

"You're an entertaining braggart, Mr. Lean, and almost surely overestimating yourself, but I appreciate the confidence," Lana said. "You may need all of it."

David said, "Let me see if I understand this plan correctly. The three of us are going to take the car across the river to Victor Herzog's clinic, keep an eye out for Blondie, and just introduce ourselves to Herzog?"

"Exactly." Lana touched her pointer finger to the tip of her nose. "We're taking Uncle Simon to see about having an unsightly tattoo removed. It brings him unspeakably painful memories, and we've heard that Herr Doktor Herzog is the best man in Europe for the job."

David looked at Simon.

Simon looked at Lana. He smiled. "My dear, I think that I may be ever so slightly falling in love with you. No offense, old boy."

"None taken," David said.

Lana nodded. "If nobody has room for dessert, let's go and bushwhack this blue-eyed goon."

CHAPTER
THIRTY-ONE

Although he'd expected more palm trees, and perhaps warmer temperatures, and while a person could hardly look left without spotting some building or other that was older than the entire United States of America, something about the feel of Madrid still reminded David of the California he'd known in his youth.

Maybe it was the color of the sky. Or the relaxed, leisurely pace of things on the street. Or the eclectic, outgoing people he encountered. Or maybe he just found himself feeling homesick for a long-ago place and time as they motored toward the lair of an alleged Nazi surgeon in a rented two-door Peugeot.

He was still reflecting on the topic when, early in the afternoon of December 29, 1961, they discovered that Dr. Victor Herzog and his legendary medical clinic no longer existed.

*   *   *

They found the good doctor's sprawling Mediterranean estate—a central two-story villa surrounded by a compound of low-slung out-buildings—just where Lana had described, nestled in a grove of chestnut trees between the west bank of the Manzanares river and the eastern edge of Casa de Campo park. A large stone sign posted at the gate read LA PUESTO DEL SOL PACÍFICA.

The Peaceful Sunset.

"I don't know about either of you," Simon said from the back seat of the rental car, "but if I really were going under the knife tomorrow, sunset is not the image I'd prefer to keep in mind."

His comment gave voice to their first clue that things here were perhaps not as they'd expected. Their second clue: all the old people.

"I'm very sorry," the administrator told them on the front lawn, a quarter of an hour later, where they stood together amid the tatters of Lana's original plan. "But I'm afraid that this facility changed hands some time ago."

The supervisor's name was Angelica Borras. She was a handsome woman, perhaps Simon's age, with a strong wide mouth, deep brown eyes, and impeccable English that sounded more melodic to David's ears than English when he spoke it himself.

"I'll be a striped baboon," Simon mused aloud, glancing around at the elderly men and women out strolling, or asleep, or being wheeled about by orderlies, all taking the cool afternoon sunlight in one fashion or another. Some appeared to notice their surroundings more than others. "A geriatric convalescence home. Perhaps we should have called ahead?"

Lana, for her part, seemed to be taking this turn of events with a surprising degree of tranquility. She said, "May I ask how the new management is affiliated with Dr. Herzog?"

"I'm afraid that there is no prior affiliation," Borras answered. "We are a private group, and very small. We received this property as part of a charitable donation last year, under the condition that we maintain a nonprofit operation."

"That's quite a donation," Lana said.

"*Claro.*" Borras nodded. "A blessing from God. We began accepting residents only six months ago."

"May I ask the name of your benefactor?"

"Isabella Herzog," Borras said. "I am told that the doctor himself left no instruction as to how his estate should be handled after his death. Isabella claimed responsibility as his only daughter. Although it is my understanding that the two of them had been estranged for many years."

David said, "Did his death come unexpectedly? Dr. Herzog?"

"*Suicidio.* I am truly sorry. One of you was a patient?"

Simon stepped in, smiling as he pushed up the sleeve of his sport coat. "I was scheduled to be. I've been on a waiting list."

Angelica Borras drew in a breath at the sight of the blue-gray digits imprinted on Simon's forearm. She touched her fingers to her lips, looking slowly from his wrist to his eyes. "You have been waiting a long time, *señor.*"

"You have no idea," Simon said.

She offered the three of them an apologetic smile. "You are not the first people to arrive here in search of the clinic since we opened our doors, I'm sorry to say. We inherited the doctor's records if you would like to retrieve your file."

David looked at Lana.

Lana remained unperturbed. From her outward demeanor, he could almost believe that they really had brought their uncle Simon in for a long-scheduled touch-up, and that this unexpected snafu merely gave them more time to enjoy the city together.

"How kind of you to offer," she said. "We'd like to do that, if you're certain it's no trouble."

"The trouble is all yours today, I fear."

"May I ask one more favor?"

"Of course."

"We'd like to pass along our condolences to Isabella," Lana said. "Do you have any idea how we might contact her?"

Borras nodded. "Of course. Real Monasterio de la Encarnación. She is a member of the order there."

Simon looked at David. All at once his face reddened. His lips clamped into a grimace. For no possible reason that David could intuit, the author's eyes filled with tears.

David glanced again at Lana, who also looked perplexed at the sudden state of their companion. Angelica Borras noticed, too; she adopted another sympathetic expression, as if to once again convey her sincerest apologies regarding his cosmetic misfortune—to say nothing of the inhumane personal history it represented.

David, meanwhile, nervously stepped over to defuse whatever outburst seemed to be building within Simon. He placed a firm hand on Lean's slender shoulder. "What's the matter, Uncle Si? Are you okay?"

It was only then that he understood that Simon wasn't crying, or choking back his frustrations, but rather struggling to keep from bursting into laughter.

"I'm terribly sorry," he said, nodding politely to Borras. He dabbed at his eyes with the backs of his fingers. "For a moment, I could have sworn I'd heard you say that Dr. Victor Herzog's only daughter was a nun."

*　　*　　*

According to Angelica Borras, La Puesto del Sol Pacífica had never been staffed to properly dispense the fifteen years' worth of abandoned business and medical records that had fallen into their possession with the donation of Herzog's grounds. But neither had it seemed appropriate to throw them all away. So, they'd moved everything to what had been, in Herzog's time, a stable behind the villa.

"Well," Simon said, gazing upon the rows upon rows of filing boxes lining the dusty, hay-scattered stalls. "With the three of us working together, I'd say this oughtn't take more than a week. What are we looking for, again?"

"Anything," Lana said. "Which is a lot easier than looking for something in particular."

"I suppose I hadn't thought of it that way."

"Meanwhile, I have an alternative plan."

Simon shook his head. "Please don't say it."

"How do you know what I was about to say?"

"You were about to suggest leaving us here on clerk's duty while you traipse off in the car to pay a visit to Isabella Herzog."

Lana smiled. "Actually, no. I need David with me."

Simon smirked at David. "Mustn't *you* feel special."

"Ask me later," David said.

Simon harrumphed. They wished him luck. On their way back to the administrative building, David looked at Lana and said, "That was surprising."

"Oh?"

"Leaving Simon Lean alone in a room full of possible clues? Seems like a towering leap of faith in the same man whose name you couldn't bring yourself to speak out loud six hours ago."

"Oh, I still don't trust him," Lana said. "Not half as far as I could throw him. But it'll work to our advantage if he believes that I do."

"Uh-huh," David said. "Also, this way he's not privy to anything Isabella Herzog might tell us."

Lana feigned innocence. "You're the one who suggested *that* notion. Not me."

"Right."

"But I will say this: If Simon Lean really does know Ernest Hemingway, I'll eat my hat," she said. "And yours for dessert."

As they crossed the lawn toward the villa, they passed a toothless old woman sitting alone in a wheelchair, staring into space. The woman's slack skin was as brown and wrinkled as a walnut hull. Thin, slate-colored hair hung limp on her scalp. She had a white afghan draped over her lap, but the blanket had slipped aside, so that it hung nearly to the green grass at her feet, exposing the hard, veiny knobs of her knees.

Lana veered over to the woman. She stooped, fetched the blanket, and rearranged it over the woman's lap.

The woman raised her rheumy eyes to Lana, then to David. Her mouth never closed. Her expression never changed. David couldn't even be sure she was seeing them. Lana patted the back of her hand, then moved on.

David wanted to ask more questions. He wondered how she'd been able to remain so calm upon discovering that their best lead had killed himself a year ago. He wondered if Nicholas Balcon had known all along that Dr. Victor Herzog was dead. David wondered all kinds of things.

As they neared the villa, he couldn't shake the sensation that the old woman in the wheelchair was watching them every step of the way. But when he looked back over his shoulder, he saw only an old woman with her mouth open, staring at nothing. Her blanket had slipped to the side again. It hung from the arm of her wheelchair like a white flag, indicating surrender.

"What if Blondie shows up here while we're here?" he said.

"Then he and Simon can spend a little quality time getting caught up with one another," Lana said.

"I don't understand."

"Something tells me they've crossed paths before, Blondie and Uncle Simon."

David thought back to the moment in Paris, in the kitchen of the ambassador's residence. When the pale assassin and Simon Lean had locked eyes. He was forced to concede that he'd entertained a similar thought then. At least momentarily.

"But that doesn't make any sense," he said.

"It certainly doesn't," Lana agreed.

CHAPTER

THIRTY-TWO

They didn't have far to travel.

Real Monasterio de la Encarnación was a centuries-old convent near the Plaza de Oriente, overlooking the Old Quarter of Madrid, a fifteen-minute drive from Herzog's estate. The convent itself was a blocky, brick-and-stone edifice with a low-pitched, clay tile roof. Except for the chiseled stone cross rising up from the peak of the central loggia, the building reminded David of the barracks he'd lived in as a shiny new boot at Camp Pendleton.

A commemorative statue of Spanish author Lope de Vega presided over the close-clipped, winter-green public lawn of Plaza Encarnación. David thought of Simon's proclivity to point out landmarks related to famous writers and wondered if he knew about this one. Part of him wished he had a camera.

Closer to the building, a polished stone tourist placard informed him that the convent housed, among hundreds of other relics, the blood of the martyred saint Pantaleon, which was said to miraculously return to liquid each year on his feast day of July 27.

"I guess we missed it," David said. "I hope that's not bad luck."

"Missed what?"

"Never mind." He looked at the locked wrought iron gate separating the convent's vacant courtyard from the rest of the world. "This place doesn't look open to the public."

"It isn't," Lana said.

"Then what do we do now?"

"We wait." Lana dug in her bag. "She shouldn't be long."

"Who?"

"Isabella Herzog," she said impatiently. "Haven't you been paying attention?"

David hadn't felt quite this lost since he'd found himself alone at a pay phone in Georgetown with a swollen trachea and the first Hitler reel stuffed in his satchel. "How will we find her?"

Lana smiled. "Don't worry. This time I really did call ahead."

He gazed past the fence toward a suggestion of movement somewhere in the shadows of the loggia's open arcade. A woman wearing a black-and-white habit emerged into the sunlight of the courtyard. She saw them waiting by the fence, paused in her tracks momentarily, then approached.

"I didn't even know nuns were allowed to use telephones," David said.

*　　*　　*

It would have been impossible for a film buff like David Toland to look at a woman like Isabella Herzog and not think of Audrey Hepburn in Zinnemann's *The Nun's Story*. Framed by her headpiece, scapular, and tunic, Victor Herzog's estranged daughter had the same slender neck, pristine cheekbones, and big, entrancing eyes. Except that Isabella Herzog's eyes looked much sadder to David than Hepburn's ever did.

"Miss Welles," she said through the fence. "And you must be Mr. Toland. Good afternoon."

"Sister Isabella," Lana said. "Thank you for agreeing to meet with us."

"It is not customary," Isabella said. "Mother Agueda has determined that my vow of obedience applies to your request. She has granted me a special dispensation to speak with you today."

"We're grateful," Lana said. "These are special circumstances indeed."

"I should make clear that our time together must be limited."

"Of course."

Sister Isabella unlocked the gate and stepped through to join them, pulling the gate closed again behind her. She slipped her ring of keys into a side pocket of her tunic and said, "Shall we enjoy the air?"

They walked a pea gravel path to Calle San Quintín, then across to the small park leading into the Plaza de Oriente. David felt an almost immediate sense of peace amid the bare trees and formal gardens of the park. He took in the manicured hedges, evergreen shrubs, and wide pebbled pathways lined with statues of Spanish monarchs, enjoying the way the long, slanted bands of setting sunlight cast everything in a golden glow. Filmmakers called this time of day the magic hour. That seemed an apt description. He thought of Simon Lean, stuck back in the stable building, surrounded by dusty old medical records, and did not wish to trade places with him.

Although he sort of wished that he and Lana could trade places with the young couple he spotted on a nearby stone bench. The couple sat with their foreheads together, seemingly carefree, enjoying the occasional kiss in the late-afternoon chill.

Some wishes seemed farther-fetched than others.

"My mother died bearing me into the world," Sister Isabella was saying. She clasped her hands behind her back as she strolled, her eyes turned toward the ground. "But I never felt a moment's blame from my father. He doted on me as a child. We played games in the evenings. He comforted me when I was afraid. I loved him deeply."

"How was it that the two of you came to Madrid?" Lana asked.

"We escaped Germany before the Allies took Berlin," Sister Isabella said. "At the time, he explained to me that he'd been discovered treating Jews in his practice. He said that we had no choice but to flee for our lives."

"And did you believe him?"

Lana's question seemed cold and strange until David considered the game she'd grown up playing with her own father: *Am I Lying?*

"I was ten years old," Sister Isabella said. "He was my father. I believed him with all my heart."

They emerged into the plaza, a wide-open square with a view of the Royal Palace, centered by a large, heavily patinaed bronze statue of a man on rearing horseback.

Sister Isabella stopped at the moss-lined fountain surrounding the statue. She gazed into the dark water for a few moments, then said, "Many years later, I discovered papers in his office. Papers stamped by the Reich. When I confronted my father, he grew angry. It was the first and only time in my life that he ever raised a hand to me."

"How did he explain the papers?"

"He claimed that he'd been pardoned in absentia for his so-called acts of treason," Sister Isabella said. "He insisted that we were safe now only because of his efforts to make us so. And that I'd been a spoiled, ungrateful brat to go snooping among his things." She sighed. "But I was older by then. He may have been able to strike me. But he couldn't make me believe him anymore."

"Did your father ever admit the truth?"

"Not until the day he took his life."

"What did he say on that day?"

"On that day, he wrote me a letter. He described the work he performed for the SS. The experiments. Described them in his own handwriting." Sister Isabella's voice developed a tremble. She paused. They waited. When she finally spoke again, her voice seemed thicker. "Worse than animals. As if they had no souls. That was how my father treated the Jews."

David was grateful that he'd thought to pick up a package of handkerchiefs at ABC Serrano, for no better reason than so that he could offer one to Isabella Herzog now. Sister Isabella thanked him and dabbed at her eyes with her bare fingers, kindly declining his offer.

"I didn't receive the letter until after my father's staff discovered his body," she said. "I was still a novitiate at that time. I feared excommunication."

"But that clearly didn't happen," Lana said.

"I was offered the opportunity to profess my vows instead," Sister Isabella said. "May I now ask you a question?"

"Of course."

"Why have you come here?" There was no rancor in Sister Isabella's tone, only curiosity. "What is your purpose?"

"My explanation may cause you pain, Sister."

"I accept your concern in the spirit you clearly intend."

Lana returned Sister Isabella's steady gaze. "Would it surprise you if I said that your father's work for the Third Reich didn't end in Berlin? That he brought it with him to Madrid?"

Sister Isabella paused a long time before she answered.

"It would come as unexpected news," she finally said. She didn't break eye contact, and her expression didn't change. But David noticed that the fingers of her left hand had grasped the fabric of her tunic. "And I would ask you to elaborate."

"The services Victor Herzog continued to perform for the Party, here in hiding, enabled certain high-ranking members of the Reich to avoid apprehension," Lana said. "He used his surgical skills to alter their appearances forever, enabling these murderers to walk freely among us. My purpose is to find them."

Or at least one of them, David thought.

Sister Isabella looked away, into the middle distance. Her eyes had gone vacant.

"I take no satisfaction in telling you this, and certainly no pleasure," Lana said. "But it's important for you to understand the gravity of my mission. Before you ask how I'm able to pursue it with such certainty, let me assure you that my information has cost me my professional career. Others have paid for it with their lives."

Sister Isabella's fingers slowly loosened their grasp of her tunic. She took another deep breath in through the nose, turning her eyes up to the statue of the man on horseback. The frozen rider towered above the three of them on his heavy stone pedestal, his royal staff drawn and brandished, his mount fixed in the act of pawing the air with its hooves.

"King Felipe IV," she said, raising her eyebrows to David. "Preparing to charge into battle."

"It's quite something," he said.

She turned to Lana. "And what do you think of this piece?"

"I agree with my colleague." Lana didn't bother looking up at the statue. David almost wondered if she noticed it. "It's very dramatic."

Sister Isabella nodded. "I think so, too. Although bronze is too soft a metal to support such a pose."

"Maybe we should move to another spot," David suggested in jest.

Sister Isabella seemed amused by the joke. "The artist himself worried, too," she told him. "He feared that the rearing horse would topple forward under its own weight within a few years' time. Do you know how he solved the problem?"

"How?"

"The Italian, Galileo, advised him to cast the stallion's hindquarters in solid metal," she explained, "but to make the front half of the animal hollow. That way the bottom is heavy, like an anchor. Meanwhile, the top is light."

"Clever."

"Galileo? As the father of modern science, I presume that he must have been."

"An excellent point."

"But his science also hides the truth."

Lana said, "What truth is that?"

"That sometimes the drama we perceive contains nothing inside."

Lana finally gave the statue a cursory glance. "How long has it been standing?" she asked.

"More than three hundred years."

"I guess they must have known what they were doing, then."

Sister Isabella nodded to herself. "Indeed." Then she straightened her slender shoulders. "And if I wish to make the same claim, I'm afraid it's already past time for me to return to my duties."

To David's surprise, Lana didn't attempt to dissuade her. They accompanied Sister Isabella back across the plaza, back through the park, retracing their steps in relative silence.

The statues of the monarchs cast longer shadows now. He wasn't sure what they'd accomplished here in the short time it had taken those shadows to lengthen, other than rattling the consecrated life of a perfectly pleasant German expatriate who surely would have preferred to be left in peace. David couldn't help thinking again of Sister Luke—Hepburn's character in *The Nun's Story*.

Sister Luke also had been the daughter of a surgeon, if he remembered Zinnemann's film correctly, which he did. The story recounted her spiritual struggle to uphold her vows during the Nazi occupation of Belgium on the eve of World War II. In the movie, Sister Luke loses this struggle after her father is killed at the hands of East German soldiers. Hepburn had received her third Academy Award nomination for her work on the picture.

What had Isabella Herzog received?

They followed the path out of the park, back to the sidewalk along narrow Calle San Quintín. Just before crossing the street, Lana said, "Sister, if you'll forgive me for asking, I wonder—"

"If I would show you the letter my father wrote to me before he died," Sister Isabella finished. She took a deep breath. The sadness returned to her eyes. "A thousand times I've held those pages over a flame. And a thousand times I've returned them to my things. I don't know why I haven't been able to destroy them."

"Perhaps you were waiting," Lana suggested.

"Waiting for what, child?"

"For me to arrive."

Sister Isabella seemed calmly intrigued by this notion. She looked at the sky, as if requesting a second opinion. At last, she seemed to have arrived at a decision. But just as she opened her mouth to deliver it, a sudden squeal of tires interrupted her.

A powerful sense of impending disaster overcame David as the hairs on the back of his neck stood on end. He wheeled to his aft just in time to see a Jaguar coupe the color of charcoal jump the curb and accelerate toward them, two wheels on the street and two on the sidewalk, bearing down on them with lethal intent.

CHAPTER

THIRTY-THREE

A roaring engine. A leering grille. Blank headlamps like twin dead eyes.

These were the details David perceived in the scant few moments before instinct overrode his response system, and he found himself tackling a nun.

He pulled Sister Isabella roughly to the ground on top of him just as the Jag rattled through the spot where they'd been standing, jouncing and shuddering on its wheels. He heard the air leave Sister Isabella's lungs in a pained blurt as they landed in a tangle on the strip of grass between the sidewalk and the park.

He looked up just in time to see Lana make her own leap clear of the onrushing car. But she was a step too late. From the ground, David could only watch in panic as Lana cleared the coupe's low, predatory front bumper by a hair's breadth. She bounced up the hood and hit the windshield with enough force to send an instant spiderweb of cracks radiating out from the smashed center of the glass. Then she rolled off the other side of the car, into the street, out of view.

Somewhere nearby, a woman screamed. Other passersby cried out, scattering as the marauding Jaguar clipped a park bench and bounced back down off the curb, fishtailing precariously. Then came another smoking squall of tires as the car corrected its course and sped away.

David could see Lana lying motionless in the street, her arms trapped beneath her, legs akimbo.

"Go...to her!" Sister Isabella wheezed, gasping to reclaim her breath. "I'm not...hurt."

David scrambled to his knees, then his feet. He sprinted to Lana, heart pounding, a sick, slippery feeling in the bottom of his gut.

But by the time he got to her, she was already pushing herself up on bloody, abraded palms.

"Don't move," he said. "Stay where you are."

Lana waved him away and stood under her own power. Just below the hem of her sweater dress, her right knee looked like a pad of ground meat; rivulets of blood trailed down over her shin and ankle. At the end of the street, they heard another moan of tires as the Jag cornered right onto Calle de Bailén, trailing a blue cloud of rubber smoke behind it.

Incredibly, Lana gave chase, loping after the car as fast as she could hobble.

"Lana!" David called. "Stop!"

When she paid no attention, he followed after her with a limp of his own. His smashed toe, still unhealed from their adventures in Moscow, had now been wrenched severely for good measure. His sock felt spongy inside his shoe, sodden with new blood.

He ignored it and limped faster.

Twenty feet ahead, Lana shoved between a pair of bystanders wearing open-faced motorcycle helmets. As David came upon them, he recognized the bystanders as the couple he'd seen kissing on the bench in the Plaza de Oriente. They'd been preparing to climb aboard a well-used BMW twin cylinder—a machine now in the process of being commandeered by a staggering Lana Welles, her purse somehow still cross-slung on one hip.

"*Oye!*" the guy called. "*Qué estás—*"

David apologized as he pushed past him. "Lana, come on. You obviously need to be examined."

Somewhere in the distance, they heard the whine of a

high-revving engine, followed by the sound of more people screaming. Now tires screeched. Horns blared. The sound of the engine suddenly became distant and muffled, as if it had dropped into a hole.

"I'm fine," she snapped, standing up on the bike's kick lever, using her body weight to fire the Beemer into snarling life. She goosed the throttle and yelled over the growl of the big boxer engine: "Stay with Isabella! I'll meet you back at the Fénix!"

When David looked back over his shoulder, he saw that Sister Isabella had already stolen across the street behind them, her tunic gathered up in her hands. She was now beating a straight path back to the convent's locked outer gate.

Another split-second decision: Lana or Isabella?

Stay with the nun or go with the spy?

In the time it took David to formulate the question in his mind, he'd already swung his leg over the back of the Beemer behind Lana. He found the passenger foot pegs just as she stomped the bike into gear. Lana twisted the throttle with her blood-smeared, gravel-encrusted right hand, nearly flipping him off the back as the bike surged forward. David grabbed onto her waist. Then they were up and over the curb, onto the walking path, now blatting back through the park, spraying pea gravel behind them.

"What the hell are you doing?" David shouted.

"He hooked into the tunnel on Bailén!" she called back over her shoulder. "Under the palace! Heading south! I can beat him!"

David almost asked what in God's name she was planning to do even if they did somehow catch up with the mystery car. Then he decided that he didn't really want to know.

Meanwhile, either Lana's decision-making was not, in fact, being undermined by an intracranial hemorrhage, as David feared must certainly be the case, or she wasn't letting it slow her down. She thumbed the horn button as they careened out of the Central Gardens, back into the Plaza de Oriente: *meeep-meeeep-meeeeeeeeep!*

Onlookers scurried aside. A woman laden with shopping bags

panicked and froze in their path; Lana countersteered and slipped past her with an inch to spare, blowing the woman's bangs back from her forehead.

They caromed around the fountain of Felipe IV, a new steel horse racing a circle around an old bronze one. Lana dragged her heel around the tight loop, correcting a brief, heart-gulping skid from the back end—otherwise known as David's sitting place.

Then she bore straight toward the looming eastern façade of Palacio Real, with its Flemish spires and great Tuscan pilasters and centuries of accumulated prominence in the neighborhood. Visigoth kings carved out of limestone stood sentinel along the roofline, quietly observing the goings-on in their plaza below.

Lana kicked up through the gears until David's windbreaker flapped behind him like a shred of torn parachute. Over her shoulder, she called out what sounded like important instructions, but David could no longer make out her words over the noise of the wind and the revving engine. He yelled back: "What?"

But she'd already made her move, leaning the bike so far to the left that their knees almost scraped the ground. David held on for dear life, forcing himself to keep from leaning the opposite direction. Whatever he could clench, he clenched it.

Lana accelerated smoothly through the turn. They popped upright again under a new twist of power, now screaming along the brick-paved pedestrian boulevard between the royal palace and the plaza.

Just ahead, a row of concrete bollards connected by hanging arcs of chain served as a divider between the pedway and the street. Lana aimed for the empty passage between the two center posts, laying on the high-pitched horn again as they slalomed between confused, stutter-stepping pedestrians.

Leaving the plaza behind, they dove off the curb and into southbound traffic on Calle de Bailén. Lana quick-shifted without pulling the clutch and wrung the throttle again, weaving in between cars, pointing the bike directly toward what looked to David like a low concrete wall in the middle of the street.

So, this is how I die, he thought. *Not in Korea. Not strangled by an assassin in a library basement. Not shot by a guard at the Bolshoi, or even drowning in a sewer tunnel. It's going to happen on the back of a 600cc German motorcycle, clinging to the hips of a psychotic lady spy.*

If Adolf Hitler really was still alive, David imagined him laughing.

Horns blared all around them. Drivers gestured angrily out their windows as David and Lana roared past them in a blur. David saw the wall—part of some kind of elaborate central median—approaching at an alarming rate. Lana was going too fast. In two more seconds, they'd become part of the wall itself, or at least decorate it with whatever came splattering out of them when they hit. David's heart tried to get a head start on the rest of his internal organs, hammering the inside of his rib cage as if attempting to squeeze through the gaps. He braced for impact.

Lana yelled, "Hang on!"

She veered hard to the right at the last possible moment, slipping in front of a taxicab with no room to spare, touching off another wailing screech of tires behind them, another blare of a horn at the nape of David's neck.

But they remained upright and intact, funneling into a narrow one-way side strip between two guardrails, just barely wide enough for a single-file line of traffic. To his left, David could see over the railing to a two-lane street rising up to meet them from underground. He realized they'd reached the exit of the Bailén street tunnel.

And exiting that tunnel, just ahead of them, was a charcoal Jaguar coupe with a shattered windshield.

David patted Lana on the shoulder and pointed. Lana made big, exaggerated nods with her head. She quick-shifted again, winding the Beemer up another gear, pulling abreast of their quarry in parallel.

The low-slung Jag shimmied on its springs as it veered from one side of the exit to another, attempting to find its way around a supermini Citroën in one lane and a delivery van in the other. The Citroën sported a wine-red cabriolet top that put David in mind of the coagulated, wind-dried blood on Lana's leg. This random association at high speed put him in mind of two things: their fragile mortality, and how high her sweater dress had hiked up in order to accommodate motorcycle seating.

Once again, David was amazed—and more than slightly embarrassed with himself—to find that the sight of her well-toned thighs was almost enough to distract him from his injuries, her injuries, their current rate of travel, and the howling danger all around them.

Then the Jag laid on its own horn, snapping him back to the moment at hand. He had an elevated view from which to watch the following strange ballet unfolding beside them.

First, the van tooted its horn politely and stayed its course. The supermini braked in apparent confusion, slowing down rather than speeding up. The Jaguar finally lost patience, cleared its throat loudly, and rammed the Citroën from behind, shoving the smaller car forward. The mini lost control of its steering, skidding into the adjacent lane in front of the hard-braking delivery truck.

Meanwhile, the Jag soared out of the tunnel, charging full-tilt toward the merger at street level where its lane and theirs met each other.

Lana leaned forward, racing the other driver to the spot.

They were on a clear collision course with the Jaguar. David forced himself not to squirm, thinking: *Please don't ram that car with this motorcycle. Please don't ram that car with this motorcycle. Please don't . . .*

But they lost the race by half a second, dropping in behind the Jag even more narrowly than they'd slipped in front of the cab— so closely that David swore he felt the Beemer's front tire graze the Jaguar's rear bumper. Lana feathered the rear brake until she'd opened an eighteen-inch cushion between them, then held steady pursuit as Bailén opened up into multiple lanes.

The Jag blew through a red light at Calle Mayor, diving through a lucky gap in cross traffic. David could see nothing of the driver through the smoked rear window.

Lana backed off a few more feet but followed closely behind. David caught a glimpse of blurred motion in his peripheral vision as a fellow motorcyclist laid down his bike and slid through the intersection behind them.

The more alarming sight came from just ahead of them, however, as the Jag's taillights suddenly pulsed red and held. The car slammed on its brakes, fishtailing to a smoking dead stop in the middle of their lane. Once again, David closed his eyes instinctively, preparing for impact.

But somehow, once again, they never stopped moving. The world tilted around him in the darkness. When he opened his eyes, the street ahead was clear. He felt a burst of elation. Another slim escape from the teeth of disaster!

On the other hand, they'd now traded pursuit for flight. David glanced over his shoulder and saw the Jaguar coming up fast behind them, its cracked windshield shimmering in the day's last long rays of sunlight, the face of the driver still obscured from view.

Lana quick-shifted back up through the gears, preloading the toe lever and blipping the throttle instead of pulling the clutch, like a Moto Grand Prix racer hitting the straightaway at Silverstone. She opened the Beemer up, weaving in and out of gaps in traffic too small for a motorcycle, let alone the car chasing them.

The Jag solved this problem with brute, steel-scraping force, jostling its way through every four-wheeled obstacle, leaving Madrid's Sunday motorists spun out in its wake.

Lana blared on, her windblown hair whipping at David's face. The streets widened. They narrowed. They narrowed still further, then widened again.

They blasted across a palatial intersection centered by yet another tall stone monument. They hooked another knee-dragging turn through a roundabout, peeling off in a new direction. The Jaguar fell behind, caught up, and pulled abreast at every opportunity, attempting whenever possible to swerve them into oblivion.

For nearly a quarter mile, Lana took to the sidewalk along Paseo de la Chopera as they entered the leafy Arganzuela District, sending pedestrians diving for doorways. Then she found the street again, the Jaguar still behind them, unshaken.

Which stuck them at high speed on a divided thoroughfare with apartment blocks on one side, a seemingly endless public park on the other, and no time to corner into one of the few alleyways they passed. David found himself hoping that the Beemer had plenty of gas in the tank. They would not be stopping—or slowing down—any time soon.

Meanwhile, each time they blew through a red light as if it were green, he felt another few months tick off his life. But Lana seemed to be a legitimate expert at handling the big bike, and her sustained success at not crashing—despite the Jaguar's repeated efforts to the contrary—was a quality he admired more with every blurred, wind-blasted mile.

Soon the parkland on their right gave way to some kind of long, redbrick façade. The façade appeared to run the entire length of the block, with a scalloped topline punctuated by circular portals. David noticed a change in the quality of the air in this neighborhood—faint at first, beneath the Beemer's exhaust fumes, but growing stronger by the moment: a heady mix of farm smells mixed with the ripe, vaguely sickening tinge of rendered meat.

Lana straightened her spine, scanning the brick expanse along their starboard side. Inexplicably, she let up on the throttle; David glanced over his shoulder and saw the Jaguar coming up fast behind them again. He thought of the heavy new Llama Model IV tucked in the back of his waistband.

Then he thought, *No.*

He wasn't ready to start shooting into a populated neighborhood from the back of a motorcycle. Even if it meant getting rammed like the little Citroën back in the tunnel—an occurrence that appeared to be imminent.

All at once he noticed what felt suspiciously like Lana's rump between his hands. David faced front to find that she'd stood up on her footpegs, still craning for a glimpse of . . . something.

Then she sat down, countersteered sharply to the right, and took the bike through a slim gap in a row of parked cars, up onto the mostly empty sidewalk. They skimmed along the redbrick wall close enough that David could have reached out and skinned his knuckles along its surface. That was when he saw what Lana had been searching for, just up ahead: a gated entrance.

The iron gate stood open. Lana double-braked hard, taking them into a yawning skid that threatened to end David's long track record of never soiling himself in public.

But she maintained perfect control of the machine, opening the throttle again, executing a near-perfect right turn in the middle of a sidewalk from roughly thirty kilometers per hour. They accelerated through the open gate, passing beneath a stone placard set into the brick archway: MATADERO DE MADRID.

That was when David first heard the mooing.

*　　*　　*

When people of comparable means spoke of wintering in Spain, Simon thought between sneezes, he doubted they envisioned long afternoons in a stifling horse barn stacked halfway to the rafters with dust-caked business records. It seemed appropriately figurative that his assignment should smell, if only faintly, of ancient manure.

He opened the big doors at either end of the structure to let the breeze through, then worked in what had once been the tack room, where he found enough passed-over office furniture amid the abandoned medical equipment to fashion an adequate study carrel.

He spent the first hour out in the main stables, excavating. He opened, closed, and set aside box after box of billing invoices, inventory sheets, and account ledgers, finally digging his way back to the boxes he wanted: the patient files.

These he lugged one after another into the tack room. Here he sat at a wobbly examination table, surrounded by a phalanx of bad office paintings leaning against the walls like unemployed freeloaders.

Simon paged through evaluations, vital statistics, and before-and-after photos by the dim light of a fritzy gooseNecked floor lamp until his own neck kinked. He took periodic walks around the barn, letting the fresh air clear the dust from his brain.

Then he'd return to his drudgery, finding himself distracted with increasing frequency by the department store artwork all around him. Soon, for each ten minutes he spent glancing through nose jobs, he'd spend five more gazing at a cheaply framed print of a sailboat on open water. He imagined that he was lounging on the deck of the sailboat instead of hunched over whichever file happened to lay open before him.

By late afternoon, the ratio had turned upside down: five minutes of liposuction and scar removal for fifteen idle minutes beside a lithographed mountain brook. One piece in particular seemed to draw his attention more often than the rest; an original painting, smaller than the others. It was of amateur artistic merit at best, yet curiously arresting in its composition and color palette. And the artist's signature seemed vaguely familiar to him, somehow.

Had a known painter been a patient here and left the piece by way of thanks? Or had the name merely wormed its way into his mind subliminally over the course of this afternoon? Or was he simply bored out of his skull?

Whatever the case, this off-kilter little painting was—again—the focus of Simon Lean's wandering attention when a hand fell suddenly on his shoulder, causing him to jump halfway out of his skin.

"Oh!" said Angelica Borras, withdrawing her hand as if his startlement had delivered its own electrical charge. "*Señor. Lo siento mucho.* I spoke, but you didn't hear me."

Simon blinked at her; it was as if she'd materialized out of thin air. He'd had no sense of another person's presence; he'd been lost in a jungle, all alone. In *that* jungle, he thought, looking back at the painting again.

And that was when it hit him.

The artist's name.

Borras said, "*Señor?* Are you well?"

Simon jumped up so quickly that his chair overturned, striking the tack room floor with a sharp wooden crack. Angelica Borras's eyes flew open as he swept her into his arms and kissed her right on the mouth.

"My dear!" he said, beaming as he twirled her. "Better than you could possibly imagine. Tell me: have you ever considered dealing art on the side?"

*   *   *

They rocketed into a large compound of dun-colored buildings and wide-open spaces. Lana bore immediately to the right, heading for some kind of rusty tank perched on stubby iron legs. She ran behind the tank, skidded to a stop, and toed the bike into neutral. As they sat there, idling, she patted David's leg rapidly. "Off," she said.

"What the hell are we doing?"

"I'm getting my gun out," Lana said, already digging in her purse. "You're going over there. The minute that son of a bitch shows himself, close the gate behind him. Hurry now."

David disembarked the Beemer, finding solid ground on not-so-solid legs. They'd entered some kind of urban stockyard— ground zero for the smells he'd picked up out on the street.

In and among the buildings, he saw pens of lowing cattle. There was another large pen in the center of the compound, fashioned out of split-rail angles into a spacious, octagonal paddock. Surrounding the octagon was a group of young brown men in loose white clothing. The men were smeared with dust and sweat. Some of them were bleeding. A few of them looked over their shoulders casually at David and Lana.

The rest of them watched two figures inside the pen. The first figure was clearly one of their fellows: a dust-covered young man wearing the same loose clothing, but with a red sash tied around his waist. He was holding some kind of spear.

The other figure was an enormous black bull with great knotted shoulders, a thick humped neck, and pair of wide, upcurved horns. The bull—its front quarters bristling with blood-smeared *banderillas*—held its massive head low, scraping at the ground with one blocky hoof as the young man in the red sash circled him.

Not a pen, David thought. *An arena.*

He thought of the sign he'd glimpsed on the way in: MATADERO DE MADRID. Then he thought of the story Simon had told them back at the hotel—apocryphal though it may or may not have been—of Cooper and Hemingway: *The two of them used to take day trips to the slaughterhouse to watch the* novilleros *practice their killing.*

David guessed this must be the place. Yet another missed attraction for Simon Lean, the poor devil, cooped up back at the convalescent home without anyone trying to kill him.

And with that thought, a familiar-sounding car engine became audible just outside the wall. A low, cruising rumble.

Lana shouted, "Go!"

Quickly as he could hobble, David took his position at the wall just as the long, sleek snout of the Jaguar nosed its way cautiously into the compound...

And then stopped there, idling. Half in and half out.

David pressed himself flat against the wall, thinking, *Now what?*

More of the *novilleros* over by the training pen began to take notice of the newcomers to the compound. David looked over at Lana. He shrugged his shoulders.

Lana shook her head at the sky, shoved her pistol under her leg, grabbed the handlebars, and tore out from her hiding spot behind the rusty tank, spraying reddish dirt behind her.

The moment she came into view, the Jag's tires barked. The driver floored the accelerator, shooting into the compound like a greyhound coursing a hare.

David hauled the gate with both hands, swinging it closed with a heavy iron clang. Every last one of the apprentice matadors turned their attention from the training pen, now—including the young man with the red sash.

The bull chose this moment to charge his opponent, coming in low, swiping its great horns in an upward arc. Through some seemingly preternatural mix of clairvoyance and athleticism, the young man in the red sash moved in the scant nick of time, leaping aside from a dead standstill. He took three running steps and flopped over the top rail of the fence, narrowly escaping what might well have been a lethal goring, had he been half a step slower in sensing eight hundred pounds of angry, onrushing beef.

Meanwhile, Lana tore across the compound, leading the Jaguar in a wide circle. The chase sent clouds of drifting dust into the air, tinting the last moments of the so-called magic hour a sanguinary hue. She geared up and opened the throttle as they came about; the Jaguar momentarily lost its traction, sliding off course. Lana used the opportunity to pull away in a sudden burst of torque.

As she sped straight back toward him, David drew the gun from under his windbreaker. He racked the slide, instinctively thumbing for a safety catch that wasn't there, then took a three-point stance.

He could see Lana's face clearly, her expression set in grim determination. He aimed past her, resolving his focus to the Jaguar, which had recovered, corrected, and resumed pursuit.

But he hesitated to pull the trigger. It was a high-risk, low-percentage shot for a handgun; if Lana zigged or zagged at the wrong moment, he could easily shoot her by mistake.

As if to validate his fears, Lana took a page from the bull's notebook, throwing the bike into a jaw-dropping, 180-degree skid, so that she faced the onrushing Jaguar. David saw her rear wheel spin, and he thought, *No, no, no, what are you doing, what are you doing . . .*

And then she went charging directly back toward the car, like an unarmed knight tilting against a Panzer light tank.

She's out of her mind!

But David was forced to acknowledge that she wasn't precisely unarmed. For a moment, he stood with his mouth open, breathing in dust and taking up space, as Lana extended her left arm, gun in hand. Controlling the bike with her throttle hand, she began to fire with the other: *blam blam blam bla-blam!*

One of the Jaguar's headlamps shattered and disappeared. Jagged bullet holes began to appear in the car's hood, marching up toward the windshield.

David took his cue, pulled his wits about him, and joined in, squeezing off round after careful round. He aimed to Lana's left, targeting the car's low front grille, hoping to hit the radiator concealed behind it.

Lana geared up and laid on more speed. David was forced to cease fire for fear of hitting her. Neither driver nor rider showed any indication of flinching.

Pull out! he shouted in his head. *For Christ's sake, Lana, pull out now!*

The sound of bullets puncturing steel gave way to a flat *pop!* as a glinting hole appeared in the Jaguar's cracked windshield. Then another. And a third, stitching across the glass from passenger side to driver's. The windshield finally gave up the last of its tensile strength, crumbling out of its frame and across the hood in a shower of safety-laminated nuggets.

The Jag finally swerved, careening to its left as Lana held her line, charging straight through the spot where the car had been, never for a moment deviating from her path.

Through the empty hole where the Jaguar's windshield had been, David finally caught a glimpse of the man behind the wheel. As he watched the man lose control of the car, barreling wildly toward the *novilleros* spectating from the practice arena, David registered the following thoughts in the following order: Lana Welles was a deranged lunatic. And she was right.

Their blond-haired, blue-eyed assassin had tracked them to Madrid after all.

CHAPTER

THIRTY-FOUR

When the dust clouds parted, David took note of the current score inside the Matadero de Madrid training pen:

Condemned bull: 1.

Jaguar coupe: 0.

Apprentice matador: did not finish.

Somehow—and David Toland dearly wished he could have seen enough through the heavy dust screen to observe precisely how—the car lay on its driver's side amid a jackstraw pile of split rails. Its rear wheel rotated lazily in midair. Geysers of white steam poured from under the hood. The driver's side, now aimed skyward, had crumpled in like a dented soda can.

Meanwhile, the injured bull had trotted away from its demolished pen to an open area of the compound, barbed and bloody *banderillas* bobbing with its gait. The animal's great head hung low as it attempted to evade the young *novilleros*, who had scrambled together to form a new human pen around it.

David and Lana raced to the decommissioned car on foot, where a dazed and bleeding blond man was attempting to crawl out through the opening where a windshield had existed previously.

"Hands flat on the hood!" Lana shouted, circling around to the front bumper, gun leveled in a two-handed grip. "Move half an inch more and I'll put one in your eye."

Blondie raised his head groggily as sirens became audible in the distance. It seemed to take him a moment to focus his eyes.

When he finally recognized the source of the instructions he'd been commanded to follow, he chuckled softly, showed his blood-smeared teeth, and then his palms. In a strained, distinctly American voice, he said, "Can anybody tell me how to get to the Prado museum from here?"

*   *   *

Using a combination of her gun, her CIA identification, and a fistful of American cash, Lana Welles convinced one of the *novilleros* to secret them out of the Matadero de Madrid in the bed of a dented, rust-eaten pickup truck with no suspension to speak of, or at least none to speak of kindly. They tied their prisoner's hands at the wrists using a borrowed length of cord, then used the livestock delivery entrance at the rear of the compound, taking to side streets as the sirens grew louder on Calle de Bailén—the tell-tale sound of law enforcement vehicles gathering one by one around the entrance to the compound.

Lying prone beneath a heavy canvas tarp that smelled of mildew and manure, each with a gun pressed against opposite sides of Blondie's rib cage, they rode hidden in the bed of the rough-riding pickup all the way back to the Hotel Gran Meliá Fénix at the center of town.

Once they arrived, Lana and David were forced to confront the problem of how to escort a bound, bloody man at gunpoint across a public street, through a hotel lobby, and up to their room. It was a problem Lana solved with somewhat alarming ease using a back-alley service entrance, the hospitality elevator, and another strategic wad of US currency.

But only partially.

"There's nothing to stop this mouthy coward from screaming bloody murder the minute we get to our floor," David said in the elevator, his gun in the man's left ribs.

"I might even start now," Blondie said.

Lana twisted the barrel of her gun in his other side.

"Ow."

"We could gag him," she suggested.

"With what?"

"Your jacket and belt."

"That won't stop him from squealing."

The assassin gave a cold chuckle. "Trust me. When you hear squealing, it won't be coming from me. And it's going to last awhile."

"I can see there are only two ways we can do this," David told him.

"I thought *she* was the muscle."

"Suit yourself." David brought the butt of his pistol down hard at the base of Blondie's skull. He felt the meaty, ripe-melon *thonk* halfway to his elbow. Blondie's clear blue eyes clouded and rolled back as he collapsed to the floor of the elevator car between their feet.

"Take it easy," Lana scolded. "I'm the one who gets to kill him."

David sighed as the elevator slowed to a halt. The floor bell rang. The doors slid open.

"I guess that means I'm the one carrying him," he said.

*   *   *

David spent most of the next half hour concerned that perhaps he really had hit their captive too hard. Especially when a faceful of cold water from the bathroom sink failed to rouse him.

But the man was still breathing. And his pupils responded to light. So they did the only thing either one of them could think to do: they tied him to a chair with drape cords and waited.

Concerned was perhaps overstating David's position anyway.

Eventually, their new captive made a long, low groan and came around. David, having had enough time to really review the past two hours in his mind, found himself resisting the urge to knock the

Jaguar-driving bastard unconscious again. It had been ages since he'd felt such a thing—the urge to willfully do another human being harm.

He didn't like it.

On the other hand, David Toland could not honestly say that looking into this particular human being's strange, arctic-blue eyes made the feeling go away.

"Nice place," the assassin said from his chair. He winced as he glanced around the room, as if the light hurt his eyes. "How's the service?"

"Discreet," David said. "I'm told they get celebrities here."

"No kidding."

"But just in case, I put in a call with the front desk. The man on duty assured me that we wouldn't be disturbed."

"Why? Are you a celebrity?"

Lana finally stepped forward, placing the muzzle of her gun against the killer's temple.

"So," she said, clicking the hammer back with her thumb. "Tell us a little bit about yourself."

Over the course of the next hour, with a surprising lack of coaxing or fuss, the man who had very recently tried his level best to run down a nun with a car revealed to them that his real name was Jeremiah Okerlund. Known best to his familiars as Jerry. He was forty-one years of age, born and raised in St. Cloud, Minnesota. And he was, in a sense, an erstwhile colleague of Agent Lana Welles.

"Come on, Jerry," David said, crossing his arms. "You can't possibly expect either one of us to believe that you're CIA."

Okerlund smiled from his spot in the middle of their hotel room, hands still bound behind his back. "Believe me or don't believe me. But feel free to check my pockets."

While Lana held her gun steady from the edge of the bed, David patted the man down until he found a wallet.

Inside the wallet, he found a Central Intelligence Agency ident card, which looked—all except for the photo and personal information—just like Lana's.

"Huh," David said. He removed the ID, held it to the light, then replaced it in the wallet. "The spooks really need to review their training procedures. Or their recruitment parameters. Maybe both."

"How's that, sport?"

"By my count, you've tried to kill us three times," David said. "And here you are, tied to a chair."

"Four, if you count that fleabag movie theater back in DC." Okerlund shrugged, never losing the grin. "Anybody can have an off week."

David offered the wallet to Lana, who shook her head. "I don't need to see it. He's telling the truth."

"How can you tell?"

"By the way he fires his weapon," she said. "And because he just confirmed what I've suspected from the beginning."

"Which is?"

"Which is that I've been marked by my own agency," she said.

"Dynamite analysis, Agent," Okerlund said. "I don't know how you were able to piece that together."

"And your mole is still at large," she said.

"Save it for the rube, honey. Though, I gotta say, I'm curious. What exactly do you think you've been up to, these past eight days?" Okerlund tilted his head toward David. "Better yet: what does *he* think you've been up to?"

David tossed the wallet into Okerlund's lap. "When you say *he*," he said, "am I to presume you're referring to the rube?"

Okerlund shook his head slowly. "You know, whatever it is you think you're involved in, I gotta tell you, fella. Me being you, in a beautiful city? In a room like this? With a woman who looks like her? I wouldn't be hanging out at a convent, if you get my meaning."

David stepped forward and delivered a bone-rattling right cross to Okerlund's jaw. He felt one of his knuckles pop and go numb. Okerlund's head snapped back.

"Mind your manners," David advised.

Okerlund shook his head as if to clear it. He opened his jaw slowly, wincing. He spat a bloody tooth onto the carpet near David's shoe. "You pack a decent punch for a pacifist," he said. "I'll give you that much."

"That was just to get your attention."

"Uh-huh. I guess the honeymoon isn't quite over yet, huh, John Davis?"

David backhanded him upside the head, square on the ear. He used his core muscles for maximum torque; Okerlund nearly toppled over sideways in the chair.

"She's asking the questions. You're answering them."

Slowly, Okerlund straightened himself upright. He grimaced as he tested a cut on his lip with his tongue. "You should ask a few yourself, pal. I could tell you stories."

"I only want to hear three things from you," Lana said. "What is your assignment? Who put you in motion? And when do they expect your next report?"

But for the better part of the next two hours, Okerlund steadfastly refused to tell them so much as a fairy tale.

David, on the other hand, slipped into a dark and disarranged frame of mind.

It was as if striking Jerry Okerlund had reignited some long-extinguished pilot light inside him—a small flame that illuminated every misshapen, ugly thought hiding in the grimiest corners of his mind. Hidden goblins that, now exposed, seemed only too happy to step out of the shadows. Gather together in a group. And take over for a while.

After the events of these past days, David found himself helpless to fend them off any longer. A single thought was all it took: the vivid, helpless memory of Lana Welles rolling off the hood of that Jaguar, then lying motionless in the street.

Save what you love.

It was as if he stepped outside himself and had become somebody else for a while. Somebody violent. Somebody who, under any normal set of circumstances, David Toland wouldn't even want to know.

Okerlund held his ground, for the most part, maintaining a steady display of general intransigence until David's hands ached from trying to wipe the bloody smile off his face. Lana seemed content— even pleased—to sit back in a chair of her own, doctoring her ravaged knee, hand, and miscellaneous other cuts and scrapes while David Toland, director of preservation for the National Film Archive at the Library of Congress, stood off to one side, invisible. Watching a figure who looked a lot like himself play the role of one-man goon squad—an unsavory doppelganger capable of doling out swift, blinding punishment for every sidestepped question, every meaningless taunt, every calculated pause.

By the time Jerry Okerlund could no longer hold his head up on his own, David was spent, exhausted, and sick with himself.

Other than that, he'd accomplished absolutely nothing.

Hill 255 came to mind.

"What's...the matter," Okerlund mumbled, head hanging, stringers of blood dangling from his swollen lips. "You giving up...already?"

"I think he's earned a rest," Lana said. She finished wrapping her knee in gauze, taped off the loose end, and picked up her gun from the side table as David sagged back into his chair. "And you've earned this."

Okerlund raised his head, looked at the gun in her hand, and scoffed. "Spanish knockoff of American hardware. Appreciate the thought, but no thanks."

Lana pressed the barrel to his sweaty forehead, nestling the muzzle in between hanging lanks of disheveled white hair. "It's what's on the inside that counts. Besides. An American gun would be too good for a traitor like you."

"Traitor." Okerlund leaned forward, spit a wad of blood on the carpet at her feet. "You're the authority. Tell me something, Irene: have you filled in the mister about dear old daddy yet?"

"My father dedicated his life to his country, you treasonous son of a bitch."

Okerlund gave her a bloody smile. "That's the story, isn't it?"

Lana's eyes went hard and cold. She cocked the pistol. Voice audibly trembling with anger, she said, "Enjoy your retirement."

David saw her finger tighten on the trigger.

He sat forward in his chair.

Someone knocked on the door.

"Room service," a muffled voice said.

CHAPTER
THIRTY-FIVE

David knew it was Simon before he checked the peephole. He opened the door and stepped back.

"Ah," Simon said. "So the two of you haven't left Spain without me, then. Excellent."

"Simon. We forgot. Sorry," David said. Without turning, he said to Lana, "Speaking of things to remember, we need to figure out what to do about the rental car. It's still—"

"Parked at the Plaza," Lana said, behind him. "I'm aware."

"Good Lord," Simon said, eyeing David up and down. "You look like warmed-over hell from a can. What have I missed?"

David stood aside so that their late joiner could see past him into the room.

"Well, well. Look who it is," Jerry Okerlund said from the chair. "I guess they *do* get celebrities here."

Simon's mouth dropped open. He looked at Lana, then at David, then back to the man tied to the chair in the middle of the room. His face twisted into a hostile mask. His hands balled into fists.

"Give him to me," he snarled. He unshouldered his satchel and charged past David, into the room, straight toward Okerlund.

David stuck out his foot, tripping Simon to the floor in an awkward, thudding pile.

Simon barked in surprise, turning to gape at David from the carpet. "What the bloody *hell* did you do that for?"

Okerlund laughed until he gurgled, then spat more blood to the carpet. "Big fan, Mr. Lean. Read all your books. Say: do you think there's any way I could get your autogra—"

There came a muffled *bang*.

David jumped. A fan of red speckles spattered the side of Simon's face.

Lana Welles stood over Okerlund's chair, a pillow in one hand, her gun in the other. A faint twist of smoke curled from the end of her gun barrel. Down feather stuffing floated in the air around her like snowflakes. The pillow appeared to have developed an exit wound.

"That was for Yegor," she said.

Simon's eyes went big. "Oh my," he whispered.

David stood motionless for a moment, disoriented. He had seen Lana Welles kill a man before. But not like this. He found himself at a loss for an appropriate reaction. He had just witnessed the execution of an unarmed prisoner. Horror, disgust, moral alarm: These were appropriate human reactions. But somehow David couldn't seem to make himself feel anything.

So he made himself useful instead and closed the door to the room. Jeremiah "Jerry" Okerlund slumped dead in his chair, head hanging, thick ropes of blood dripping into his lap. His blizzard-white hair glistened with crimson.

"Oh my," Simon repeated.

Lana looked at David. "You or me?"

"I'll take this one," David said.

He withdrew his gun and pointed it at Simon. "Stand up slowly, keep your hands where I can see them, and go sit the hell down over there," he said.

*   *   *

At first, Simon didn't move a muscle. He just stayed on the floor looking bewildered.

"Now," David said.

"But I . . . you . . . what on God's earth is happening?"

David placed his thumb on the hammer and dipped the barrel forward, letting the weight of the gun do the cocking for him. "Please do as you've been told."

Slowly, like a puppy who has no idea why he's being scolded, Simon pushed himself to his feet, raising his hands up beside his ears.

David followed as Simon tiptoed around the dead man, making his way toward the empty chair David had vacated. When he glanced over, Lana shifted her eyes elsewhere. But he caught a glimpse of the expression she'd been wearing.

He could have been mistaken, but it looked to David like pride.

"If you'll forgive my saying so, old man, I rather think you've lost control of yourself," Simon said.

"Lost, yes I am. Out of control, no."

"And here I thought that you and I had developed something of a rapport."

David waggled the gun barrel. "Sit."

Simon sat.

David reached inside the older man's sport coat, pulled the Welrod, and tossed it on the bed. "Now talk."

Simon stared queasily at the man with a ragged, gaping hole in his forehead three feet away. "I'm quite sure I haven't the faintest idea what you'd like to hear me say."

"Why don't you start by explaining how Okerlund managed to track us to the convent?" Lana suggested.

"Who?"

David pointed at the dead man.

"How on earth would I know that?"

"Because you're the only other person on earth who knew we'd be there," David said.

"Ah. I see," Simon said slowly. "Information I must have passed along to my accomplice." He looked back and forth between them. His expression changed from confused to wounded. Then came indignation. "Is that honestly the thinking here in this room? After all we've been through as a group?"

"If I were you," Lana said, "I'd wipe the scowl off my face and try very, very hard to convince us otherwise."

"For heaven's sake! He probably followed you there!"

David shook his head. "Nope. He would have attacked as we headed into the park. Not after we came back out."

"Then maybe he beat us to Herzog's in the first place," Simon countered. "Paid Angelica Borras to keep him informed. Or even threatened her."

"Wrong again," Lana said. "I told Angelica Barros that we'd be visiting Isabella next week, not this afternoon. And she was in the other room with David when I used her telephone. Well out of earshot, and certainly not listening in on another line. Nor was anyone else, or I'd have known. As far as Angelica Barros knew, we were returning to the hotel for your medication, just like I told her. I also told her we'd be back before the dinner hour to take you away peacefully."

"Well, then, only the most obvious possible explanation remains."

"Which is?"

"Which is that Blondie," he said, glancing at the dripping corpse, "or Okerlund, or whatever the bloody hell his real name is, clearly managed to do what *you*, love, did not."

"Oh, please." Lana spoke as if she were chewing the words and spitting them out. "Do elaborate."

"His homework!" Simon shouted. "Either he knew enough to speculate what Balcon must have told you, or whoever he's been working for did. Either way, he already knew your next destination." Simon began counting on his fingers for dramatic effect. "He already knew that Victor Herzog was a year dead in his grave. He already knew that the clinic was gone, and he already knew that Isabella had thrown in with the nuns. And he was very nearly successful in beating you to her."

Lana tossed the ravaged pillow aside. It landed on the carpet near Jerry Okerlund with another puff of feathers. One of the feathers floated up and stuck to the jagged red place where the retired assassin's orbital ridge used to be. She glowered at Simon.

Simon took a deep breath through the nose, then let it out slowly. He uncrossed his arms and rested his hands in his lap.

"Let me ask the two of you a question for a change," he said. "If I were working against you—and, I must say, it still pains me to think that either one of you could believe such a thing, after what I showed you in Moscow—then why in the name of Jesus Christ and all the saints in heaven would I bring my findings back here to you?"

Lana finally looked at David.

David said, "Findings?"

"In the hallway," Simon sighed. "Leaning against the wall where I dropped my bag. Bring both. I'll wait here. Assuming I still don't have your permission to move."

Lana stalked over to the door and yanked it open. She stooped to grab Simon's bag from the floor where it had fallen, then peered around the edge of the jamb. Finally, she straightened. She shouldered Simon's bag and looked both ways, up and down the hall.

Then she reached down and brought a large, rectangular parcel back into the room with her, kicking the door closed behind her.

David said, "What's that supposed to be?"

"I can think of at least one way a person might find out," Simon groused.

The package was flat. Perhaps twenty-four inches by eighteen, wrapped in brown paper, taped at the seams. Lana brought it to the bed, placed her gun on the coverlet next to the Welrod, and began tearing off the paper.

"It's a painting," she said.

"A painting of what?"

"I don't know. It looks like a building. Hang on."

Simon said, "I found that in the tack room back at the clinic. I told Angelica Borras that I was quite taken with it, and I offered her five hundred *pesetas* for its purchase. She countered my offer by giving me the piece free of charge. 'I should pay you' were her exact words."

"Why?" David said.

"I presume she had no use for it."

"I mean why did you offer to buy a painting you found in a horse barn?"

"That's what I'm preparing to explain."

Lana finished removing the wrapper and let the paper fall to the carpet, exposing a colorful canvas in a gilded wood frame. She stood over the painting a moment, then tilted it up on its edge so that David could see.

What he saw was a vaguely impressionistic portrayal of a Renaissance-style edifice with a central dome in green and gold.

"Another palace," David said. "Swell."

"I think it's a cathedral," Lana said.

"That's not a cathedral," Simon said. "And it's not a palace, either. Nor a state building, nor a museum."

"Then what is it?" Lana snapped.

"It's an opera house," Simon said. "Quite a famous opera house, in fact. I'm surprised that neither of you recognizes it."

David pressed the muzzle of his gun to the top of Simon's left knee. "And I'm surprised that a man in your position seems not to be taking our requests for information very seriously."

"Teatro Amazonas," Simon said. "That's a portrait of Teatro Amazonas. The theater in the jungle. Oil on canvas, if I'm not mistaken."

"Why are we looking at it?"

"Look at the artist's signature," Simon said. "Lower right corner."

Lana stooped, squinting. "Who's Carl Denham?"

"One of Dr. Herzog's patients. If you'll open my bag, you'll find his medical file."

Lana did as Simon suggested, retrieving two items from inside his satchel: a plain manila file folder and a large, leather-bound photo album. She flung the satchel onto the bed and quickly opened the folder.

"This is empty," she said.

"Yes. I noticed that, too."

She held up the album. "And this?"

"Before and after photos," Simon said. "Of the good doctor's handiwork. I found an alphabetical set of them in the stable. That scrapbook contains the D's."

"The D's."

"*All* the D's," Simon confirmed. "Unless I missed a box, you're holding volume one of one."

Lana let the empty Denham folder float to the floor. She opened the photo album. Mounting curiosity—aggravated by some distant, nagging spark of recognition, somewhere deep in his mind—pulled David over to the bed to look over her shoulder. Each black paper page contained, just as Simon had disclosed, a before and after Polaroid snapshot mounted in adhesive corner tabs.

David scanned the altered faces, necklines, bustlines, hips, thighs, and buttocks of dozens of men and women. All shapes and sizes. All very clearly pleased with their results. He saw varicose veins vanished, deformities deleted, and burn scars smoothed. Occasionally, they crossed a photo of a cleft palate or underdeveloped ear corrected in a child. Danvers. Delacroix. De la Cruz. De la Fuentes. Delgado. Dennison.

But no Denham.

And David Toland smiled.

Because he had it now.

"What?" Lana said. "What are you grinning about?"

He kissed her on the cheek. "Carl Denham," he said.

She touched the spot on her cheek reflexively. "What about him?"

David looked at Simon. Who also was smiling now.

"I'll let you tell her," Simon said. "It's really more your area."

Lana planted a fist on one hip. "I'm waiting."

David became aware that his heart rate had elevated. Suddenly he felt almost buoyant. "You know, I've always found it ironic that all this started with a can of film," he said, "given that Adolf Hitler was known to be a lifelong cinephile."

"Yes. Mass murderer and movie nut," Lana said. "What the hell does that have to do with anything?"

"The Führer's very favorite film of all was a little motion picture called *King Kong*," David said. "You may have heard of it. 1933. Directed by Merian C. Cooper and Ernest B. Schoedsack, screenplay by Ruth Rose and James Ashmore Creelman. It's a perennial candidate for preservation at the archive."

"I swear I'm going to shoot you," Lana said, "if you don't get to the damned point."

David felt his smile widening. He couldn't help himself. He felt almost giddy. "Carl Denham," he said, "was the name of the main character in *King Kong*. Other than the ape, I mean."

Lana stared at him.

Then at the painting.

David said, "If memory serves, wasn't Hitler also a painter?"

"An amateur," Simon confirmed from the peanut gallery. He nodded toward the bed. "Although not an entirely unskilled one, it seems. Technically speaking."

Lana looked from the painting to Simon. Then back to David again. Her expression had gone blank. The color had drained from her cheeks. She appeared to be speechless for a moment. Then she found two words: "Surely not."

David decocked his pistol, tucked it back under his windbreaker, walked over to Simon, and offered his hand. He'd found two words of his own.

"I'm sorry," he said.

Simon looked him in the eye for a long moment, then accepted David's hand. "I suppose I can't fault your thinking," he said. "Though I won't lie. You did hurt my feelings."

"Good old Uncle Simon." David felt himself grinning like a fool as he hauled Simon up to his feet, wrapping the author up in a big, backslapping hug. "Cagey devil. I don't know what else to say."

His enthusiasm must have been contagious, because Simon Lean laughed, patting David politely on the back.

"Now this is the David Toland I prefer," he said. His chuckling sounded like water flowing under a bridge. "Please don't squeeze me to death."

David retrieved another one of his brand-new handkerchiefs and handed it to Simon as a peace offering—something he could use at least to begin the task of wiping Jeremiah Okerlund's blood from his face. Then he clapped him manfully on the neck, smoothed his rumpled lapels, and returned to Lana. "Well? Aren't you going to say anything?"

Lana seemed lost in the painting of Teatro Amazonas, the theater in the jungle. "I don't know where to begin," she murmured.

David felt as if a thousand-pound weight had been lifted from his head. As if he could hardly keep his feet on the floor without it. "The first question is, where's that theater?"

"The theater is in Brazil," Simon said. "Manaus, to be specific." He appeared to go slightly green around the gills as he looked again at the corpse tied to a chair with drape cords. "If you ask me, the *first* question is, what are we going to do with him?"

CHAPTER
THIRTY-SIX

Tomorrow, there would be another plane to catch.

But first: some light room cleaning.

David and Simon wrapped Jerry Okerlund's body in the plastic shower curtain liner from the bathroom while Lana ran out for supplies. David would not have believed that the dead assassin could have looked any paler than he had when he'd been alive.

When they were finished, they adjourned briefly to Simon's room to retrieve an item the author felt might be useful to their efforts: a large, tweed-covered steamer trunk with polished brass hardware.

"Where did you get this thing?" David asked. "*When* did you get this thing?"

"From a charming little *tienda de viaje* I passed this afternoon at ABC Serrano," Simon said proudly. "An impulse purchase. I had it delivered to the room. Isn't she a beauty?"

"You certainly travel light."

"I travel in style, dear boy," Simon said. "Grab the other end, will you?"

They lugged the trunk back to David and Lana's room. Having spent ten minutes in fresher air, David was immediately struck by the smell upon re-entering. The room had a meaty, coppery odor that put him in mind of some of the slaughterhouse smells he'd picked up on the breeze back at Matadero de Madrid.

They folded the plastic-wrapped corpse more or less in half and shoved it into the steamer trunk. David sat on the lid while Simon latched it. The door to the room opened just as they were finishing.

"Well," Simon said. "That was unpleasant."

"We're just getting started," Lana said on her way in.

"At least the worst is over," David said. "You're sure you won't mind finishing the rest?"

"Har har," Lana said, tossing him a package of heavy rubber dish gloves.

The three of them spent the next hour armed with sponges, spray bottles of bathroom cleanser, and ice buckets filled with hot soapy water. They worked together to remove every trace of blood spatter they could find from the furniture, bedspread, and surrounding areas.

The carpet was another matter. And there was plenty of matter to contend with. Blood. Gobbets of Jerry Okerlund's brain. Tiny shards of slick, gleaming bone. More blood.

When they were finished scrubbing, dousing, soaking, and scrubbing again, the beige-colored carpet looked like someone had dropped a pot of coffee in the middle of the floor and allowed the stain to set in.

But it appeared to be the best they could do. Lana stripped out of her gloves, looked around the room, and said, "John and Irene Davis would definitely be getting a bill for this if they had a real address."

"I wonder if either of you noticed the dinner menu," Simon said.

"God," David said. "I couldn't eat a thing."

"What I noticed about the dinner menu," Simon continued, "is that the kitchen of this hotel makes its own sorbet. Supposedly famous for it. According to the dinner menu, that is."

"I don't want any ice cream, either. Do they make their own whiskey?"

Simon only chuckled. He went to the bed, picked up the remnants of the painting's brown paper wrapper, and folded it into a manageable square. "Back in a jiffy," he said.

He returned fifteen minutes later, still carrying the paper, now tightly wrapped around a five-pound block of dry ice. He nodded to the trunk and said, "Would you?"

David stooped, unlatched the lid, and opened it.

Simon dumped the ice block on top of the body, trailing tendrils of fog. He kicked the lid closed, stooped, and latched it again.

"There," he said. "I'll be pouring a stiff drink in my room if anyone cares to join."

*   *   *

"A steamer trunk," Lana said some time later, as Simon refreshed her whiskey from the in-room bar. "I wonder. Can that possibly work?"

"If it does, you can bet I'll be using it in a novel one day," Simon said.

David concentrated on sipping his drink this time, rather than gulping it down the way he'd done with his first two. His hands had only just stopped trembling. "Neither one of you," he said, "is crazy enough to actually attempt traveling with that trunk. Which leaves us with the same question we had before."

A wicked glint came to Lana's eye. She reached over, swiped the pad and pen from the nearby phone table, and scribbled something down. She worked the pen with one hand while she held her drink in the other.

Then she tore off the sheet and handed it to Simon. "Have the hotel ship it here."

Simon took the paper, read it, grinned. "Bloody brilliant," he said.

He handed the page to David, who read the note once himself. Then he read it again. He shook his head in amazement.

"Makes sense to me." He raised his glass wearily. "Cheers."

Lana and Simon responded in kind as David looked at the note one last time.

She'd written down the address to CIA headquarters in

Langley, Virginia. To the attention of Assistant Deputy Director Roger Ford.

"I hope you won't mind if I use this in the book as well," Simon said.

*   *   *

The first available flight from Madrid to Manaus didn't depart until 6:13 p.m., the following evening. First thing in the morning, David and Simon retrieved the abandoned rental car while Lana stayed back at the hotel, making phone calls. The three of them spent the remainder of the time left to them at Biblioteca Nacional de España, Madrid's public library, and the sole legal deposit for all of Spain. It was, in a sense, the Spanish Library of Congress. Under different circumstances, David might have liked to meet the director and perhaps discuss the state of their film archive, starting with whether or not they currently maintained one.

Instead, they skimmed everything of use they could find about their next destination, focusing especially on Teatro Amazonas—the improbable cultural jewel in the middle of a billion-acre rain forest. According to one encyclopedia David found, the opera house—built during the nineteenth-century rubber boom—owed its existence to sheer will, lofty patronage, and architects from Lisbon.

Soon enough, it was time for the three of them to go and see it for themselves. As per custom, Simon Lean sprung for first class, while Lana economized in coach.

It was to be nearly a whole day of flying via Africa and across the Atlantic, their path almost perfectly describing the invisible boundary between northern and southern waters. David spent most of it looking at the insides of his eyelids, dreaming of absolutely nothing at all.

But they were traveling in the general direction of the United States for the first time since leaving New York just over a week ago. After a decade preserving films, David honestly had forgotten how much life could be lived in just a week's time. But something about the feeling of moving west instead of east for a change seemed to put his hot nerves at ease.

"You know that's all in your head," Lana told him during the dinner service, which consisted of stale ham sandwiches, rubbery carrot sticks, and tiny foil packets of unsalted peanuts. "We're traveling more south than west anyway."

"Not to rain on my parade or anything."

"You're right. I'm sorry."

He nudged her with his elbow. "I thought you didn't believe in apologies."

Slight grin. "I don't."

"Getting soft on me?"

"I'm glad you were able to get some rest." She took a mammoth bite out of her sandwich. "You need it."

"I'm not the only one. Have you even closed your eyes since we boarded?"

"Off and on," she said.

"And if we were playing a game of *Am I Lying?* right now," he told her, "I'd win this round."

But she must have found peace enough to drift off during the night, because she was asleep on David's arm as sunrise set the clouds outside their cabin window afire.

David watched the world turn green below them as they descended beneath the cloud deck—an ocean of trees as far in every direction as he could see. Except for one bare patch in the midst of it all. And a fat, black snake winding its way through.

A city on a river in the middle of a jungle.

David tracked the black snake with his eyes until he found the place he'd read about at the library, just to the southeast of the city. This was the spot where the Rio Negro joined the Rio Solimoes to form the mighty Rio Amazones—the Amazon River.

Lana began to stir as the plane banked over the confluence of the two tributaries, descending, bringing the ground below them into sharper relief. She yawned cavernously, stretched, and had a sip of water. Then she joined David in peering out the window, taking in the aerial view of a curious natural phenomenon.

For several kilometers, the black waters of the Rio Negro met the sandy brown waters of the Rio Solimoes but did not mix. It had something to do with opposing temperatures and densities of sediment. David couldn't exactly remember—the previous afternoon's research had already gone fuzzy around the edges in his mind. Lana put her head back on his shoulder as they watched the peculiar two-toned flow from above.

"That makes me want a black-and-tan," David joked.

"It doesn't make me want anything," Lana said. "It only makes me feel sad."

And here was that aura of melancholy again. David couldn't help noticing that it seemed to flare up in hotel rooms and on airplane flights. Anywhere with downtime and a window, really. He wanted to help her, but he didn't know how. He supposed that it was probably the height of what they now called male chauvinism to presume that he could.

As he turned to her, she sat up in her seat and looked into his eyes. She smiled at him, took his face in her hands, and gave him a long, tender kiss.

"Thank you," she said.

David held her gaze. "For what?"

But she didn't answer.

It was time to prepare for landing.

PART IV

Meeting of the Waters

CHAPTER
THIRTY-SEVEN

Brazil

H ot. Steamy. Vibrant. Roiling. Underprivileged. Overflowing. Wild.

These were David's initial impressions on the ground in Manaus. It was a surprisingly crowded city despite its geographic isolation, or possibly because of it, a boom/bust town only just beginning to emerge from decades of poverty. According to the history books—at least the ones he'd encountered in the stacks back in Madrid—the hardships that had befallen this particular spot on the globe had been brought on by the seed smugglers who'd stolen the rubber monopoly and moved it to plantations in Southeast Asia. Once among the wealthiest cities on the planet, Manaus had enjoyed electricity before most of Europe; after the rubber barons had fled, the people who made their homes here couldn't afford to turn on a lightbulb for generations.

They took rooms in a hotel under renovation in Praça de São Sebastião, San Sebastian Square. They chose the spot because of its location, directly across from Teatro Amazonas—the opera house of fable, fact, and at least one amateur oil painting even now on its way to an unsuspecting curator David knew at the Library of Congress.

That such a building existed here, in the midst of a verdant jungle, rising above the rain forest in grand Belle Époque style, struck David as both a triumph of art and the height of human folly. The building itself seemed a physical manifestation of sheer ambition and indulgence taken to extremes. Which led David to wonder: if the painter Carl Denham and the dictator Adolf Hitler indeed were the same person, were these the qualities that had drawn him to Manaus in the first place?

"An interesting thought," Simon said as they left the plastic-draped lobby of the hotel, stepping bleary-eyed into the hazy sunlight of a humid Brazilian morning. "If one cared to understand the innermost mind of a soulless, slaughtering maniac. Which I do not."

Lana said, "You're a thriller writer. I thought that was part of your job."

"I write fiction, my dear," Simon answered. "None of my monsters are real."

They crossed Rua Dez de Julho as a trio, navigating the short, boisterous, exhaust-fogged walk from their hotel to the square. Simon looked every bit the part of the lily-white South American traveler: sky-blue seersucker suit, jaunty straw fedora. Given the state of her bandaged knees and shins, Lana had opted for loose white slacks and a colorful, sleeveless blouse. David—still in his chinos and checked button-down—apparently had been the only one among the three of them who'd failed to shop ahead to his next change of clothes.

For the dual purposes of climate control and weapons concealment, he'd traded the windbreaker for the leather satchel he'd purchased in Madrid, replacing the one he'd left behind in Moscow. He'd found the bag at the same men's store where he'd bought the handkerchiefs—of which he was now down to his last. By the time their cracked, weedy strip of sidewalk led them to a brick promenade, he'd already taken out that sole surviving hanky to dab the morning's first droplets of sweat from his brow.

He gave a handful of *cruzeiros* to a gaggle of gangly, brown, barefooted boys panhandling on the corner. As if in reward, they received a slight but welcome breeze as they entered the tree-ringed square. In the center of the square was the latest in a seemingly endless string of monuments in the centers of squares, this one a tribute to the city's ports cast in marble and bronze. Cobblestone pavers covered the small Praça de São Sebastião in wavy, alternating bands of charcoal and beige that played tricks on the eyes, echoing the so-called "meeting of the waters" just a few kilometers to the southeast. Speckled pigeons cooed and warbled as they pecked at the cracks between the stones.

"Now there's my kind of lunacy," Simon said as Teatro Amazonas came into view, presiding over the square with its rosy Italianate body and striking, mock-Byzantine dome. "I don't know who in their right mind would pay to build such a thing in such a place. But isn't it wonderful that they did?"

"Remarkable," Lana muttered. "Let's see how it looks from the inside."

They crossed the square and climbed the ascension of granite steps leading up to the front of the building.

Upon entering, they found themselves in a grand marble lobby inlaid with tropical hardwoods. Large overhead fans circulated the air. A stooped, elderly custodian with skin like David's satchel leather looked up from his work, nodded to them, and returned to mopping the floor.

Simon stopped at a lobby card propped up for display on an easel just inside the doors. The card advertised tomorrow night's opening performance of Wagner's *Parsifal*.

"A young hero seeks the holy grail," he said, smiling at David. "Fitting, don't you think? Maybe we can learn something."

"I just did." When Simon looked at him questioningly, David nodded to the card and said, "It didn't occur to me until just this minute what day it is today."

Simon read the date of tomorrow's performance: *Uno de Enero.* January 1.

"Well, I'll be stuffed," Simon said. "It's New Year's Eve."

"Don't forget to make your resolutions."

"Oh, I've made them already, you can be sure of that."

Meanwhile, Lana had moved on to a glass display case hanging on the wall nearby.

David and Simon went to join her. The case displayed the photographs and names of the theater's board of directors. Lana was transfixed by the portrait of a polished, silver-haired gentleman presiding over the rest. The engraved brass name placard below the photograph read:

C. DENHAM, PATRÓN.

David felt a spike in his pulse rate as Simon Lean drew in a sharp breath behind him. Even Lana reached out and took his hand. The three of them stood there together, staring.

"That must be the after photo," David said.

Simon Lean leaned in until his nose almost touched the glass. "My God, Herr Doktor Herzog was good."

*　　*　　*

Running on a strange, heady mix of jet lag and adrenaline, they regrouped in the umbrella shade of an outdoor table at a café within view of the opera house.

Everyone was too wired to be hungry, and it was too early for lunch anyway. They ordered three glasses of strong, ice-cold *maté* tea, intending to plot their next move. Instead, they ended up sitting together in high-strung silence for the better part of an hour.

"Well, we know what Denham looks like now," David finally said. He could scarcely believe the seismic implications of such a simple statement.

"Knowing what he looks like and finding him are two entirely different things," Lana answered.

For the past half hour, Simon Lean had been wearing the beatific expression of a man who had lived to see his life's greatest longing come to be within reach.

"Whoever wants to understand Germany," he said, "must know

Wagner. Do either of you know who said that? I'll give you one guess between you."

Neither David nor Lana said a word in reply. They didn't need any guesses. Adolf Hitler had a favorite movie. He also had a favorite composer. This was really happening—David felt the certainty of it in the very marrow of his bones.

"Who else fancies a night at the opera?" Simon said.

"If I can believe what I'm seeing right now," David answered, "we might not have to wait that long."

Simon and Lana followed his gaze across the street to the polished, silver-haired gentleman approaching the opera house from the east. The man was dressed not unlike Simon himself, wearing a white linen suit and a trim straw fedora. He carried an ivory-topped walking cane in one hand. At his side trotted a beautiful, blond German Shepherd, its pink tongue lolling.

David thought instantly of Jerry Okerlund.

Lana sat bolt upright in her chair.

Simon froze like a statue. He didn't blink. He no longer appeared even to be breathing.

The man and the dog took the granite steps up to the building as the three of them sat there in the shade, glasses of forgotten *maté* tea sweating puddles on the table in front of them.

C. Denham.

Patrón.

"I . . ." Simon whispered.

He trailed off without finishing his thought.

They watched Denham and the dog meet another man, roughly similar in age to Denham himself. The two men appeared to exchange pleasantries, then disappeared together inside the theater.

A minute later, two additional gentlemen in summer suits appeared. They greeted another pair on the steps and headed for the entrance.

None of these newcomers appeared quite so well-heeled as Denham. But still they seemed, by all appearances, to be successful men of Manaus.

"The one on the left," Lana said tightly, her spine like a ramrod, eyes watchful as a falcon's. "With the chin whiskers."

David leaned forward. "What about him?"

"His picture was in the display case," she said. "In the lobby."

"The board must be convening."

"They do have a curtain tomorrow."

"They have a curtain now," Simon said, rising from his chair. His hand had already disappeared inside his seersucker jacket.

Lana reached out quickly, grasping his wrist. "No," she hissed.

Simon jerked away, bumping the table, rattling their glasses. Customers at nearby tables took notice of the sudden commotion.

"Simon," she said, rising halfway to meet him. "Please."

Simon's apparent serenity had vanished. His face had flushed. Fat veins bulged in his neck and forehead. He looked as though he were about to burst.

He looked, for perhaps the first time since David had met him, like he meant business.

Lana clearly sensed it, too. "Please," she repeated.

He pushed her aside. "That man slaughtered my family."

She stepped back into his path. "We're too close."

"On that we agree. Now stand away."

David tensed in his chair.

"Simon! I can't imagine the pain you've endured. But we mustn't make a mistake now." She gripped him by the shoulders, looked directly into his eyes. She lowered her voice to a whisper. "We are too close."

"Too close to *what*?" Simon shouted, drawing still more attention to their table. "How dare you ask me to stand down now? My God, woman, *why*?"

"Because he's alive," Lana said calmly. "And so is everything he represents. Simon, like it or not, if our countries hope to exterminate that evil once and for all, we need to understand how any of this is possible. So does the rest of the world."

"Then let the rest of the world perform the autopsy."

Lana stood her ground. For a long, queasy moment, David thought that Simon Lean might actually yank the Welrod free of its concealed holster and shoot her in the stomach, right there in broad daylight, in front of every bystander within view.

But their companion finally exhaled. His shoulders loosened. He removed his hand from his jacket, took another deep breath through the nose, and sat down again. Lana squeezed his shoulder. She returned to her own chair. David released the breath he'd been holding.

"All right," Simon said, clearly still struggling to gather himself. "Then what now?"

"Now we use every last ounce of our willpower," Lana answered, "and wait."

*   *   *

Thousands of miles across three continents by plane, train, and horse-drawn wagon. Lies peddled. Untold currency distributed. International laws violated. Liters of warm blood spilled, spattered, and smeared. And in the end, all they had to do to find the most ruthless butcher in recorded history was to sit down and order tea.

The longer they sat there, watching the opera house from a distance, the harder it became for David Toland to believe that any of this was actually true. As the café filled up around them with lunch-hour traffic—locals and tourists alike, going about their affairs—he had the vaguely fuzzy, hypnotical sense that he'd woken up from a dream, only to realize that he was still sleeping.

Finally, just over an hour later, Lana pointed and said, "There."

The same half dozen men in summer suits, ranging in age from David's to Simon's and a fair few years beyond, began to reemerge from the opera house and go their separate ways.

Denham and his dog were the last to appear.

"Meeting adjourned," Simon growled under his breath.

Denham touched the brim of his hat to an elderly local woman on the sidewalk. Then he and the dog strolled away, back in the direction they'd come.

Lana gathered up her bag, threw some money down on the table, and stood up. "Let's go," she said.

They hurried across the street, dodging rattletrap delivery scooters and belching taxicabs, struggling to keep Denham in view. They passed more street kids panhandling along the curbs. They passed an aromatic *tacacá* stand on the corner. They passed a blind man selling woven mats from a threadbare blanket spread out on the ground.

Up ahead, Denham turned a corner. They quickened their pace, hurrying along a chain-link fence interlaced with weeds. They turned another corner, then another, always just catching one last glimpse of Denham before he disappeared ahead of them.

Eventually, they found themselves entering a crowded, open-air market, filled with noise and color and a rich, confusing mix of smells both appetizing and questionable.

They hung back and tried to blend in as Denham stopped at one merchant's stand or another, inspecting the fresh produce on offer, perusing the handmade goods. Then they hurried on again, care-ful to keep their distance without losing sight of Denham's hat in the crowd. When they couldn't see the hat, they scanned for the flash of his white suit amid the vibrant skirts and wraps, loose-fitting *bombachas*, and bright headscarves crowding the narrow street from curb to crumbling curb.

"I never would have imagined Adolf Hitler doing his own shopping," David said.

Simon glared straight ahead. "A real man of the people. He should have been dead an hour ago."

"This is bigger than one man," Lana said.

"Not for this man, it isn't."

They followed on. The crowds thinned. The neighborhood changed. Soon they'd entered a far less-populated area of blighted buildings, graffitied walls, and weedy, buckled sidewalks. Their surroundings made the task of following Denham undetected all the more difficult, forcing them to hang farther and farther back. All at once, far up ahead, Denham turned abruptly, mid-block, and disappeared from view again.

"Damn it." Lana broke into a trot.

David hurried to catch up. "Do you think he spotted us?"

"Does it really matter, at this point?"

David thought that it probably did, but he elected not to say so. They came to a narrow, garbage-strewn alley. The alley separated two dilapidated buildings that appeared to be constructed primarily of stucco and water-stained plywood.

At the far end of the alley, perhaps fifty meters away, they saw Denham and his dog getting into the back of an impeccable white limousine. David stretched out with his arms, pulling Lana back around the corner just as Denham glanced over his shoulder.

"Think he made us now?" he whispered.

"If he did, so be it," Lana whispered back. "Let me go."

A car door slammed. The sound of the limousine's engine changed pitch. David peeked around the corner just as the long car pulled out of the alley and turned right onto the cross street.

"Hurry!" Lana said, sprinting up the alley.

David followed on her heels, Simon right behind him. They lucked into a cab that smelled like a bath house and appeared to have delivered its prime years of service before any one of them had been born. Lana shoved a fat wad of bills into the driver's gnarled hand and said, *"O carro branco. Siga por favor."*

The driver showed the half dozen yellowed snags he had for teeth. When he stepped on the gas, the entire car shuddered as if preparing to fling its own parts into the gutter.

"Did you just tell this cab driver to follow that car?" Simon chuckled tightly, seeming to have reclaimed at least some slim shred of his usual sense of humor. "And people say my books aren't true to life."

Follow that car they did, winding their way through the narrow streets and markets to Avenida Brasil, a major thoroughfare that took them roughly northeast out of the inner-urban crunch. They kept to this route for perhaps a quarter of an hour, at perhaps a quarter mile's distance, through rows of graffitied tenement buildings, past cluttered vacant lots, into a trash-blasted industrial area.

Up ahead, the wide, black expanse of the Rio Negro came into view. The landscape opened up as they neared the waterfront. Soon, a large green overhead sign welcomed them to the southbound entrance of Ponte Rio Negro: a long bridge connecting Manaus to a hazy green tree line in the far distance.

"Iranduba," the driver said, pointing ahead through the bug-spattered windshield. "Iranduba?"

"*Sim*, Iranduba," Lana answered. She shoved another wad of cash into a frayed elastic band that had been attached to the dashboard by what looked to David like rusty wood screws.

"What's Iranduba?" he said.

Lana said, "I think it's a town."

The bridge spanned a distance of four or five elevated kilometers over the wide, flat water. David could see ramshackle commercial barges, rust-streaked fishing boats, and small private dinghies making their way down below. Lana said a few more words to the driver, who eased up on the gas for a short while, putting a bit more distance between them and Denham's limo. They passed beneath a peaked confluence of suspension cables marking the center point of the bridge's considerable span.

And then they were descending toward land again, a gallery of shaggy palm trees waiting to greet them. The rural tropic landscape on this side of the river made David think of the scores of young Americans now heading over to Southeast Asia to fight another new war—this time in Vietnam. The thought occurred to him: *Will catching this gray-haired, cane-carrying, limo-riding son of a bitch really change a thing?*

After a few more kilometers, the limousine turned off the main road, into a lowland area dotted all over with palms and mangroves.

The road narrowed and roughened. Puddles of rainwater stood in the ruts, cracks, and chuckholes in the decrepit asphalt.

Lana spoke to the driver again. They increased their distance to half a mile, passing through a sparse, decaying shantytown that looked somehow both decades old and suddenly improvised at the same time. They inadvertently increased their following distance again, forced to stop for an old man herding goats across the road.

Simon said, *"This* is Iranduba?"

Up front, the driver laughed, shook his head, and pointed out his own open window, indicating a direction they no longer traveled.

"Iranduba," he said.

Soon after that, what passed for pavement ran out altogether. They proceeded another kilometer through grassland, along what amounted to a washboard track. The cab jounced, rattled, and splashed over the ruts in the road. The landscape changed again around them, becoming denser and darker, tinted with shades of sepia and green as they entered a mangrove forest. Far up ahead, the limo's tail lights pulsed red as the long car slowed, turned right, and disappeared from view, as if the driver had decided to proceed directly into the forest itself.

When they reached the spot, they discovered a narrow, unmarked road leading into the trees. The cab driver stopped, wrangled the shift lever on the steering column into park, and said, *"Não mais."*

Lana turned to him, wide-eyed. She spoke a few halting words, stopped and scowled, then tried again, gesturing vigorously toward mangrove road.

The cabbie finally interrupted her, raising his palm and shaking his head. *"Sinto muito. Não mais. Sinto muito."*

Lana attempted a few more words of appeal. The cabbie shook his head steadily, clearly unmoved.

David didn't need Portuguese to understand that the cabbie did not want to travel the mangrove road. He tried what little Spanish he knew, figuring it was close enough: *"Por que?"*

Why?

The cabbie looked at him. His eyes widened slightly as he whispered a single word in reply: *"Monstros."*

Lana barked in frustration, pounding the seat with her fist. She and the cabbie exchanged a flurry of heated words. She reached out and grabbed back the wad of bills she'd stuffed into the cabbie's dashboard strap. Then she shoved out of the car.

David scrambled after her. "What's going on? What did he say?"

"He says he won't go any farther. He says he's *sorry*."

"What did you say?"

"I asked him how much farther he wouldn't go."

"And what did he say?"

Lana snorted, pointing up the mangrove road. "Two more clicks that way. Or so he claims."

As Simon got out to join them, David reached down, snatched the money out of her hand, walked over to the cab, and handed it through the window, back to the driver.

Lana called, "Hey!"

The driver showed David his yellow teeth. He dipped his head in appreciation.

David turned back to Lana. "Now ask him if he'll wait here for us. And try to be nice."

Shooting daggers with her eyes, Lana crossed her arms and refused to budge.

"You're not being helpful," David said.

She sighed.

As soon as the driver saw her reapproaching his cab, he clunked the car into gear and headed back up the road in reverse, bald tires flinging clods of mud.

Lana took off after him, hollering at the top of her lungs.

Simon and David stood there, slapping at bugs and watching their ride go away.

Lana finally gave up and came trudging back. Her shoes were caked with mud, blouse half-untucked, hair hanging limp in the sultry heat.

"Well," Simon said. "I guess that's sorted."

"I hope he hits a damned tree," Lana said, glancing only once back over her shoulder at the cab, still weaving and wandering its way backward down the road.

"He certainly seems to be doing a yeoman's job so far," Simon observed. "He'd fare well in London."

"Pun intended, I'm sure," David said.

Simon took off his hat and swatted at a large, persistent, faintly humming cloud of gnats with it. "What's the plan, then?"

"Apparently it involves us walking," Lana groused.

"At least you wore flats," David said. "Come on."

*   *   *

The bugs did not get smaller, the farther they walked into the gnarly mangroves. They didn't bite or sting less frequently.

Nor did the heat subside. Or the terrain get smoother. Or the road dry out beneath their feet.

In fact, the mangrove forest slowly began what seemed to David like a gradual transition to mangrove swamp. The air was like breathing through a washrag. The smell of earth and vegetation clung to the sinuses like some invisible organic paste. The ruts in the road sank in spots to ankle depth; the occasional exposed tree root tripped each one of them at one point or another. They could hear things moving in the trees—sometimes large-sounding things, sometimes small-sounding things, sometimes things on the ground, and sometimes things in the canopy overhead. Strange birds called and answered each other. Tree frogs trilled and warbled. And the bugs.

Dear Lord in heaven, the bugs.

"At least it's not raining," Simon said.

On they trudged, slapping at their foreheads and necks, until they heard a faint sound in the distance. Something mechanical, David thought. A small, stationary motor chugging dutifully along.

"Sounds like a generator," he said. "Or a water pump."

"In other words, civilization," Simon agreed.

Lana stopped dead in her tracks. When David looked back, she made a sharp, silent gesture toward the timber to their right. Then she followed her own direction, slipping off the road and into the mangroves, silent as a wraith.

"If it's all the same to you, old boy," Simon said, "I believe I'll stay on the road."

"Suit yourself," David said. He followed Lana into the trees.

By the time Simon Lean caught up with them, Lana had led them five hundred meters farther on ahead, creeping without a sound over ground the consistency of a sponge, through the dark woods, keeping them parallel with the road. Finally, she stopped and crouched behind a fat trunk encircled by vines.

"There," she whispered, pointing through a gap in the timber. "Two out front. Assault rifles and sidearms."

David had already spotted them: two guards in jungle green on the other side of the road, standing post on either side of a tall iron fence. For the first time, he noticed the vine-covered brick wall extending into the trees on either side.

"Well," Simon said. "It's a good job I didn't stay on the road."

Quietly, Lana opened her satchel and retrieved a pair of compact field binoculars.

David said, "Where did you get those?"

"Madrid. Same place I got the guns. What were you two doing that whole time we were supposed to be shopping?"

"Shopping," David and Simon said in unison.

She rolled her eyes and raised the binoculars. She peered through them for a minute, then handed them to David.

The eyepieces were already damp from her sweat. In the magnified field, he could see the swarthy, stubbled faces of the two guards. Between them, a cast brass sign, affixed to the gate and framed in creeper vines, read CAVE DA ÁGUIA.

"My turn," Simon said over his shoulder.

David handed back the binocs. "Cave da Águia. What does that mean?"

"The Eagle's Basement," Lana said. "Or something close. My Portuguese is rusty."

David thought immediately of Kehlsteinhaus, Hitler's famous mountaintop retreat, perched high above the little town of Berchtesgaden in Bavaria. During the war, allied troops had referred to this fortress as the Eagle's Nest. Somehow, the faded, vine-covered sign on this gate struck him as the most incredible thing they'd encountered so far.

Physical proof that Adolf Hitler, the once-unstoppable megalomaniac, had a perversely self-deprecating sense of humor.

David checked his wristwatch. The crystal had fogged over in the heat, but he could still read the time. It was nearly three o'clock in the afternoon. "What now?"

Lana accepted the binoculars back from Simon and returned them to her bag.

"We need to go shopping again," she said.

CHAPTER
THIRTY-EIGHT

They hiked several clicks through the heat, all the way back to the edge of the shantytown, where they came upon an elderly woman tending to a mangy burro. The woman's tarpaper shack looked as swaybacked as the animal she cared for, surrounded on all sides by a wide range of detritus, both natural and man-made.

From her, Lana was able to negotiate the purchase of three rusty bicycles. Throughout their business dealings, the woman looked up at the three of them from under the hanging ledge of her own brow, her chin nearly touching her knobby collarbones. They paid more money than she was likely to have seen in the past decade, a more than fair price in any country for three bikes with nary a tire among them. David only hoped that, in doing so, they hadn't made her a target for *bandidos*—or for that matter, her fellow villagers.

They rode the bikes on bare rims all the way back over the bridge to Manaus, hailing the first cab on the waterfront they could find.

By the time they got back to the hotel, David felt as though he'd been dragged there on a rope by the old village woman's burro. The cab ride had stiffened his joints until he felt like the Tin Man before the oil can. The heat had wilted his clothes, and his sweat had soaked them, though neither condition had prevented the bugs from chewing him alive.

His feet hurt. His great toe throbbed like a bass drum. He smelled like a water buffalo. And if the hotel meant to add air-conditioning with the renovation currently underway, nobody had gotten around to hooking it up yet.

They parted Simon's company at the third floor, taking the elevator up to the building's fourth and final level, where they found their room to be stifling with cooped, late-afternoon heat. A ceiling fan with blades shaped like palm fronds turned lazily, barely stirring the soupy air. Lana pulled open the shutters, pushed open the windows, and went to the bedside telephone.

David—without pausing or changing his stride—walked straight to the bathroom, shedding his grimy clothes in sodden piles behind him.

He stepped under a lukewarm shower, leaned his forehead against the tile, and let the water rain over him. It ranked among the most glorious showers he'd experienced in his life. That ranking climbed sharply a few moments later, when Lana peeled back the curtain and stepped in to join him.

"Well," he said. "Hello there."

"Hi."

"I would have held the door for you, but I was in a coma."

"Let's see if this wakes you up," she said.

She stepped under the water, pressing full length against him. David enjoyed that for a few moments, then cupped his hands under the water. He released what he collected over her slender shoulders.

"Mm," she said.

She closed her eyes, turning her face up to the spray. David leaned down and kissed the hollow of her neck. Lana opened her eyes, stood up on tiptoe, and did the same to him in return. He felt an electric tingle. Felt her taut, slick skin beneath his palms. Two minutes ago, he would never have thought he'd had the energy to rise to such an occasion.

Two minutes ago, he would have been wrong.

They kissed tenderly for a few moments, cupped more water over each other. Then, just as things began to escalate, Lana turned her back and settled against his chest. He wrapped his arms around her waist. They stood together under the cooling spray.

"You know, when I first read your file, I really was not a David Toland admirer," she said. "I suppose you probably picked up on that."

"I was never completely sure why," he said. "Especially since you came to me in the first place."

"It's because you were a warrior."

"Not much for men in uniform, huh?"

She chuckled softly. "Men in uniform I can handle. But you walked away. That was what bothered me most: knowing that your country offered your choice of meals on a silver platter, and you chose ice cream."

An interesting way to phrase it, David thought. He did like ice cream.

"You thought I was a quitter," he said.

"I thought you were a coward."

"Ouch."

She caressed his forearm with her fingertips. "I'm only being honest. And only because I don't think that way about you anymore."

"What do you think now?"

She turned to face him again, still in his arms, her skin sliding against his. "Now I think I envy you."

"Envy me? Why?"

Lana rested her wet hair on his chest, gripped his elbows, and pulled his arms tighter around her.

*   *   *

Some time later, while Lana succumbed to a short nap on the bed, David washed his clothes by hand in the tub. He considered hanging them in the sun on the balcony, but he doubted they'd get very dry very fast in the tropical heat. So, he called down to the concierge and arranged to have them dried in the hotel laundry.

Sixty minutes after that, they met Simon downstairs in the hotel café as planned.

The café was already filling up with patrons getting a start on the evening's festivities. Most of the customers were guests of the hotel, although a few tables appeared to be occupied by locals. All of them, to a person, were decked—somewhat inexplicably to David—in white clothing. As if everybody in the joint had coordinated their attire en masse.

The café itself was decorated all over with glittering streamers, bowls of colorful flowers, and festive mini-shrines to Yemanjá—mother of the waters, spirit of the moonlight, and matron saint of fishermen.

"And shipwreck survivors," Lana said, taking David's hand in hers as they moved. They were getting to be, he thought, almost like a real couple.

"Shipwreck survivors," he said. "That's us. Metaphorically speaking."

"If Yemanjá wants to bless us, I won't argue with her."

They made their way toward the back, passing a makeshift air conditioner consisting of a large oscillating fan blowing cool air across a buffet tub filled to the brim with salted ice. It was a nice touch.

Simon Lean apparently thought so, too. They found him already occupying a corner booth near the ice table, reading a local news-paper. "Well," he said. "Don't you two look fresh as a pair of spring daisies?"

"Amazing what a shower can do for a person," David said, feeling Lana's fingernails dig into his palm.

"Quite." Simon smiled. He folded the newspaper back on itself and dropped it on the other side of the table for Lana to see. "Can you read this, now that you've had a chance to brush up on your Portuguese?"

They sat down and looked at the paper. Simon had presented them with the front page of the social section, which featured a thumbnail photograph of none other than C. Denham, patrón.

Lana read bits and pieces aloud from the accompanying story item, which revealed that the wealthy Teatros Amazonas board president would indeed count himself among the attendants of tomorrow night's opening of *Parsifal*.

"And me without my lorgnette," Simon said. "Or my tuxedo."

"Let's not get fitted just yet," Lana said. "I've been thinking."

"Is that so?"

She began to outline a tentative plan that involved her attending the opera herself. Alone.

"I already don't like it," David said.

"You haven't even heard it yet."

"I heard the part about us splitting up."

"You have incursion experience. And I can't trust Simon anywhere near Denham. No offense, Simon."

Simon raised a palm. "Fair enough, dear."

"And I'm a better actor than both of you."

"I still don't think we should split up," David said.

Lana gave his hand a squeeze. "You're very sweet. Now will you be quiet and hear me out?"

David sighed. While he and Simon listened, Lana went on to explain her idea.

She would pose as an art dealer from London. She would approach Denham about his work, claiming to have purchased his painting of the opera house on the auction market some months previously. She'd claim that the quality of the work—especially from an artist unknown to the establishment—had inspired her to investigate its provenance. This effort had, quite naturally, led her to Manaus, but her time here was limited. It could be good for both of their careers if Denham would consider granting her a viewing of his more recent pieces tonight, after the opera.

Meanwhile, David and Simon would return to the Eagle's Basement, infiltrate the grounds under cover of night, and look for anything they could use to prove Denham's true identity to the world. They would be there waiting when she and Denham arrived.

"I see," David said. "What do we do with him once we have him?"

"Once we have him," Lana answered, "our options will exponentiate, believe me."

"Well. If it was that simple, why didn't you say so in the first place?"

Lana smirked. "Do I detect a hint of sarcasm, John, dear?"

"Who, me? None at all. I'm just waiting to hear the next part of the plan."

"Which next part?"

"The part where you tell us how exactly we might hope to accomplish this little incursion, as you call it. While you're sitting next to Adolf Hitler. Alone."

Lana folded her hands primly on the table. "Refresh my memory of your file, Captain Toland. Did you or did you not lead the insertion team that sabotaged a critical North Korean supply bridge at Sunchon?"

"Not with two pistols, no intel, and a few hours' planning in a sweaty hotel room, no."

Now Simon cleared his throat. "Three pistols," he said.

David nodded. "My mistake. *Three* pistols, no intel, and a few hours' planning in a sweaty hotel room."

"Thank you. Meanwhile, my experience in the field—amateur though my status as a swashbuckler may be—suggests that there must be a precinct official who could be persuaded to furnish us with any residential building plans that may be on file."

"At six p.m. on New Year's Eve?"

Simon's buoyant expression sank a little.

"Don't get discouraged," Lana said. "I like the independent thinking."

"You're too kind, my dear, as always."

She leaned forward. "But as long as we're brainstorming, what else do you think your experience might get us in the next twelve to fifteen hours?"

Again, David indicated his disapproval of this overall line of strategy. If Simon or Lana noticed, neither one of them seemed overly concerned.

"Why don't we put our heads together and make a list," Simon said, "and then we'll see?"

*   *   *

By nightfall, David had learned that white clothing was a well-known New Year's Eve tradition in Brazil.

White symbolized the wish for peace in the coming year, according to an English-speaking bartender they encountered. Revelers wore it with accent colors meant to attract various brands of luck: green for health, red for passion, purple for inspiration, yellow for money. This went a long way toward explaining why the merriest young men of Manaus kept offering to sell David the literal shirts off their backs: his was predominantly blue. The color of melancholy and faded bruises.

"And water," Simon suggested helpfully. "That should put you in good stead with Yemanjá. I wouldn't worry, old man."

"It's not Yemanjá I'm worried about," David said. "What worries me is that nobody who can help us is going to trust me looking like Howdy Doody from Dum-Dum, USA. How did you two know how to dress?"

"I'd have worn this anyway."

"Me too, actually," Lana said.

David examined their outfits. After cleaning up, Simon had changed into white slacks and a beige linen sport coat, with a pale violet shirt open at the collar. Lana wore a white jumper with sandals, a yellow gerbera from a street vendor in her hair. The flower reminded David of the picnic dream he'd had: Lana in yellow, a daisy behind her ear. He caught her and Simon exchanging a glance of amusement at his expense.

"I get it. Everybody laugh at the lab guy," he said. "That's fine. Knock yourselves out."

"Don't be sensitive." Lana patted his arm. "You have your own sense of fashion, that's all. Besides, by the look of this town, our campaign planning may be postponed until morning anyway."

The three of them made their way through the crowd lining Rua Dez de Julho. There was a raucous street parade underway, just north of the opera house. On the parade route, David saw a woman in feathers carrying a three-toed sloth in her arms like a sleepy toddler. The woman was followed by a samba troupe surrounded by ribbon stick dancers. Walkers carrying sparklers brought up the rear, leaving sizzling neon squiggles in the dark as they tossed candy and trinkets into the crowd.

David liked all of it very much. While he soaked in the scene, he pointed up ahead to a pair of street kids working the crowd. One of the kids carried a large white sign laid out in some kind of pictographic grid. The other kid—taller, and a few years older by the look of him—collected money from curbside partiers.

"Those two," he said. "Anybody know what kind of game they're running over there?"

"*Jogo do bicho,*" Simon told him. "The animal game. It's illegal in Brazil, but that doesn't stop the mobsters from running it anyway. Or the grandmothers, for that matter."

"You sound like an authority."

"I'm a crime writer. I research these matters."

"Follow me," David said. "I have an idea."

Ignoring the exchange of skeptical looks between Simon and Lana, David headed over and beckoned the *jogo* boys to a marginally quieter spot away from the parade route. He was already doing business with them when Lana and Simon caught up.

The boys—possibly eleven and fifteen years old, or thereabouts—each had their own role to play. The older, taller one held out his hand. When David handed the older boy a *cruzeiro* note, the smaller boy—the one holding the sign—handed David a card in exchange. The card was about the size of a baseball trading card, the kind that came in packages of bubble gum back home. It had a picture of an eagle on it.

David perused the sign a second time. It looked like an oversized advent calendar, with cardboard flaps opening on square windows. Each available square contained a picture of an animal: horse, pig, rooster, elephant, monkey, peacock, and so on. Some of the flaps had already been closed. The boy now closed the flap over the eagle while David browsed.

"Having fun?" Lana asked him.

He handed her the eagle card. "Here, this one's yours," he said. "An eagle for a patriot. How does this game work, anyway?"

"It's like a lottery," Lana said, looking her card over, front and back. "Each animal has a set of numbers. If any of your numbers come up in the drawing, you win."

David nodded. "Come on, Uncle Si, let's you and me pick out our animals. I don't think they're going to talk to us if we don't."

"What if I wanted to be the eagle?" Simon said.

"In that shirt, you can be the peacock," Lana answered.

"This shirt is Dior. And it's within the palette of the occasion. He's the colorful one."

David shook his head as he studied the board. "Na. I'd rather be the butterfly."

Lana smirked and handed two more bills to the taller boy. "O pavão," she said. "E a borboleta."

The boys took Lana's money, then handed Simon and David their cards: one pavão and one borboleta. Closed went the flaps over the peacock and the butterfly.

"Now we're getting somewhere," David said. He spoke to Lana as he handed the taller boy a whole fistful of bills. "Ask them if they know a pilot."

Lana and Simon both looked at him. Something twinkled in Lana's eye. She turned to the boys, cleared her throat, and said, "Sabe um piloto de avião?"

"Sabemos que um piloto," the smaller boy answered. "Um piloto branco."

"They know a pilot," she told David. "A white pilot, no less."

Simon said, "When did we start looking for a pilot?"

David peeled off another short stack of bills and showed it to the boys, but did not hand it over. "Ask them if they'll introduce us to their white pilot."

Lana pointed to the bills in David's hand. *"Você vai nos levar agora?"*

The elder boy pointed to the ground and said, *"Você esperar aqui. Uma hora."*

And then, just as Lana opened her mouth to counter, the smaller boy snatched the bills out of David's hand. He tucked the *jogo* board under his arm quick as a flash, and the two of them ran off into the night.

"Perhaps this is my privileged Western perspective revealing itself," Simon said, "but I think you were just robbed, old boy."

"Actually, he claimed they'd be back in an hour." Lana turned to David and smiled a slow smile. "Smart thinking. I'm slightly angry that I didn't come up with it myself."

David polished his nails on his inappropriate blue shirt. "Aw shucks."

"Well," Simon said. "I won't pretend to understand what the devil you two are grinning about. But at least we have some time to enjoy the parade."

*　　*　　*

They never saw the *jogo* boys again.

After the first hour had passed, the parade and the bystanders had essentially merged to create a general carnival atmosphere all along Rua Dez de Julho. David, Lana, and Simon wandered along the edges of the festivities, sipping *cachaça* cocktails, watching the people, and scanning for signs of the young hustlers.

After the second hour, David began to think that they'd been taken for a ride after all. And not in an airplane by the pilot the *jogo* boys had promised. But he found himself getting swept up in the general mirth of the evening, and it felt like ages since he'd had any kind of fun. So, he decided he'd wait until morning to be depressed about the wad of Brazilian cash he'd forked over.

At 11:55, the fireworks started. Screaming rockets shot up from San Sebastian square, exploding over the opera house in cascading blooms, tinting the upturned faces of the crowd in reds and greens, blues and golds.

Four minutes and forty-five seconds after that, the fireworks abruptly paused, pulling a sudden drape of silence over the crowd.

Then, from the silence, came hundreds of voices rising in unison:

Dez...nove...oito...sete...seis...

David slipped his arm around Lana's waist and did his best Clark Gable impersonation, pulling her to him with manful authority. "Pucker up, beautiful," he told her. "There's a kiss coming right at your mouth."

...cinco quatro três...

Lana looked up at him, smiling. "Unhand me, you fiend."

"Never."

...dois um!

David kissed her, pulling her closer as the fireworks resumed over their heads, whistling and booming and turning the dark Brazilian night to sizzling, multicolored day. He felt her lips part against his as the crowd erupted into cheers of celebration all around them. He could taste *cachaça* and lime on her tongue.

Then the samba music kicked in. David looked into Lana's eyes and said, "Happy new year."

She looked back into his. "And to you."

A nearby tourist turned to Simon and said, "I wish I had somebody to kiss like that at midnight."

"Well spoken, friend," Simon said. "Well spoken indeed."

The tourist—a fair-skinned, well-built man in his forties, with a vaguely South African lilt to his voice—raised the glass in his hand and said, *"Saúde."*

"To auld lang syne," Simon said. "Cheers, mate."

After they drank, the tourist offered his hand and said, "Ranier Van Tonder. Pleasure to make your acquaintance."

"Simon Lean. And you as well."

David broke his clinch with Lana, shook Ranier Van Tonder's hand, and said, "John Davis. This is my wife, Irene."

"Happy new year," Lana said.

"Many returns," Van Tonder said. "Now that we know each other, I'm told you Yanks are looking for someone to take you up in the air."

CHAPTER

THIRTY-NINE

New Year's Day

On the first day of 1962, retired USMC captain David W. Toland, fugitive CIA agent Lana Welles, and bestselling author Simon Lean prepared to resurrect a dead man.

They started before sunrise, splitting up to cover the most possible ground in the least possible time: Simon in the direction of supplies and tactical equipment, Lana to prep her cover story and to reconnoiter the theater, and David, by cab, to a small, private airfield ten clicks west of the city.

"Good luck," he said to Lana on his way out. Something had changed between them overnight, he sensed. Somehow, this morning, David could almost believe that if the two of them lived through the day, they just might have some kind of future together. In fact, he found it increasingly difficult to believe that his feelings were one-sided. "And be careful."

"You too," she said, kissing him once to seal it. It was a good kiss. "Because if we don't get this done today, we'll be looking for dishwashing jobs in Manaus."

"Say again?"

"I gave the last of our operating cash to our friend from Cape Town," she said. "And I won't be able to get more without going back on the grid."

He nodded. "Then let's get it done today."

An hour later, at the airfield, he found Ranier Van Tonder fueling up a 1951 Piper Cub with bullet holes in the side paneling and no tail number.

"Looks like she's seen some action," David said, tracing a puncture with his finger.

"That she has, mate," Van Tonder said. "And I'll make you a deal: don't ask what kind of action, and I won't ask why you need a bloke to fly you over Papa Denham's place at the crack of dawn."

David looked up and said, "Who?"

Van Tonder laughed. "Good man. Ready to shove?"

Fifteen minutes later, as they lifted off the runway and climbed toward the lightening sky, David said, "How did you know we were flying over Carl Denham's place?"

Van Tonder's voice crackled back over his headset: "Between the river and Iranduba, you said. In the rain forest. That'd be Cave da Águia."

"Do you know Denham?"

"Everybody in Manaus knows Denham, mate," Van Tonder said. "He built the new hydroelectric plant on the river. There are stories, mind."

"What kind of stories?"

"Oh, scary stories." Van Tonder pantomimed a shiver. "They get scarier every time you hear them, too. Probably none of 'em are true."

David thought of what the cab driver had said on the mangrove road: *monstros*. Translation: here be dragons.

"On the other hand, nobody knows exactly why he lives all the way out there in the jungle. With armed guards, no less. Nobody I know is dumb enough to go flying in his airspace, either."

"I guess that makes me dumber than I thought."

"That's how I knew you were American. That and the shirt."

"I've been told I have my own sense of fashion."

"So what are you, then? CIA? NSA? Private sector?"

"All good questions. How long have you been a smuggler?"

Van Tonder laughed as he banked over the river, leveling off around a thousand feet. "I knew I liked you. Your gear's in the bag on your left."

David retrieved the small duffel from the floor well beside his seat. Inside the bag, he found a battered Nikon F camera fitted with a 200mm Nikkor telephoto zoom lens—more or less exactly as requested. "You do quick work," he said. "Am I locked and loaded?"

"Ready to shoot. As long as you work as quickly as I do."

They bore to the southeast, the long span of the Ponte Rio Negro visible in the distance, shrouded in morning mist. Even at this altitude, the tops of the trees looked almost close enough to reach down and touch. Which was, David thought, under the circumstances, a cautionary illusion if ever there had been one.

It didn't take long to reach their destination: a sudden clearing in the trees a few clicks south of the river. In the clearing was a compound centered by a sprawling villa in the Mediterranean Revival style, surrounded by various outbuildings, miscellaneous vehicles both heavy-duty and light, and what looked like a private fuel tank. A handful of small-scale men with miniature guns on their backs could be seen milling about, sipping from tiny white mugs in the first light of dawn.

David raised the camera and began shooting frames, first in master, then in close-up, pulling focus and selecting shots by instinct, hoping that he was managing to counteract the bounce and vibration of the aircraft well enough to produce legible results.

Especially when Van Tonder rocked his wings without warning: a wave to the armed men on the ground, all of them now looking toward the skies. Through his lens, David saw one of them raise his mug in acknowledgment. He snapped the man's photograph for posterity.

And then the clearing disappeared beneath them as they growled away over the rain forest. David craned as far as he could to his right, snapping one last shot out the window, mostly blocked by the Cubbie's wing struts.

"Can you turn back and make another pass?" he asked.

"Sorry, mate," Van Tonder said. "Told you to be quick. Those fellows down there know my plane all right, but if they see it come over a second time, it won't be coffee they're raising. If you take my meaning."

David took his meaning. He only wished he'd managed to take more than a handful of shots—some or all of which might not even turn out to be usable—of this guarded location he was meant to breach, preferably without dying, fifteen hours from now.

"In that case," he said, "do you happen to know of a good photo counter in Manaus that's open on New Year's Day?"

* * *

They reconvened at the hotel, in Simon's room, at noon. They ordered up a plate of *bauru* sandwiches for lunch and stayed in all that steamy afternoon, sweating over the plan.

"The show begins at eighteen hundred," Lana said. "Twelve minutes before sunset in Manaus, according to my naval tables. That means you'll have full dark by eighteen thirty."

"Great," David said. "We could be dead by intermission."

"I'm almost never awake for the third act anyway," Simon said.

After eating, David stripped down to his A-shirt and laid out his morning reconnaissance photos on the dining table. He'd hastily developed the half dozen eight by ten prints in the back room of a warehouse on the waterfront, near the ports—a shady, unnerving space owned by a shady, unnerving associate of Ranier Van Tonder's. It occurred to him, as he arranged the results for Simon and Lana, that he'd now seen the inner workings of the pornography industry on two different continents. It was an unexpected accomplishment.

Meanwhile, Simon laid out the product of his scavenger hunt on the bed: a pile of old T-shirts, two Zippo lighters, a flare gun, boxes of ammunition for the Welrod and the Llama, two KA-BAR-style military knives, two heavy-duty flashlights, two dark green safari vests, two rucksacks, a pair of long-handled bolt cutters, two extra sets of field

273

binoculars, and a tin of black shoe polish. Over by the window, he'd already lined up a ten-liter jerry can of gasoline and half a dozen empty wine bottles.

"No helicopter gunship, alas," he said.

"I guess we'll have to make do," David said.

He picked up one of the knives and unsheathed it. He tested its edge by shaving a patch of hair from his own forearm, then began slicing one of the T-shirts down into strips.

Lana, standing over the photos, tapped a fuzzy close-up he'd taken of the rear foundation of the main house. "You're using this as your entry point?"

"It's a thought. Though I'm open to suggestions."

"Nope. I like it. Good cover. Clear egress to the rear wall. Light guard, if any. And you've got the bolt cutters."

"Those took some getting, by the way," Simon said. "And I thought bullets would be the challenge."

"Good thing we didn't need pruning shears," David said. "Are you going to fill bottles or help me cut rags?"

*　　*　　*

Eventually—ready or not—it was time.

David helped Simon load up the rucksacks, then returned briefly to his own room.

He found Lana standing in front of the bureau mirror, pinning up her hair. She wore a simple champagne gown, sashed at the waist. Her jewelry included a necklace made of small, delicate shells, which she'd purchased on the street here in Manaus. The overall effect was elegant with an artistic, globe-trotting quirk. The spell it cast on David was swift and complete.

He stepped up behind her, placing his hands on her waist. "Wow," he said.

"All things considered," she said, "I'd rather be wearing the other tac vest."

"You'd pull it off better than Simon."

"Sweet talker."

David turned her gently and took her in his arms. Before he could open his mouth to say what he'd come in here to say, she covered his lips with her fingers and shook her head. "Don't."

"How do you know what I was going to say?"

"You were about to tell me to be careful," she said. "Or something even worse than that."

"Actually, I was going to say that when all this is over, and they offer you your choice of meals on a silver platter, I'd like to take you out for ice cream."

She smiled at him. But David couldn't help noticing the hint of sadness in her eyes. It was the same wistful melancholy he'd glimpsed on the plane ride into Manaus, as they'd looked out the window together at the meeting of the waters. It had replaced the almost domesticated look of contentment he swore he'd seen on her face this morning, after the New Year's celebration.

"That sounds nice," she said.

She'd even done her best to sound sincere. David could tell. "Then it's a date," he said.

He kissed her once, then released her and headed for the door. On his way out, he looked over his shoulder and said, "I almost forgot."

"Yes?"

"Be careful."

"You rat."

He blew her one last kiss, then went downstairs to join Simon before his favorite author found a way to accidentally blow up the hotel.

CHAPTER

FORTY

In an unsolicited gesture of camaraderie—on what grounds, David found himself unable to speculate—Ranier Van Tonder had offered them two spots in the back of a cargo truck bound for Iranduba early that evening.

His first instinct was to mistrust the proposition. On the other hand, they had nothing of particular value to steal; if Van Tonder meant him harm, he'd had more than ample opportunity already, and catching a free lift in the back of a thriving scoundrel's armed transpo truck seemed appreciably more covert—and somehow marginally safer—than their rattletrap commercial taxi ride carrying two rucksacks stuffed to the zippers with Molotov cocktails assembled in a hotel bathtub.

Not to mention cheaper.

So he and Simon made their way to the ports at the appointed time, with the appointed verbal passwords. There, at the appointed warehouse slip, they were loaded into the back of a diesel-belching Daimler deuce-and-a-half. They sat against bales of what the men called *maconba*, which David identified, by smell alone, as quite a large volume of unprocessed reefer.

Sixty bone-rattling, *maconba*-reeking minutes later, they were crouching their way back through the rain forest, full packs on their backs, their faces and arms smeared with shoe polish. The shoe polish served as improvised camo paint to break up their silhouettes during these last rays of daylight, and to blend in with the dark when nightfall came. As it happened, it worked as a reasonably effective insect repellant as well.

David couldn't get over how immediately familiar—even comfortable—the whole commando routine felt to him. Like putting on an old pair of shoes. Almost as if his past ten years in the subterranean film stacks at the Library of Congress had been the dream, and not the other way around.

"Hey, Simon?" he said as they moved along a well-trampled animal path through the trees.

"Still here, lad," Simon panted, perhaps ten meters behind him. "Don't slow down on my account."

"Didn't you tell me you'd researched the Amazon for *The Jaguar Hunters*?"

"Ah. My first crack at the Big List, yes. I was always partial to that one."

"Are the snakes in this region poisonous?"

Simon chuckled. "A fair few. There's the bushmaster, of course—deadly, but shy. Now. The fer-de-lance, on the other hand, is a serpent of an altogether different stri—"

"Okay, thanks," David said, looking quickly away from the slithering movement he'd been tracking in the vegetation off to their left.

"Why do you ask?"

"No reason."

They forged on. After thirty more minutes trudging through heavy cover—David poking at the ground ahead of him with a long stick every step of the way—they neared the hiding spot Lana had discovered yesterday. They crawled the rest of the way on their hands and knees, sacrificing pace for stealth. They did their best to avoid fallen limbs, snarls of tangled vines, and anything else that might announce their approach with an ill-timed rustle or snap, sticking to soft beds of peat moss wherever they could.

And then they were there.

Cave da Águia.

There were no guards posted at the gate this time.

Simon whispered: "Maybe this will be easier than we thought."

David held up two fingers to shush his companion, then quietly opened his rucksack. He retrieved the binoculars, raised them, and scanned the trees on the far side of the forest road.

There.

He wiped sweat from his eyes and raised the binocs again, fine-tuning the focus wheel with his index finger until he zeroed in on the subtle movement he thought he'd seen. A figure emerged from a stand of tall ferns and stepped into his field of view.

A guard. He appeared to be patrolling the perimeter of the compound along the vine-covered brick wall, rifle slung on his shoulder. He had a cigarette in his fingers and was moving steadily their way.

David tracked the guard all the way to the road, then lowered the binoculars. He and Simon watched the guard return to his post.

"Half as difficult," Simon whispered. "At least there's only one of them."

David motioned for Simon to lean closer. When he did, David pressed his sweaty, stubbled cheek against Simon's sweaty smooth one. In his lowest voice, he spoke directly into Simon's ear: "Stop making sounds with your mouth."

"Ah," Simon whispered. "Too right."

David raised the binoculars one more time. He scanned the trees, and as far along the wall as he could see, for security cameras.

At half past six, the guard stood to attention. A moment later, they heard the sound of an approaching car engine.

The guard turned to his left and opened a lid set into the brick beside him, revealing a keypad. David fine-tuned the focus, training in on the guard's hand. He steadied the binoculars with one hand, using the fingers of his other hand to display each code number as the guard entered it—both for Simon's benefit and to help commit the numbers to memory himself.

Five fingers...four fingers...five fingers. Three. One. Two. Nine...

Oops. He'd just have to remember that last one.

Enter.

The gates clanked, then whirred, then opened. A gleaming black luxury car rolled into view.

The guard stood aside and snapped a brief salute as the car passed through the opened gates and turned out onto the road. Visible in the back of the car was a behatted, sharply dressed Carl Denham.

David crouched lower. He could feel Simon tensing beside him as the car passed their position, cruising smoothly away.

But David kept his focus on the guard, who stepped into the compound, reached back through the iron gate, and punched more numbers into the keypad. David checked his work through the binoculars.

4-9-7-7-5-6-2.

As the gates began to close, the guard slapped the lid closed over the keypad, hiked his rifle, disappeared into the compound.

Simon said, "What's the plan?"

An excellent question. David had been thinking very hard about that. He would have hoped to have come up with some better ideas by now. Then again, "better" was a debatable concept in this situation.

"They were completely different," he said, half to Simon, half to himself.

"What was completely different?"

"The code numbers. Seven positions to open the gate, a different set of seven to close it."

"That fact," Simon said, "does not seem useless."

David couldn't remember ever having wished quite so dearly that he'd thought to bring along a pen.

*   *   *

The plan: Using everything he could remember about operating an extreme-stealth mission—which was, he hoped, more than he'd forgotten—David would breach perimeter security, infiltrate the compound, and make his way into the house via the rear cellar door shown in the surveillance photos.

Simon, meanwhile, would remain in position and monitor the front entrance, taking action only under the following circumstances: somebody came home early, or David signaled for help with the flare gun.

In either scenario, Simon would take a position atop the outer wall and go to work with the Molotov cocktails they'd prepared back at the hotel, aiming for maximum diversion, and hopefully—if luck was on their side and a hundred different variables landed in their favor—giving David the time he needed to escape over the wall.

After that, they'd be alone in the rain forest at night, almost certainly under heavily armed pursuit. That was more or less where the plan ended.

"May I ask one question?" Simon said.

"Lay it on me."

"Our operative at the theater aims to capture this man. I aim to kill him. If, in the course of our activities this evening, you find yourself in a position to choose which objective you support...do you know your answer?"

After a long pause, David said, "The only objective I support is keeping the three of us alive until our activities are concluded."

Simon Lean grinned. "Well spoken, old man. I'm in the presence of a born leader."

"Then God help you," David said.

*   *   *

An hour after dark, he made his move.

After watching a fat black howler monkey run along the top of the perimeter wall at dusk without triggering any alarms, David chose the same route for himself, rather than risk the disruption of opening the gate. Fewer passcodes to remember anyway.

Once he'd dropped inside the far back corner of the grounds, he discovered something else that increased his hopes for success: while the Wolf was away, the sheep would play.

Cards, specifically. In a bunk building separated from the main house. David counted eight guards there, carousing around two different tables, with plenty of rum and *pinga* to go around.

He crept slowly past the barracks into the heart of the compound, using the outbuildings and maintenance sheds for cover. Wherever possible, he avoided the wide pools of sodium-arc light thrown by power poles stationed periodically about the grounds.

For nearly a quarter of an hour, he crouched amid a row of expensive, freshly washed cars in front of a large stucco garage, waiting for a two-man patrol team to finish their cigarettes and head over to the barracks to join the others.

At the upper corner of the garage, a mounted security camera covered the open space between the garage and the house. David used his knife to sever the feed, then braced himself for a reaction.

When none came, he unfastened the bolt cutters from their tie-down on his rucksack and sprinted toward the back corner of the house in a silent crouch.

It was true that he'd conducted plenty of other missions in his previous life, from hastily conceived objectives in the heat of live combat to covert operations under cover of night. High-risk, high-reward scenarios. High-risk, low-reward scenarios. High-risk, high-risk scenarios.

Cut to January 1, 1962.

Getting into Hitler's house was much, much easier than any of them.

David would think back on that, later.

CHAPTER

FORTY-ONE

He stashed his rucksack in the cellar, amid the many crates and tarp-covered shapes stored in the climate-controlled dark down there. David made his way up to a pantry, which opened on a warmly lit kitchen no larger than David's entire apartment back in DC. The stone tile floor surrounded a center island, where the house staff busied themselves with the final stages of cleanup from the evening's meal.

He held position for nearly half an hour, praying that nobody needed any dry goods. At first opportunity, he slipped quietly across the large open kitchen and into a darkened side hall.

David followed the hallway deeper into the darkened house, pausing in shadowy nooks and alcoves whenever he heard voices. He proceeded in quiet flashes, moving from one hiding spot to the next, grateful for the smooth flagstone floors underfoot—no creaking floorboards. The house smelled of recently cooked food and old damp wood, a rich and effective mix for covering his own noticeable bouquet after four hours in the rain forest.

He checked rooms as he moved, looking for one that passed for a study. He hoped to avoid moving to the upper level, where there *would* be creaking floorboards to contend with, but after twenty minutes inside, he began to lose optimism.

And then, deep in the southeastern quadrant of the house, he finally found the room he was looking for, dimly lit from within by a stained-glass desk lamp.

It wasn't hard to determine that he'd found the right place.

Carl Denham's home office was nearly an exact reproduction of the private study David had seen through his loupe while working on the Führerbunker film. Only this version of Hitler's study could have doubled as a temporary exhibit at the Louvre.

Since the end of World War II, much had been written, in newspaper stories and history books, about Hermann Göring's Kunstschutz unit. Theoretically charged with preserving the art and culture of enemy nations during armed conflict, the Kunstschutz had become infamous for its systematic plunder of European treasure. Paintings. Statuary. Religious and ceremonial artifacts. Thousands of other miscellaneous *objets d'art*. And gold.

Lots and lots of gold.

Despite Allied postwar recovery efforts, great volumes of Nazi loot remained unaccounted for, the subject of worldwide speculation and pursuit.

David believed he'd just found some of it. Amid the shelves and built-in bookcases, he saw paintings that were either astounding reproductions, or original works by the likes of van Gogh and Rembrandt. He saw Greek and Egyptian artifacts displayed tastefully under concealed spotlighting. On the corner of a big mahogany desk, he saw a decorative bowl filled with gold coins, set out like a candy dish.

These items were simply the highlights that first drew his eye. David could have spent hours browsing the furnishings and décor of Carl Denham's inner sanctum. The historical importance of this room was palpable.

Hell. It was nearly overpowering.

Awestruck, he moved to a cluster of silver-framed photographs on the corner of the desk. He picked up one frame in particular.

Under the glass was a black-and-white photograph of a smiling blond girl, perhaps four years old. The girl sat upon the knee of a very familiar dark-haired man with a very familiar toothbrush mustache. Despite the difference in their hair color, the family resemblance between the man and the little girl was undeniable.

Tucked into the lower corner of the frame—outside the glass—was a recent Polaroid print of the woman the little blond girl clearly had grown up to be. A photo so recent as to have been taken only the previous morning: former CIA agent Lana Welles.

The inside of David's head was a shell filled with airy black noise. A chilling weight sank to the pit of his stomach. He went numb all over.

The snapshot depicted Lana standing on the sidewalk outside their hotel near San Sebastian square. David could see his own shoulder at the edge of the snapshot. He recognized the blue-checked fabric of his shirt.

So stunned was David by the photograph he now held in his trembling fingers—so utterly poleaxed—that it took him a moment to register the metallic clicking sound he heard behind him.

David looked over his shoulder.

Where he found Simon Lean holding him at gunpoint.

"Sorry, old boy," Simon said.

FORTY-TWO

S imon, what the hell are you doing?"

Simon Lean sighed. When next he spoke, David couldn't help noticing that his accent had changed. Gone was the refined English gentleman, replaced by...East End cab driver? Cockney street thief?

"Afraid I've been less than a hundred percent straight with you, mate," he said. "Name's Rupert Allenbee. The real Simon Lean is a fat middle-aged woman somewhere in Wisconsin. And they say the English have bad teeth! Do you know, I don't even know the woman's real name?"

Slowly, David turned to face Simon.

Or Rupert.

Or whoever. "What are you talking about?"

"Me, I don't even write letters. Though if I did, they'd at least make sense."

David hadn't felt so mistrustful of his surroundings since the first day he'd found himself sitting in a conference room at Langley. Once again, he half expected the *Candid Camera* crew to crawl out from under the desk. Surely the David Toland episode they were filming would go down as their most elaborate setup ever broadcast. "But I've read your books. All of them."

The imposter chuckled. "If you think I'd waste my prime years writing such a steaming pile of piffle as all that, mate, you really haven't developed an accurate sense of me at all, have you?"

"What?"

"I believe I mentioned the homely woman in Wisconsin? She's the one who writes that silly pulp." Simon/Rupert grinned. "Me, I'm just the pretty face."

David couldn't think. His head was spinning. "I don't understand."

"You like fairy tales, here's one for you: Ten years ago, I met a publisher in a Chelsea pub. We knocked back a few pints, went out looking for trouble, knocked back a few more. By the time we were finished, he'd gotten himself a bright idea. Bought me a suit of clothes and hired me to pose for an author photo. Something a touch more dashing than what they had on offer." Rupert Allenbee vamped a piercing, intellectual look for David's benefit. "Somebody the paper hats would believe could have written all that fat-arsed suburban fantasy adventure drivel. Maybe even from experience."

"The face that's been promoting the Simon Lean books ever since," David said.

"Now you're catching on."

David didn't know which betrayal seemed more difficult to contemplate, let alone comprehend: Lana's face in these photographs, or the face of the man pointing the gun at him now. "Who *are* you?" he said.

"Told you already. Name's Rupert Allenbee. I'm a treasure hunter by trade."

"A treasure hunter."

"Well. Mum stuck me in the am-drams as a biter, but really. Comes the time for a man to face brass tacks. The acting just wasn't working out."

Since the Simon Lean books became international bestsellers, he explained, he'd been able to use his now-famous face to grease his way into rarefied company all over the world in his pursuit of riches.

"It's come in handy, I can tell you—though never quite so handy as this." Allenbee swept his arm around the study. "Can you Adam and Eve it? I'd almost put *these* stories down to fairy tales myself. Cheers to you, mate."

He tipped his gun forward.

"But now I'll have your weapons. Blade as well as barrel. Slowly."

David looked at the photographs in his hand.

Carefully, he tucked the Polaroid back into the corner of the frame. Then he tucked the frame inside his vest.

"I'll be needing that back as well," Rupert said. He waggled the barrel of the Welrod. "But let's take things one step at a time."

David removed his own gun from his waistband. He unsheathed the combat knife from his belt. But he made no move to hand them over.

As Rupert extended the Welrod in warning, David nodded toward the other man's exposed forearm. "What about the digits?"

Rupert laughed. "Five quid to a tattoo artist in Brixton. On the ground at your feet with those, please."

David stooped, placing his weapons on the woven rug at his feet, mentally calculating the distance between himself and Allenbee. He assessed the parameters of the room. He thought: *Two seconds.*

That was how much time he thought he needed to make a move and make it count. Just a two-second window. One Mississippi, two Mississippi. All he needed was a distraction. Any kind of distraction at all.

Just then—almost as if he'd willed it to happen—his opportunity presented itself in the form of a low, animal growl from the doorway behind Rupert.

It was an opportunity that required no action on David's part, however. Rupert Allenbee turned toward the unexpected sound at approximately the same moment that Carl Denham's blond German Shepherd barked sharply and launched itself like a furry torpedo.

Allenbee—aka Simon Lean—issued his own bark of surprise as he tried to bring the Welrod around in time. But he was too late. The dog hit him full-force in the chest, bowling him over backward to the ground.

David heard a scream, followed by a gurgle, followed by much kicking and thrashing. But by the time Rupert fired a meaningless round into the ceiling, the snarling Shepherd had already torn out his throat. David stood there, flat-footed, disbelieving his eyes; the whole thing had happened so quickly that he could only marvel that it had happened at all. A cloud of red mist rose up as the dog thrashed its head, shaking Allenbee's body by the neck like a movie prop of a man.

Then a new voice called out: "Johannes! Achtung!"

Instantly, the dog released Rupert's lifeless body. The animal stood to attention like any good soldier, still growling deep in its broad, blood-spattered chest. The dog fixed its eyes on David, crimson teeth bared, its wet blond maw dripping with gore.

Carl Denham entered the room.

With Lana at his side.

Father and daughter both were still dressed for evening: Denham in a tux with his walking stick, Lana still breathtaking in her simple champagne dress, her necklace of delicate shells. David stared at her.

She wouldn't meet his eye.

Denham surveyed Rupert's bloody corpse, took a long look at David, and clucked out a *tsk* sound, as if expressing disappointment in a child.

"Herr Toland," he said, shaking his head slowly. "Such a mess you've made in my home."

CHAPTER

FORTY-THREE

It was no wonder that he'd had such an easy time breaking into Carl Denham's jungle hideaway, David thought.

No wonder that Lana had insisted on going to the opera alone.

No wonder he'd felt that the last words she'd spoken to him, when he'd mentioned their future back at the hotel, had sounded to him like an unspoken goodbye.

And yet none of these things seemed possible, even in this moment.

"Lana," he said. It was all he could come up with.

"You were right," she said. "It's almost over now."

"Tell me I'm dreaming."

Lana opened her clutch, removed her Walther PPK, and pointed it at him. "I'm not going to pinch you."

David realized that he hadn't seen this weapon in her hand since Moscow. Hadn't even thought about it, in fact. He'd completely lost track of things.

"Then talk to me, Lana," he answered. "Please."

*   *   *

Dear Diary, David thought later, long after the misery and regret had settled in for a good long stay. *Today I learned that Adolf Hitler and*

Eva Braun had a secret child. Can you believe it? Cute as a bug. They sent her to America to be raised by friends of the Party, away from the dangers of war. Her adoptive parents groomed her for a career as a CIA mole, and for years now, she's been working as a double agent for a secret council of Nazi collaborators scattered throughout the corridors of American power. I can hardly believe it myself, Diary. Boy. Life sure is crazy sometimes.

"When the Führerbunker film surfaced," Lana told him, "the rumors burned through both worlds like a grass fire. My bosses at the CIA scrambled to restore the film even as my bosses at the Council sought to destroy it. Ironically, my assignment from both sides was the same."

"Recover the film," David said. "And then kill me."

"Until we were attacked together at the Uptown, yes."

Unbeknownst to Lana, the Council had already put another double agent named Jerry Okerlund into play. Okerlund's mission: kill David, destroy all traces of the films, and keep Lana from the truth that her father was alive. Along their journey, as Lana kept in touch with the Council, it had been the Council who relayed their every movement to Okerlund.

"You're the mole," David said. "That's why you've been running from the CIA. Roger Ford has been onto you since DC."

"Roger Ford," Lana spat, "is a blind pig who tripped on an acorn."

"Maybe the Council should have kept better track of their acorns."

"The Council lied to me," Lana said. "In Moscow. In Paris and Madrid. In Washington. My whole life long. I've spent every moment of it believing that my true parents were dead."

Now Denham stepped forward. He touched his daughter's face with the backs of his fingers.

"Lana. *Meine schöne.*" He smiled tenderly. "Only until you were ready to learn the truth. It was for your protection."

"My protection?"

"So that you could grow into the woman before me now." He

caressed her cheek lightly, pride in his eyes. "If you had learned too soon that your *vater* was alive, that knowledge could only have altered your course. But you were needed. You are needed still."

"I could have been killed before I found you."

"Perhaps," Denham told her. "But you were not."

"Then all this has been a test?"

"All this has been a complication. Orchestrated by the traitor Tarkovsky. It should have ended in Moscow."

"But, Father. I . . ."

"Ruhe bitte," Denham snapped, softening again almost at once. "That is enough for now. In time you will understand."

Lana gazed into her father's new face. A face she'd never seen before now. Not as a grown woman, nor as the little four-year-old blond girl, smiling on his knee. For that moment, her attention was focused entirely on Denham.

One Mississippi. Two Mississippi.

This time, David seized his opportunity. He dove for the gun, fumbling it, then holding on tight with both hands. As he sprang to his feet, the gun fell easily into his shooting grip. He pointed it at Lana.

Lana renewed her focus, shifting her aim to his new location. And there they stood. Aiming at each other's hearts as Rupert Allenbee's dead body cooled in a lake of blood on the floor between them.

Denham, meanwhile, watched the scene as though observing a social experiment. Johannes trotted over and took position beside his master's leg.

"Lana," David said. "Don't do this."

"I have no choice," Lana said. The slightest tremble had crept into her voice. "And neither do you. Lower your weapon."

David took a deep breath. Let it out slowly. He willed himself to relax. To breathe.

It didn't work. Nothing reduced the gallop of his own pulse in his ears. He tried his best to offer her a smile of his own. It was a poor attempt, but he tried. "What about that ice cream?" he said.

Had her eyes softened? She pulled back the hammer of the Walther with her thumb.

"Lana," David said. He struggled to keep his own voice steady. "I've seen you kill a man with your hands. And I've seen you give an old lady a blanket. I've seen everything you're capable of. And I love you."

When her eyes began to glisten in the stained-glass lamplight, David finally knew he was reaching her. He could feel it.

"I love *you*," he repeated.

That was all it took. Her focus sharpened. The eyes went hard again.

"You haven't seen everything I'm capable of," she said, and pulled the trigger.

CHAPTER
FORTY-FOUR

At first, there was only darkness.
Then pain.
Then lots more pain.

I'm blind, David thought, as if from a great distance. *This is how dying feels.*

Then came smells, and sounds, and the sensation of rocking, punctuated by thudding jolts and washboard rumbles that slipped daggers of new pain between his ribs.

When David Toland finally regained full consciousness, he came to understand that he was locked in the trunk of a moving car. His chest was on fire. His head felt like it had been cracked open. His clothes were soggy with blood. And he was face-to-face with a corpse.

Each new bump and jostle touched off flashes of hard lightning behind his eyes. David's jangled brain spun into overdrive. His breathing quickened and shallowed. His heart hammered in the base of his throat, sending more pain up his neck and down his left arm like thorny vines. He couldn't move. Claustrophobia gripped him in its talons. He was panicking.

Yes, you are, a voice in his head confirmed. The voice sounded like Lana's. *But you're also in shock.*

David closed his eyes.

Your organs aren't getting enough oxygen, she told him. *You're going to lose consciousness, or vomit into your own trachea, or both, and then you really will be dying, so stand the hell down, soldier. Stand down and breathe.*

He focused on unclenching his fists. Then his arms. Then his teeth. He focused on drawing in breaths, just one of them at a time, smooth and easy. Every time the car hit a new bump in the road, he imagined that he was floating on a cloud.

And all the while he was doing these things, David thought: *Lana.*

*   *   *

He could remember the sound of her gunshot. He remembered the look on her face, illuminated by the flash of fire from the muzzle of her gun. He remembered the sensation of being kicked in the chest by an invisible horse, and he remembered falling. Right up until the moment his head exploded.

The rest was darkness.

But there was a knot at the base of his skull the size of a golf ball, which seemed to tell at least part of the story. Touching the spot caused new warping waves of pain and nausea. So David stopped touching it.

He'd hit his head on something, that much was obvious. The floor? The edge of Denham's desk? The rude, unforgiving, concrete ledge of betrayal?

It didn't matter. He'd sustained a serious concussion at the very least, and it was the very least of his concerns.

David fumbled in an outer vest pocket for the Zippo lighter Simon had procured for each of them, to be used in the event that they were forced to start hurling firebombs. *Allenbee*, he thought. *Not Simon.*

At first, the lighter was too slippery with blood to operate. David used both trembling hands, desperate to avoid dropping the lighter in the dark. But the more he handled the metal, the stickier it became, until finally he managed to force his numb, dumb fingers to click open the lid, scratch the rough wheel, and produce a flame.

The first thing he saw in the flickering light was Simon's dead, staring face, inches from his own. An open mouth. Flat, glassy eyes. A gory ditch for a throat.

Not Simon.

Not the man David Toland had come to think of as a friend.

Some stranger named Rupert Allenbee.

He was too cramped to change position, so he worked on ignoring the leering corpse instead. David tore open his vest and held the lighter over himself, craning his neck to get a visual assessment of his wounds, fearful of what he was prepared to find.

What he found was a bullet hole in his chest. Struggling to move his pinned left arm, holding the lighter in his other hand, he lifted his blood-sodden A-shirt, probing gently around the edges of the pulpy, dime-sized hole over his heart. The hole didn't appear to be bleeding anymore. In a moment, he understood why.

There was a slug buried in his left *pectoralis major*. David could feel it with the tip of his index finger: a hardness lodged deep in the flesh and muscle, maybe an inch beneath the surface of his skin. The slug had mushroomed on impact, creating a ridge around the entry point, like an insect burrow. But it had penetrated no further.

What he couldn't understand was *how*.

Lana had fired a Walther PPK from a distance of perhaps six feet—not quite point-blank range, but close enough—and had struck him center mass. The Walther was a light weapon, yes, but it was hardly a pellet gun, firing a .32-caliber ACP round at a muzzle velocity of more than eight hundred feet per second. Based on shot placement alone, he should be dead as Davy Crockett. David couldn't imagine what trick of ballistics had prevented that outcome.

Then the car rumbled over a vicious, jarring hole in the road, extinguishing the lighter and banging his brain against the walls of its smooth bone bowl. Something hard and heavy fell out of his vest, clattering to the floor of the trunk beside his hip.

When he could manage it, David scratched a new flame, reached down, and grasped the object, knowing what it was even before pulling it into the light: the solid silver picture frame from Denham's office.

With a neat hole in its perimeter.

If his head hadn't hurt so badly, David might have laughed. If Lana's bullet had struck him an inch to one side or the other, he'd most likely never have had the opportunity to laugh again. And with that thought, the film in his mind rewound and played again:

The sound of her gunshot . . . the look on her face, illuminated by the flash of fire from the muzzle of her gun . . .

But wait.

In the split second prior, had her eyes flicked down to the tell-tale bulge of an object in his vest? Had her bullet struck him exactly where she'd intended all along, aiming to give him the slimmest of chances? Was it even possible? Even if she'd wanted to, was she that good a shot?

Or was it nothing more than wishful thinking on his part? The kind of wish only a lovelorn sap might dream up? A wish only a movie could fulfill?

Lana.

Somehow, her childhood photograph remained intact under unbroken glass.

It dawned on him that he wasn't the only one who thought he should be dead. Why else would Denham have had him loaded into the trunk of this car with the other dead guy, like oversized pieces of luggage?

I love you.

The last words he'd spoken to her.

Lana.

*   *   *

Biting down on the stainless-steel Zippo to keep from screaming, tasting his own coppery blood on his tongue, David went to work

296

on himself in the dark, squeezing and massaging and prodding and digging until he'd worked the flattened slug out of his chest muscle with his bare hands. He hoped it wasn't acting as a cork.

No sooner had the pulped hunk of shrapnel slid down his freshly blood-slickened rib cage, catching somewhere in his waistband, then the car began to slow down. In a moment, David sensed his captors pulling off into what sounded like tall grass along the roadside.

Then the sensation of forward motion finally stopped. He heard doors opening, then slamming shut. He heard men's voices over the crunch of heavy boots outside the car.

An airy lightness began to creep around the edges of his awareness, evolving into what felt almost like some kind of delayed motion sickness. David realized that he was starving for oxygen again. This time because he was holding his breath.

Quickly, he tugged down his A-shirt, closed his vest, and stuffed the Zippo back into its outer pocket. He tried to do his best Robert Allenbee impersonation.

Think like a corpse.

Your motivation is to not become one.

Somewhere in the distance, he heard the sound of another engine approaching. Meanwhile, a gruff voice spoke outside the trunk, not five feet from where David played possum: *"Die entsorgung der organe."* A commanding tone.

David heard the grind and *thunk* of boot heels snapping together on dirt. A younger voice—also male—said, *"Jawhol!"*

He didn't know German. But if he'd been forced to take a guess, he would have guessed that some kind of commander had just ordered some kind of underling to get rid of some bodies. And the underling had responded with a dutiful *Yes, sir!*

The sound of the new engine drew nearer, then idled. David heard footsteps moving away. In the middle distance, he heard different car doors open and slam shut again. The new engine revved and receded.

The crunch of boots resumed, stopping just outside the trunk.

David held his breath again in the pause that followed. He couldn't help himself.

Then a rush of humid tropical heat filled the space around him as the trunk opened. He caught whiffs of live human body odor and hot sour breath as someone leaned in and, with a grunt and a heave, dragged Rupert's corpse roughly from the cargo space. He heard the sound of dead weight hitting the ground outside the car, like a 180-pound sack of potatoes falling out of the back of a wagon.

Somewhere out there, in the big yawning darkness beyond his cramped little world, he heard the sound of flowing water. David cracked one eyelid as two men conversed briefly in German a few feet away. It was still dark outside.

Fortunately, his eyes had already had plenty of time to adjust. He saw a narrow, rutted road stretching into the night behind him, a quilt of stars in the sky above.

He also saw one of the men returning for him.

A young guard in uniform. Blond hair: check. Red armband with swastika: check. Crusher cap with iron cross pin: double check.

David closed his eyes and went limp. *You're a corpse*, Lana's voice reminded him.

You're dead.

*   *   *

Looking back, everything from that point on seemed to happen in slow motion. Yet it was over in moments, and in retrospect, David couldn't separate the individual details. It all blended together. Like a long, liquid dream that dissipates into vapor upon waking.

But the general details, which would recur in such dreams of his for years to come, were these: The moment he felt rough hands on his shoulders, David grabbed the guard's wrists and pulled him off balance, into the trunk on top of himself. He found the guard's chin with his palm, grabbed a fistful of hair, and twisted with all his might. He felt the young Nazi's neck snap like a dry limb in his hands.

David shoved the body away. He was already scrambling out of the trunk when the second guard came rushing around the rear fender of the car. David made his fist into a wedge and drove it into the second guard's windpipe. As the guard stumbled and squawked, David clamped a hand over his mouth, snaked the guard's feet with one leg, and shoved him forward into the cargo space. He slammed the lid on the guard's neck and head until the guard's legs spasmed and went slack.

Moving as if on autopilot, David stripped both guards of their pistols and spare clips. He stuffed both bodies into the boot of the car, in the same space he and Rupert Allenbee had occupied only moments ago.

Which left not enough room for what was left of Rupert himself. David slammed the hatch and dragged Allenbee's body over the road. He opened the back driver's side door, hoisted Rupert up by the waist, and shoved him into the back seat.

The keys still hung in the ignition. David climbed in, fired up the car, and pulled it farther off the road, into a stand of prehistoric-looking ferns that grew taller than a man. He killed the engine, slammed the door, and trudged back to the road. Every step was like a jolt to his brainstem.

Only then did he finally take stock of his surroundings, dimly illuminated in the ghostly light of a full moon high overhead.

The service road ran atop the northern bank of the mighty Amazon River. On his left: jungle. On his right: big, wide water, wrinkled and black in the moonlight. Somewhere above him: the distant sound of a chopper. A big Huey, if David hadn't lost his ear, but he couldn't be sure. He couldn't tell if the chopper was approaching his position or flying away.

And behind him: more headlights. Most definitely approaching.

The sound of the chopper faded. Quite possibly carrying Adolf Hitler himself somewhere far out of reach.

Pinned out in the open, David looked to his left. Looked to his right. Looked behind him. The headlights only grew larger as the oncoming vehicle rounded a bend in the road. The sound of a big diesel engine only grew louder.

He chose right, racing for the edge of the riverbank, stuffing the pistols into his vest as he moved. *This is a terrible idea*, Lana's voice whispered in his ear.

He dove in anyway.

CHAPTER

FORTY-FIVE

The truck rumbled past without slowing, kicking up clods of damp road in its wake. In the moonlight, David caught a glimpse of a company logo on the truck's passenger door: Hidrelétrica Amazonia.

If the personnel inside had noticed anything amiss en route to their destination, they didn't stop to investigate. Apparently, the truck and its passengers had more pressing hydroelectric business elsewhere.

And so did the others that followed it. One every five or ten minutes, growling and rattling and farting out black clouds of diesel exhaust. David couldn't imagine where all the trucks were coming from. Nor did he care.

He only wanted to know where they were going.

So he kept to the reeds along the shore, moving silently through the tepid water, trying to remember what he knew about gators and piranha—specifically, whether or not they hunted at night. He stayed with the current of the river, once stepping in a deep hole that submerged him over his head. He came up choking and disoriented. He stepped more carefully after that.

Despite the bullet hole in his chest—not to mention the fear being eaten alive by things full of teeth that could smell his blood in the water—David found his mind drifting like the river itself as he slogged and paddled along. He kept thinking of Ronald Reagan as Lieutenant Brass Bancroft in *Code of the Secret Service*. He remembered the way Bancroft had used a hollow reed as a breathing tube while hiding from the Mexican army. He thought: *Could that really work?* Only one way to find out.

Answer: no.

The movies really were full of it.

As he rounded a long, gentle bend in the river, David saw the eastern sky beginning to lighten with the first hint of dawn. All cover provided by the night would be gone soon enough.

But no—fuzzy and unfocused as his thinking had become, that didn't seem right.

It *couldn't* be right. For one thing, it couldn't have been much past ten p.m. when Denham had returned home with Lana at his side. David had lost a good deal of blood since then, he'd taken a bad blow to the head, and he had no idea how much time he'd spent with his molars rattling together in the trunk of the car. But any experienced field medic would tell you that sustained unconsciousness lasting more than six hours wasn't simply a black-out anymore. It was a coma.

Besides, at second glance, the hazy corona of light he saw over the jungle downriver was nothing like morning twilight after all. It was too bright, too white, and too localized. The kind of light you might see over a twenty-four-hour construction site. Or a nighttime baseball game.

Or a hydroelectric plant, Lana's voice said in his head.

It wasn't much longer after that before David first saw the submarine.

*   *   *

Eventually, the long bend in the river scooped around to a small, secluded cove, which served as a riverside entry point to a man-made clearing in the trees.

The whole area was lit up like a surgical theater by klieg lights mounted atop a twenty-foot security fence. The ground inside the fence had been paved edge to edge with asphalt. Upon that slab was a large warehouse surrounded by vehicles and armed personnel, its cargo bay an open mouth. A wide steel dock jutted into the cove like a tongue.

Little by little, David began to accept the fact that he was looking at a modern-day Nazi installation masquerading as an energy plant in the middle of the ancient Amazon basin. But that wasn't the most jarring, surreal thing that David Toland had ever witnessed.

The most jarring, surreal thing that David Toland had ever witnessed was the topline of the German U-boat moored next to the dock, waiting patiently under the lights at zero ballast, zero trim.

Men in uniform joined men in factory clothes to form a human ant trail from the warehouse to the sub. The men carried crates and bags and objects wrapped tightly in plastic, as if they'd been evicted from the premises and had elected to vacate in the night. David watched their activity, utterly transfixed, until another sight commanded his attention on shore.

Two figures walked across the asphalt toward the warehouse building, arm in arm. He couldn't see their faces at this distance. But one of the figures appeared to be an older man with an ivory-topped walking stick. The other appeared to be a younger woman with raven-black hair. And they appeared to be the only two people in this part of the jungle who were dressed for the opera.

From his spot in the reeds, submerged in the river to his chin, David watched Denham and Lana accept a sharp *sig heil!* from a guard standing post at a ground-level side door. Then they entered the building together.

He hauled himself out of the river and collapsed on the muddy shore. He suffered there a few minutes, exhausted and significantly unwell, wondering why he hadn't taken to the jungle instead of the river. Made his way back instead of forward.

But of course he knew why.

So he pulled himself together before the act of moving again became impossible. He pushed himself up from the mud. Struggled into a low crouch.

And set out to finish this.

CHAPTER
FORTY-SIX

The third man David Toland killed in 1962 was a young guard with pale blond freckles who could not have been far into his twenties, if he'd yet reached his twenties at all. The guard—apparently a member of the light-fingered side of the employee spectrum—had snuck away behind a fueling station to stuff his trouser pockets with gold coins from the lockbox currently under his care.

David strangled him to death from behind, then dragged his body inside the supply shed to steal his clothes, along with his sidearm and military knife.

The fourth man—the one who abandoned his post at the side door just long enough to take a leak behind the warehouse building—was easier and quieter, if somewhat messier. David had the knife by then.

He didn't have to kill the fifth man until after the shooting started.

After that, David lost count.

*　　*　　*

Six feet inside the building, he came upon an iron staircase. David took the stairs up to a catwalk overlooking the warehouse floor.

The voices and footfalls and echoing clangs of activity seemed louder up here, the cavernous interior of the warehouse serving as a kind of industrial amphitheater as men hustled in and out through its open bay doors. Another theater in the jungle, David thought. No books had been written about this one yet.

At the first corner of the catwalk, he encountered a rail-thin man in mechanic's bibs coming the other way. David snapped his best *sig heil*. The man looked at him like he was an idiot and kept on walking.

David shrugged and did the same, following the catwalk around to the small, large-windowed office he'd spotted at the far end, where he found Carl Denham and Lana Welles emptying file cabinets in their evening wear. David tried to read her body language. Was she thinking of him? Did she hope he was alive? Again: one way to find out.

"Evening," he said, pointing a gun at each of them as he entered the room.

Lana's face brightened the moment she recognized him. Relief flooded her eyes. She moved reflexively, taking three steps toward him before realizing her error and stopping in her tracks, halfway between David and Denham.

David's heart thumped in response.

Her display of emotion was not lost on her father, either.

Denham looked at David.

He looked at his daughter.

"Keep your hands where I can see them," David advised him, "and step away from the desk." He kept the gun in his left hand trained on Lana. "You stay right where you are."

"Why?" Lana said softly—almost to herself. Then, louder, directly to him: "Why, why, *why* would you be so stupid?"

Calmly, Denham stepped away from the desk. Looking steadily at David, but speaking only to Lana, he said, "You love this man. I can see that now."

"Father." Lana straightened her spine. "Don't be absurd."

Denham smiled. He walked around the desk toward Lana as if the two of them were still alone together in the room. As if David had never entered.

"One more step ends your life," David said. He trained both guns on Denham. One trigger per trigger finger.

In response, Denham gave the oiliest, most derisive grin David had ever received. It was a look that expressed what all three of them knew full well: that shooting Denham now would be akin to sealing David's own fate. He would never leave this jungle alive.

But David had already prepared himself for just that.

Meanwhile, Denham came to stand before his daughter. *"Meine liebe,"* he said. A kind, paternal murmur. "You cannot deceive me."

Lana dropped her gaze, unable to meet her father's eye. "I'll kill him now, if you ask."

"Then kill him now, please."

David said, "Lana, don't move."

But she did move, quick as a viper, plunging a hand inside her father's opera jacket and retrieving a Luger pistol. She turned on David, pointing a gun in his direction for the second time this evening—this one belonging to the father she'd been searching for since the moment David had met her.

David searched her eyes. He found deep sorrow there, but no evidence of mercy. "You don't have to do this, you know. You still have choices. Make a different one."

"You already made it for me."

And with her response, at last, David finally felt his will slipping away. He was beyond exhausted. Empty. For the first time in his life, he didn't have the energy to care what happened next.

"Fine," he said. He dropped his guns and kicked them aside. He tore open his ill-fitting Nazi disguise down to his bloodstained A-shirt, then let his aching arms hang. "Here's your second chance. Either take it, or stand with me. But I'm coming toward you at the count of three."

Now it was Lana's finger tensing on a trigger.

"One," he said.

"Wonderfully dramatic, Herr Toland," Denham said. "The opera has come to us this time. How enjoyable."

"Two," David said. "Am I lying?"

"I don't play that game anymore," Lana said.

"I never did," David said. "I will never lie to you, Lana."

The Luger's thin barrel began to tremble. "The saddest part is, you don't even realize that you just did."

She shifted the gun to her other hand and thumbed back the hammer.

"Three," David said.

Lana moved before he did.

She wheeled around and pointed the gun at Denham.

This time, she squeezed the trigger without hesitation.

CHAPTER
FORTY-SEVEN

lick.

That was all.

Not a bang. Not even a whimper. Just a flat, mechanical snap as the Luger's hammer fell on an empty chamber, followed by a silence so chilling that David actually froze in his spot.

He could see his guns on the floor, ten feet away, up against the base of a filing cabinet. *Move!* he shouted to himself, but the signal in his brain seemed to decay before it reached his limbs. He might as well have been one of those statues in the park outside Isabella Herzog's convent.

Denham only sighed. He shook his head slowly, as if his heart had been broken.

Lana dropped the gun. She hung her head, defeated, as the Luger hit the floor with a meaningless thud. She understood that she truly had been tested, just now. And that she'd failed with flying colors.

"Meiner schöne," Denham said, spreading his arms. He stepped forward to pull his daughter into his embrace. Then, in a whisper, he added: "My child, who stinks of betrayal."

As Lana lifted her head from her father's shoulder, Denham pulled the handle from his walking stick, unsheathing a concealed dagger.

David saw it happening, but he could do nothing to stop it.

309

He heard himself shouting. Felt himself lurching forward. Heard Denham say, even as he plunged the dagger to the hilt between her shoulder blades, "I have no daughter."

David shouted, "Lana!"

With one last look into her widened eyes, Denham twisted the blade free of her back, pushed her into David, and fled.

*　　*　　*

David sagged to the floor with Lana in his arms. She looked up into his face as he smoothed her hair.

"I've got you," he said. "Lana, stay with me, I've got you. Lana! Stay right here."

Lana coughed. Bright red blood spattered her lips and chin. She tried to smile, then stopped trying.

"Don't give up on me now," David said, pulling her closer. "I've got you."

"I'm sorry," she murmured. Her first apology.

"Hey. Hey. No." David gripped her tightly. "No, no. Come on."

But she wasn't listening to him anymore.

She almost never did.

CHAPTER
FORTY-EIGHT

David lowered Lana's body gently to the floor. He brushed his fingers over her flat, glassy eyes, closing them for good.

Then, with a howl of grief that came from some deeper place than he was equipped to navigate, David grabbed his discarded guns, sprang to his feet, and gave chase.

From the catwalk, he spotted Denham running across the warehouse floor, straight toward the open bay door. David got off three shots, scoring one high on Denham's left shoulder. Denham staggered, then stumbled. But he kept running, shouting orders to his men, gesturing angrily toward the catwalk as he moved.

David vaulted the railing and dropped down to the roof of a Hidrelétrica Amazonia cargo truck, which he'd come to recognize as nothing more than a repainted Unimog heavy series 6×6—among the favored troop transport vehicles employed by the East German military. He landed hard, rolled off, dropped again to the concrete floor, then scrambled to his feet and resumed pursuit.

On the warehouse floor, pandemonium erupted. A bullet whined past his ear; David widened his field of vision, found the onrushing guard who had fired the round, and shot him in the face with the pistol in his right hand. He shot another guard twice in the chest with the pistol in his left. Turbocharged by adrenaline—by a primal rage that bordered on madness—he lowered his shoulder like an

NFL fullback and bowled the next guard off his feet. Then he reached back and shot him, too.

By the time he made it outside, Denham was halfway across the compound, racing for the dock with a hobbled gait, listing noticeably to his port side. David gave chase, making it about halfway himself before rifle shots began kicking up chips of asphalt around his feet. He maneuvered evasively, zigging and zagging, firing his pistols until they were empty, no longer hitting a damned thing.

Up ahead, Denham shoved bewildered workers out of his path as he limped up the dock toward the U-boat. David tossed the pistols away and poured on every last ounce of speed he had, closing the distance as bullets *pinged* and *whanged* off the dock around him. He didn't bother zigging or zagging anymore.

He was locked on target. Full speed ahead.

Denham reached the end of the platform. With no time to board the vessel, he wheeled around. He threw the shaft of his walking stick aside, brandishing the dagger once again. David could see the blade glinting in the bright overhead light, still wet with Lana's blood.

He ducked a vicious, sweeping slash from her killer and spun around to face him once and for all. The gunfire thinned out now, as if the men in charge of stopping David feared hitting the boss by mistake.

But David wasn't out of guns himself yet. He pulled the pistol he'd taken from one of the guards on the road. Denham charged at the same moment, cutting an arc through the air with his blade, laying David's knuckles open to the bone.

David sucked in a sharp gasp of pain as the gun flew from his bleeding hand. He clenched the hand into a fist as Denham charged again, dagger raised over his head. Even wounded, the old survivor was stronger and wilier than David could have imagined.

But he'd had his time as a member of the human race. And now he was going to die.

David sidestepped the rush, turning his body away but extending his leg behind him. Denham tripped over the leg and went sprawling on his belly, propelled by his own momentum, his feet kicking up over his head like a scorpion's tail. But his stinger—the dagger that had killed Lana—went skittering across the dock, dropping over the edge and into the water with a faint *plop*.

Boots thundered up the dock. Voices shouted: *"Kapitulation! Hände hoch!"*

David glanced quickly over his shoulder. He saw men pointing guns at him. He considered diving into the water and taking his chances in the river again. It had worked once.

But no.

No. He'd finally reached the end of the line: So be it. David Toland vowed one last thing to himself, to Lana, to the idea of a Simon Lean he'd never really known, and to every marginally decent soul on planet Earth while he was at it: wherever he was going from here—from this very spot at this very moment—he was taking this murdering, false-faced son of a bitch with him.

"Well done, Herr Toland," Denham said, struggling to his feet. He offered David a smug, bloody smile. "But alas. It would seem there is nowhere left for you to go."

David looked down at his slashed hand. Blood dripped from every finger, spattering the surface of the dock at his feet. He wondered how many more drops of the stuff he had left in him. Gradually his focus lengthened, resolving past the blood dripping from his fingers to another object, three feet away: the gun he'd dropped when Denham had slashed him. It had slid across the dock but hadn't gone over. The weapon now leaned precariously against a steel anchor post.

"How would one of your American cowboys say it?" Denham said. "You've reached the end of the line."

What the hell, David thought, raising his hands in false surrender. At least he wouldn't need to hassle with stitches.

He dove for the gun, flipped over, and shot Carl Denham in the throat with it.

Denham made a choking sound, clutching at his throat with both hands. Blood oozed between his fingers as he slowly sagged to his knees.

David would have been content to savor the look of surprise on Denham's surgically altered face for the rest of his life, however little of it remained.

Instead, he delivered a jarring kick to the center of the older man's chest. Denham pinwheeled his arms, eyes wide as he pitched off the end of the dock and into the water with a heavy splash.

David stood at the end of the dock, waiting for the bullets to tear into his own back as he watched Denham flail in the river. Then the man—this dying old man who had overseen the systematic extermination of millions—screamed: a high, keening shriek that curdled the blood. The muddy water began to churn violently all around Denham. The screaming went on and on.

An explosion of pain ripped across the backs of David's legs as a guard batoned him from behind, dropping him to his knees. Rough hands shoved him forward, facedown on the dock. A knee landed in the center of his spine, forcing the air out of his lungs. More hands grabbed his arms, threatening to twist them out of their sockets. He heard a ratcheting sound, felt the bite of hard metal cuffs crimping one of his wrists, then the other. Men screamed at him in German. Combat boots crossed his field of view. Another bomb went off in his right side. Then another. And then another, this time accompanied by the deep pop of snapping ribs.

All the while, David kept his eyes on the water. In the bright light, David saw the glint and flash of silvery bodies breaking the surface, but it still took him several moments to understand what he was witnessing: a school of piranha. Previously gathered, perhaps, in the dark, sheltered waters beneath the dock.

Now engaged in a feeding frenzy.

Little by little, Denham's horrid screams died away as his arms went limp. His body bobbed and jerked in the water, tugged this way and that from below. His head lolled back, face forever frozen in a mask of agony and terror. Then his head jerked back still further, submerging in the water.

Before long, he was gone. The swirling water grew calm again. Almost as if he'd never been there.

Then all hell broke loose.

CHAPTER

FORTY-NINE

I n his memories, David would sometimes conflate the remainder of that night in Adolf Hitler's rain forest stronghold with the long-ago mission he'd led into the North Korean mountains, almost a decade previously. Only this time, he was on the receiving end of the extraction effort.

He would never forget the awesome, terrifying, spine-shaking sound that surrounded him as the jungle erupted with the lethal *chat-a-chat* of automatic weapons fire.

He'd never forget the sight of Nazi militiamen turned to bloody tatters in the spotlight beam of a Bell UH-1 attack chopper.

He'd never forget the sight of United States Marines pouring into the clearing from all sides, engaging in very brief, 100-percent-nonnegotiable firefights with any combatant who attempted to resist or flee. Or the sight of the survivors throwing down their weapons, dropping to their knees, and shoving their hands in the air.

But the sight he'd remember most vividly—the sight forever emblazoned on his mind's internal cinema screen in rich, Technicolor detail—was Assistant Deputy Director Roger Ford stepping out of that same Huey chopper, striding the length of the dock toward David. David thought of the distant chopper he'd heard, out on the river road.

"Captain Toland," Ford said. "You're a hard guy to keep up with, if you don't mind my saying so."

"I've hardly been able to keep up with myself," David said. He felt heavy. Like he was generating his own gravity. Talking took almost more energy than he had left. "How the hell did you find me?"

"One of my junior analysts cross-referenced the names John and Irene Davis on three different passenger manifests between New York and Madrid." Ford removed his Panama hat and wiped his brow with his sleeve. "We've been a day behind you since you left Moscow."

David tried to imagine how many mass transit lines must operate out of each major city they'd visited between home and here. He couldn't.

"Fortunately for you, our narcotics division has a resource in Manaus. Guy by the name of Van Tonder. I'm given to understand that you've met?"

"Our paths have crossed." David tried to make a quick calculation in his head, couldn't manage it, and gave up trying. The sound of automatic weapons fire in the background had receded to occasional bursts. Like punctuation. "But only in the past twenty-four hours. How are you here?"

"We scrambled this unit out of Panama City. I've only been here an hour myself." Ford pointed behind him, toward the jungle. "We've been staging three clicks that way since we missed you at Denham's place." He put his hat back on. "Sorry we were late."

"I forgive you," David Toland said, moments before collapsing, unconscious, into the man's unexpecting arms.

EPILOGUE

April 1962—Washington, DC

T he cherry blossoms around the Tidal Basin appeared even earlier than usual that spring, followed by the magnolias and redbuds, and finally the dogwoods, until the whole city was abloom, shrugging off the last shreds of winter, fragrant with the promise of a new season.

David spent his days the way he'd always spent them: at work in the archives during the day, alone in his apartment at night. He wasn't what he used to be at the splicing table, at least not yet—he'd undergone two surgeries on his dominant right hand to repair the tendon damage inflicted by Carl Denham's blade, and his two middle fingers remained stiff and clumsy. They ached whenever it rained. It had been a rainy spring.

He still thought of Lana Welles at least several times a day. In the final postmortem analysis, David was given to understand that she'd come under suspicion within the agency some time during the course of her dealings with Sergei Tarkovsky. The truth was that any junior analyst could have been assigned to babysit David during the restoration of the first Führerbunker film. Hell, somebody from Langley's custodial staff could have handled that much. It seemed that her father and the Council hadn't been the only ones testing Lana Welles. Something about that made him very sad.

Meanwhile, it was a matter of some irony that she and Jerry

Okerlund each had been working as double agents for the exact same people—the CIA on one side and the Council on the other. As far as anyone could piece together, each of them had remained unknown to the other until that night their assignments converged at the Uptown. Only in retrospect had David come to realize how extraordinarily hard Okerlund had worked to avoid killing her along the way, only to die at her hand instead. More irony, he supposed.

But he didn't care about irony. He didn't care who'd known what when. He didn't care who'd double-crossed whom, or even why. He only wanted to remember Lana the way he remembered her: with a daisy in her hair.

Some days he wished those memories would fade. Most days he didn't know what he wished. He didn't know how he felt, or what he'd learned. And on those days when the weight of not knowing became too heavy to bear, David searched for solace the only place he'd ever been able to reliably find it: at the movies.

Always at the Uptown, of course—newly refurbished, reopened, and better than ever. Ironically, the violence that had befallen the building ultimately had brought Myron Burbage's fondest dream to fruition, allowing the old curmudgeon to buy the place for a song.

Still, it was mid-February before David could trick the man into speaking with him again. When Myron finally did, he didn't stop for an hour, concluding, "And you owe me another Bolex, too. Same model as the last one, and not a day newer. You can put it back in the damned storage closet where you found it."

David took him out to lunch on his birthday, same as last year.

The third week in April, Myron ran a three-day revival of *Casablanca*, one of David's very favorite films—Tuesday through Thursday, matinee only. David was in his regular seat for all three screenings, despite the discomfort the film now caused him. Or perhaps because of it.

In truth, David wasn't entirely sure why he insisted on torturing himself. He only knew that skipping the opportunity to view this film on the Uptown's newly replaced seventy-foot screen would have felt, somehow, like snatching defeat from the jaws of victory, and he wasn't about to give the monster who'd called himself Carl Denham the satisfaction. Even posthumously. Even if an embarrassing lump did rise in his throat every time Rick looked at Ilsa and delivered one of the classic lines in all of cinema: "We'll always have Paris."

On the third day, after the credits rolled, David left the theater and went to a nearby café for pie and coffee. He thought of Meg Jenkins and wondered what she was doing now. He wondered how his life might have proceeded if they'd managed to make it here to this café on their proposed date together. If Lana Welles had never crossed his path in the first place. He wondered how different the world might have been. Or if it would have been one damned bit different at all.

As he brooded over these questions, a man sat down on the other side of his booth, directly across the table. "Mind if I join you?"

David looked up to find Roger Ford smiling at him.

He placed his fork next to his empty pie plate, wiped his mouth with his napkin, and said, "I'm almost afraid to ask. What can I do for you, Roger?"

"That's what I'm wondering." Ford pulled a battered film canister from the leather satchel beside him. He placed the can on the table between them.

David shook his head without hesitating. "Absolutely not."

"If this really is what we think it is, I'm willing to bet you'll feel differently." Ford pushed the film can an inch toward David. "Welcome back to the fight. This time I know our side will win."

David smirked. Ford was quoting *Casablanca*. Paul Henreid's last words to Humphrey Bogart. Two characters who, each in their own way, understood more about saving what they loved than they had at the beginning of the movie.

"How long have you been following me, Roger?"

"I wouldn't say following, exactly. I'd say—"

"Actually, never mind." David raised his left palm like a traffic cop. He was getting better with that hand all the time. "Forget I asked."

Ford slid the film can another inch.

After a long deliberation, David sighed, took the canister, and placed it next to him on his side of the booth.

Roger grinned at him. "This could be the beginning of a beautiful—"

"Don't even say it," David said.

ACKNOWLEDGMENTS

Our names might be on the cover, but like a movie, it took an incredible crew to make this book a reality. Thanks to our editor, the ever-enthusiastic Wes Miller, and to Meriam Metoui, who always kept the trains running, as well as Jordan Rubinstein and Joseph Benincase. To the irrepressible James Frey and our phenomenal coconspirators, Sean Doolittle and Greg Ferguson, as well as everyone at Full Fathom Five. Dana Kaye and Julia Borcherts, for your sage guidance. To our personal Mega-counsel, Michael Gendler, for always having our backs. And the incredible folks at WME, Ari Greenberg, Eric Simonoff, Marc Korman, David Stone, Lindsay Aubin, and Meyash Prabhu. Last but certainly not least, our ever-patient wives and families.

ABOUT THE AUTHORS

Alfred Gough and Miles Millar are prolific screenwriters. They met at USC film school and sold their first script in their last semester. The duo has been writing together ever since. Among their many credits is the iconic television series *Smallville*, which they created, as well as the classic Jackie Chan and Owen Wilson film *Shanghai Noon* and Sam Raimi's *Spider-Man 2*. *Double Exposure* is their first novel.